ARDEN PARK

ARDEN PARK

For Paddy
An introduction to
the west coast...

Rick Kantola

To order additional copies of this book, contact:
Xlibris Corporation
1-888-795-4274
www.Xlibris.com
Orders@Xlibris.com
25270

CONTENTS

In memory of Don Stensaas.

Thanks to Margot Lyon, Danielle Starkey,
Mary Ann Robinson, and Mary Bisgay,
who read early versions of this novel
and provided useful suggestions.

Chapter 1

Cynthia Ward's Good Fortune

In the early 1970's, Cynthia Anne Ward, a California high school teacher's daughter, had the good fortune to capture the fancy of David Gannon, fourth generation descendent of Theodore Gannon, younger brother of the founder of the Gannon Oil Company. For Cynthia, it was a superb match.

The portion of the Gannon fortune David could expect to inherit would be diluted to a few hundred corporate shares, scarcely enough to be of greater than sentimental value, but David had inherited other financial interests, and his family's social position was far superior to the Wards'. Moreover, as a child Cynthia had suffered from a tiny lisping of her T's, for which she'd been shunned by schoolmates. Even in her middle school years, after both the lisp and childish prejudices had retreated, she had remained quiet. She was no longer disliked by her peers, but she was not popular. Mostly, she had been happy to be ignored.

Adolescence brought her superbly proportioned legs, long for her 5'6" height, and larger breasts than she quite knew what to do with, all while her wary childlike eyes retained their doe-like size and brightness. She was at first puzzled by the lingering looks that boys began to let fall on her, but as luck would have it, it was at about this time she discovered girls' magazines, beginning with *Seventeen* and moving on to *Cosmopolitan* and *Vogue*. She read intently, completed each self-evaluation survey faithfully, and soon learned to appreciate the value of her assets.

She understood that she was not particularly gifted in conversation and lamented that her mediocre grades were something of an embarrassment to her father, yet she had received without effort what other women so coveted as to undergo painful and costly surgery. Surely, this was not for nothing. Fate, she intuited, must hold some uncommon purpose for her. When she regarded her high school's cheerleaders and songleaders, displaying—without risk of rebuke—rear views of bare thighs and panty-clad tushes which could not match up to the one she saw in the mirror when she looked over her shoulder, her mission became clear. She lacked the tumbling skills for cheerleading, but surely she could learn the steps of songleading. Surely her figure would compensate for any lack of agility.

The second happiest day of her life—the happiest at the time—was the day she read the roster of songleaders selected by the rally committee. The rest, it seemed to her, had been inevitable. She attracted David and, with the helpful advice of her magazines, held his attention through his remaining year of high school and his four years of undergraduate education—all while denying him ultimate access to the tush that fascinated him.

The day following his graduation from Stanford, the *most* happy day of her life, they were married. His curiosity was quickly satisfied. Not disappointed, he began medical school, and Cynthia began the life of domestic tranquility which fate had intended for her.

Cynthia had two younger sisters. The elder of the two was named Christina, though she always used the diminutive form Tina. She was not so attractive as her older sister, but she used Cynthia's connection to advantage and married an acquaintance of David's, a dental student named Franklin Stubbs. Dr. Stubbs was not independently wealthy as Dr. Gannon was, nor did Tina consider a dental degree to carry equal weight as an M.D., but the world in the late 1970s was not so well supplied with families of fortune as it now is; and, after all, dentists held the title of doctor and earned comfortable incomes. Later, when the two men had finished their training, the couples had relocated to the same street in Arden Park.

Despite being nearly directly across from the Gannons', both the Stubbs's house and the lot on which it was placed were noticeably smaller. Even so, it was only with the help of the Gannons that the Stubbs had been able to afford their down payment. Cynthia, seeing advantages to having her sister live nearby, had asked Dr. Gannon if they might be able to offer the Stubbs financial assistance. Dr. Gannon, always deliberate, considered and agreed, but not before stating to all his concern for "their future relationship if events were to occur that would prevent repayment."

Thus, the two families, despite the considerable difference in their wealth and consequence, shared the same friends, were members of the same athletic club, attended the same parties, and were much in each other's houses. It happened also that both the Ward sisters' parents and David Gannon's died prematurely, causing the families to rely even more on each other for family support than is perhaps typical for siblings.

Tina's attachment to the Gannons only increased when her husband, a mere five years later, came home complaining of a headache, took himself to bed, and proceeded to die of a cerebral hemorrhage. Tina, a woman of robust disposition, recovered quickly from her initial shock and began to see the blessings of her changed situation. Her husband had given her no children, his profession had caused him to grow heavy and soft, dyspepsia had rendered him petulant about the promptness and gustatory qualities of his meals, and his two subjects of diatribe, a relentless advocacy of universal water fluoridation (which Tina found altogether too selfless) and a lament against a common tendency not to think of dentists as doctors despite their spending nearly identical time in training, had grown tedious to her. Moreover his practice had not flourished.

Dr. Gannon, who had been executor of Dr. Stubbs's estate, assured her that her insurance and inheritance would be adequate to allow her to maintain her current standard of living and to keep her home. Nonetheless, Tina adapted with alacrity to her widow's role, setting a regimen of strict economy. She promptly sold her home, forgetting about the loan from the Gannons, which her brother-in-law had rather guiltily hoped might be repaid with the proceeds, and moved to a smaller house on the edge of Arden Park.

As to her social life, she devoted herself to Cynthia's son and two daughters—especially to the elder of the two girls, Chrissie, whose given name, like Tina's, was Christina. Cynthia's enthusiasm for community activities had been left behind with her pleated songleader skirts, and Tina often filled in for her less energetic sister, as a volunteer at school pageants and fund-raisers, a chaperone, or a driver for the children. Not having children of her own, she experienced no opportunity for jealousy or resentment. A Gannon was a Gannon after all—and David's stature had only increased when he became known as a key advisor to the Governor and began to appear on television as a pundit of public health issues. A practical woman, Tina preferred life in the Gannons' reflected light to remaining entirely in the shadows.

The youngest of the three Ward sisters, DeeDee, had lacked her siblings' good judgment. In truth, she was prettier than Tina, nearly as pretty as Cynthia herself, but she did little to enhance her appearance. Nor had she learned to conceal flaws with a mesmerizing smile. Active and impulsive in nature, she allowed only minutes to grooming tasks her sisters could ponder for hours, could make do with a wrinkled or poorly matched blouse in a pinch, and wore makeup so seldom that she developed no skill in its application. She preferred comic books to her sisters' magazines, which in Cynthia's and Tina's judgment explained why she was so unprepared when the mating instinct struck. She was especially attracted to the Negro boys with their muscular frames and aggressive smiles, and became uncontrollable by her parents and disdainful of her more timid sisters, who, if they sometimes envied her reckless fun, never doubted her foolishness. She began to socialize with a group of older boys from the university—most from the athletic teams—and the day after she finished high school, she secretly married Marcellus Johnson, a young Negro man from Tennessee, who had come to California to play football. She delivered her first child six months later.

DeeDee's parents, though already declining in health, tried to be philosophical about their daughter's circumstances and assisted her as best they could. Cynthia, secure in her future with David and soon to be a mother herself, visited DeeDee on several occasions and cooed sincerely over her baby nephew's silky curls. Tina, however, was at that time still unsure of her dentist and felt the full force of social stigmatization that having a poor, teenaged mother for a sister implied. She avoided all contact with her, until they one day met accidentally in the driveway of their parents' home. Tina's anger then overflowed, and she charged DeeDee with stupidity, malice toward her family, and general sluttiness, all of which DeeDee might have been able to endure had Tina for one moment acknowledged either the very real beauty of her child or the possibility that she loved her husband.

DeeDee, ascribing Tina's feelings to the rest of her family, broke off communications, and, when her husband injured a knee and dropped out of college, she followed him back to Tennessee. The family heard nothing of her for more than two years, when she sent a brief letter informing them that she was again pregnant and that her husband, his knee having recovered to the satisfaction of the military doctors, had joined the Army.

A half-decade passed before their next communication. Cynthia received a very formal note—coldly formal, Tina thought—from Mr. Johnson's grandmother. DeeDee and her husband had been killed in an accident on the autobahn in Germany. Their ashes had been returned to Tennessee, where the family had conducted a memorial service and burial. It was regretted that DeeDee's family could not be located earlier, but her parents being deceased, her sisters having taken their husbands' names, and DeeDee having left no contact information among her papers, their initial efforts had failed.

"Why couldn't DeeDee have called us?" Tina lamented to Cynthia. "If she'd given even the smallest sign that she would be open to a reconciliation . . . ."

"I wish that I'd done more to encourage her," Cynthia said.

"You did. You did so much. We both did. We were always willing to bend over backwards for DeeDee, from the time she was a little girl, but there was something in her nature that made it impossible for her to come even half-way—to come even part-way."

Cynthia did remember having sent several unanswered Christmas cards in years past, but the guilt she'd experienced when first hearing the news of DeeDee's death was only partially allayed by Tina's arguments.

"None of us, I imagine, is entirely perfect," she said.

"We never expected her to be perfect," Tina objected. "We only asked a tiny piece of consideration . . . . And even that, if she tried, if she had been able to reach out, we would have forgiven everything."

Cynthia considered this for a moment, not quite certain what it was they'd needed to forgive. Then, with a sense of shock, she remembered DeeDee's children.

"Goodness," she said. "Do you think her children died too?"

"Surely not," Tina said doubtfully. "They would have told us. There was a boy. He would be eight or nine by now, wouldn't he?"

"Very nearly the same age as Thomas. And there was a younger girl."

"And possibly others we never heard about."

Suffering the financial and social indignities of widowhood had broadened Tina's social view—that and being associated with the household of a well-known Democrat who came from a renowned liberal family—and she was now quick to voice sympathy for the poor and indignation at their neglect.

"What this government does to those without a financial support network," she said with a shake of the head, "it's impossible . . . ."

What exactly was impossible was to remain unspoken, however, for Cynthia had now been moved by the awesome possibility of their own niece and nephew being left as orphans, and she interrupted, saying, "And we may be the only family they have to turn to!"

This having been acknowledged by both sisters, they agreed that something must be done. They sent off a letter immediately.

A week of melancholy but perversely stirring speculations about the state of the children followed, then came to an end when they received a second note from the children's great grandmother in

Tennessee. Since their parents had not wanted to disrupt their educations by taking them to Germany, the two children, William and Jasmine, had already been living with her for six months at the time of their parents' death. After observing that the children were especially in need of a stable home in their time of distress, the grandmother pronounced herself able to provide for them and noted that the parental claim of attachment, even when extended by two generations, was stronger by natural law than that of any sibling.

"Of all the nerve . . .," Tina said. "You'd think we were children."

Cynthia, who was both less inclined to detect condescension and much less vulnerable to it, said, "But isn't it a relief to know that they had someone to hold them while they cried."

Tina could hardly deny this.

"I'm sure their grandmother loves them," Cynthia went on, "and isn't it more common for Negro children to live with grandparents? I think it's more accepted in their communities."

"I'm sure it is," Tina said, with a dignified lift of her chin.

"After all, it may be best that they remain where they are. Still, I don't know how DeeDee could have done that—leaving her own children behind."

Tina was now stung by what seemed to her to be a reference to her own lack of children. "Those who have always had enough sometimes don't fully appreciate how hard it is to be poor," she said.

"Do you think she was very poor?" Cynthia asked.

Tina murmured mournfully, then said, "Necessity sometimes leads us to places we would never have imagined. I'm sure that they were doing the very best that they could. Of course, it wouldn't be fair to expect DeeDee's children, growing up as they have, with DeeDee sometimes as careless as she was, without the advantages your children have had . . . ."

Cynthia murmured in agreement before what could not be expected could be stated directly, preferring that vague images of barefoot, southern Negro children, dressed in cotton sacking, not be brought too clearly into focus.

Another seven years had passed with only an occasional haunting reference to their lost cousins being made in the Gannon home, when Tina and Cynthia received letters on the very same day from the Tennessee Department of Child Welfare. Mrs. Johnson, the great grandmother in Tennessee, had died.

The older child, William, had already for some time been receiving financial support from a benefactor, a military friend of his father name Robert Taylor. Even prior to the grandmother's death, Mr. Taylor had seen to placing the boy in the same private military school in Virginia which he himself had attended. Now, he had applied for legal guardianship. Mr. Taylor, however, was an unmarried military man and did not judge himself in a position to care for a younger child—especially not a female child. The girl's name was Jasmine. She was now eleven years old. Could either of them take her in?

The sisters sat at a table next to the Gannons' pool, pondering the two letters which sat open on the table in front of them. Though the water hadn't yet warmed enough for swimming—David considered the price of heating it during the winter profligate—it was a gorgeous day, and Cynthia, in spite of the portentous letters, had not forgotten to pull back her hair to sun her face. Her Pomeranian sat on her lap, its eyes nearly closed against the bright light.

"Think of the tremendous advantages we'd be able to offer her," Tina suggested.

Cynthia, having a husband with rather definite opinions, was hesitant to develop her own. Thus, she answered as she often did, by endeavoring to clarify what was already obvious to all. "If we were to take her in?" she said.

"Think of the tremendous opportunities we could make available to her if she were living here with us in Arden Park."

"Living here with us?"

Tina, using the best method she knew to force a more definite response from her sister, nodded and waited.

"It could be quite a shock," Cynthia finally said, without clarifying whether the shock would be more to herself or the child.

"It would be unthinkable to do anything else," Tina said. "She has nowhere else to go."

"But there must be other relatives in Kentucky . . . ."

"Tennessee."

"Yes, of course. But the old lady . . . the deceased . . . was DeeDee's husband's . . . Marcellus's grandmother. Where in the world might his parents be—the children's grandparents?"

"It may be that they don't want her."

"Why should they *not* want her?"

"Of course they *want* her, but it's impossible to know what it's like to be poor when you've always had enough," Tina said, a slight trembling in her voice.

"Surely, though," Cynthia replied, shying from contemplation of the exigencies of poverty, "the child would rather be with people she knows. Couldn't we just send them money?"

"I'm sure the social services people would have looked for grandparents first. And even if they are living, they might live far away. She might not know them very well at all."

"And she doesn't know *us* at all," Cynthia said. "Or us, her. For all we know she could be a . . . a . . . ."

"A what?"

Cynthia shook her head vaguely against the unpleasant possibilities.

"Yes, she could," Tina said, raising her head from the reclining patio chair. "She could be slow. Or rebellious. Possibly even handicapped. But if she is, doesn't that mean she needs us all the more?"

Now further upset by speculations she had not before considered, Cynthia gathered the courage to state her original concern. "Don't we need to . . . Shouldn't we . . . Don't we have a responsibility to consider that she has been raised in a Negro household."

"I, for one, think it would be shameful to let skin color be an issue," Tina said, looking every bit as shocked as Cynthia had feared she might.

"It isn't skin color," Cynthia said, "not exactly."

"What else could it be?"

"There are different customs. Perhaps she would find the adjustment too difficult."

Tina's reply was a tearful, disparaging sigh, and Cynthia, who had little confidence in her own judgments and often revised them at the first sign of resistance, relinquished her argument. Instead, remembering that David had turned down the high school's request that they house a Japanese exchange student for six months because of the disruption it would cause in their household, she settled the issue in her mind as one of family privacy and intimacy.

"It would be such a disruption to the family. And Thomas is already in high school . . . ."

"Yes, it would be an *inconvenience*," Tina said, the flatness of her facial expression an indictment that even Cynthia could not ignore.

Cynthia considered what David's response might be in this case. Perhaps disruption, as much as she detested it, would not seem enough cause to abandon a close blood relation to an orphanage. Nor would David's answer to charities not on their standard list—"If we give to all worthy causes, we'll soon be one ourselves"—answer here. The girl was, after all, her own sister's daughter.

"I suppose we could discuss it with David," she finally said, confident he would be better able to articulate her own apprehensions.

That evening, before dinner, the two women presented the letter in Dr. Gannon's study. Dr. Gannon was an inch or two over six feet tall, with colorless, brush-cut hair. His blue eyes could be penetrating and cold, but when he was at home, they more often appeared tired. He was almost excessively thin, but his well-tailored suits disguised this shortcoming, and there was nothing to offend in his Anglo Saxon facial features. Almost any woman—at least any woman who was aware of his name and financial wherewithal— would have considered him handsome. Cynthia considered him very handsome indeed, Tina somewhat less so.

If there was one irritating characteristic in Dr. Gannon's nature, it was that he habitually deliberated silently before pronouncing judgments, a habit which to Tina suggested pomposity and for which his children sometimes secretly mocked him. He now demonstrated this by reading the letter through two times before looking up. Then, even when he lifted his eyes, he studied first his wife's and then his sister-in-law's eyes for a moment. Neither said a word, and it is possible that he mistook their reticence for mortification over their sister's family's indigence. In any case, he didn't respond as Cynthia had expected.

"Of course, any niece of yours," he said, not forgetting to include Tina with a nod and glance, "is worthy of the best we can offer her."

"I don't think that you should in any way feel obligated," Cynthia said. "After all, she's half-grown and none of us has ever been allowed to see the girl."

Dr. Gannon knew this last to be somewhat disingenuous, as they had never actually sought an opportunity to see the girl. Nonetheless, he understood his wife to be commenting on the remoteness of the family connection and did not contradict her.

"Sometimes circumstances confer obligations that we don't really seek, but they are obligations nonetheless," he said.

After a silence, Cynthia said, "And you realize that she'll be dark-skinned," not daring to glance toward Tina.

"Yes," he said. "I suppose she will."

Cynthia looked at him beseechingly, waiting for him to continue, but Tina interjected, saying, "I think it would be shameful to let race play any part in this."

David paused long enough for Tina to regret her outburst before saying, "I wish it were so simple, but I believe her being Negro must be considered."

David and Cynthia were the last people on earth Tina knew who publicly used the term Negro, and she winced inwardly when she heard it now. "Perhaps it would be better all around if we adopted a more current term, African-American or even black," she suggested, trying to soften her correction with a smile.

David regarded her evenly. "It would seem to me that any offense taken at the term 'Negro' would be a reflection of the prejudices of the offended."

"Oh, I agree totally," Tina said quickly, reacting as much to his tone, as to his actual words, which she found impenetrable. Then, she grew embarrassed at her easy capitulation and spoke up again. "There is nothing whatsoever wrong with the term *per se*. But sometimes I think we need to adapt to the conventions of the time—that is, if we don't want to be misunderstood." David nodded, a sufficient acknowledgment to assuage her wounded dignity, and she went on. "'Mixed race' I think would be a more accurate description in any case. After all, her mother is exactly as white as Cynthia and I are."

"Thank you for your correction," David said, settling again into measured political tones. "I'm aware of the current trend to credit all strains of a person's race, and I approve of it. Nevertheless, we live in California where such things are accepted more readily than in other parts of the country. It wasn't so long ago that anyone with even a far distant African forebear was considered Negro or colored. And in parts of the country, I imagine that convention still holds."

"I would hope that we could be larger than that," Tina said.

"And I would hope so too. Nonetheless, I think it would be naïve not to give care and consideration to the racial issue and how it may affect the child's happiness. As well-intentioned as we may be in such an undertaking, there are those who would regard our adoption of a Negro child as a racial injustice."

"Are we to be so swayed by the opinions of others?" Tina asked.

"Whether we choose to be influenced by them or not, I think it's useful to understand them. How she regards us and how she is regarded by our friends and neighbors will directly affect her happiness. While we might wish that the race issue would disappear, and while I think by-and-large it would be the best strategy to treat it as a non-issue, I think we need to realize that others may not dismiss it as easily as we do."

"I, for one, have always believed that a person should be judged not by skin color but by the content of their character," Tina said, quoting the line from Martin Luther King as though she had first-uttered it herself.

"Agreed," said David, a degree of forbearance beginning to show in his voice. He looked toward Cynthia, who was brushing desultorily at her Pomeranian's golden coat.

"I take it then," he said, "that Tina speaks for you as well."

"That she speaks for me?" Cynthia said.

"Yes," he said, continuing as he typically did, and as she counted on him to do, to guess at her thoughts, "that the girl is your, rather *our* niece, and that racial considerations, and these other considerations, shouldn't be prohibitive issues."

Often, Cynthia would seize on his first guess to her thoughts, on the assumption that it was the one he preferred for her, and claim it as her own. This time she dared to question once more, saying, "That they shouldn't be issues?"

"That they don't preclude us from taking any action," David replied.

"I'm sure that we are free to take any course we like," Cynthia said, running her fingers through her dog's coat and looking down to pick apart a mat of fur.

David studied the top of his wife's head for a moment, sighed, and misinterpreting what he could read from her scalp, said, "Well, it's agreed then, assuming that the details can be worked out satisfactorily." He turned to Tina. "Of course, we'll accept our share of the financial burden. But I imagine that you would enjoy having a companion in your household."

Tina coughed, then met his gaze. "Yes, but wouldn't it be so much better for the girl to live under the influence of other children. Cynthia and I have often talked about what good influences Thomas, Chrissie, and Julia are on their friends. Besides, I don't have room for her. You know my house only has three bedrooms, and I have to keep one for an office." She paused for a moment, perhaps performing a small piece of arithmetic and went on, saying, "And I need to have a guest room for visitors. Friendships are so important to a woman in my position."

Though he could not remember any instance in which his sister-in-law had invited overnight guests into her home and could not imagine what clerical duties she undertook that would require an expanse greater than her dining room table, David nodded in acknowledgment. After sealing his lips with one finger for a moment, he continued, "Then, we would be the first to house her. So much the better. I would have thought you would have enjoyed the companionship . . . ."

"I would have," Tina interrupted, "but don't you think it would be better for the girl *overall* to live in a more active household?"

David was not as certain that experiencing the undivided attention and affection of one parent, surrogate though she might be, who could unreservedly devote herself to the education and moral development of her charge, would not be of greater benefit to the child than growing up in direct competition with three modern, sometimes selfish children, who would by right of birth have first claim to their parents' attentions; but it was not a point that could be argued gracefully.

"In that case, there is another issue I believe we need to consider. Thomas is no longer a boy," he said. "I realize that he is only fifteen, but as immature as he may sometimes seem to us, physically he has come into his manhood. He is *sexually* mature."

"Oh, goodness," his wife replied, jumping up from her seat, "Pom may have a tick!" Then she scurried out of the room.

David turned somewhat reluctantly to Tina, who now softened her voice in deference both to David's apparent irritation and to the delicacy of the subject. "I understand your concern perfectly, and I fully agree with the necessity of confronting it openly. The world has simply gotten too dangerous to let things go unsaid. And I agree that generally it would be foolhardy to place two young people, not of the same family, in too close an intimacy. But isn't this a special case? The girl coming into the household so young— four years younger than he—Thomas could hardly think of her in any other way than as a sister. Then, she is his cousin, and I think that the time of cousins being romantically involved is long past. Moreover, even at eleven, the girl will have reached an age for modesty. Certainly, the situation isn't nearly as troublesome as occurs with so many families where step-siblings and half-siblings all live together who knows how. The relationship lines here will be too clearly drawn for someone of Thomas's good judgment to confuse them."

Though less sanguine than his sister-in-law about the judgment of his son, Dr. Gannon was inclined to agree and nodded his assent. He then turned to his wife, who had returned in the middle of her sister's speech and was now snipping delicately at Pom's coat, the tick having proven to be made of hair.

"Would it be best to have her share a room with one of the girls, then?" he asked. "She's only a year younger than Julia. Or should we put Chrissie and Julia together?"

Cynthia offered her usual question. "To have her share with one of the girls?"

"Oh, no, no, no," Tina interjected. "I don't think that would be necessary at all."

David waited expectantly, and even Cynthia's eyes rose from the quivering ball of yellow hair that now perched on her lap.

"She can move into Mrs. Compton's room," Tina continued, referring to their occasional nanny who, seeing that her services were no longer needed, had taken another position the previous fall.

David waited for Cynthia. "Dear? . . ." he asked.

"Yes?"

"Mrs. Compton's room, then, do you think?"

"Mrs. Compton's room?"

"Yes."

She thought for a while, then said, "That would have the advantage of preventing the children from having to share."

"And I believe the physical distance from the other children—considering the issues that we've been discussing—would be an additional advantage," Tina added.

"It seems a little far away for a little girl," Dr. Gannon said.

"And the downstairs wing can be chilly in the winter," Cynthia added.

"Nonsense," Tina said. "The girl's eleven. It's not like she's an infant. And we can put in an electric heater. I'm sure she'll value her privacy. Children need time to themselves."

"Very well," David said, "but I do make one proviso. If there is something deeply disturbed in her character, we would have to terminate the arrangement."

"Of course, we couldn't allow any deeply harmful influences on Chrissie," Tina said, instinctively thinking first of her older niece, who was her goddaughter and favorite. "It wouldn't be fair to her—it wouldn't be fair to anyone in the household. But I believe that the force of good examples and good education will prove very powerful. And DeeDee, for all the poor decisions she made, was certainly very intelligent. The girl should be bright enough."

"It's decided then," Dr. Gannon concluded. Then he directed himself toward his sister-in-law. "Would you like to make the necessary phone calls to confirm arrangements?"

When Tina didn't answer immediately and Cynthia failed to look up from her dog brushing, David suggested, "Or perhaps I should?"

"After all, that might be best," Tina said, "since you will, of necessity, be providing the finances."

"May I expect that you will go and bring her to us, then?"

"Is that really necessary? Chrissie and Julia were flying off alone to visit their Gannon cousins well before her age."

"I think we need to consider the circumstances," Dr. Gannon said. "The girl's grandmother only died this month, and, relatives or not, we're perfect strangers to her."

Cynthia moaned in sympathy and caressed her Pom more adoringly.

"She may need a comforting hand," Dr. Gannon continued. "I will consider the price of your ticket well spent."

Tina brightened. "How thoughtful of you, David. Of course, you're perfectly right. I was only thinking of sparing you the expense. Airline tickets have gotten so expensive, especially when you can't get an advance fare. Even so, everything considered, I'm sure it would be best if I went to meet her and established right off what types of expectations we'll have for her."

They all smiled at each other then, until Cynthia said, "I hope she's doesn't tease Pom. It seems like Julia has just gotten past the tail-pulling stage herself."

Chapter 2

The Advent of Jasmine Johnson

Despite her well-meaning sentiments, Tina Stubbs was not the most felicitous choice of family ambassador. While she'd been much around Cynthia's growing children, she'd had none of her own, had never spent more than five minutes cuddling an abject child, and understood little of the secret fears and shynesses that can strike a child mute. Nor, as she flew east, did she spend a great deal of time considering traumas the child might have suffered with her great-grandmother's death. Rather, she looked forward with satisfaction to the miraculous transformations life among the Gannons would induce in such a benighted soul.

When Jasmine was first presented to her at the children's home, she was alarmed at how gray the mere slip of a child appeared and dismayed that she could not be induced to raise her eyes from the floor to look at her; nonetheless, she was confident that kind words and hugs would soon bring her around. When the child at first positively refused to take her extended hand, however, instead emitting a faint, but prolonged and bizarrely inhuman squeal and clinging desperately to the hand of her fat social worker, seeds of doubt were planted. Tina began to suspect sullenness and to fear intractability. Nonetheless, she applied kind words and attempted several times to draw the child close to her, though she did so with little assurance that the gestures would succeed. The child remained stiff and unyielding. Nor was she much appeased when the girl finally took her hand as instructed and followed her out of the door, as it was clear she only did so with the greatest reluctance.

How deeply mistaken Tina was! While there existed unusual gaps in Jasmine Johnson's understanding and certain eccentricities in her speech, under more normal circumstance, her manners could not have been faulted. What Tina took for willfulness or ignorance was in fact incapacity. When she first met her aunt, the child was no more capable of displaying her childhood training than a champion runner with a broken leg is capable of displaying his speed.

Jasmine's great-grandfather, Charles Johnson, husband of the Mrs. Adelle Johnson with whom she had lived for the past six and one-half years, was for many years a servant in George Washington Vanderbilt's Biltmore estate in North Carolina. Though Negro servants were the exception in the house, he had, against all odds, risen to an under-butler's position. From the English butler who presided, he had acquired a very strict and already somewhat archaic view of proper manners, honorable behavior, and decorum; and from resisting the mockery his fellow employees directed toward his punctiliousness and their employers' pretentiousness, adamantine dignity.

Mrs. Johnson had been trained as a teacher at the Tuskegee Institute and was much devoted to the principles of self-improvement in general and of Booker T. Washington in particular. She and her husband met at the African Methodist Church in Knoxville, where Charles had traveled with his employer on a visit to Vanderbilt University. They were impressed with each other's manners and began a two-year, epistolary courtship. When Mr. Johnson was able to transfer his employment to the chancellor's residence at Vanderbilt University, they were married.

Mrs. Johnson opened a school for girls in the basement of their home. Their only child, a precocious, talented girl, was exceptionally bright and learned quickly, first in her mother's classroom then in the local high school. Having noted the high value the Vanderbilts and their peers placed on a European education, Mr. Johnson agreed to send his daughter to Paris for a year of art education. So in 1937, a time during which Mr. Johnson's steady employment made him relatively wealthy, the girl boarded a ship and left her parents. She didn't return until the very eve of the Nazi occupation.

In Paris, the girl had developed a great love of jazz and the nightclub life that quickly set her pining when she was back in Tennessee. Immediately after the war, she moved to New York, where she associated with performers and artists. A decade later, she gave birth to a son, Marcellus. She refused ever to name the child's father. She later moved to California and died at the age of forty-nine under unpleasant circumstances that her parents were never able to unravel.

Marcellus came to live with his grandparents during his last year of high school. Both Johnson's were by this time retired. Humbled both by age and by what they perceived to be their failures with their daughter, they at first allowed the boy to follow his own course. He played sports instead of studying, slept in the old school room in the basement, dressed sloppily (as seemed to be the way with young people), and talked in popular, ungrammatical jargon, the likes of which had never before been heard in their household. Eventually seeing an error in their ways, they sought to reform him, but the boy proved every bit as stubborn as his mother. He defied them, ignored them, and generally went his own way, neither consulting them for advice nor informing them of his plans and whereabouts. When they had all but relinquished hope for his future, they were amazed and delighted to learn that he would be attending a university in California, though perplexed that football playing could be the purpose of it.

Their hopes again foundered when he came home less than two years later, with few university credits, a very young wife, and an infant child. The wife, a pretty if somewhat awkward girl, spoke a youthful but otherwise grammatical and well-bred English. As they were firm believers in the superficiality of skin color and the shallowness of those who dwelled on it, they would never have allowed themselves any disappointment in her whiteness. Moreover, they were pleased to see their color-blind principles mirrored in the adoring looks the girl poured out on her husband and child.

For a time, while DeeDee worked as a waitress and Marcellus considered possibilities, the three of them lived in the basement. Sometimes the grandparents heard them arguing, but knowing Marcellus as they did, their sympathies were typically directed toward his wife. They considered it to be her good influence that persuaded him to join the military. As it seemed to them, the army offered a good opportunity for the boy to develop the discipline and good manners which their daughter had neglected to teach and which they had tried to teach in vain. While they'd had higher ambitions for their offspring, they could not, given past developments, be disappointed.

Shortly after Marcellus's enlistment, Mr. Johnson died. His wife retreated into seclusion, disappointed in many ways—in the loss of her daughter, the modest aspirations of her grandson, the state of education in general, and the neglect of elocution, good manners, and honorable behavior in particular—but secure in her principles. The corrupting influences of the world may have defeated her, but she never doubted the nobility of her cause.

When Marcellus was later stationed in Germany, it was both a convenience and a financial blessing to the couple to place their children with their great-grandmother, though they would not have done so had they not also believed that they were doing the lady a good turn. Children, they thought, would draw her back into society and enliven her old age.

The old woman was only too happy to have the children put in her charge. These children were young enough that she could reverse her previous errors. She would raise them to the highest levels of scholarship, character, and honor. She'd been a teacher, trained virtually at the knee of Booker T. Washington, and was perfectly capable of educating them—in fact, at the age of eighty-five, she believed she was the only person still alive capable of educating them properly. As for herself being drawn out, however, she felt no such compunction. Exposure to the world had done little for her daughter or grandson. Instead of these children drawing her out, she would gather them into her seclusion.

In actual application, Granny Johnson's teaching was uneven. William and Jasmine learned to write in elegant, smooth loops and to do basic figures well enough, but Mrs. Johnson was more interested in the geography of the soul than the geography of the world. In her view, literature was the atlas of human potential, each poem and novel a new map, and in her enthusiasm for these arts, she neglected higher mathematics and the sciences. The children read well, beautifully aloud, and from perpetual reading of nineteenth-century verse developed both old-fashioned linguistic habits and a vertiginously heightened sense of the importance of elegant expression and personal honor.

The house in which this education took place was as old as Mrs. Johnson herself, and in Jasmine's mind, the woman and the house would always be inseparable. The once-white siding was flaking and skirted with mold, the pastels of the interior rooms had turned leaden gray, and the two children were often sent into the attic during rainstorms to place enameled wash basins and porcelain chamber pots. The neighborhood, like the house, had seen better times. Abandoned lots were strewn with cans, broken bottles, and food wrappers, and some neighbors had resorted to putting up woven wire fences to keep out passers-by.

Others might have judged the house dismal, but the old lady was able to overlook the flaws and see the beauty that once was, just as she managed not to see cracks in the otherwise beautiful china in her cabinet. After all, the flowers on the cracked cups were hand-painted, the crooked banisters still shined when oiled, and the scarred planks of the floor were of narrow-grained, old-growth oak. There might be no telephone, as Adelle Johnson found the intrusion of a ringing phone impertinent, but they enjoyed the benefits of electricity, and there was nearly always water enough for a hot bath.

Jasmine had grown up neither in rags nor in a hovel—all was serviceable enough—and with the aid of the patchwork quilts she and her grandmother stitched together, she'd always been warm in winter. William, nearly four years older than Jasmine, could perceive that the house was irregular, though he respected and loved his Granny far too much to say so, but to Jasmine it became the very definition of home.

The children's education in manners had been extraordinary. At ten, Jasmine could pen an elegant note in remarkably mature handwriting, understood the importance of clear enunciation, had learned that she must always ask after the health of others and their relatives at every meeting, and had accepted that when she reached the age of fourteen she would wear a hat whenever leaving the house. Moreover, she'd repeatedly practiced making introductions in the proper sequence, meeting the eyes of adults with both humility and interest, shaking the hand offered to her with a dainty but marked pressure of her fingers, and even curtseying with a book balanced on her head.

Only the presence of her great-grandchildren had given Mrs. Johnson the strength to endure the death of her grandson; only the presence of Jasmine gave her the strength to accept William's departure for Virginia. All her investigations of the school, all her searching for some disqualification, had been disappointed—indeed, the school had as fine a reputation as any in the country. Even so, she would have barred the door to William's departure had she not misunderstood the circumstances under which Mr. Taylor had promised to serve as his guardian. She believed Mr. Taylor to be responding to a deathbed request of her grandson rather than to what in fact was a promise extracted in the last hour before a tavern's closing—after an evening spent fretting over William's excessively feminine upbringing. Mrs. Johnson could not ignore the weight of a deathbed request. She must give the boy over to Mr. Taylor's care. Poor William, only fourteen years old, left them! And poor Jasmine was left behind, deprived not only of a brother but also of her sole friend, companion, and confidant.

This then was the life experience of the child who was presented to Tina Stubbs at the Knoxville Children's Home. Of course, the girl knew all too well that it showed appalling manners not to speak up to her aunt, that instead of hiding her chin in her shoulder she should have curtsied or at least offered her hand, and that her grandmother would have been very disappointed in her for not doing so. Nonetheless, everything was so new, her grandmother's death so recent, and her disappointment at not having seen her brother at the funeral so sharp that all speech seemed to have been tied up in a great knot in her stomach. When she tried to say, "Yes, ma'am," no air rose to propel the words from her lips. That she knew she was behaving abominably only made her misery deeper. Words seemed to have buried themselves deep inside her. Her limbs felt as though she were pulling them through honey.

Her aunt said many kind things to her, and she wanted very much to say something nice in return, but she felt as though all the strength would go out of her if she so much as opened her mouth, leaving her to collapse in a puddle on the floor. She knew by how her aunt tugged at her arm and said "Come along now" that she was becoming more and more displeased, and she pushed hard at first to keep up with her clacking heels; but when her aunt spoke sharply to the nice lady from the children's home, who had held her hand throughout her Granny's funeral, the honey engulfing her grew darker and thicker. Then, when her aunt scolded the driver of their car for handling her suitcase too roughly, the honey sealed her up completely.

Jasmine had hoped that her aunt would take her back to her house, but it was not to be. Instead, she found herself in a great noisy, crowded room and then being led down a ramp into what, from looking out the window, she realized to be an airplane. She had never been on one before, and when the engines began to roar, the noise terrified her, pushing her into a near coma.

Tina had hoped to present to the Gannon family a sweet and grateful child who already regarded her new aunt as a strong ally and even as something of a savior. That she could not do so—that the child had rejected her overtures of love and kindness—wounded her. It was now her belief that the girl was rude and defiant and would need to be treated with firmness until her manners improved.

It was indeed a forlorn figure that Tina presented to the Gannon family: a girl wearing an unfashionable, sleeved shift, who was slightly small for her age, with rather long and awkward limbs, who scarcely raised her head to glance up from the floor, whose face seemed locked in perpetual mute expression, and whose skin had turned gray, flaky, and bloodless from the dryness of the plane and general terror. Dr. Gannon suspected a degree of autism.

All were not so discouraged, however. Cynthia, being herself a person who might sometimes have preferred to retreat into her own silence, found encouraging signs. The girl's features were even, and the waves of her black shining hair, the rigorous morning and evening brushing of which even terror had not induced her to forget, were striking as curved shards of obsidian. Her lips were delicate, her nose narrow, her hair between wavy and kinked, and her skin of a color that she would have described as Caribbean or perhaps Polynesian. It would glow beautifully when brightened by a little California sunshine, and her slim legs would look lovely out by the pool. Best of all, she was not fat. Cynthia was delighted that she wasn't fat.

On the children's part, Chrissie and Julia were pleased that she didn't have an appearance that would embarrass them. Thomas found her little more than a pleasant curiosity.

Jasmine was terrified of them all. Her Aunt Cynthia's first smile had produced a glimmer of remembrance of her mother, or at least of the woman in the photo that was buried in a packet of William's letters in her suitcase, and had loosed in Jasmine a momentary impulse to bury her face in her lap, but the smile was so invariable that no deeper remembrance grew. Her Aunt Tina had long since attained the petrifying power of an ogre, and her uncle seemed the most severe and enormous eminence she had ever encountered. She could not bring herself to raise her eyes high enough to see the color of his hair and knew him primarily from the sound of his voice. Thomas was nearly as huge as his father, and his light eyes seemed unusually cold. She was unable to distinguish between the two sisters in the blond, blue-eyed blur they presented to her fleeting eyes.

The Gannons tried, but nothing could cajole the girl out of her silence—not being encouraged to pet Pom, not being presented with several of Chrissie's and Julia's old Barbies, and not being offered a treat of ice cream or Coca Cola. Finally, she was led to her room, with the echoed suggestion that she must be very tired. She lay on the bed and cried, wishing her grandmother was with her to repeat their nightly prayers but believing herself too ill-behaved a girl to be worthy of repeating them on her own, and remembering the ray of hope she'd had when she'd seemed to see her mother in her aunt's smile. Oh, how she wished that William was there with her! Why hadn't he come to Granny's funeral? Why didn't he come to get her now so that they could move back home?

The night before, with her aunt in the hotel room with her, she hadn't dared to cry, and she'd lain awake for hours. Now the tears rumbled up from her very center making her whole body shudder and soaking the pillow. Ten minutes later, the web of wires she'd strung to hold herself together collapsed. Her eyes fell shut, her thin little cheeks lay slack, and she sank into oblivion.

She woke in the morning and peeked out of her window onto a shining swimming pool and an expanse of bright green grass beyond. After the quiet, shady dark of her Granny's old house, everything seemed sharp and hard, and she'd just managed to snuffle up the last of a new springing of tears when she heard footsteps coming down the corridor outside her door. One of the blond-haired girls from the night before—she could not be certain if there had been two or three—thrust the door open and yelled, "Come eat."

Thus she was introduced to a California breakfast of sugary cereal and milk, eaten in haste with little or no conversation, whereas at home she would have had hot cereal followed by a boiled egg perched above the purple violets painted on her own porcelain eggcup. Oh, what would happen to her little eggcup now!

Neither her enormous uncle nor her Aunt Tina had yet appeared, and she managed now to say, "Yes, please," and "Thank you," though her words seemed out of place in a room where the only other sounds were a sullen bickering over who should have which sections of the newspaper. Her Aunt Cynthia still smiled on her in a kindly way, and relieved that she would not be positively called upon to speak or act, Jasmine was able to down six spoonfuls of cereal before her uncle entered the room.

Dr. Gannon, dressed in suit and tie, asked her if she'd had a good night's sleep.

"Yes, sir," she managed to mumble.

"Ah," he replied, "I see that you can talk, but I think it would be better if you called me Uncle David." No doubt he intended his words to be light, but his complete lack of a smile, the formality of his dress, his height, her own overly sensitized state, and the fact of his being an adult male, a species with which she'd had very little experience, conspired to make her feel accused. She tried to mumble an apology, for she knew an apology was due, but the same paralysis of the night before prevented her, and she created only the odd squealing sound. He looked at her steadily and left. Chrissie, the taller one, smiled in amusement; Julia, the one who never smiled, scowled, and Jasmine shrunk in shame, unable to eat another bite. Instead, she retreated to her room, buried her head in her pillow, and cried yet again.

Jasmine was neither intellectually impaired nor autistic—on the contrary she was both a quick learner and, under normal circumstances, highly attuned to the feelings of others—but she had suffered a shock; and even the healthiest human organism, young and resilient as it may be, requires time to heal itself. Time, fortunately, the Gannon house afforded her. Her cousins' summer was heavily scheduled. During the first days after Jasmine's arrival, one activity after another—swimming, art classes, basketball clinics, parties, soccer practices, and overnights with friends—kept them all much out of the house. She was never completely alone—one of her aunts or cousins was always somewhere about—but the hallways and patio were often deserted, and the house was so large that it could seem very quiet indeed. Her Aunt Cynthia, who had herself known the sting of childhood loneliness, provided an unguent of kind smiles and gentle caresses, just as often as she remembered to do so; but nothing was demanded or expected of Jasmine, and seldom was she sought out. She was allowed many hours of quiet contemplation.

Parts of the house—her uncle's office, for example—she never ventured to enter, but inch-by-inch she began to explore those

areas that seemed least forbidding. What she saw offered little
warmth or consolation: the hard granite counters in the kitchen,
the untouched expanses of white carpeting in the living room, the
cold tile in the entry. She found she preferred her own little room,
isolated and barren though it was.

The family sensed that she was most comfortable being left
alone, and since it was typically most convenient for them to leave
her alone, they did. What they didn't know was that she spent
many of those hours crying, despite her best efforts to steel herself
and stand up and do what her grandmother would have expected
of her. She longed for her Granny, for her guidance, for her
comfortable lap, and for her reassuring voice, and for her mother,
for whom an old longing had been renewed by seeing her in her
Aunt Cynthia. Most of all she ached for a letter or visit from her
brother.

Chapter 3

Cousin Phillip

Three weeks after Jasmine's arrival in Arden Park, the household
began to anticipate a young visitor. Chrissie happened to share a
birthday with a Gannon cousin from San Francisco. The two families
had endeavored to build upon this coincidence and maintain an
ongoing friendship between the two children. Thus, since they
were small, each had spent at least two weeks per year, and often
longer, in the other's home. The two children being of different
temperaments and genders, however, the connection between them
had become less intimate as they'd grown older. As the John
Gannons of San Francisco were more direct heirs to the family oil
fortune than were the David Gannons and considerably richer,

Tina Stubbs had been particularly interested that the exchange be continued, and Cynthia, compliant in most things, had proved sensible to her arguments. By urging, supplicating, and moralizing, the sisters had induced the two young people, who were now thirteen, to continue the traditional exchanges at least one time per year.

Though Mrs. Stubbs attempted to disguise her anxiety, the impending arrival was a source of constant concern and animation to her. Meals, outings, sleeping arrangements, parties, and even movie selections were discussed, planned, and rediscussed, and the infernal dullness and oppressive heat of Arden Park were regretted. When Chrissie suggested that they just wait and see what Cousin Phillip wanted to do, with the added suggestion that "he might just want to hang loose around the pool," Tina assured her that her plans amounted to nothing more than possibilities and that every arrangement could, of course, be changed up to the very last instant if that was what Phillip preferred; then she would ask Chrissie if she remembered whether or not Phillip liked barbecued food and, finding out that he did, whether he preferred chicken or beef.

"We ate hot dogs when we went to Santa Cruz."

"You did?" Tina said, noting the fact on her shopping list. "Were they any special kind? Beef? Pork?"

"They were so burned up I don't think anybody could tell," Chrissie said, smiling at her aunt's look of frustration. "We also had gooey, flaming marshmallows. Plus, Kool Aid, which was terrible."

"Kool Aid? Do you think his parents no longer allow him soft drinks?"

Chrissie huffed at the ridiculousness of the suggestion.

"Perhaps we should keep only juice in the house. I wouldn't want to do anything that would make John and Margaret unhappy."

Tina proceeded to make notes on the shopping list, and Chrissie, aware that she was her aunt's favorite and safe in the knowledge that only a few additional moans and huffs would be required to overrule any of her plans, held her tongue.

While Jasmine's grief at this stage was still too new for her to feel any good fortune at finding herself in Arden Park, she did not doubt for a moment that her situation could materially worsen at a moment's notice. Thus, she regarded the boy's arrival with some trepidation: her room might be needed for him and she would be sent away to an orphanage; he would not like her and she would be required to stay in her room, where he would not be obliged to look upon her; or she might even be removed to her Aunt Tina's home, a prospect that filled her with horror.

By the date Phillip was scheduled to arrive, she had magnified him to a height that put his head in the same clouds where Jack in the Beanstalk's giant resided, and she was very nearly certain that, if Phillip didn't eat children, he was very likely to step on them. As a consequence, her first view of him proved befuddling. The vaunted Phillip was no more than a slim, dark-haired boy who was inches shorter than Chrissie and appeared younger. Moreover, while he was able to answer his aunts' and uncle's questions with a calmness to his eyes and steadiness to his voice that Jasmine much admired, he was reserved in manner. He smiled politely when told who Jasmine was and met her eyes with such unfeigned interest that she was induced to offer her hand. This might have resulted in real mortification for this gesture drew a clearly audible snicker from Chrissie. Phillip, however, never acknowledged his cousin's outburst, and instead took the offered hand, pressed it thoughtfully, and said, "I guess it isn't every day you get a new cousin. Cool." Tina then made short work of ensconcing him in Thomas's room—empty because Thomas was on a school trip to Mexico with his Spanish class—all the while plying him with questions about what he would most like for dinner.

Over the next few days, Phillip was re-introduced to Chrissie's friends, taken with Chrissie, Julia, and several companions to two movies, and escorted by Tina to the state capitol and railroad museum. These diversions over, however, and Chrissie's friends not yet being of an age to find wealth a sufficient compensation for small stature and reticence, he soon began to spend much time in Thomas's room reading, while the sisters and their visitors lounged by the pool.

Thomas's room was directly above Jasmine's, and when Thomas was home she often heard the scraping of his chair, the thump of his gym bag hitting his floor, the bantering tones of his voice as he talked on his telephone, and almost continually, either music and voices from his television or the rumbles and thumps of his video games. Phillip was much quieter. If he turned on the television at all, he played it so low she could not hear it, and he seemed to be very light-footed. In fact, she would scarcely have been aware that he was above her had she not frequently sat on a stair just outside the corridor leading to her room.

Her room, placed as it was at the end of the air conditioning ducts, grew too warm when the afternoon sun beat on it, but the stoop, located between the house and fence and shaded overhead by a sycamore tree, received no sun at all and remained comparatively cool and damp. From there, when Phillip had his window open—which he often did since her cousins preferred to keep the upstairs air conditioning set to frigid temperatures—she could hear him turning the pages of his books.

One day when she was outside, she heard Mrs. Stubbs knock at his door and urge him to come out for ice cream sundaes on the patio, where Chrissie and Julia and several of their friends were gathered. Expecting her aunt to include her as well and preferring that she not discover her quiet place in the alleyway, Jasmine stood up, ready to step inside as soon as she heard Tina's footsteps in her own corridor. No footsteps came, and an overwhelming and all too familiar hurt and sadness pushed tears out onto her cheeks. The ice cream was not important; in fact, though she had no objection to sweets in general, she would have preferred doing without to facing Chrissie, Julia, and their friends. But to be ignored and neglected, to have no one in the house for whom she was of first and unforgettable importance, made her heart ache.

She had returned to the step and was looking up into the leaves of the sycamore, longing for her grandmother's quiet, tree-lined street and gently crying, when Phillip came wandering along the path. He drew close before he looked up, his mouth fell open, and he began to back away. Jasmine tried to stifle her tears but broke immediately into sobs. Seeing that she was crying in earnest, he stepped forward and sat beside her on the stair.

"Have you hurt yourself?" he asked.

She managed to shake her head.

"Did something happen? Has somebody done something to you?"

"No," she said, her tears now flowing.

"Did someone say something?"

Jasmine again shook her head. "I miss my Granny. And I miss William."

Phillip, almost as bewildered by Jasmine as she had been by him, had imitated Chrissie and Julia in leaving her to herself. Being of a more compassionate temperament than his cousins, however, he now perceived—and felt—both her loneliness and his own lack of sympathy. He sat down beside her.

"Who is William?"

"William is my brother," Jasmine sobbed. "He lived with me and Granny."

"You must have been very close to him then."

Jasmine nodded.

"And where is he now?"

"He's at a school far away . . . . When he went away, he said he'd write to me every week, and until Granny died, he did. But I haven't had a letter since."

"Maybe he doesn't know where you are. Did you send him your address?"

She shook her head.

"Why don't we write him now. Or, better yet, why don't we call him up?"

"Call him?" Jasmine said incredulously, thinking that such a call must be wildly expensive.

"Sure, we'll just get on the phone and call him. Do you know his number?"

"He sent it in a letter once," she said softly.

"Could you find it?"

As she knew not only which letter it was in, but exactly which page of the letter it was on—and that it had been written in blue ink and once been scratched out—she could only say, "Yes."

"Cool," Phillip said. "Then it's a slam dunk."

Jasmine had become more accustomed to hearing slang since coming to California, but she was still surprised to hear it from Phillip. Her grandmother had always viewed use of slang as a form of intellectual laziness and an invariable sign of poor character. At the moment, however, she was exquisitely sensible to Phillip's kindness and to the sweet tones of his voice, and therefore could only regard his informality of speech as something akin to the private language she and William had shared when they were younger. She wiped away a last sniffle.

"But how much would it cost?" she asked.

"I don't know. Not enough to worry about." Jasmine was unable to voice the joy that lifted her, but Phillip appeared to see it, as his eyes met hers with wide-eyed delight. "Why don't we go call him right now?" he said.

"Wouldn't we have to ask my uncle first?"

"I'm sure it's okay," Phillip said, without a moment's hesitation. "It's not that big a deal."

Jasmine, picturing the forbidding countenance of her uncle and wanting never to have it cast admonishingly on her, could accept no such easy justification. "I couldn't do it without getting permission first," she said.

"That's what we'll do then. I'll ask Aunt Cynthia." Phillip then stood and reached out his hand. "Come on."

Phillip quickly received Cynthia's permission, even her enthusiastic approval, though it being the best hours for suntanning, he didn't induce her to stir from her lounge chair. Unfortunately, they had less success reaching William. The number was an emergency number that could only deliver messages, and under no circumstances were phone calls allowed from anyone other than parents. The school official suggested writing a letter.

Jasmine's disappointment was tempered by her having regarded a phone conversation with her brother as too fond a hope to be real and by Phillip's sitting down with her immediately to help her compose a letter to her brother.

"Why didn't you write him earlier?" Phillip asked.

"I didn't have paper," she whimpered.

He regarded her curiously for a moment. "There's paper everywhere. I'll bring you all you want. And you can get a stamp out of Aunt Cynthia's desk," he said, showing her the niche in the desk where the stamps were kept.

Jasmine's look showed that taking a stamp was something she could never do.

"Here," he said, detaching five stamps from the roll and handing them to her. "When you run out of these, come to me, and I'll get you more."

"Thank you," she said, cradling the curl of stamps in her hand like a baby bird. "You'll tell Aunt Cynthia that you gave them to me?"

"I'll tell her and when I tell her, she'll probably give you a whole roll of your own."

They then composed the letter. The letter sounded to Phillip like it came from his mother's *Best Loved Poems* book, from which he had sometimes taken pieces for reciting in primary school. She began with "My Dearest William," and he assumed for a moment that she was being satirical, as his sisters and cousins would have been in using such a greeting, but she sat rapt over her writing, occasionally dabbing the trace of a tear from her cheek, and he soon concluded that she was in earnest. She wrote of her grandmother's death, its having come suddenly of a stroke, which she explained to be the same as apoplexy, and of having found her on the floor, conscious but unable to speak or move. "You can imagine how frightened I was and how heartbroken I was for Granny. Never in my life have I wanted you more. But I took solace in trying to do exactly what you would have done in every situation, and sometimes I felt almost as though you were there with me." Phillip corrected a few misspellings and helped her blot a smudge where a tear had fallen. He was touched by her obvious affection for both her brother and grandmother and the many expressions of her hopes for his success and happiness. Moreover, he detected a potential delight in having the type of sister who would call him "dearest," rely on him for advice, and sign letters to him with "all my love."

Jasmine's speech had seemed odd to Phillip, but he attributed this to her having come to Arden Park from a southern state. Her written language was undeniably bizarre. After considering this for a time, Phillip concluded that her language was only old-fashioned—like the poems in his book—and that it might not have seemed at all odd fifty or a hundred years earlier. In this he was wrong. Living in isolation as she had, in a southern state, with a grandmother whose tastes ranged from Edwardian to Victorian, and having read and been read to from books that spanned the nineteenth century but only peeked into the twentieth, she spoke a dialect never before heard on earth. It blended usages from every decade of the nineteenth century and dipped occasionally into both the eighteenth and twentieth. No person who lived at any time would *not* have considered her speech unusual.

The more tempered tones she had used in writing of the Gannon family suggested to Phillip how unhappy she'd been in Arden Park. "Our uncle and cousins are all very tall, and I was at first a little frightened of them, but no one has spoken a harsh word to me, and my Aunt Tina has helped me to remember how fortunate I am to have found a place in such a prosperous and well-respected household. I know that she is right, but I can't help missing you anyway." She concluded by writing, "I believe our Aunt Cynthia may strongly resemble our mother."

As he finished a final reading of the letter, Phillip wondered for a last time if she were mocking him. He looked into her dark, expectant eyes, observed her slightly open, questioning mouth, and gave over all cynicism. His heart danced with a curious joy.

After he had provided an envelope, Jasmine fixed one of her treasured stamps to it, and, since the mail had already been delivered to the house for the day, they walked to a corner mailbox to assure that the letter would get on its way as quickly as possible. When they reentered the yard, and Phillip had accepted Jasmine's profusion of thanks, she began moving toward the wing of the house that she alone occupied. Phillip sensed the loneliness that she had experienced there, and, finding it unbearable to think of, called out to her. He led her into the garage. Hanging from the rafters were four bicycles of various sizes and gearing.

"When Chrissie and I were your age, we used to ride bicycles all over the neighborhood."

He took one down, a girl's model, saying, "Chrissie used to ride this one." Then he located the pump and began filling the tires. When he'd hosed it off and wiped it with a rag, he held it out to her.

"There," he said.

"But it's Chrissie's."

"She won't care. Chrissie's way too cool for bicycles anymore."

"I couldn't ride it without permission," Jasmine said.

"It's okay. Nobody's going to care."

"But I care," Jasmine protested. "Granny said that I must never take anything without permission."

Phillip hesitated, realizing on further thought that Chrissie, having certain unpleasant tendencies to selfishness, was not quite beyond developing a sudden attachment to an old bicycle that was at risk of falling into someone else's hands. He reclimbed the ladder and took down an older, wide-tired, single-geared bicycle, which had once belonged to Thomas, but which, in more recent years, had been ridden only by Phillip.

"This one is mine," he said, as he began cleaning it. "And I'm giving it to you." Then, when she didn't smile as he had expected, he stopped his wiping and looked up. "What is it now?" he asked.

"Granny didn't think it was proper for a girl to ride a bicycle on her own."

"Your granny sounds like she was a little old-fashioned." Jasmine didn't answer this, finding it impossible to say anything disrespectful of the grandmother who had loved and cared for her, and Phillip continued, saying, "I can tell you that it's completely okay for you to ride a bike in this neighborhood."

When the bike was clean and the tires were inflated, he stepped back and held it towards her, saying, "For a while, maybe you should stay inside the neighborhood gates, but Thomas, Julia, Chrissie, and I always rode everywhere. To the park, and the store, and to the pool."

"But there is a pool here . . . ."

"To the big pool. No one's ever taken you to the club?" he asked, referring to the family's athletic club, where until the previous summer the young people had swum and socialized nearly every day. "It's pretty cool. It has a slide, a high board, and a low board."

She again looked desolate.

"What is it now?" he asked.

"I don't know how to swim."

Phillip shook his head in mute silence. "I guess that's why you're never out on the patio."

"Aunt Tina said that I shouldn't go near the pool until I learned to swim."

"You never had swimming lessons?"

Jasmine shook her head.

"Don't you like the water?"

"I like to drink water," Jasmine said seriously, remembering her grandmother's oft-stated opinion that water was best used for drinking and washing; yet Phillip's answering smile was so spontaneous and warm that Jasmine couldn't help laughing in reply.

"Swimming's easy," Phillip said, leaning the now clean bike over toward her. "Easier than riding a bike. You'll learn how really fast." He mounted the old bike of Chrissie's. "Okay, let's ride. I'll show you all my old favorite routes."

She looked at him hopefully then whispered, "How do you do it?"

"Do what?"

She nodded at the bike. "Ride."

"You mean you don't even know how to ride a bike?"

She shook her head.

"Wow," Phillip said, "that's a little weird." He leaned his bike against the garage wall. "Okay, so we'll start some lessons. I think you're too big for training wheels though. I'll hold you up."

From that day forward, Jasmine began to grow more comfortable in her new home. Her riding lessons gave her many opportunities to be with Phillip and to sit in the shade of a tree and talk about her Granny, her brother, and what she remembered of her mother and father. They discovered that they both loved books and discussed those few classic titles read by boys and girls alike. Jasmine's first ride on the streets was to the library. Learning that Phillip secretly hoped someday to be a teacher, Jasmine said, "My Granny was a teacher," and quickly adopted the same goal for herself.

She had found a friend, a kind and sympathetic one. She knew that she could speak with him about her problems, and though she was careful never to be critical of her aunts and cousins, she felt that he understood the loneliness she had suffered. Moreover, the entire family was grateful that Phillip seemed so pleased to spend time with her, as they'd worried that he might be bored or discomforted by the lack of a true companion in the household; and, as there was no active malice among them, they were all happy to see Jasmine smile more often.

The family began to regard her not as feeble-minded, but only very quiet and perhaps a little intellectually slow, and even after Phillip had returned home, she was occasionally invited to accompany one of her cousins to a movie when no more fashionable companion could be found, asked to join in a game or other activity when another participant was needed, or encouraged by one of her aunts to admire one of Julia's or Chrissie's new outfits. Her position could never be equal to a Chrissie or Julia, of course, but Phillip's preferences could not be disregarded, no matter how eccentric, and when she received letters from him, she was looked on with something like astonishment.

Her brother, once he had learned her address, had become an even more faithful correspondent than Phillip, and she greeted their letters with nearly equal joy. She always carried them off to her room to be read, reread, and memorized in private, and saved them together in a discarded jewelry box of Chrissie's. William's offered news from his own life, recollections of Granny, and affection. Phillip's provided reassurance and gentle advice for living in Arden Park, observations on books he was reading, and recommendations for her own reading. She borrowed from the library not only the books he recommended to her but those he read as well. That he was nearly three years older than she and a boy and that she had difficulty understanding some of the books bothered her not at all. She filled her letters to him with long lists of questions—questions which he faithfully answered.

Her cousins still snickered at the awkwardness of an eleven-year-old who was only just beginning to learn to swim and bicycle; but as more and more of their discarded clothes passed down to Jasmine, they began to find her appearance less embarrassing. In general, however, their lack of attention to her seemed less callous and more natural than one might suppose. While Chrissie was not quite three years older than Jasmine and Julia something less than two, the two sisters were tall, robust girls, without the least bit of shyness, and so unquestioningly confident of their places in the world that they were little prone to introspection. The differences in their physical maturities and worldly sophistication were so striking as to seem to place them in a different generation.

As for her Aunt Tina, Jasmine suspected that she continued to hold some ill will toward her for her bad behavior on her trip from Tennessee. She tried on several occasions to steel herself to make a proper apology, but her good intentions wilted when confronted with her aunt's impatience.

It was, after Phillip, her Aunt Cynthia who became her most sympathetic companion. Cynthia was indolent, and she instinctively resisted the disruption that any change might bring to her daily schedule, but she liked to be liked, and her smile was a great comfort; nor, after seventeen years of marriage, was she the least insecure of her husband's affection, her own good appearance, or her social position. Once she had assured herself that Jasmine would not tease Pom, she discovered it was soothing to have the quiet girl sitting near her in the kitchen or reading out on the lawn while she sunbathed in one of the patio chairs. It was also a convenience to have a willing and gracious child to find Pom's brush, the tanning oil, a fresh towel, or her slippers and robe, or to bring refreshments from the kitchen. Indeed, after discovering that Jasmine had remarkably mature handwriting for a girl of her age and that she was perfectly able to address and stuff envelopes, she began to take on charitable chores from her children's schools which required her to pen personal notes. She valued pretty handwriting, found herself very pleased and satisfied to see Tina carrying the evenly stacked envelopes off to the school or post office, and celebrated by offering Jasmine shimmering hugs.

Her niece performed her tasks so cheerfully that before the summer was out Cynthia had begun almost to prefer her company to her sister's. Tina seemed always to be pushing some issue of household reform or some improvement of the children's education, just when she wanted most to be at her ease. Jasmine's presence soothed.

Chapter 4

Jasmine's Schooling

As September approached, a decision needed to be made concerning Jasmine's education. Would she attend the same private school which Julia attended and from which Chrissie had just graduated—the one to which Cynthia's own parents had sacrificed to send her—or the public school on the edge of Arden Park? Though she had missed the required entrance exam, the girls' school would almost certainly make accommodations if a Gannon were to ask for special consideration, but Tina argued for the public school. It would be an injustice, she explained, to force Jasmine to compete with better prepared students. Her formal education was almost non-existent. What was to be gained by placing her in a situation where she was certain to fail? Moreover, she was not a Gannon and could never expect to be one. Since her future couldn't be known with certainty, wouldn't it be cruel to begin setting unrealistic expectations?

Though it seemed to Cynthia that Jasmine displayed a depth of understanding that in many respects surpassed that of her own older daughters, she'd long since begun deferring to Tina in matters of her children's educations. She'd been only an average student herself and claimed no expertise in such matters and, more importantly, knew that academic ability could only carry a person so far: it had contributed almost nothing to raising her to her own current position. Rather than risk a confrontation with her sister, she allowed her to present the matter to David.

Dr. Gannon had himself attended a public school. Like his father before him, he believed in the democratizing influence of universal, public education and was a strong political supporter of public school funding. Indeed, Thomas had spent his first years of schooling at the neighborhood school, and David had expected that all his children would continue with public schooling through high school. As the time for Chrissie to begin school had drawn near, however, his sister-in-law had begun to present arguments for private education. She argued, quite rightly, that public schools had declined: buildings were not being maintained; classrooms were overcrowded; the best teachers were leaving; and, due in part to an influx of immigrant students and in part to the general decline in standards, teachers were obliged to set their expectations appallingly low.

For months, Dr. Gannon resisted these arguments. Then, Thomas's second-grade class suffered the chaos of a different substitute nearly every day for four weeks. First Tina's then David's attempts to intervene with the principal met only frustration: the ailing journeywoman teacher was on the verge of retirement and refused to accept a replacement; union rules precluded quick action;

permanent substitutes were more costly than temporary ones; the regular teacher would in any case return soon. When the situation had still not been remedied at the end of the school year, Dr. Gannon himself made the decision to transfer his son to a private school. The girls would follow.

Now that David had been converted, he had assumed, like his wife, that Jasmine would attend the same private school as his own children. He was surprised to learn that Tina felt otherwise. She pointed out that a good many Arden Park children attended public grammar schools (though not, of course, the high school) and that a new school board had done much to improve the outlook for the city's schools. Most importantly, Jasmine had not taken the necessary private school exam, and there was no assurance that she would have passed it if she had. Her status was as yet unsettled. She was making a difficult adjustment. Wouldn't it be best to place her in a less stressful academic environment?

All these arguments had influence, but the issue of the missed exam nettled most. Dr. Gannon, chary of making unfair use of his name, was very reluctant to ask for special considerations. He would ask none for Jasmine.

Secure in her triumph, Tina patted Cynthia's arm, saying, "There are so many more African-American girls at the public school. Don't you think she'll be more comfortable among people who look more like she does?"

"Our Jasmine?" Cynthia said, momentarily befuddled, as she attached negative stereotypes to the term African-American and associated none of them with Jasmine.

"Yes, our Jasmine. She is half African-American after all."

"African-American?"

"Certainly," Tina said, smiling condescendingly.

"But I never think of Jasmine as anything at all."

"I know you mean that to be kindly," Tina said, "but she is partly of African descent, and, as David has said, it would be naïve not to consider what that implies about her social position."

"My goodness," Cynthia said in reply, still a little astonished that anyone would think of Jasmine as being Negro.

While it was true that a number of Arden Park families sent their children to public schools, these were nearly all families that lived in the district on the north side of the neighborhood. The Gannons lived in the southern district, where all but a handful of families either circumvented rules and attended schools on the north side or enrolled in private schools; nor could they be much criticized for doing so. The south-side school was overcrowded, and nearly half of the students were from immigrant families and had limited English skills. Most teachers went through their days as though punch drunk, never able to find solid footing and wobbling from one failed lesson to the next. A Gannon could hardly bend the rules without detection, however, and it was to the south-side school that Jasmine went.

Even under such difficult circumstances, Jasmine did not go unnoticed. Her teachers were only too happy to have a quiet student who made no fuss, who turned in her work on time and progressed more than adequately, and whose parents were never known to complain. Despite their surprise and consternation, all her teachers, especially in their current degraded status, were secretly pleased to hear themselves addressed as "sir" or "ma'am," and some even confessed their delight. That Jasmine was part African-American was all the better. Her steady progress and good behavior were examples to the other children; and, though her skin was a little light, she was living proof amid a sea of failing students that black children could do well.

She attended school faithfully, riding on the old-fashioned bicycle (which she wouldn't have given up for anything, since it had once been Phillip's), sat quietly, completed all her lessons, then left school in one direction, while most of her classmates headed off in the other. If she had difficulties with her homework, she wrote to Phillip and awaited his reply.

Up to this point in her life, Jasmine had experienced little of racial prejudice. The public schools in her Knoxville neighborhood had long since been desegregated, but Jasmine, of course, had not attended them. Her grandmother had seldom taken her and William out at all, and when she did they'd been almost entirely among other Negro people, even at the church they attended each Sunday morning. In the months she'd been in Arden Park, she'd been entirely among white people, and, while she had certainly felt herself an odd fish, she'd never felt skin color to be the reason. There was perhaps an excess of sympathy in those who knew her circumstances, but she welcomed their kindness. Strangers always treated her with courtesy.

At school, where the races mixed, skin color was much more of an issue. She seemed odd to the dark-skinned girls. Her skin was light enough that they did not know if they could consider her black, she talked more like a white girl than most of the white girls, she never braided her wavy hair, and she lived in a neighborhood where they never ventured and believed they would be greeted with hostility if they did. The small group of white girls at the school, having felt the sting of racial snubbing and insult, were furtive and insular.

No girl in the school of any race had grown up in a household as well-educated, liberal, or affluent as the Gannons. Most were accustomed to hearing the bluntest racial generalizations spoken at home in plain terms and, among girls of their own races, often would voice them themselves. Consequently, girls of every group felt constrained in Jasmine's presence. Moreover, she did not listen to music, showed no interest in boys, and rode a bicycle to school, a mode of transportation suitable only for primary school. All this, plus her habitual reserve, made it easiest to ignore her; and after a time, not knowing exactly how to see her, the other girls ceased seeing her at all.

She did make one friend. A girl named Amy Shi, whose family had recently immigrated from Taiwan, began occasionally to confirm homework assignments, test dates, and other instructions with her. Like Jasmine, she was industrious, quiet, and polite without exception, and her father, like Jasmine's own, had been in the military. They began to eat lunch together, and Amy's brief, thin smile became a source of great comfort to her.

Their friendship, however, never extended beyond the school boundaries. Amy's parents were strict and very ambitious for her education. They distrusted outside influences and were too new to the community to feel the influence of Jasmine's connection to the Gannons. Circumscription of their friendship was agreeable to Jasmine as well. The Gannons' household was not an isolated one like her Granny's, but her Uncle David and Aunt Cynthia both valued quiet and privacy.

Jasmine was not discontent. Chrissie and Julia were happy to include her in activities when a third was needed and just as happy to leave her out when she wasn't—and, in truth, Jasmine usually preferred to be spared. Thomas, whose teasing had never ceased to distress her, began more and more to ignore not only her but everyone else in his family as well. Her Uncle David seemed always pleased to learn of her accomplishments. When he said, "Well done, Jasmine" or "Good girl," it gave her real pleasure, and had he learned ever to speak such words with more tenderness or to accompany them with a gentle kiss on the forehead, she might have learned to love him. Her Aunt Tina was always quick to note those aspects of her character, grooming, or manners that needed improvement, and to remind her of her good fortune in being part of the Gannon household—if not part of the Gannon family.

If David and Cynthia Gannon could be faulted for not involving Jasmine more in family and community activities—for not encouraging her more forcefully to share in the family's prestige and prosperity—they also deserve our understanding. It is all well and good for those who have never raised a child to proclaim that successful child-raising is a simple matter of treating each child consistently, fairly, and equally. Yet it is not so. The same Draconian rules that spare one child a prison cell may cast the other into a dungeon of isolation and despair. Your daredevil may thrive among his friends and joyfully immerse himself in one group revel after another, while your shrinking violet, if forced into the same circumstances, will soon grind her teeth to the gums. Even parents who nurture only two children, if those children be of even modestly differing temperaments, soon learn the virtue of flexibility. For those parents who have harbored among their brood a true eccentric—a sport of nature, an odd fish, or genius—the idea of equal treatment is quickly disposed of as absurd.

Jasmine was certainly eccentric—it would have been impossible for a girl raised in a nineteenth century household, who has had that home ripped away from her in a matter of hours only to be plopped down in a thoroughly modern household, who is by nature contemplative, and who is of unusually agile intellect, not to be eccentric. Thus, if Jasmine was not treated identically to her cousins, as much of the cause may be attributed to the nature of the child as to the intentions of her guardians.

Having lost one home, Jasmine clung strongly to the next. She was at nearly all times most content in her own room or wandering her own yard. Moreover, she was unusually orderly in her habits and instinctively put to rights any disorder she encountered. This tendency to habitual picking up was at first resented by her cousins for it seemed to reflect badly on them; but, especially as she never suggested that they should share in her tasks, they soon began to accept such behavior as natural to Jasmine. As for her guardians, Jasmine was performing without prompting chores that no amount of exhorting could induce her cousins to perform. Ought they to discourage her?

It must be said that Jasmine herself would never have faulted her guardians—especially not her Aunt Cynthia. The gentle kindness of Cynthia's smile, the intimations of her mother she found in her soft touch, gentle kisses, and kind eyes, and the safety she felt when sitting within her quiet space had allowed her the time and comfort she needed to heal. It was her Aunt Tina who had gathered her up in Tennessee, and it was her Uncle David's wealth that supported her, but it was Cynthia who had rescued her. She reciprocated her aunt's love and welcomed opportunities to assist her and be near her. She was deeply attached and grateful.

From the outside, it might have appeared that Jasmine was less than a full member of the household—even that she was sometimes treated like a maid—but the view from the inside was different. Not to have allowed her to serve her household or to have forced her to leave the comfort of her home would have been a cruelty.

Indeed, Cynthia grew increasingly dependent on her niece, relying on her for such tasks as decorating tables, picking up the discarded flowers she culled from the garden, and calling to make Pom's appointments with the veterinarian and groomer, all chores which she never could have induced her own children to perform; yet she enjoyed Jasmine's quiet companionship as much as she did her usefulness. After she discovered her niece's sewing skills, they spent many winter evenings quietly piecing together quilts from the children's old clothing. That her aunt was indolent Jasmine well knew, but her smile was kind, her manner was never sharp, and her dependence on Jasmine was a type of affection in itself.

Chapter 5

William

Once having learned of Jasmine's attachment to her brother, Dr. Gannon had worked conscientiously to arrange a holiday visit. He was able, with considerable difficulty, to contact the young man's guardian at his current station in Saudi Arabia. This Mr. Taylor impressed him as being an honorable man, but one whose attachment to the boy was not as close as might be wished. He and Marcellus Johnson had struck an acquaintance, and, in some late-night session, Mr. Johnson had expressed concern about his son growing up entirely under his grandmother's dominion. Mr. Taylor had agreed that this might not be entirely desirable, and Marcellus had extracted a promise from him that if anything should happen to him and his mother he would see to the boy's receiving a proper education in manly virtues. Anyone but a military man might not have felt honor-bound to fulfill a promise so casually given, yet Mr. Taylor had arranged for William's admission to the military school and faithfully made his tuition payments. He was a very enthusiastic military man, sought always to be assigned to the most active theater of operations, and therefore was seldom in the United States. He had, in fact, never met William.

A constant though very slow correspondence had passed between the school, Mr. Taylor, and the Gannons. Dr. Gannon assured all involved that he would cover the expenses of a visit and guarantee the boy's proper supervision, yet Mr. Taylor remained guarded. The doctor surmised that William's father had expressed some dissatisfaction with his in-laws—it would have been remarkable if he had not—and he wondered as well if there might exist some racial distrust in Mr. Taylor's reluctance. The doctor persevered, and entreaties on behalf of the two siblings, assurances as to the deep affection they held for each other, and suggestions as to the importance of maintaining sibling alliances eventually prevailed. Nevertheless, the much-awaited reunion would not occur until Jasmine's second Thanksgiving in Arden Park!

Jasmine, who was allowed to miss school for the occasion, met her brother at the airport with her uncle, trembling with joy and anticipation. She discovered what to her seemed a fully grown man, rather imposing in stature and formality. The old-fashioned manners he'd learned from their grandmother were now borne on the rigid spine of a military man, and while Jasmine could not help being pleased that Dr. Gannon seemed favorably impressed with his appearance, she was a little frightened by how changed it was.

William held her by her shoulders, tested her arm muscle, and pronounced her fit enough to be a cadet. Then, as tears began to fill his eyes, he hugged her. Upon seeing this, Dr. Gannon had the kindness to walk on ahead of them, and the two walked through the airport arm-in-arm. They were soon consumed as much by laughter as by tears, and in an hour's time, it was as though they had never been parted.

For five glorious days, they walked the streets of Arden Park, remembering all they'd seen and learned in Granny Johnson's house, describing every detail of their current lives, and sharing their dreams for the future. William had described in letters how agonized he had been when he could not attend Granny's funeral—Knoxville authorities had been slow to inform his school, and his commander had been at a loss to obtain a guardian's permission, as none had as yet been appointed. It was heartrending to Jasmine to hear this spoken from her brother's own mouth. She could feel now that his agony and frustration—not to mention sorrow—had been as great as her own. She would never have admitted any failing in her brother, nor even the tiniest lack of love or loyalty in his behavior, nor would she ever have questioned his actions, but to hear these words from him and to see the deep feeling with which he said them was a blessing to her.

"The commander apologized to me," he said. "He offered even to take me back home himself, but by then Granny was buried and you were already here."

William was pleased to learn that Jasmine had done well in school. He too had experienced some difficulty in keeping up in math and science. "But for all the funny things about Granny," he said, "she was a good teacher. All the time other kids were watching television, we were reading and reciting. We need to always be—excuse me, *always to be*—grateful for that." His own school was very strict, he told her, and at first he'd been frightened, but now he saw it all to the good. He would turn eighteen in the spring, graduate from his current school, and follow his father's path by joining the military. He would then be able to earn his own living and begin paying back Mr. Taylor's expenses. He hoped to attend university someday, which would be necessary if he were to become an officer, but he was not yet certain how this might be accomplished.

Though there was no whisper of complaint in Jasmine's description of her life in Arden Park, William was much too close to his sister not to suspect how unhappy she had sometimes been.

"But, after all," he said, consoling her with a gentle smile, "we're so lucky in some ways. The Gannons have been very good to you, and Mr. Taylor has been very good to me. They've given us a great deal. And no matter what happens, no matter how far apart we are, we'll always have each other."

The visit was over much too soon, and Jasmine was left to review and replay in her mind a hundred times all the things that he had told her, all the secret dreams he had shared with her, and the warm kiss and hug he had bestowed on her before turning to walk onto the plane. Had she not been supported by the knowledge that they would meet again in May, before he took his first military posting, she might have collapsed on seeing his broad shoulders disappear through the doorway to the plane ramp.

This separation would be for six months, and in this interval David and Cynthia would see more changes in their niece, at least in appearance and demeanor, than they had since the first weeks of her arrival. In addition to spurting an inch in height, she adopted the California habit of wearing shorts, flip-flops, and T-shirts when at leisure (as opposed to wearing dresses and leather shoes, as she had previously insisted on doing), increased the frequency of her much valued smiles, developed a more equal, if still not particularly warm or intimate, relationship with their own daughters, and trimmed the more prominent eccentricities of her speech. It seemed to both David and Cynthia that she appeared happier, healthier, and more normal, in every way.

In discussing these improvements with his wife, Dr. Gannon attributed much to William's visit. He had brought with him sandals, sweatshirts, athletic shoes, T-shirts, and shorts—a wardrobe, which while astoundingly clean and wrinkle-free, was otherwise conventional—and he had conversed freely and in good humor with Thomas, Chrissie, and Julia. That his manner with his elders had remained extraordinarily formal, mannerly, and respectful hardly seemed a fault. All in all, they felt he had been a very good example for his sister, and Dr. Gannon was satisfied that his persistence and months of correspondence had produced a useful end.

In truth, the changes these six months brought were more external than internal, as William soon discovered when they again walked in Arden Park. This visit occurred in the spring, when the last of the azalea blooms displayed their many colors in every garden about the neighborhood, and spring flowers were in full display.

As they walked, Jasmine stopped to admire particularly artful displays. Their Granny had taught her the proper names for Tennessee flora—lessons in which William had been remiss—and she had used her aunt's otherwise neglected gardening books to learn the California species. William asked the names of each new flower, as much to be impressed by his sister's thorough knowledge, as out of any real desire to learn names.

"Phillip doesn't know his flowers either," Jasmine said, in response to William's query concerning the ubiquitous violas.

"Who exactly is this Phillip?" William asked.

Jasmine had shied from speaking or writing too much about Phillip to William, and her current reference had been inadvertent. She very much wanted them to like each other, however, and she now accepted this opportunity to present his best qualities, describing in particular detail how Phillip had helped her in her first weeks in Arden Park and how kind and thoughtful he had been.

"I think of Phillip as my best friend," she said, "which probably seems funny since I only see him a few times a year."

"Not so funny. I think of you as my one and only sister."

"But that's different."

"It is different," he admitted.

"He likes to read, as we do," she said, "and he is always suggesting new books."

"As your Anne of Green Gables would say, it sounds like you've found a 'kindred soul.'"

"Yes," she said, then added quickly, "but he could never mean to me what you and Granny have meant."

"No," he said, "I wasn't worried about that"; but in this he did not quite speak the full truth, for Jasmine was the only soul in the world with whom he had an exclusive and unalterable connection. As it had been invaluable to Jasmine to know that she had a brother who loved her, valued her, and shared her ideals, and who would never abandon her, it had been invaluable to him to have a sister who admired, trusted, and even exalted him. He understood that he took strength from her just as she took strength from him, and his heart clouded at the idea of sharing her loyalty and affection.

They were now before one of the few empty lots in Arden Park. It was home to a profuse display of golden-orange California poppies, and William bent and picked one.

"My first summer, when I brought a bouquet home, Julia told me that it was against the law to pick poppies. She said I would be arrested."

William cupped the blossom to hide it against his chest, and Jasmine laughed.

"When Phillip found me crying," she went on, "he explained that it was the state flower. It's one of those stories that somehow takes hold among children . . . like eating watermelon seeds will cause a watermelon to grow in your stomach."

"I'm very careful about watermelon seeds," William admitted.

"And picking wildflowers may actually be against the law, though, of course, it's nothing that's enforced. Poppies aren't very good for picking anyway. If you look at the one you have, you'll see it's already wilted."

He exposed the flower. Its petals, though still of the same bright color, were already drooping. He set it back in the field.

William, picturing his little sister huddled in her room listening for sirens or a policeman's knock at the door, could only be grateful that someone of Phillip's kindness had been present to reassure her. Besides, despite her growth and despite the alterations California life had made in her dress and speech, he'd been with her enough now to know that she was not much changed. She never spoke in slang, disdained disorderly dress or grooming, refused to waste even a pea of toothpaste, never gossiped, and cared much less for the good opinion of her peers than for her good opinion of herself. She bore all these qualities with honesty and compassion, and seeing them displayed in the slim figure of his own sister made him both proud of her and determined to be deserving of her love. Most of all, he knew that he could and must trust her judgement, for it was superior to his own.

Chapter 6

High School

As Jasmine had matured and grown more capable, Cynthia's reliance on her had increased, and, as is natural in such situations, so had her affection. Though Jasmine would never have suspected it was so, her aunt's fondness was perhaps exceeded by that of Dr. Gannon. In part, he secretly enjoyed the continual reminder of his own charity which her presence offered, but he also took pleasure in her manner and appearance. Her timidity and her extreme reluctance to displease him allowed him opportunities to exercise a gentleness which was not typical in his nature and for which there had been little need since Julia's infancy. Her presence flattered him and also delighted him, in the way that watching any young, innocent creature incites tender feelings. Thus, when Tina began making arrangements for her to enroll at the public high school for the following year, he suggested that she instead be enrolled in the private school with her cousins.

Tina thought this unwise. Though she could not directly contradict her brother-in-law, she began efforts to circumvent him by discussing the issue privately with her nieces. Chrissie cared not at all. She would be a junior, and the comings and goings of freshmen were of no consequence. Besides, Jasmine's discretion could be relied on. She never snitched. At first, Julia was non-committal.

"Don't you think it would be difficult for Jasmine there?" Tina prompted her.

"There's a lot of really dumb girls at our school," Chrissie said, as Julia still did not respond.

"Oh, come now. They wouldn't have been admitted if they were slow, and even the weakest students have had the benefit of attending very good schools, something Jasmine hasn't had."

"You think she might flunk out?" Julia asked.

"I think it's possible," Tina said.

"That would be pretty awful," Julia said.

"There was a girl in my class who got kicked out," Chrissie said.

"Who?" Tina asked.

"Sarah Robinson. She went to Roosevelt. She didn't think it was so bad. They let you dye your hair any color you want there. And you can wear tank tops. She said they're just happy if you show up. She figured she could probably go naked if she wanted to."

While having an attractive and popular older sister for a schoolmate was sometimes a social asset to Julia, she was less certain about Jasmine, who was only a grade behind. Jasmine was flat-chested, gangling, and funny-looking. She was hard to explain to friends, said odd things, and made other kids feel uncomfortable. Coming from the school where she did, she could hardly be a very good student, nor was she likely to be much of a success in anything else. She did not have many friends—certainly not any important or cute ones—and she might even want to tag along with her. All together, Jasmine was not likely to prove much of an asset. There was no doubt that she would be a hindrance when it came to boys.

"I'm not sure that Jasmine would fit in," Julia ventured, then detecting an encouraging look from her aunt went on, saying, "I don't know if it's the right place for her . . . . I mean, I don't know if she would like it there."

Chrissie squawked incredulously.

"I really don't think she'd like it," Julia protested.

"Of course. She very well might not," Tina said, turning to Chrissie. "I think Julia deserves credit for speaking up, even when it's something that's difficult to say. We wouldn't want to make a mistake and send Jasmine to the wrong school. Sometimes it's a disservice to people to be over-sensitive."

Chrissie cast a smirking, satirical look, but knowing that her aunt favored her and therefore detecting that there might be some useful purpose to her aunt's designs, held her tongue.

"And it really might be too hard for her," Julia ventured, glancing quickly toward Chrissie. "It really might."

"She hasn't had algebra," Tina said. "That would put her behind to start."

"Not really," Chrissie mumbled.

"But you both completed algebra in eighth grade," Tina said.

Chrissie looked at them both, noted a warning in Julia's eyes, and acquiesced, letting her sister know from a eye lift of her own that this was something that would deserve repayment. "That's true," she said, not adding that such was not the case for at least half the girls in the school.

So armed, Tina felt herself prepared to discuss the issue with Dr. Gannon. She went to him in his study, as she always did when serious matters were to be discussed, and found him seated behind his desk reading a medical journal. After apologizing for her interruption, she explained that both his daughters felt that the workload at Riverbend would overwhelm Jasmine.

"Neither wanted to say anything negative or anything critical about Jasmine, but eventually I was able to get it out of them. They both think the schoolwork would be too hard."

"I think we may sometimes give Jasmine too little credit," the doctor answered, in his usual, deliberate manner.

"There's not a doubt in my mind that Jasmine is a very capable girl," Tina said quickly. "It's no reflection on her that the curriculum at her school is sub-par."

"I've never heard Jasmine complain when asked to undertake a difficult task."

"I'm afraid that may be because so little has been expected of her in the past. For things to change so extremely, so quickly, overnight . . . ."

"What I intended to imply was that I believe that she would gladly undertake the increased work."

"I have no doubt that she would. But the fact remains that she hasn't learned one x or y of algebra."

"I see," Dr. Gannon said, regretting now that he'd originally agreed to allow his niece to attend the public grammar school.

Seeing him falter, Tina ventured on. "Isn't it for the best in any case that she remain among her friends?"

"Wouldn't it be just as well for her to be with her *cousins*?" he asked.

"It's never quite the same," Tina replied, shaking her head knowingly.

Dr. Gannon had great faith in Jasmine's abilities, and had he felt infinitely wealthy, he might have dismissed his sister-in-law's arguments. It happened, however, that there had occurred at this time a certain diminution of the Gannons' income. The doctor had decided to give up his medical practice and assume a position in the governor's administration, and his income would drop nearly by half. At the same time, Thomas would now be attending college at a cost of more than $30,000 per year. He was no longer insensible to the $10,000 per year tuition charged at Riverbend. While it occurred to him that the high school tuition fees might be spent more effectually on Jasmine, who would avail herself of every opportunity the school offered, than on one of his own less appreciative daughters, he could not deny a first obligation to Chrissie and Julia. He reluctantly, and somewhat guiltily, agreed that Jasmine would continue her education at the public high school.

Tina was aware of the Gannons' changed financial circumstances, and she referred to them later when she justified her position to Cynthia. "We really shouldn't lead her to expect a lifestyle beyond what we can provide for her. Unless we're prepared to provide her with all the same advantages we do for Chrissie and Julia—cars, private universities, and they'll have to be sent on a trip to Europe soon—wouldn't it be inconsiderate—almost cruel—to encourage her to have expectations which are beyond our powers to fulfill?"

Cynthia had never suspected that they would provide Jasmine with anything less than what her own daughters received; but then, she'd never before had much occasion to consider the possibility of limited resources. She made no reply to her sister.

Jasmine was not disappointed—she did not relish the possibility of attending school with her cousins and, if asked, could honestly have said that she preferred the public school—nor did she think enough of her position to have objected had she wished for anything else. Nonetheless, she was warmed, even privately elated, when her Aunt Cynthia roused herself to accompany her to her eighth grade graduation ceremonies. There Jasmine won awards for citizenship and attendance, a Young Author's citation for an imaginative, if somewhat over-florid, essay on freedom and responsibility, and was listed on the honor roll. She also took advantage of the opportunity to introduce Amy Shi to her aunt, and Amy in turn introduced her parents. They spoke in accented, ungrammatical English, dropping the s's from plurals and verbs, but were otherwise models of deferential courtesy and goodwill. Cynthia insisted that Amy must visit them in Arden Park during the summer, in the warm and completely sincere manner that, while completely inoffensive, was equally meaningless.

When the day was over, Cynthia gave Jasmine one of her longest and fondest smiles, and at dinner announced the news of her awards to the family. Dr. Gannon told her that he found her success "very gratifying," assured her that she had every reason to be proud, and resisted an impulse to change his decision about her future education. Julia and Chrissie, consumed by preparations for their end-of-the-year parties, paid no attention, and the news was greeted by Tina with the observation that it was appalling how far the public schools had declined.

To Cynthia's surprise and consternation, Jasmine had received one additional honor: she had been nominated to represent her school at a summer session for promising minority students to be held at the local university. Cynthia never thought of Jasmine as a "minority" and therefore had assumed she would decline. Her Aunt Tina, however, who was the most faithful of her Gannon relatives in reminding her that she must never forget her African-American heritage, insisted that she attend. This Jasmine did, with the hope of new ventures in literature or possibly even an introduction to the science of computers. To her disappointment, the program proved to be more sociological in nature. While she and her classmates were reassured that they could succeed in higher education, they were also informed that racial discrimination in admissions would make it impossible for most to gain admission, that an under-funding of black studies programs and black dormitories would make them feel unwelcome if they did gain admission, and that a systemic bias against black graduates would make it impossible for them to obtain top positions in their fields if they did graduate.

In describing the instigators of these injustices, her instructor frequently used the term "white supremacist." At first, Jasmine did not quite understand to whom he referred, as the term produced for her an image of short, pale men with shaved heads and tattoos on their arms. It was only on the second day that she came to realize—and then with astonishment—that they were referring to the very people she encountered daily in Arden Park. Was it possible her instructors knew so little about white people?

Forewarned is forearmed, yet to Jasmine this all seemed too much like excuse-making—excuse-making in advance but excuse-making nonetheless—something her grandmother had abhorred. Miserable with it all, she decided to withdraw, though she found herself ashamed to admit the true reasons to her aunts. Instead, she gave the explanation that she didn't feel justified in holding a place in a program that was designed for more disadvantaged students. This argument was rejected by Tina and elicited a stern reminder: "Jasmine, you must not think of yourself as not being disadvantaged. David and Cynthia are your guardians, not your parents. You are an orphan. You are a minority. You fully deserve every privilege which that entails." To Jasmine's surprise and great relief, Cynthia rose to her defense, saying, "What does any of this have to do with Jasmine anyway?" The withdrawal was allowed to stand.

While Jasmine had no doubt that Tina meant well, she could not completely take her admonition to heart. Many of the students in her grammar school had actually lived in poverty, a circumstance that they typically tried to conceal but which was revealed by their eligibility for free lunch programs, their inability to procure the proper gym gear, and a general repetitiveness in dress, which they pretended to be a preference, but which, when extended to worn-out shoes and lack of a coat on cold mornings, revealed itself as an act of necessity. Moreover, many of these children had grown up with no books in their homes, guardians who either did not read English or simply did not read anything, and absent, drug-addicted, and sometimes incarcerated parents. Considered in this light, it was clear that she had suffered no disadvantages at all—that, in fact, despite the loss of her parents, her life had been very much blessed.

Jasmine knew that her range of experience was limited. She had lived a sheltered life in Arden Park, and there were evils in the world of which she remained innocent. Her instructors, who described a conspiracy of white people that would labor to prevent her success and thwart her happiness, seemed very sure of their arguments; yet she had no personal experience from which to verify what they said. Her Granny had told her that she must not judge people by what others said about them but from her own experience. From her own experience, she very much doubted that she would ever believe her Uncle David to be a white supremacist.

This then was the Jasmine Johnson who entered high school, a girl with an unusually observant and contemplative nature, a grace and repose that showed well in any circumstance, a lively intelligence, and a purity of character that was often mistaken for immaturity. There, she impressed her teachers with both the conscientiousness and intelligence of her work, and, following Phillip's example, joined the cross-country and track teams. She was gratified when her fellow students began more often to exchange greetings with her and sought to develop rapport. Still, adolescent society is governed by a desire to belong, and most students use the convenient category of race to find their groups. Jasmine could not think of herself as *not* Negro, because to do so would have been to reject her Granny, whom she loved more than anyone else in the world; nor could she think of herself as *not* white, as to do so would have been to reject both her mother and the aunt and uncle who cared for her. Amy Shi remained her only close friend.

In the spring of Jasmine's sophomore year, a fateful change was to occur in the Gannon household. Dr. Gannon was offered a position in the Presidential administration that would require him to be in Washington for a minimum of two years, effective immediately. David felt the significance of this honor, welcomed the increased power and influence it would afford, and was keen to accept. He first proposed a temporary relocation of the entire household to Washington D.C., but this proposal was met with near hysteria by both of his daughters, and it was soon withdrawn. Instead, Cynthia would remain in Arden Park with the children, and Dr. Gannon would use the small enhancement in his income to rent an apartment in Washington. He would fly back and forth as often as was practical.

The conduct of a household is the product of all the forces acting on it, and Dr. Gannon, despite his frequent absences, had been recognized as a powerful influence by every member of his family. With his absence, alterations began to occur, not instantaneously, sometimes almost imperceptibly, but steadily, in the same way that a once-tidy drawer reverts to chaos or a garden plot fills with weeds. Already during his first summer of absence, his daughters' bikinis had shrunk to strings, and they often left the house in tight, bare-midriffed tops that gave abundant display of their shapely bosoms. Meals began to be taken more often on the run in the kitchen; a second and then third hole appeared in the lobe of Julia's ear; Thomas, who was home from college for the summer, would sometimes sit out by the pool late at night, drinking beer with his friends; and the occasional crude expression, which only would have been whispered when Dr. Gannon's presence was more closely felt, came into common usage. A few actual profanities began to be heard.

Dr. Gannon had preferred to maintain a private household; and Cynthia, too, had discouraged the children from having visitors, both out of respect for her husband's wishes and out of fear that children would tease her Pom. Now, there occurred an escalation in both the social activity and noise levels about the house. Most prominent among the summer visitors was a young man named Jeremy Blunt, Pudge to his friends, whom Chrissie had procured as an escort to her senior year functions and who was now considered her steady boyfriend. Most of his summer seemed to be spent beside the Gannon pool.

The ensuing fall brought yet another departure. After much turmoil, Chrissie had accepted admission to a college in Arizona. Her father, and even her aunt and mother, had argued against this choice, as she would be attending a state university, where as an out-of-state student she would pay tuition almost equivalent to a private school, but without garnering equivalent advantages in prestige or quality of education. Chrissie, however, had set her heart on Arizona and had mounted a relentless campaign. What had begun with sullenness and silence had advanced to slammed doors, weeping, and vitriol. Tina was the first to be won over. She came away from a closed-door meeting with her niece convinced that the girl's happiness had to be put foremost. Cynthia, who loved her peaceful days, soon capitulated at well. Dr. Gannon could perhaps have resisted his daughter's silence and hostility, especially at a three-thousand mile remove, but his wife's tearful phone calls he could not. He gave way: Chrissie would have her own way—this despite her having never made clear why she had set her heart on Arizona! If it was, as Julia suspected, because the weather would allow her to wear spaghetti-strap tops the year round, she had possessed the wisdom not to say so.

For high schools students of the most ambitious sort, the junior year is considered the most difficult, in part because the various curricula conspire to torment them, and in part because this is the year that will most influence their future academic prospects. Admissions committees may dismiss deficiencies of freshmen and sophomores as youthful folly. Back-sliding by seniors typically occurs too late to affect decisions and is, in any case, not completely unexpected. It falls upon juniors, however, to demonstrate that no academic resource would be wasted upon them. This they must do by earning excellent marks, maintaining an unblemished disciplinary record, and undertaking a load of community service and extracurricular activities, which, if done with a completely pure heart, would confer sainthood. The young are robust, and a surprising number succeed in accomplishing all this with neither physical nor emotional breakdown, though inevitably a tear or two falls. Jasmine continued with her running, both on trails in the fall and on the track in the spring, tutored primary students at her old school, earned marks unblemished by B's, and was elected secretary of her student council. (That she was uncontested in this election members of those admissions committees need never know. Amy Shi was president.) It can be supposed that Jasmine endured all this with less than typical angst, as she suffered less from social anxieties than most of her peers and wasted little time on the telephone. Nonetheless, a tear or two did fall, though only twice outside the privacy of her own room: once upon William's arrival on the day of Christmas Eve and again upon his departure on the evening of Christmas Day.

His bearing had become so dignified and manly that she feared for a moment that he might have grown distant to her; then, when he kissed her, his eyes were so divinely sweet that she burst instantly into tears. He soon proved himself still to be her loving brother, and both her fear and her tears soon passed. Yet when he left her at the airport gate, she was struck hard by an awareness that he was a soldier and might be killed. Her eyes remained overflowing until she had said prayers for him and laid her head on her pillow.

Chapter 7

Max and Sherry Hill

The following summer brought two events that would further change the household and also promise to make the school vacation much more interesting for Jasmine. The first concerned Phillip. His father had long been a contributor to conservationist charities, and with his youngest son out of the home, he had taken the opportunity to assume a more active role. Having procured the

temporary directorship of a rain forest ecology experimental camp
in Brazil, he was eager to begin his new duties. Could Phillip stay
with the David Gannons during his summer vacation? The answer,
of course, was "yes," and much to Jasmine's delight, Phillip would
visit for twelve uninterrupted weeks.

While Phillip's stays had continued to be spoken of as visits to
Chrissie, with each passing year he had spent more hours in
Jasmine's company. During the day, they talked, rode bicycles,
and swam, but they could most often be found reading under the
shade of an oak tree out beyond the pool in the farthest corner of
the yard. With Jasmine now sixteen and Phillip nearly three years
older, they no longer rubbed shoulders as they sat on the couch
reading, and they discussed more delicately those book passages
about adult relationships which they once would have passed over
with youthful obliviousness. Two years before, however, they had
ventured to approach the baby grand piano in the living room—a
Gannon family heirloom—and discovered it could serve for more
than gleaming statuary. They had soon found themselves competing
to see who could learn tunes from Chrissie's and Julia's instructional
books most quickly. Each had continued practicing independently,
and when they sat at the piano bench demonstrating what they
had learned, they not only bumped shoulders but touched hands
as well.

This summer's visit would be especially sweet, as Phillip had
spent the last year attending college on the east coast. It was not
that she'd seen him much less often—he only visited on two or
three occasions per year in any case, and he had spent a day with
them in Arden Park over Christmas—and distance seemed not to
have impaired his letter-writing; yet she had still grieved to picture
him so far away. Time had not diminished her appreciation of her
cousin. Even now, she could see only one flaw in him, a tendency
to be overprotective that she attributed to her skin color, but of
even this she could not be truly critical. She found him perfectly
handsome and intellectually brilliant, knew him to be kind, loyal,
and charitable, considered his judgment in all things to be wise,
and believed that she could tell him anything at all about herself

and receive a sympathetic hearing. Her reading of literature had taught her such perfection could not be sustained for any merely human being, yet she was not altogether certain that Phillip *was* merely human.

The second major event of the summer involved a Mr. and Mrs. Lee who had purchased Tina's former residence, across from the Gannons' home. The family had long accepted that the Lees were somewhat eccentric, and even suspected encroaching dementia, but they had little direct knowledge of their personalities, as the elderly couple was generally private and had resisted involvement in neighborhood affairs. While no animosity existed between the households, little more than nods and waves had been exchanged between them in the decade-plus they'd lived in Arden Park. Shortly before Phillip's arrival, however, Mrs. Lee stopped Tina's car as she pulled from the driveway and announced that her grandchildren were coming to spend the summer with her.

"Sherry's the most beautiful little thing you ever saw," she said. "Such a nice figure, and she's so sweet to me. I think it's because she so takes after me. And Max is simply a splendid actor. You know his stepfather is a movie producer, which is going to help him tremendously. He's not tall though. I wish he were taller, but then that's how it is with actors now. Not like it was. Bogey was short—Lauren was hardly more than a child, but she knew enough to dip her head so he'd looked taller than she was—but Jimmy was six-feet at least, and Cary and Clark and Errol and, of course, Duke were all taller than he was. Errol was really quite tall . . . ."

Despite the car that waited in the street behind her, Tina's interest was piqued by the older lady's reference to acting. She managed a parting suggestion that the young people meet when Sherry and Max arrived in Arden Park, and the following week, when she'd had opportunity to observe that Sherry and Max both were sufficiently attractive, Tina offered an invitation to dinner. Thomas, who now was in college and could only intermittently be found in residence even in summer, happened to be at home, and Tina invited them for the evening of the day of Phillip's expected arrival, in order that the Hills might meet the entire entourage of young people.

Thus it was that Sherry and Max Hill, accompanied by their grandparents, presented themselves to Tina at the Gannons' door. It happened that Phillip had for the first time driven his own car to Arden Park, and this provided the first opportunity for conversation. An older Porsche that his father had restored two decades earlier and then put into storage after finding it too ostentatious to drive, it had been presented to Phillip as a graduation present. The emerald-green car now sat in the driveway, displaying a rarity and perfection that could not go unremarked—not even among those accustomed to swank automobiles.

"Lovely car," Max Hill said, his voice surprisingly deep for his small frame.

"It belongs to our nephew Phillip—Phillip Gannon from San Francisco."

It would have been crass to query Phillip's relationship to the Gannon Oil Company, as it perhaps was of Tina to so pointedly emphasize his name, but it was apparent from Max's and Tina's discreet but understanding nods that no query was necessary. No doubt, his grandparents had informed him of the crucial details.

Like her brother, Sherry Hill was small of stature, but she was darker-haired—and, Tina observed, lively-eyed and very cute indeed, with a perfectly proportioned, if petite, figure. "It's such a beautiful green," the girl said. "You feel like you could just dive down and swim in it."

Sherry had been holding her grandmother's hand ever since her arrival, and she now guided her down the hallway into the living room, where the two young people were introduced to Cynthia. This task gracefully accomplished, the two Hills followed Tina out to the family room to meet the young people. The Hills understood good manners and good conversation. They gave brief but unapologetic address to the customary forms of introductions and pleasantries in much the same way a young aristocrat might wrap a loosely cinched tie around his neck for a family party; then when Tina had departed, their conversation advanced quickly to compliment, ironic social commentary, and even the slightly ribald. For one brief moment when Max commented about the rural character of the city, the proximity of farms to the city limits, and the row-upon-row of box-like houses that were being plopped down in the middle of bare pastures and fields, Chrissie and Julia suspected he might be haughty. Such an attitude could not have been maintained. The sisters did themselves condescend instinctively but could only treat condescension directed toward them as utterly ridiculous and worthy only of contempt.

"Arden Park, though," Max went on, "it's so beautiful and quiet. It's like an English country estate here." Arden Park was not, of course, in any way like an English country estate, but the girls were appeased by the comment. Haughty was acceptable, as long as they were safely ensconced among the high.

Otherwise, the conversation was accomplished with such ease, with such deep interest in the views and habits of their hosts, and with such admiration of their tastes that nothing offensive could be found in it. The Gannon children, having so infrequently been exposed to people of such effortless manners, were much impressed. They found themselves enraptured even by the story of the circumstances that had placed the Hills in Arden Park.

The two had been living with their mother in Los Angeles, but their stepfather had taken a financial role in producing a movie and was temporarily relocating to a small tropical paradise to be near the movie set. The children, who were not fond of their stepfather, didn't wish to be marooned with him, not even in paradise.

"He's a crook is what he is," Max said.

"He is not," Sherry corrected.

"Maybe not a crook exactly," Max said, "just a chiseler. The unindicted co-conspirator." Sherry shrugged and smiled pleasantly at this, and Max continued. "The house is actually in Bel Air. It was our mother's and father's originally. No doubt Jerry's found a way to mortgage it for more than it's worth. He says he's planning to loan it to some British actor or another who's in LA for a film. Really, I think he's planning to lease it. Needs the money. Otherwise, they'll probably lose the place."

"Max exaggerates," Sherry said, "but Jerry is a gambler—at least when it comes to films he is. And his finances are complicated beyond belief. He could be worth millions."

"Or more likely that's what he owes."

"I'm sure *you* don't know one way of the other . . . . In any case we were both living at home, though Max had the caretaker's cottage . . . ."

"And we were put out on our ears."

"Mom suggested I come stay with Gram and Gramps, which I thought was a wonderful idea, and Max has sort of tagged along. In fact, I have almost no idea what Max is doing here."

"Neither do I," he admitted with a shrug. "All that work . . . finding a new place . . . . Who can be bothered?"

"Maybe we both needed a vacation from Los Angeles for a while. Sometimes you live there and begin to think it's the only place in the world. I know a change will be good for me. It's so peaceful and beautiful here, and I had no idea that Gram and Gramps had such interesting neighbors."

The meal was taken outside by the pool. While the Hills conducted themselves with more formality with the adults present, they appeared to be at their ease and to enjoy themselves—as well they might, considering that Esmeralda, the cook who had begun to appear in the Gannon house with increasing frequency since Dr. Gannon's departure, had prepared a lusciously colorful, sweet, and refreshing fruit salad to accompany salmon fillets with caper sauce.

The current plans and accomplishments of all the Gannon family, excepting Jasmine, were reviewed, commented on, and duly praised. Cynthia explained Jasmine simply as, "our niece, who lives with us and helps me with the flowerbeds." In discussing Max's involvement in the film industry, the subject of stepfather Jerry again arose, and Tina commented that it must be very helpful to his career to have such a strong connection in the industry.

"The danger is he'd get me in some schlocky B-flick that would set my career back ten years."

"Stop," Sherry said. "You're giving our neighbors the wrong impression . . . ."

"Or some later letter of the alphabet," Max said, looking out from under his eyebrows.

Most did not take the reference until Thomas blurted out, "Like x?", with a rather horrible laugh. This was met by embarrassed laughter from nearly all.

"Jerry is a completely reputable filmmaker," Sherry corrected, with a stern but loving look towards her brother. "Early on he made some B-films that Max likes to make fun of. But since then, he's done some very good and very innovative work. Max likes to think of himself as a serious artist. Occasionally we have to remind him that it's just movies, after all."

All were curious about the names of the Hills' stepfather's films and whether they might have seen them, but something in Sherry's tone made them not want to ask. Many other questions *were* asked, however, and much was learned about the film industry. The meal did not conclude until after nine, when the Lees pronounced themselves tired, and Sherry took her grandmother's arm and led the household home.

Max and Sherry having proved to be fashionable in taste and to possess undeniable social graces, and their stepfather being in a position which suggested at least glamour if perhaps not wealth, Mrs. Stubbs was eager to extend the acquaintance. Beneath this interest lay an unspoken understanding that Max, while perhaps a two or three years too old for her at the moment, might someday make an ideal match for Julia. It being discovered that the filter on the Lees' pool was not functioning properly, Tina was quick to invite them to use the Gannons' whenever they might need it, and the Hills soon became frequent visitors.

Sherry often sat out in the sun, her wet, dark hair pulled back from her forehead and gleaming. Despite her petite figure, she showed little modesty about how it outlined under her bathing suit, which was of a dingy-appearing beige, a little stretched, and inclined to droop and cling unpredictably, or how transparently or openly her blouses draped. All together, except for a certain physical grace which created a more mature impression, she would have been judged ravishingly cute. Indeed, had she been blond, taller, and more generously proportioned, and had Julia and Chrissie not been utterly secure in their own beauty, they might have felt some threat from her.

The sisters' original disappointment at Max's rather too average appearance had not been completely allayed by their first dinner. In addition to his small stature, his skin didn't tan as well as his sister's, and he often wore a long-sleeved, white shirt draped over his shorts. He was not the least athletic, and smoked an occasional cigarette—of some exotic brand—which they generally found repulsive. Moreover, he held his fingers with an off-putting artistic delicacy that might have seemed feminine if not for his very deep, unusually smooth voice, which had already earned him several jobs narrating for television and radio.

Even had his voice been high, however, all his shortcomings would eventually have been redeemed by his knowledge of the best clubs in Los Angeles, his stories of meeting young actors at parties, most of whom he regarded with disdain, the perfect teeth which seemed to be a family trait, and his gift for conversation. He was only three years older than Chrissie, but the manner in which he was able to talk about the most intimate of subjects, whether it be sex, drugs, or the affairs of one's parents, caused both girls to feel daringly sophisticated. There was no denying that he lived in a richer, more adventurous, more glamorous, and altogether better world than they.

By the end of their first week of acquaintance, neither sister would have judged him either too short or too plain. By the end of the second, both found him to be one of the better looking men they'd ever met, and Chrissie was urging the well-bronzed Pudge to purchase a Brooks Brothers shirt to wear poolside to cover his bulging girth.

For a time, Tina contemplated a large party to display the Hills, but not yet feeling secure in their special affections, she eventually satisfied herself with enhancing the elegance of the usual Gannon entertainments. The young people still regularly dined on the patio, but the tables were now draped with linen and decorated with flowers, the silver had begun to be used, Esmeralda was often asked to stay on and help serve, and the fare grew more exotic, including items such as endive salad, Thai satay, shrimp, and frozen fruit drinks. The Hills greeted these efforts with proper appreciation, though certainly without awe, Max displaying a surprisingly robust appetite, and it seemed to Tina that everyone appeared for the better amid the bright tablecloths and shining silver. Thus, the young people spent many hours at the side of the pool, sipping drinks, sampling tasty dishes, and conversing.

Jasmine, while she usually didn't join them at the pool edge, often sat under one of the umbrellas, listening from afar. On one such evening, just as the sun was setting and the shadow of the umbrella was becoming too dark for reading, she had put her book down and paused for a moment to let a breath of cool breeze waft across her face, when the conversation at the pool edge drew her attention.

"It doesn't matter at all what kind of car a person drives," Max was saying, apparently in response to some comment by Chrissie.

"On the other hand, you wouldn't be caught dead in a Plymouth," his sister said.

"A Plymouth," Max said with an abashed look that caused the Gannon sisters to laugh aloud. Then he incited more laughter when he gathered himself, sat straighter, and said, "I'd be immensely proud to be the owner of such a noble vehicle."

"The whole point is that it isn't the least bit noble," Sherry said quickly, "and the only way you'd drive it was if you could make people think it was."

Max looked at his sister and pondered, but didn't grant her point.

"Max would make it noble," Julia said.

"He would," Chrissie added. "Any car Max drove would be noble."

Max gave Chrissie a light touch on the chin, which made her beam with pleasure.

"But that's just the same as saying that clothes don't matter," Sherry said, "and in the real world, they always do. If somebody is dressed in some awful way, they've got no chance. And if Max were driving a Plymouth, it would be just the same as if he was wearing Bermuda shorts and knee socks."

Chrissie and Julia laughed at the idea of Max so clad, and even Jasmine, from her seat in the distance, silently admitted such an idea to be ridiculous.

"'Clothes don't matter,'" Phillip now said, "it's one of those axioms that we silently applaud and pretend are true, but which don't hold up to close analysis."

"Like which axioms?" Pudge, who had been listening passively, now asked.

"Love conquers all," Phillip said.

When this statement was met with quiet, though perhaps somewhat reluctant, acceptance, Phillip said, "Two heads are better than one."

"Almost never true," Max agreed. "Idiots just get in the way."

"If it saves even one life, it's worth any cost," Phillip said.

"Nah," Max said quickly. "There wouldn't be many traffic deaths if we all walked instead of drove, but it wouldn't be worth the cost."

"All men are created equal," Phillip said.

This statement created an embarrassed silence, as, while it was not intended to refer to racial differences, the axiom had become so closely associated with racial arguments that the issue immediately became apparent. No one was completely certain how closely Jasmine was listening.

Sherry, feeling the uncomfortable silence, attempted to mitigate any potential hurt, saying, "God knows I could never pass one of Phillip's physics classes if I took the course ten times. And Max could run every day for the rest of his life and never catch up with him on the track."

In fact, Jasmine had been listening, but it was not the final axiom that had disturbed her. She fully understood that the common understanding of Jefferson's assertion was delusional; people were not equal in any way. Nor were aptitudes, talents, and skills distributed equably or even randomly. Now, as the silence had resumed, she looked up from her book and offered her opinion, one that she had learned directly from her grandmother's mouth. "I believe that Jefferson only intended the statement to mean that all men, including King George, were created equal before God and that laws and governance ought to apply to them all equally, even the King."

"All except black people," Phillip now said.

Thomas Jefferson had been presented to her by her grandmother as a hero of human progress, and she now went on in his defense. "The idea that common men were equal to the king was far from self-evident to almost anyone but Jefferson. That *led* to the idea that common people were equal to each other, which led to the idea that African common people were equal to European common people. Without Jefferson, there couldn't have been a Lincoln, and without Lincoln there couldn't have been a Booker T. Washington."

This last reference was lost on most of the young people, though they were wary enough of their own ignorance—and Jasmine's intelligence—not to ask the question which first occurred to them: What interest had President Lincoln taken in funky jazz? Phillip, however, knew who Booker T. Washington was, and on previous occasions having heard Jasmine refer to her grandmother's reverence for him, had read *Up From Slavery*. "And without Booker T. Washington," he now said, "there could have been no Martin Luther King."

Chrissie now said, "Really, we all just believe what we're brought up to believe anyway."

Phillip turned to her quickly. "I refute that," he said. "That sort of reasoning is being used to defend all types of prejudices that any logical person can see are ridiculous. Aren't there some standards of reasoning that are independent of our upbringing? Aren't there some objective measures of fairness and right and wrong?"

No one wanted to answer his somewhat heated inquiry, and Phillip answered for himself. "Even if we are all subject our own prejudices, we have to at least try not to be. We have a moral obligation to do the best we can."

"Maybe that's just another prejudice," Max said, inciting doubtful laughter from Chrissie.

"If so, it's the one universal prejudice we all ought to accept."

Jasmine remained silent, contemplating the course of the conversation. She was not much troubled by most of it. Like the others, she'd long since given up the idea that all people were endowed with equal talents. She felt certain that the others overemphasized the importance of clothing—many millionaires, famous scientists, and saints were well known to have paid very little attention to their appearances; Einstein was reported to have sometimes forgotten to wear socks—yet as a brown-skinned girl, she'd had even more opportunity than her cousins to observe the effects of tidy skirts and pressed blouses on the behaviors of store clerks, gatekeepers, and even teachers. She could hardly deny that first impressions had a powerful, sometimes even insurmountable influence on people's judgments. She felt they'd too easily dismissed the value of a human life, but could not deny that safety had necessarily to be balanced against cost. Two heads were most certainly not always better than one. Indeed, it was Phillip's first example that had caused her the most distress. She very much wanted to believe that her parents' and grandmother's love, which she believed had persisted even after their deaths, the love she and her brother felt for each other, and even her love for Phillip could, if perhaps not conquer all, endure all tribulations.

Such grave considerations had now passed far from the others' minds, however, for the conversation had moved on to evaluation of the essential elements of a good name for a rock-and-roll band. On this evening, however, they were unable to reclaim the gleeful and exuberant joy they usually found in exploring the inane and trivial. Max and Sherry left before midnight, more than an hour earlier than had become typical for them.

Max did not at first talk to his sister on their walk home, and Sherry feared what effect the dull evening might have on him. While they had both found the Gannons to be better acquaintances than they had hoped for in the out-of-the-way backwater of Arden Park, her brother was easily bored. She suspected that he had accompanied her to their grandparents to escape some temporary unpleasantness—whether financial, legal, romantic, or some combination of the three she did not know. Such crises usually passed quickly with him, and she was concerned now that dullness would drive him away. She enjoyed his company and he hers, and she questioned whether Arden Park would be very pleasant without him. Unfortunately, she could make no claim to influence over his behavior.

When they had crossed the dark street, she broke the silence, saying, "I'd have thought you'd be back in LA by now."

He murmured an assent.

"Still sizing up the possibilities?"

"So to speak."

"Big girls, aren't they?"

"I'd say," he replied.

"I'd say so, too, if falling out of their bathing suits qualifies."

"Don't you just love that?"

Sherry laughed. "Not as much as you do, I'm sure. But why not? They'll be big as their mom in a few years. I'd say they're ripe for the plucking."

"The plucking, you say?"

"The plucking," she repeated, laughing again.

"Actually, their mother's pretty prime herself," Max said.

"God, Max, that's completely gross. She's got to be at least forty-five. But the way she saunters out to the pool, you'd think she was Miss America. She'd probably wear diamond-studded slides if it wasn't just too ridiculous."

"I wouldn't be surprised to learn she'd been a Miss America. She's certainly got the rigging."

"And that thousand watt smile . . . . It's a thing I don't understand about men, why they can be so attracted to all that flesh."

"Have no fear," Max said. "In the long run, you'll hold up better."

"Oh, I know that. I'm perfectly happy with my looks . . . . But of the two, of the two sisters, you like Julia better, right?"

"Chrissie's got a better ass."

"But you prefer Julia."

Max laughed and wrapped an arm around his sister's shoulders. "If you say that I prefer Julia, I prefer Julia."

"Pudge could snap your little neck with one hand."

"Pudge I suspect is too dim a bulb to know which necks need snapping."

"My God, you're hopeless," Sherry laughed. "But I'm completely serious. Julia and Chrissie are both very sweet. They've been nothing but good to us, and they'll be right across the street all summer. It would be awful to do anything to mess that up."

"Do you think I'm such a jerk that I need this type of lecture?"

"Yes, I do."

He laughed again. "Julia it is then. I'll set my sights on Julia. Too bad for you Phillip isn't a little hunkier."

"He's hunky enough," Sherry demurred.

"If his father wasn't worth a hundred million, you'd never look at him."

"Is he worth that much?"

"Give or take fifty . . . . Did you know he wants to be a school teacher?"

Sherry nodded. "I admire him for that."

"It's still boring."

"There's nothing wrong with wanting to help other people. Just because you don't do it, and I almost never do, doesn't mean we have a right to ridicule those who do. I think altruism is really very wonderful, especially when it comes from someone who has as much money as Phillip . . . . Besides, it's something I'm sure he'll grow out of when he begins to see other possibilities."

Max laughed again. "Meaning that it's wonderful, but you don't want to have anything to do with it."

"Meaning that I'm not sure I'm as good a person as he is."

"Good, bad, indifferent, or whatever—you'd die living the life of a school teacher's wife."

"That might be true," Sherry said thoughtfully, "but if it is, it's not something I'm proud of."

Max guffawed. "Please spare me."

"I won't spare you. The truth is, as much as I love you, you're a very selfish person, and I'm not that much better. It's how we were raised, but that doesn't make us right, and it doesn't make us better than someone else. In fact, it probably makes us worse."

In truth, as much as she enjoyed the intelligence and ingenuousness of his conversation, Sherry would have liked Phillip to have been more handsome and dashing. She had only in the past year become consciously aware of an instinctual, ever-active mechanism in her that automatically grouped the boys and men she met: First, there were those who were repulsive and those who were not. Those among the unobjectionable were further divided: there were boys with whom a girl might flirt, whom she might date, and with whom she might even let go once in a while; then there were boys who might someday be a husband. A husband need not necessarily be rich and famous, but he must be rich. If she were going to live with someone, that someone ought to be able to provide her with the means to do the things her friends did, to live as they did, and to buy the houses, clothes, furniture, cars, wine, and vacations that made life enjoyable. Phillip, thoroughly to-the-manor-born, was safely in this marriageable class. If he'd also generated more excitement, he would have been too good to be true.

"Go easy," she now advised her brother. "Someday, you know, you're going to want to marry some girl. And Julia Gannon wouldn't be a bad catch."

"What is it with women and marriage? Every marriage you've been around has been a failure."

"I think it's that women understand something about marriage that you don't."

"Oh?"

"The world is made for married people. There's no other choice. Everything else eventually dries up. You'll have to give in to it someday. It's the way the world works."

"It sounds damn boring."

"I imagine it would—to you, who can't even keep a girlfriend through two menstrual periods. But it's not like marriage has to be a cage," she said.

They were now entering the front door of the house. Sherry stopped inside the door, and though their grandparents were usually sleeping by nine o'clock in the evening, she dropped to a softer voice. "Mom and Dad are no happier now than they were when they were together. No one ever is. They should have just stayed together and had affairs. It would have been so much simpler."

"Is that what you're going to do?"

"It's better than a divorce."

"What if your husband turned out to be mean? Or gay?"

"No one would dare be mean to me. And as long as he was rich, I wouldn't care if he was gay. In fact, that might be better. We could be friends. We wouldn't provoke each other."

After Max had poured himself a glass of brandy from his grandfather's decanter, they sat in the dark on the leather couch in front of the fireplace.

"But it's not the same for men," Max went on. "Living with some pooch would seem like a losing bargain, even if she was rich and all that. I think it would be better for me to be one of those men married women have their affairs with."

Sherry shook her head. "No married woman with an ounce of sense would have anything to do with a single man . . . . Plus, old bachelors just seem completely ridiculous. Can you imagine anything more awful than Hugh Hefner limping around his house in his bathrobe with his bony chest hanging out? That's just totally disgusting. You'll have to get married. The thing is to plan."

Chapter 8

We Learn More of Max and Sherry Hill

One evening when Thomas was again in town for a weekend, a discussion arose at the dinner table as to whether—now that the children were older and Chrissie and Phillip were to be away at school—wine should be offered to all at the table.

"There is something to be said for learning moderation in the home," Max said, not fearing to meet both Mrs. Gannon's languid and Mrs. Stubbs's more piercing eyes. "With every kind of drug imaginable readily available to any high school student . . . ."

"In grammar schools even, so I've heard," Tina interjected, tossing a quick glance toward Jasmine.

Max nodded solemnly, saying, "It's come to that," and Jasmine, who was sitting on one side of him, noticed that his sister, who was on his other side, reached under the table and pinched his leg. His countenance never quivered.

"But is alcohol really all that different from other drugs?" Julia interjected.

For a moment, all eyes were on Cynthia and Tina, who both enjoyed afternoon cocktails, wine with dinner, and occasional gin and tonics by the pool.

"I think it is," Max said evenly. "Alcohol is very much a part of our culture and our western traditions. Abuse can be dangerous, just as abuse of anything can, even food or television for that matter, but we have well established rituals, rules, and traditions for the use of alcohol. Those rules, if we learn them—if parents don't abdicate their responsibilities to teach them—allow us to experience the pleasure of alcohol without allowing it to become a burden."

"I never have drinks before five," Tina said. "And I know that Cynthia rarely allows herself more than one drink in an entire evening."

In the course of an evening, Jasmine typically carried out to her aunt at least two and not uncommonly three glasses of wine, but no denial was forthcoming from Cynthia.

"Exactly my point," Max said. "You've established rules to assure that alcohol is kept in its proper role. Isn't it just like the rules of courtesy? Just as there exist certain boundaries that you don't cross with your friends and neighbors, there are certain boundaries you don't cross with alcohol. As long as one stays within the bounds of tradition and proper usage, alcohol can remain a source of great pleasure, just as one's friends are. It's when one begins to impose too much that problems arise."

"With friends or with alcohol?" Thomas suggested.

Max laughed. "Both of course."

"There's something in that, isn't there?" Tina said to her sister.

"Something in it?" Cynthia said.

"But I'm not so sure that instruction is as important as example," Sherry suggested quickly. "I'm sure none of you," she continued, looking around to the three Gannon children, and then to Jasmine, "would ever have a problem with alcohol abuse, as you've always had perfect models to emulate. Max and I . . ."

"Yet," Max interrupted, "it's still possible to make mistakes. Wouldn't it make more sense to have those first experiments with alcohol occur here in the home rather than in who-knows-whose house—or, heaven forbid, even in a car? Don't you agree, Thomas?"

"It seems reasonable to me," Thomas said, with a smile. "I could tell you stories of some things that went on when I was in school that would curl your hair, Mom."

"Please, don't," Cynthia said.

"Dad's always said that we have a responsibility to set an example for others," Chrissie said.

"It comes with the roles we occupy, doesn't it?" Max said, nodding to Chrissie. "Let's face it. We've all been very privileged. We've grown up with all we've needed, always been able to attend the best schools, and, while Sherry and I can't make equal claims with your family, we've been granted the wonderful gifts of health, good appearance, and certain talents. I think with those gifts comes a leadership responsibility. And I know of no family anywhere that's done a more admirable job of accepting that responsibility than the Gannons. Dr. Gannon has sacrificed his medical practice for public service. And I've seen how often you, Mrs. Gannon, are working on one charitable project or another, and, Mrs. Stubbs, you've sacrificed so much for the welfare of your nieces and nephews, who, I must say, are a true credit to the family name."

While Jasmine appreciated the Hills' handsomeness, their adept and intelligent minds, and their quick wit, she sensed that there was something not right about the way they spoke with adults. Using the polite form of address, "Mrs. Gannon" or "Mrs. Stubbs," correct forms of who and whom, and an almost English-sounding accent seemed to excuse them from any accusation of impropriety in thereafter offering their opinions and proposing activities exactly as though they were of equal rank.

Thomas, who regarded most of the household goings-on with bemusement, now laughed aloud, saying, "And what exactly does this have to do with wine at the table?"

Max laughed joyfully along with him. "I did get a bit on my high horse didn't I. But it's all true nonetheless, and the point is this: The best families have to take leadership. We shouldn't allow this to become a battle between the prohibitionists and the booze pushers. It's only one example, but it's demonstrative. We have a responsibility to speak up for moderation and good sense."

"You know, there is more than a little truth in what Maxwell says, Thomas," Mrs. Stubbs said. "There are decisions and judgments that your mother and father have had to make as adults, which you've been unaware of—situations where they've been obliged to sacrifice their own welfare, and even sometimes that of you children, for the general good. Dr. Gannon being in Washington is a perfect example." She turned to her sister. "I think what Max has said makes good sense, and knowing David's character as I do, I'm certain that if he were here, he would approve as well. Why don't we, Cynthia?"

Mrs. Gannon let her eyes fall first on Max and then Sherry. "Is this an arrangement that you've had in your own home?"

"Oh, yes," Sherry said quickly, "forever. But then mother was French, and she always has said that the French are much more open and matter-of-fact about a lot of things."

Mr. and Mrs. Lee, who were the parents of Sherry's and Max's mother, did not seem at all French to Jasmine, but she supposed Sherry might be referring to some stepmother by way of her stepfather.

"It's something we could consider," Mrs. Gannon replied.

"It is," Mrs. Stubbs said. "Of course it is. The French view really is much more mature than our American ways. Prohibition certainly would never have happened in France. Jasmine, why don't you set out additional glasses."

Jasmine had been amazed when her Aunt Tina suggested that Dr. Gannon would approve. Though her uncle took a glass of wine with dinner and an occasional brandy late in the evening, she was aware that he looked askance on his own wife's cocktail glasses and had more than once declined offers of drinks rather pointedly, with a sharp glance at his wife. Moreover, he had often warned his children about the effects of alcohol on moral judgment and of the sometimes mortal consequences of its abuse, and had even suggested that its banishment from the face of the earth would be to the benefit of all. Nor would he have overlooked the legal consideration that providing alcohol to minors was against the law, just as consumption of it by them was. Jasmine believed that he would not only have been opposed, but would have been adamantly so. She set the glasses with a troubled conscience, skipping only her own place; and a half-glass of white wine was poured in each, swirled, sniffed, and sipped. Phillip, Jasmine noted, took only the smallest taste, that is, until Sherry raised her glass and cast her bright smile across the table at him.

"Such wonderful friends we've found here, so generous and kind. To think, that before we came we worried that it would be a lost summer. Now, I can't think of anyplace I would have preferred to be."

The catch that came into her voice and the tears that gathered in her eyes made her sincerity apparent. Phillip's face reddened, the pleasure glowed out of it, and he followed her lead in taking a deeper draught of the wine.

Perhaps in part because she was aware of her close friendship with Phillip, Sherry was always considerate of Jasmine, frequently being the first in the group to invite her into conversation. That evening, after dinner was over and the young people had moved out to the patio, Sherry deliberately took a seat beside her.

"I could see that you were upset about the wine," Sherry said.

"Upset?" Jasmine said, then realizing that she was imitating one of her aunt's less attractive mannerisms, went on before Sherry could respond, "I didn't think that my uncle would have approved."

"And you don't approve either."

Jasmine didn't reply.

"There's no reason you should," Sherry said. "Max was only trying to see what he could get away with. I'm sure he doesn't believe any of it."

While Thomas was apt to act against his parents' wishes, he always did so secretly. Never had Jasmine seen so bold a deception played out in the Gannon household. The realization of it made her feel much as though a wall of the house had fallen down.

"It's like there are two of him," Sherry continued. "When he gets bored, his evil twin comes out. But it's not really him. Though I see how somebody who doesn't know him like I do might think so."

"Is Arden Park really so boring?" Jasmine asked.

"No, of course not. It's just that in comparison to Los Angeles . . . ." She broke off, gave Jasmine a long, studied look, and began again, "But enough about Max, I want to know more about you." She then proceeded to ask many questions about Jasmine's circumstances and expressed much admiration for the maturity with which she'd handled such changes in her home life and rearing.

"Max and I have been through some stuff ourselves, though not like you have. I think my *current* stepfather has been the worst. He's just not a very good person—plus, he's pretty stupid—he's a real bastard is what he is," she said, lowering her voice as she did. "It's only his money that's gotten him places, and now I think most of that's gone. He's horrible to our mother. I don't know why she puts up with it. I never would. Then, of course, she wasn't so nice to Dad either. Honestly, I think both my parents acted like children."

"I hadn't known that your mother was French," Jasmine said.

"Oh, she wasn't really," Sherry said with a laugh. "But she lived in France for a while when she was a girl, and she spent a year there when she was in college. All that just seemed like too much to explain at the time."

When the subject of Jasmine's brother was raised, Sherry listened with rapt attention, gazing into her eyes. "You must love him very much," she said.

"I do," Jasmine said. "More than anyone. He and Granny were everything to me."

"Yet you haven't seen him in how long?"

"More than two years. He's only been able to visit three times. He's in the military now. He looks wonderful in his uniform."

Sherry interrupted to ask if she had a picture of him, and they were soon in Jasmine's room gazing at the photo that always sat on her dresser.

"He's very handsome," Sherry said.

"He's only an enlisted man now, but he hopes to become an officer. He's applied to a special program that would pay his way to attend university. He says that he knew of one private who was even able to get appointed to the military academy in West Point."

"I'm sure he'll do it," Sherry said. "I can tell just by looking at him that he's the type to succeed."

While Jasmine was unusually resistant to fulsome praise of herself, she was vulnerable to any such praise of her brother, and she now felt very warmly toward Sherry Hill for her kind words.

When they were once again back at the pool, Phillip joined them at the table. Sherry had the habit of approaching more closely than normal when conversing, and she now drew her chair within a few inches of Phillip's and leaned toward him, saying, "We've been looking at pictures in Jasmine's room. Jasmine's brother is quite the hottee."

Though the statement referred to William and not to Phillip, Sherry's tone and smile made it feel to Jasmine as though she were speaking just as much about Phillip himself. He apparently felt this, too, as he reddened and smiled with pleasure and embarrassment. As Jasmine watched him writhe in the grasp of Sherry's smile, she felt something like loneliness. The warmth of her gratitude toward Sherry cooled.

The changes in Phillip in the last year and a half had been remarkable. While still not tall and not conventionally handsome, he'd grown at least two inches. His hair had darkened, and his nose, which had not been at all prominent before, now created the strong, straight profile of a statue. His sideburns were thick, and his face developed a shadow of beard in the evenings. Moreover, running had developed his posture, and he displayed a quiet, athletic confidence, which appeared to have been much enhanced by his year of independence at college.

"Chrissie tells me that you got up in the middle of the night to run," Sherry was now saying to him.

Phillip laughed. "It was after six. Maybe to Chrissie that's the middle of the night. It gets too hot after that."

"I bet you're very fast," Sherry said, leaning yet closer.

"I'm okay," he said. "I'm not great."

"You're just modest."

"One of the advantages of running," he said, "is that you always know just exactly how good you are. Stopwatches don't lie. If somebody in Timbuktu is better than I am, there's no denying it. I was okay in high school. If I keep running and get better, I can be good in college. I'm not going to the Olympics."

"I wouldn't bet on that," Sherry said, and despite the complete reasonableness of what he'd just said, and the assurance with which he'd said it, Phillip wasn't able to suppress a smile.

Jasmine had seen Phillip's face transformed before when Sherry directed comments at him and on other occasions had noted him studying her when he thought himself unobserved. Now, as she watched him react to Sherry's attentions, the experience of loneliness she'd felt earlier expanded into a sharper sensation with a edge of humiliation to it that was completely new to her, an emotion she was able to identify as jealousy only because reading novels had prepared her for it. "So," she thought, "this is what it feels like." Shamed, she sought to quell her upset with reason. It was natural, she told herself, that Phillip would be attracted to Sherry. They were put much together, and Sherry's figure, as they were often swimming or sunbathing, was often much on display. Sherry was very pretty, intelligent, witty, and good-humored, and she was skilled in flattery.

"How far do you run?" Sherry now asked.

"It depends. Some days three or four miles. Some days more."

"So far? Never in a million years could I run that far."

Sherry's slim body was wonderfully flexible and healthy. While she could lounge about the pool for hours with lioness-like indolence, she could also chase down an overthrown Frisbee with remarkable acceleration and snatch it out of the air with effortless dexterity. Moreover, she was a gorgeous diver. "I think, Sherry, that you could do it very well if you wanted to," Jasmine ventured.

"Not if it required putting shoes on before noon," she replied.

"You could run barefoot like the Kenyans," Phillip said quickly.

Their sharp burst of laughter tailed off into silence, and Jasmine once again detected that type of awkwardness she'd so rarely before experienced in her Arden Park home. She wanted to say something to relieve it, as she knew that many Kenyans, some of them among the fastest runners in the world, did indeed run barefoot, and felt that neither Sherry nor her cousin had said anything at all wrong or offensive, but no words came readily to mind.

"It's like anything else. If you do it every day, you get better. Like playing the piano . . .," Phillip said, nodding to Jasmine.

"Well, I can't even imagine doing it one day," Sherry said, "though I certainly admire you for it."

Jasmine already had detected an excess of compliment, and even Phillip's more willing belief was at risk of being exceeded; but Sherry was too keenly observant to let her flattery extend further. She now directed the conversation to less personal subjects, albeit still finding frequent opportunities to defer to his wider experience and deeper wisdom—this despite their being of nearly exactly the same age.

Later, when Max and Thomas had gone off somewhere in the car, and Chrissie and Julia had gone inside in something of a pique, Sherry too took her leave. Phillip and Jasmine were left alone, serenaded by the gurgling of the pool filter, their faces lit by the pool lights.

After some quiet minutes, Phillip said, "Sherry seems pretty cool."

"She's has a good sense of humor," Jasmine said, "and she speaks beautifully."

Phillip laughed. "Your grandmother would have approved then?"

Jasmine, who had come to appreciate how eccentric her grandmother's views seemed to others, could now reply without defensiveness. "Granny believed that good elocution leads inevitably to the higher virtues of sincerity, humility, and compassion," she said, adding silently to herself, *And so do I, Granny*—for she had discovered that, while many of her schoolmates could speak in two dialects, one for the classroom and one for their friends, those who knew only poor grammar and slang were not only ignorant but often boorish as well.

"But I suspect that you're not convinced it's reached its inevitable conclusion in Sherry's case," Phillip said.

Jasmine hesitated. Gratified as she was with Sherry's interest in William, she had been troubled by the way she spoke of her parents. She treasured the few memories she had of her own mother and father, knowing that if they were still alive, she would have been able to forgive any shortcomings for the sake of their love. Moreover, she was aware of a certain carelessness in Sherry's behavior to others that might lead to hurt feelings, just as her aunts would be hurt if they were ever to understand how Max had manipulated them on the subject of the wine. This had been Max's doing, not Sherry's; nonetheless, it seemed to Jasmine that Sherry could have done something to stop it.

Only for a moment did Jasmine consider voicing her concerns. She'd withheld her misgivings in the past. Given that her own jealousy might now be influencing her judgment, it was even more imperative that she do so now.

"Sherry has been very thoughtful in asking after William," she finally said, "and I know she has a great capacity for kindness. She's wonderful to her grandmother."

"But you're not sure about her."

"I haven't meant to create that impression."

"Of course, you haven't. You're too good for that. But I can sometimes see things about you others don't. The way you sometimes look at Sherry and Max with that blank look you have—to others, it's just you. To me, it says that you think they're clueless."

"I don't think that, though," she protested honestly. "I think they're both very good looking and amazingly well-spoken, and I often find their conversation delightful. I know they're more clever than anyone else I've met. And they're very much *not* clueless."

"Not clueless, you're right. That's the wrong term. But you still find something not exactly right?" Phillip waited for her denial, a denial that did not come. "You're too good to say it, but you can't deny it."

"I don't think we should ever say things we're unsure of about others. It settles them in our minds. It makes it too easy for us to see what we expect to see."

Phillip did not deny this. "It looks like they have everything," he said, "but you have to think about the environment they've grown up in. They were hurt by their parents breaking up, and Sherry says that their stepfather is a real jerk. And LA isn't like here. It's more fashionable. People are more interested in glamour and money. Given where they've grown up and how they've been raised, maybe we should be surprised that they're as nice as they are."

"I think it's important to be sympathetic to the circumstances of other people's lives," she said.

"But you think I'm being too easy on them."

"I don't know."

"You mean you won't say."

"I mean that I don't know," Jasmine said, now with some vehemence in her voice. "I don't know them well enough to criticize, and I don't know my own feelings well enough to speak them."

"No, you don't criticize. But you don't like the way they talk about their parents, or sometimes even about Cynthia and Aunt Tina when they're not around. And you're right. She shouldn't talk about her parents like that," he said, unconsciously switching back to speaking of Sherry alone, "and she shouldn't have gone along with her brother on all the stuff with the wine. What a bunch of bull that was . . . . And I know she's sometimes too quick to make fun of other people. But I don't think she's bad. I really don't. I think all we need to do is give her a chance. She's only not careful about what she says—she's very natural. I don't think deep-down she's really mean."

"I'm sure that she isn't," Jasmine said, relieved that she could speak completely truthfully.

Phillip replied, "She is really good-hearted about some things."

"She *is*," Jasmine reaffirmed. "And I never hear her say any but kindly things about her grandparents."

Phillip accepted this last statement with a thankful smile, which it would have been cruel to snub, and Jasmine smiled in reply.

Heretofore, Sherry had distributed smiles, dipped eyelashes, and compliments almost equally among Thomas, Phillip, and even Pudge. But as the summer days passed and Thomas was seen less often in Arden Park, Phillip became her established target. Jasmine watched Phillip's countenance brighten under Sherry's attentions and observed that as his confidence grew, his wit quickened.

Jasmine understood that she held no claim to Phillip's romantic affections and could impute no blame to him; nor could she help feeling a painful loss. As he and Sherry often went out together in his car, her walks and bicycle rides with him became less frequent. When he and Sherry were at home together in Arden Park, they were often in close conversation, their heads bent together to deny access to anyone else.

One evening, as Jasmine sat in the quiet living room reading *Emma*, she heard a burst of girlish laughter out on the patio and looked up to see Sherry reach out to touch Phillip's arm. Apparently contented with each other's company, they frequently appeared oblivious to those around them, and Jasmine would have been very surprised to learn that on this occasion, she was the subject of their conversation.

"I don't quite understand who Jasmine *is*," Sherry had been saying to him.

"She's my Aunt Cynthia's niece."

"Yes, but she's lived *here* for five years. Doesn't it seem odd that she hasn't become more a part of the family?"

"She's part of the family."

"Not like Chrissie or Julia."

"Jasmine's Jasmine."

"Do your aunts *not* want her to go out on dates?"

"I don't think they say anything about it one way or the other."

"Why doesn't she then? Chrissie and Julia go out."

"Jasmine's still a girl."

Sherry regarded him curiously then said, "You'd better look at Jasmine again."

Phillip glanced toward the house. "She has grown a lot," he said, looking back to Sherry with a boyish nonchalance that caused her to emit the laugh which Jasmine heard come through the door.

In fact, Jasmine had grown three inches in less than a year, and a pleasant expansion of her figure enhanced the perception of her stature.

"She's striking," Sherry said.

"You really think so?" Phillip said. "I guess I just don't see her that way."

It was only a few days later that Jasmine, while out in the yard one morning to help Cynthia pick flowers for the dining room, bent forward to pick up a faded zinnia blossom Cynthia had discarded. As she began to rise, she discovered, reflected in the glass of the window in front of her, a wild-looking figure standing behind her. Alarmed, she froze for a moment, before realizing that it was only Phillip, just back from his run. Aware that her backside was perhaps pushing too prominently outward, she bent her knees, dipped into a crouch, and turned to face him. His hair stood directly upward, the neckline of his gray T-shirt was ringed with perspiration, his face was red, and his chest was still visibly rising and falling with each quick breath; yet his embarrassment was apparent. His mouth fell slightly open. His eyes seemed to fill with fear and then darted everywhere but to hers, before he looked sheepishly down and shuffled his running shoes.

Jasmine, whose grandmother had always recommended modesty, had never before so well understood its importance. Her shorts, where they pulled high up on her thighs, suddenly seemed to leave only a tiny margin of decency. She became instantly aware of the dipping scoop of her collar, and straightened to make it press flat against her chest.

As confused as Phillip, she was unable to reassure him in any way. Her face flamed hot, and she was unable to speak, not even when their eyes met for a brief, bewildering moment. Instead, she blushed more deeply still.

"I guess I'll take a shower," he mumbled, while turning away.

"Do," Cynthia said. "Esmeralda is already squeezing oranges"

Lewd and boorish behaviors were common at Jasmine's school. Boys leered at girls, gestured, made noises, and shouted mocking commands. No girl was immune; even the less attractive girls were subjected to indecent invitations and ridicule. Considering neither the taunters nor the taunts to merit her attention, Jasmine did her best to ignore them; and since it seemed that the girls who most displayed their figures were subjected to the crudest and most aggressive behaviors, she always dressed plainly and modestly.

Jasmine was, therefore, well aware of how powerful a force display of the feminine figure could be, and she was far too observant not to realize that even the more gentlemanly boys were vulnerable to it. Nonetheless, she was alarmed to discover this same type of response in Phillip and ashamed of herself for having incited it.

She very nearly dreaded meeting him at the breakfast table and was hardly aware of what her own hands were doing as they arranged the new-cut flowers and placed them on the table. He arrived late, his hair still wet, and did not at first look at her. Finally, he met her eyes and asked about an incident in *Emma*. She answered, her voice foreign and confused to her. Yet, when he followed up with a further question, relief began to flood over her, and her skin and voice felt her own again. Clearly, he planned to make no acknowledgment of what had occurred in the yard. Jasmine was happy to follow his lead in considering the incident to be forgotten and immediately saw that it was the only possible course. If they were to continue their friendship, which provided her with the most treasured moments of her life, any suggestion of something other than brotherly affection was impossible.

"You grow a lot better flowers here than we can in San Francisco," Phillip was saying to Cynthia.

"It's only because it's so damned hot here," Julia said, looking up from her cereal.

"Goodness!" Cynthia said.

"It's true though. Maybe it's good for flowers, but half the time it's so hot you can hardly breathe."

"Well, they're certainly spectacular flowers," Phillip said.

Indeed, they were a showy display. Cynthia had no particular skill in flower arranging—had the tones of the wild array of colors been produced by any other artist than Mother Nature, the effect would have been ghastly—but the mixed zinnia, delphinium, marigold, and petunia blooms were individually perfect, and their bright, cheerful abundance was nearly magnificent.

"The garden's so lovely in the morning," Cynthia said, "it's a joy just to go out and pick them. It's wonderful how such a small investment of time in the spring can yield such an abundance of pleasure in the summer."

"You didn't do squat, Mom," Julia said.

"My goodness!" Cynthia repeated.

"It's true. The gardener planted them. All you did was pick them," Chrissie said, adding, somewhat incredulously, as though seeing them for the first time, "They are pretty though."

In fact, Cynthia's labor investment had amounted to little more than selecting flowers for picking, the planting and weeding having been done by the hired gardeners, and Jasmine having removed the culls and cut the preferred blossoms. Jasmine had observed in both her aunts a tendency to treat work carried on at their instructions as having been done by their own hands. Nevertheless, in this case, Cynthia had provided both the initiative to plant the seeds and the impulse to bring the natural beauty to the table, where it made such a joyful display. Jasmine felt that for this her daughters might have given her more credit.

Chapter 9

The Young People Consider
the Question of Free Will

Everyone—or nearly everyone—was delighted to discover that Phillip was smitten with Sherry. Mrs. Gannon saw nothing objectionable in it, and Chrissie and Julia were only too delighted that a romance might create a closer connection between themselves and the Hills, Max Hill in particular. Mrs. Stubbs was the most eager of all for its success.

Prior to his lengthy absences, Tina's natural instinct for command had been constrained by Dr. Gannon, whose authority she rarely dared to challenge directly. His views, which he stated infrequently but with an objectivity and assurance that no one else in the household possessed, had to be respected, even when unwelcome. It was due to his authority that the girls never left home in revealing clothing, the family dined together at least three times per week, with a semblance of good manners being maintained at the table, music—especially songs which were profane or otherwise offensive to good taste—was played at moderate levels, crude language was not heard, and discussions of teenaged sexual, alcoholic, or truancy escapades were only whispered between Julia and Chrissie.

In theory, the children understood that they could bring any problem of any nature to their parents, but in practice only the most dire circumstances would have compelled them to take a problem to Dr. Gannon. Moreover, they were reluctant to take any delicate problem to their mother, because she was prone to relaying such conversations to their father. Thus, in practice, when touchy issues were involved and adult involvement became unavoidable, they went first to their Aunt Tina. When Thomas had been caught with a quantity of malt liquor in his school locker, it was Tina who had devised the strategy that had prevented his expulsion: complete denial of any responsibility for the presence of the liquor, insinuation that certain jealous enemies had planted it, and implied threats of litigation if disciplinary action were taken. The school, threatened with a scandal that the Gannon name would place in a spotlight, had already decided not to pursue the matter further by the time Dr. Gannon was informed, and Tina was able to convince him that this action proved that his son was innocent.

Similarly, when Dr. and Mrs. Gannon had been warned that Chrissie was likely to receive a D in her calculus class—or possibly worse—and Dr. Gannon had threatened to restrict her from attending volleyball practice, dances, and other extra-curricular activities, Tina had managed to deprecate the abilities of her teacher sufficiently that Chrissie's culpability was obscured. Instead, a tutor was found to help her with her homework—indeed, to complete a good portion of it for her—and, without giving her specific instructions to cheat, Tina had made clear to her that she would need to take extraordinary measures to improve on her exams. Thus Chrissie was able to improve on her grade without giving up the critically important social events that would allow her to attract the most desirable friends and dates.

In the past, Tina had accomplished what she could through suggestion, careful politicking, and quick action, and she'd been able to exert considerable influence by assuming roles Cynthia and David were likely to neglect, such as artful scheduling of Thomas's and the girls' activities and quick frightening off of their less seemly acquaintances. Still, she'd been helpless against any unequivocal statement of preference from David. Now, given his distance and Cynthia's docility, she was able to exert her influence more actively. She had always felt that David was far too scrupulous—even naïve—in not encouraging his girls to take full advantage of both their family name and their beauty. She encouraged them to consider acting or modeling careers. More realistic and progressive than David, she allowed her nieces and nephew to understand that their more daring behaviors, including Chrissie's escalating relationship with Pudge, would not meet disapproval. Now, in order that Phillip's and Sherry's romance suffer from no misunderstandings or other impediments concerning family, fortune, or suitability, she felt the necessity of presenting herself as an emissary to the Lees.

While Mrs. Lee had for a number of years maintained a household that conformed to the conventional, good, and expensive tastes of Arden Park, like many women of her generation, she had reverted to frugality. She had been a child during the Great Depression, and in old age, with her social status solid as stone in her own mind, she'd reclaimed old habits. This process, which had begun with a trading down from their larger house in which they'd raised their daughter to the smaller Stubbs residence, had proceeded to more minute economies. She washed and reused plastic bags, did without when the market had no day-old bread, and had worked her way to the bottom drawers of her dressing table to reclaim several decades worth of half-used lipsticks, eyeliners, creams, and powders. Nor did she any longer see reason to replace perfectly usable clothing. Her tastes had once been very good indeed, and her dresses were beautifully tailored out of the finest fabrics, but they were nearly antique and had in any case been designed to display a more youthful figure. The combination of lumpy cosmetics, especially when applied by one whose eyesight was failing, and unconventional garments often conspired to create startling effects. Even the ever-polite Dr. Gannon had once described Mrs. Lee as "mutton dressed up like lamb."

While his wife had lost the ability to discard, Mr. Lee had developed an abhorrence to clutter. The annual city refuse collection days often found items of furniture in the street in front of the house, items which were invariably picked up by scavengers before the city trucks arrived. Only the heaviest and most durable furniture remained in the living room: two velvet wing-chairs, the brown leather chesterfield Max was wont to plop himself in, mahogany end tables, and a matching coffee table. No rug covered the floor, which Mr. Lee had had refinished in a very dark stain.

Her visit to Mrs. Lee marked Tina's first return to the house since she had sold it. She had herself furnished the room in minimalist glass and leather and bleached the oak floors to near white, and she was, of course, affronted by the changes, as we all are when we see our own fine taste overthrown. She had prepared herself to confront horror, however, and given both the many years since her departure and the age of her successors, was able to contain her dismay and compliment Mrs. Lee on the fine, old wing chairs.

"They have good structure," Mrs. Lee admitted.

"They do. They very much do."

"It's so much easier when something has good structure. There's nothing to hide, like when a woman has good facial structure. There's just no substitute for good bone structure."

Tina, though in some doubt about her own bone structure, agreed that this was so.

"Your girls have very good bone structure, though I might like to see their cheekbones a little more prominent. We wouldn't want their eyes to look sunken, though, would we?"

Tina agreed that they would not.

"Sherry's cheekbones, now, are perfect."

"Sherry is a beautiful girl."

"That girl will go far," Mrs. Lee said, with a raised, prognosticating finger.

"I couldn't agree more," Tina said, moving forward in the massive wing chair, which made her feel uncomfortably small and childlike. "She will go far. She's pretty and talented and intelligent, and has all the makings of success."

Mrs. Lee beamed with pleasure and nodded in agreement.

"She has everything," Tina continued. "Still, I think it's important that we encourage our children to establish the right kinds of associations early on. The world has gotten so much more complicated. It's too much to expect a child to find her way alone. Affairs of the heart can be so very unpredictable."

Mrs. Lee, who believed unreservedly that her grandchildren were the most handsome in the world and that their good appearance was exceeded only by their virtue, agreed. "Yes, yes," she murmured, leaning forward from the matching chair and touching Tina's hand, "it's not at all as it was when we were girls."

Tina, though not ready to place herself in the same generation as Mrs. Lee, was eager to be agreeable. "There are so many more dangers for them. Yet, it is just at this age when they expect their guardians to take a diminished role. It seems to me that children now need guidance more than ever. Even I sometimes feel myself at a loss as to what exactly is the best advice."

"Well, I'm sure you always know the right thing to say to influence them for the good," Mrs. Lee said, again patting her hand.

"I do think I have a certain rapport with them. Being the girls' aunt allows me an entré into their feelings. There are some things a girl prefers not to discuss with her mother."

"Do they not get along well with their mother?" Mrs. Lee asked.

"Oh, there's no problem there at all," Tina said quickly. "None whatsoever. I only meant that there are certain types of topics a girl prefers to talk over with someone who can act more in the nature of a friend, or sister."

"I think that's so important," Mrs. Lee said.

Though precisely what Mrs. Lee thought important was not apparent to Tina, she nodded her agreement and moved on to a new topic, saying, "Sherry seems unusually mature for her age."

"Oh, yes. Oh, yes. But not like we were. Girls don't grow up as fast as we did. When I was a girl, a girl of seventeen was considered perfectly fit for marriage. Romeo's Juliet, you know, was no more than thirteen, and the Virgin Mary not a day older. I don't know how girls these days manage to wait so long."

Tina, who had accepted Dr. Stubbs's marriage proposal out of fear that a better one would not come along, had come to believe that if she'd waited longer or calculated only a little better she would have made a match every bit as good as her sister's. Now, in the interest of bolstering this gratifying perception, she ventured a gentle challenge to Mrs. Lee.

"But in some ways it's so much easier for girls now that it's acceptable to wait. They can tell so much more about a boy when he's more established. Like Max. He's done so well. No one could ever doubt his prospects, not with his fine manners and intelligence."

"Oh, yes, Maxwell is a darling," Mrs. Lee said, beaming at the compliment.

Tina felt obliged to point out that Thomas, too, had wonderful prospects, but Mrs. Lee disappointed her by failing to gush when she alluded to the fine reputation of his university.

"And Phillip is, of course, John Gannon's son, so it was in the natural course of things that he would attend an Ivy League school."

"Oh, yes," the old woman said. "A university education is always a wonderful asset, though I must say I wonder sometimes. Mr. Lee never took an interest in higher education, yet he was so successful in his business affairs without one. Perhaps it's sometimes a bit overrated."

"Certainly we must always make exceptions for exceptional people."

The conversation proceeded into stories dating from the Hill children's youth, including descriptions of their walking, talking, and toilet training ages, somewhat sketchily remembered. Having never been a mother, Tina found all this especially tiresome, and she came away from her meeting rather detesting Mrs. Lee. Nonetheless, she was satisfied with its outcome. Mrs. Lee was perhaps not sufficiently impressed with the high standing of the Gannons, but her forces were too scattered to present resistance.

Sherry's interest in Phillip drew him further into the social group that assembled around the Gannon's pool; and, as Sherry took a very real interest in Jasmine and had no wish that she suffer from a loss of Phillip's companionship, she often drew Jasmine into activities as well. Thus, Jasmine spent more and more evenings sitting next to the pool, listening to others' conversations, and to others' music as well. On one such evening, when Pudge was absent due to a family party, Sherry and Phillip sat on one side of the table and Thomas across from them, while Jasmine sat alone on the side facing the pool. Max had seated himself at the pool edge, and Chrissie and Julia had taken places on each side of him. All three dangled their feet in the water. Sherry had been describing her stepfather's scandalous behavior to her mother and offered the opinion that he was an alcoholic. Phillip, trying to be kind, had suggested that no one could be fully blamed for alcohol addiction. This comment had led to a discussion of free will in general.

"Logically," Phillip said, picking his words carefully, "there can be no free will. We're born with a set of genes that determine our physical characteristics, not just our body types, but even the configuration of the neurons in our brains. We then undergo a series of experiences that determine how our genes express themselves. What we eat, how we exercise, and our environments in general determine how we mature and grow old, and every experience we have determines how the neurons in our brains configure themselves. Given our genes and the series of experiences we've had, every decision, every action, every thought is predetermined. If any two people could have exactly the same genes and the same set of experiences they'd behave in exactly the same way. Anything else is impossible."

"We have no choice in anything?" Sherry queried.

"Logically speaking, no," Phillip replied. "Any decision we make is predetermined by our genetics and prior experience."

"Then criminals aren't to blame for what they do, and saints don't deserve any credit," Sherry replied. "So, what's the point then?"

"It's completely absurd, but there may be no point."

Phillip's and Jasmine's past conversations had often turned philosophical: they were of an age where discovering absurdity in life was more stimulating than dismaying; and it was not uncommon for them to stay up late in the night in deep discussion about such subjects as politics, success, happiness, and death. What made Phillip's current behavior different—and disturbing to her—was that he now displayed an element of pride in his tone, an intellectual showmanship, that she'd not before detected.

Thomas, who was already a firm Republican in spite of the views of his father, said, "Even if there is no true free will, the only people in the world who are worth a damn are the ones who act like there is."

"I agree with that," Phillip said softly, "but that may only mean that one of the experiences of their lives—that is, of the people who are worth a damn—was to be taught that their decisions matter. True or false, they believe in free will. That's what makes them different."

Chrissie, who had been splashing her feet desultorily, said, "This is all ridiculous. I can jump off the edge of the pool and swim now or I can stay sitting where I am. It's entirely up to me."

"Nobody questions that we *experience* free will," Phillip said. "But is that experience an illusion?"

"What does it matter if it's an illusion or not," Max said. "For example, I could or could not pinch Chrissie right now . . . ."

"If you do . . .," Chrissie warned, raising a clenched fist in front of her. Max quickly turned away, then just as quickly turned back and firmly pinched her side.

Chrissie howled in delighted protest, reached to push him off the pool edge, and a brief hand-to-hand tussle ensued, drawing them for a moment chest-to-chest, before Chrissie fell across his legs.

"Completely beyond my control," Max said.

"Yeah, the devil made you do it," Chrissie replied. This caused general laughter.

Chrissie struggled a little longer against Max's legs; then Julia inserted herself into the tussle, saying, "You're lucky Pudge isn't here."

After a moment's delay, Chrissie sat up, but Max still held her wrists. She leaned close to his face, their noses almost touching.

"You *are*," Chrissie said to him, her eyes still flashing with delight. "Pudge will do anything I tell him. If I sicked him on you, you'd be meat."

Max released her hands and drew back. "Spare me the wrath of Pudge," he said.

Jasmine, who had hitherto said nothing, now said, "When the Bible says that God created man in his own image, does that not refer to free will?"

Continuing his fierce eyeplay with Chrissie, Max said, "I'm sure Chrissie thinks it refers to the God-like Pudge."

Chrissie guffawed and feinted a slap at him, which he caught in mid-air and held, but the others, now seemingly ashamed of themselves, went silent.

"I know it's ridiculous," Sherry said, "but when I hear the word God I picture that bearded dude in the Sistine Chapel."

A discussion of images of God now ensued, suggestions including beams of light shooting through clouds, deemed even more dubious than Michelangelo's muscular figure; Zeus and his thunderbolt; and— this offered by Max—a graphic image of a voluptuous Mother Nature, who guarded the whole of the earth under her skirts.

When the laughter had quieted, Jasmine spoke again, this time with more resolution in her voice. "But isn't it in just that, the unknowable, where God lies? Of course, all our suggestions are ridiculous, but don't they all have a little bit of truth to them, too. Don't you like the way God's hand reaches out in the Creation and don't we all feel something in Nature? We don't know what it is, but we feel it."

"What's unknown today is just what scientists will discover tomorrow," Julia observed.

"The word Jasmine used wasn't 'unknown,'" Phillip pointed out. "It was 'unknowable.'"

"Like what?"

"For example, why there is something rather than nothing."

"Goodness, aren't we the deep one," Chrissie now said, peeved that her play with Max had been interrupted.

"I just can't get behind all this gooky stuff about God," Julia now said. "Angels and cherubs and devils and all that. It's just too ridiculous. I don't see how anybody could believe that. And people are always praying 'Let God's will be done' on one day, and praying the next day that God will change his mind and take away their cancer. It's so hypocritical."

"Ninety-nine percent of the wars ever fought in the world were over religion," Max now asserted.

"You think, then," Phillip said, "if God exists, he's a pacifist?"

"Well, if God's so good and wonderful, why would people kill each other over him all the time?"

"Possibly he's not so good," Phillip said, "at least not in the way we normally think of it."

These were arguments that Jasmine had heard before, but now, listening to them here in the dark, the pool filter gurgling in the distance, she was struck by a sensation of strangeness. Here they were, all with their own hopes, ambitions, fears, each of them breathing air in and out of their bodies, their thoughts tangled into the complex web that was their lives, caring so much about every little event and every tiny success and failure of their days. She herself even at this moment understood that she was deeply unsettled by an invisible, as yet indefinable, barrier that she knew to be building between herself and Phillip. Yet how could it all seem so important if it could just as easily not have existed at all? In fact, it made more sense for it not to exist. It was only existence that was strange.

"In the end, Jasmine has us," Phillip finally said.

"I'm not sure about that," Julia replied.

"But she does," Phillip said. "Our logic takes us up to the really difficult questions and then abandons us, so we give up and say it's absurd. She at least keeps trying."

"I think God is just a superstition," Julia said.

"At least it's a superstition we somewhat agree on," Phillip said. "Isn't that better than having everybody choose his or her own set of prejudices?"

"Who knows?" Max offered, giving Chrissie a shove into the pool as he did.

Chrissie began immediately to try to drag Max off the edge by pulling on one of his legs. Julia, not about to let Chrissie have him to herself again, stood up and began pushing him from behind, and a moment later the three of them were all tangled together in the pool. Even in the darkness, it was apparent that Max was concentrating his defenses more on Chrissie than Julia, and he'd soon gotten his arms around her from behind and was holding her close against him, all while she struggled ineffectually for release. A moment later, Julia jerked herself up out of the pool and stomped—as well as her bare feet would let her—across to the house. Chrissie and Max stopped their thrashing to watch her walk away, but Jasmine observed that he didn't release her until Julia had passed under the porch light and into the house.

Chapter 10

A Trip to the Lake Is Planned

Tina had been aware that Pudge's family owned a famed property that sat on the shores of Lake Tahoe. She had hinted to Chrissie occasionally about it, asking whether the family often traveled there, how much time they spent on their visits, and whether they went in the winter for skiing. Chrissie had, in turn, grown somewhat resentful that he had never offered her an invitation and ended by demanding one.

Pudge, who had only been slow in taking Chrissie's earlier hints because he considered life at the lake to be dull, was happy enough with a junket to the lake, especially when his mother insisted that the whole Gannon enclave should be invited. It was arranged that they spend the Fourth of July holiday at the Blunt lakeside estate. They would leave on the Friday before the Fourth and return on the Sunday after.

It was assumed that Chrissie, Julia, and Phillip would go; and Pudge, having already consulted with his mother, could concur whole-heartedly when Chrissie suggested that Sherry and Max be included. On the next occasion when the Hills found themselves

in the Gannon kitchen, the invitation was offered and accepted. A
discussion of which cars would be taken ensued.

Dr. and Mrs. Gannon were not car-proud people, and by Arden
Park standards, their driveway made a poor showing, a source of
real mortification to their children. All three children had argued
for a time that their family really "needed" a sports utility vehicle
of one ilk or another. Dr. Gannon had answered that no person
could consider himself to be a good neighbor who drove an
ostentatiously large, irresponsibly expensive car that polluted the
air, crowded parking lots and traffic lanes, and threatened others
with bodily harm or death in the incident of a collision. His children
considered these arguments to be so eccentric as to be unintelligible,
especially as at least one such vehicle graced nearly every other driveway
in the neighborhood, but they had received no support from their
mother. The doctor had prevailed. While five vehicles were now at the
disposal of the family, not including Tina's Toyota sedan, none was an
ornament to the household. Dr. Gannon's Volvo station wagon was
comparatively respectable, but it was more than a decade old; Thomas's
European sedan was merely a Volkswagen; the silver paint had faded
on Chrissie's luxury import, which had been acquired from a neighbor
and was even older than the Volvo; and Cynthia's van, purchased for
transporting soccer teams and children's party invitees, utterly lacked
distinction. Only Julia had done better. She had conspired with a
friend who had received a new Beetle as a birthday present to arrange
purchase of the girl's old Mustang. The Mustang had the advantage
of being a convertible, but was, after all, only a Ford.

Julia had taken it upon herself to lead the car discussion. "Pudge
and Chrissie's BMW, of course," she said, nodding to Chrissie,
who, caught between reflected pride of ownership and reluctance
to be stuck alone in a car with Pudge for the long trip up the
mountain, regarded her with a non-committal tilt of the head.
"But, of course, that only takes care of two, and there's how many
of us?" Julia counted the people around the table, Chrissie, Julia,
Phillip, and the two Hills, then turned hesitantly to look into the
adjoining family room, where Mrs. Gannon, Mrs. Stubbs, and
Jasmine were seated.

While Pudge was not always quick to understand a situation, he was gallant in protecting others' feelings, once he comprehended them. "We can't leave Mrs. Stubbs and Mrs. Gannon here alone for the holidays," he now said. Then, lifting his voice and directing it to the family room, he went on. "Mrs. Stubbs, Mrs. Gannon, we need you to come to that lake with us over the Fourth and keep us out of trouble."

Tina now rose from her eavesdropping, stepped toward the table, and petted Pudge's shoulder with real gratitude. "I know you think it's a joke, but we older folks never quite get over the idea that you kids need taking care of."

Chrissie and Julia groaned in unison.

"I know, I know," Tina said quickly. "It's completely unnecessary, but . . . ."

"My folks wouldn't have it any other way," Pudge said, for which he received another affectionate pat from Mrs. Stubbs.

"But isn't that getting to be an awfully large party?" Chrissie asked hopefully. "Where would everyone sleep?"

"It's not a problem," Pudge said.

"But it's nine people . . .," Chrissie protested.

Pudge shook his head. A slight, wry smile indicated to Chrissie the naïveté of her remark. She quieted.

"I imagine you'll take Chrissie with you in your car," Phillip said to Pudge. "If we take Cynthia's van, the rest of us can all fit."

Chrissie allowed a gasp of displeasure to escape as she pictured the fun all the others might have riding up together in the closely packed van, and Tina, who was uncomfortable with the idea of arriving at the lake in so unfashionable a vehicle, rose to her support. "Oh, no," she said, "the van is so uncomfortable. It would make much more sense to take your car, Phillip, and maybe David's Volvo. Don't you think, Cynthia?"

Cynthia, who was not nearly so interested in the young people's conversations as was Tina and who had only belatedly begun to pay attention to the goings on, said, "The van is very noisy."

"And with all those windows, it heats up unbearably," Tina said. "We'll have to take the Volvo."

"But will we have enough seats?" Julia asked. She did a second count. "Nine, counting Pudge . . . . Do you think Thomas will want to come?" No reliable projection could be made for Thomas, who often spent time with fraternity brothers in Los Angeles and whose exact whereabouts were now unknown. "The BMW and Porsche hold two each and the station wagon holds five. If he does, we're one place short."

Cynthia, seeming to realize for the first time that she was expected to accompany them, said, "Oh, goodness me. I couldn't possibly go."

"But you have to, Mrs. Gannon," Pudge said.

"No, Jeremy," Cynthia said, smiling especially brilliantly because she was secretly pleased that he had adopted the Hills' habit of addressing her as Mrs. rather than calling her by her first name. "It's very kind of you, but I really couldn't."

Julia, who had been surprised that her mother had seemed earlier to acquiesce to making the trip, quickly began finalizing arrangements, saying, "Okay, that's it then. Chrissie and Pudge in their car, Phillip and Sherry and the rest of us in the station wagon."

Pudge, however, interrupted, turning to Jasmine and talking across the room to her. "What about you, Jaz? Don't you want to come?"

Pudge was the only person in the world who called her Jaz, and, while she did not at all mind him doing so—and was perhaps even a little flattered by the familiarity—she was always shocked to hear her name thus shortened. After a moment, she said, "When I was small, I was scared nearly to death of skiing. Cynthia was always kind enough to leave me home with our nanny."

"There's no snow now," Phillip said, with a smile.

Pudge, having identified another maiden in distress, continued his insistence, and even Sherry joined in. "Of course, you're coming," she said. "I won't go if you don't."

"But we have just enough seats as it is," Tina said.

"I could drive the van," Phillip said. "That would be even better because we could put bikes on the top."

"That's very thoughtful of you, Phillip," Tina said, turning to Pudge, "but Jasmine isn't expected. We couldn't really force an additional guest on your parents, Jeremy."

Pudge began by insisting that no such problem existed, and given that Tina and the Hills were no more expected than Jasmine, this could hardly be denied; but Tina offered him a stern look which struck him mute. "I just couldn't enjoy myself imagining Cynthia here alone over the holiday," she said. "She needs Jasmine to stay with her."

"I do love having you here with me," Cynthia said to Jasmine.

Phillip turned to his aunt. "Why don't you come too, Cynthia?"

Cynthia's reply—"absolutely not"—closed off his argument. After a moment's thought, he turned to Max. "What are your grandparents doing on the Fourth?"

Max shrugged, but Sherry answered for him, saying, "Nothing. And I've been worrying about leaving them. If I could be sure they were spending the evening with you, Mrs. Gannon, I'd be so relieved."

Cynthia, who was perfectly happy to visit with the Lees as long as it entailed no added labor to herself, agreed. "I could have Esmeralda prepare something, and we could have a quiet evening beside the pool."

"That's it, then," Phillip said quickly. "Jasmine's coming."

"And you'll be sure to take the bikes," Tina said, seeking to confirm that the choice of the van would appear purely utilitarian.

Phillip nodded. "Mine, we'll get one for Max, and how about you, Jasmine? Would you like to take a bike?" Jasmine nodded her agreement, and Phillip turned to Pudge. "Will you have beds for everyone, or should we book some rooms?"

Pudge dismissed the question with a shrug and shake of the head.

"There may be ten of us," Tina warned.

"Not a problem."

Jasmine's past exclusions from alpine adventures had not been so pitiless as it might appear. The last family skiing trip had occurred during Jasmine's first winter in Arden Park, when her guardians still vividly remembered her frightening condition on arrival. While they had felt it would be better for her if she traveled with the family and made every effort to convince her that she should, she had reacted with mute terror. Not wanting to risk a relapse, they had relented. In subsequent years, Thomas or one of his sisters had always found themselves too busy for such family trips, and Cynthia, who really grieved at having to take her Pom to the kennel, had welcomed the excuse of childcare—whether it be for Jasmine or her own children—to remain at home. Jasmine did not feel herself to have been mistreated, and she did not now wish to imply that she did by showing excessive eagerness. Nonetheless, her excitement and anticipation grew feverish as the weekend of the Fourth approached.

She read every word in the encyclopedia about the deep, clear waters of Lake Tahoe and the high mountains that surrounded it. She'd learned that Pudge's family had a sailboat, and while the glories of actually riding out onto such a lake under sail were beyond imagination, she thought that she might sit somewhere along the shore and watch the white sails glide past. To be out of the heat of Arden Park, sitting next to a cool lake in a pine-scented breeze, surrounded by steep, forested mountains, seemed a pleasure almost beyond description. She might have packed her bag early had she not feared tempting fate: perhaps the Lees would take sick and be unable to join her Aunt Cynthia on the holiday, or one of the cars might break down, or the others, having seen the lake so many times before, might settle on another outing that interested them more. She contented herself with mentally packing her bag each night before she went to sleep, imagining how each piece of clothing would be folded and how she would tuck the small items in to fill each corner. She then dressed every morning in her least favorite clothes so that those she liked most would be sparkling clean when they fitted into the suitcase.

In actuality, Jasmine need not have worried about the trip being cancelled. If no one else anticipated it quite with Jasmine's level of anxiety, all were eager that it take place. Chrissie had developed a deep curiosity about the lakeside estate and looked forward to the extended feeling of ownership which a young lady who is attached to a young man is entitled to enjoy. Julia, assured that Pudge would be in steady attendance, expected to use the time to draw closer to Max, and Sherry had the pleasurable attentions of Phillip to anticipate. Phillip was delighted with the trip as well, in part because he looked forward to bicycling down the bare ski trails above the lake, but even more because the presence of Sherry Hill was sure to enliven every moment.

Jasmine's assumed exclusion from the Tahoe trip had not escaped Sherry. From Phillip and Jasmine herself, she knew the facts of her birth and childhood, yet her story remained intriguing. When Thomas was home for a weekend, she tried quizzing him about his cousin. Thomas was of a type Sherry understood well. He was handsome, but he maintained an arrogant tilt of the head and an almost perpetual smirk that led those girls whom he scorned to say "yuck." Whether it was because he was actually shy or because he feared rejection, he stayed aloof and did not engage girls often, unless perhaps the girl was of a reputation that made him sure of his ground in advance. He could not have been described as either especially sympathetic to others in his personal relations or particularly democratic in his view of society, but he did pride himself on being a realist.

"But she did celebrate holidays with the family?" Sherry asked, after confirming the factual circumstances of Jasmine's position.

"Of course," Thomas said, adding with a chuckle, "Did you think we were going to send her to the children's home?"

"Did she receive the same kinds of gifts as everyone else?"

"More or less. I remember getting her a mirror and comb one year. Or maybe that was Julia. It might have been a cup and saucer, or something for a doll . . . . There were a lot of little girls in this house. I couldn't keep up with it all."

"She showed me her room. She has books lined up on all her shelves."

"Phillip always gave her books. Dad, too. Seemed like the easy way out to me. What kid really wants a book anyway? I just let Mom pick out something."

"What about bikes and skates and all those things?"

"There was always plenty of that stuff around. Plus, she didn't seem very interested . . . . No doubt, she got screwed-over occasionally. God knows, Chrissie and Julia weren't going to get the short end."

"Why doesn't she have a car?"

"Is she old enough?"

"Nearly seventeen."

"She probably hasn't begged enough."

"How old were Chrissie and Julia when they got their cars?"

"Sixteen probably. I don't remember. Look, if you're trying to turn this into some kind of a bleeding heart social cause, you can save your breath. If she whined as much as Chrissie and Julia, she'd get whatever she asked for. If you haven't noticed, my sisters are sometimes nasty little _____"

"They are not," Sherry said, not managing to interrupt him before he emitted an extreme vulgarity. She giggled in spite of herself and offered a quick, impish flaring of her eyes before resolutely changing the subject. "Jasmine is so sweet," she said. "Was she very unhappy when she first came here?"

"She was a little-bitty thing," Thomas explained. "She didn't talk for six months. We all figured she was some kind of moron. So, when things started to get better, we just let her alone."

"So she was treated differently?"

"Yeah, she was. We all thought she was going to go wacko or something."

"It's very hard to imagine Jasmine going wacko."

"Sure, now it is."

Sherry nodded thoughtfully, then said, "She doesn't seem to be bitter or anything."

"She's got it pretty good here," Thomas said matter-of-factly.

Sherry now leaned closer and, nearly whispering, asked, "What about the racial thing?"

He regarded her pitifully. "Nah. Just doesn't play."

"But it has to," Sherry said.

Thomas shook his head in complete dismissal. "It's equal

opportunity snobbery in this neighborhood . . . . Aunt Tina occasionally goes on a tear, telling us how we have a responsibility to prepare Jasmine for the racists, and she occasionally sits Jasmine down for little talks. But it's a non-starter."

"Plus, being pretty makes up for a lot for a girl."

"Jasmine pretty?"

"Yes, she's *very* pretty."

Thomas chuckled. "Women. Any hippo's pretty as long as she's not a threat."

"Jasmine's hardly a hippo."

"No, she's a skinny little string bean with the sex appeal of a hockey stick."

Sherry reflected on how common it was that boys—as opposed to men—needed to be told of a girl's prettiness before they could see it for themselves, but she made Thomas no reply.

Thomas had spoken to Sherry of Tina's "little talks" with Jasmine, and indeed, prior to departing for the lake, Mrs. Stubbs once again felt the need for a special chat with her niece. Jeremy's father, Mr. Harold Blunt, was a very wealthy man. He had built through his own industry a small manufacturing company, and then, through finance and acquisition, had expanded it into a corporation with more than one thousand employees, while remaining the majority stockholder. In more recent years, however, he had devoted himself to conservative political activism. His name had appeared on a highly publicized tax cut initiative, and newspapers frequently quoted his statements in opposition to one government program or another. This placed him in a category of politicians whom antagonists were likely to portray as bigoted, and who sometimes are. Tina knew no more of Harold Blunt's politics than what she had read in newspapers, but given the relationship between Chrissie and Pudge, she dreaded the possibility of an incident. On the evening before they were to depart, she found Jasmine in her bedroom, led her into the rarely used living room, and sat her down.

"Now, Jasmine," Mrs. Stubbs began, "we have not taken you out much into social situations. I hope you understand that our intention has been to protect you from . . . certain things. But I suppose we can't protect you forever. And I think that it's good that you will be making this trip with us. Yes, I think it's very good."

"I hope that it will be," Jasmine said. "I'm very much looking forward to it."

"As you should. As you should. But I should warn you that there will be situations in your life when you move outside the Gannon family—and even outside Arden Park altogether—where you may encounter prejudice."

To this, Jasmine made no reply.

"Yes," her aunt continued, "some people will judge you to be black—African-American—and use that as an excuse to treat you as an inferior. I, of course, and all of us in the family consider that an appalling prejudice. Nonetheless, it's a truth we must confront. You know, until not so many years ago, people with even the smallest amount of African-American blood were considered to be black, or 'colored,' as people used to say then."

Jasmine was fully aware of the diversity in her ethnic background, and while she wrote in mixed race on her school applications and objected to the term 'person of color' for dividing the world into camps of the colorful and colorless, she acceded comfortably to being considered African-American, black, or Negro.

"I believe that I am very nearly half-Negro, and my grandmother always described my brother and I as 'colored,'" she said, "so no one would be much mistaken in labeling me so."

"And you understand that in this country, in this era, that label can be a heavy one to carry, a heavy one indeed."

"I understand that I will meet prejudice everywhere I go," Jasmine said, her grandmother's formal, old-fashioned diction advancing to the fore, as it always did when she wanted to speak especially precisely. "Ill-bred people will always attempt to use race to divide people and gain power over them. But I have suffered no such usage here in Arden Park. In fact, I suspect that I have sometimes been treated with special kindness by our neighbors because of it."

"And that must seem a burden to you."

"I haven't found it so. Indeed, I think that it's only natural. Our neighbors in Arden Park are considerate, well-mannered people. They are aware that I might fear acts of prejudice, so they make special efforts to reassure me that they won't commit them. I've always thought of it as a kindness."

"Yet isn't that over-kindliness itself a form of prejudice?"

"I can hardly criticize someone for kindness, even if it is sometimes beyond what is necessary. Much is said about the prejudice Negro girls experience. Living here as I have, I've met with very little of it."

Tina, who did not like the word "Negro," had inwardly winced upon hearing it from Jasmine. "Why must you continue calling yourself a Negro?" she asked.

"My Granny used it."

"I find the term . . .," Tina began, then started over again. "The term has come to be seen as degrading."

"I can't control how others think of the word, but for me, it recalls my grandmother's home and the love and tenderness she always showed toward William and me. I can't hear it without feeling a warm remembrance."

"William and I," Tina corrected.

Jasmine nodded thoughtfully, not acknowledging an error because she knew perfectly well she had not made one, but not wanting to call attention to her aunt's error in correcting her.

"I do not know Pudge's parents well," Tina said. "I have no reason to believe they will be anything but cordial to you."

"I have found that when you expect the best from other people, you often find it."

"Yes, but we're not living in a world of clichés now," Jasmine's aunt replied. "You've lived a very protected life here in Arden Park."

Jasmine had often been surprised at how quickly and thoroughly her aunts were able to forget that she had attended classes for nearly seven hours per day, nine months of the year, in schools where most students were Negroes, and almost all of the rest were of Latin American or Asian descent. There her light skin had led her to experience not only social isolation but also occasional accusations of racial disloyalty, haughtiness, or prejudice, and, not uncommonly, sexual taunting as well. Yet she could not help but acknowledge that her life at school sometimes seemed so far removed from her life in Arden Park as to be unimaginable.

"I've had the wonderful good fortune," Jasmine now said, "to grow up among prosperous, well-educated, and courteous neighbors. I could never thank you and my aunt and uncle enough for that opportunity."

"I worry that we may not have prepared you for the types of difficulties you are likely to encounter."

"If there is anything I've missed in my upbringing, I'm sure it is the result of my inattentiveness, not your neglect."

"There are people who will seize on any flaw you show them."

"Dr. Gannon has always emphasized the importance of acknowledging our shortcomings and learning from our mistakes."

"Some people I'm afraid may be inclined to find flaws where none exist."

"I hope not, but, if so, I would hope to change their feelings with time."

"Centuries have not been enough for some people."

"I don't know that it would be fair to hold people responsible for the failures of their ancestors. I know nothing of my father's family prior to Granny. If I were to learn that one of my forebears had been a pirate, I don't think that I would like to punished for it."

"I'm sure there are no pirates in your family tree . . . . But if there were, you would want to give back the gains that were passed down to you. What I want you to understand is that many people refuse to acknowledge the piracy of their ancestors. White people kept black people in slavery. That's every bit as bad as piracy— worse. That must be repaid."

"I shouldn't like to take money from strangers, especially since I can't feel that I've earned it."

"You have earned it. Your ancestors paid for it with their slavery."

"What if the ancestors of the slave owners are themselves poor?"

"Then it would be impossible."

"Really, I've been so fortunate in everything. I don't need it."

Tina had before been frustrated by Jasmine's inability to take the great social view of events, and she now wished somehow to bring the girl to a more realistic view of the world. "But you may someday need it," she now said. "There's no guarantee that that you will always live in Arden Park. Indeed, it would be very surprising if you did."

This was a possibility that Jasmine had often pondered. She'd had much time to compose her thoughts about her future and was now able to speak with exactitude. "Though it's sad for me to think about," she began, "I know that it would be wrong for me to continue to impose on the generosity of my uncle forever; however, I hope to be able to finish high school while still in this household. Beyond that, I console myself with the observation that no one can foresee all the eventualities that life will present. I can only trust in the habits of character you have taught me and in God."

Tina, stymied by this appeal to divine guidance, fell silent, but she was not completely satisfied. Jasmine was to her a symbol of the inequity of a world that would allow her own sister to be so well-to-do, respected, and prominent, while she had herself been left a widow with an income that required scrupulous management. The girl had a social responsibility to maintain some degree of indignation. Of course, Jasmine had more reason to feel satisfied with her position than she herself had: the girl had been all but adopted into the Gannon family, out of a family that had offered very dismal prospects, while she had herself remained a poor relation, despite the many years she'd devoted to the nurturance, support, and guidance of the Gannon children.

She was left with a sour impression of ungratefulness on Jasmine's part. After all, it was she who had insisted on taking the poor child in when her grandmother died; it was she who'd had the courage to speak out against the racial prejudice that might have left her stranded; and it was she who had taken the exhausting flight across the country, grappled with all the tawdry social service agencies, and finally led the sullen child to Arden Park. Now, to find her pretending to genteel moral sentiments as though they were her birthright was galling.

"In the end, we must all adapt to our own circumstances in life," she finally said. "I certainly have, and I can't describe for you the hardships of a widow with limited means. Eventually, you will have to come off of that rosy, pink cloud you are now sitting on and make your own accommodations."

"If I am being unrealistic in what I have said, I would appreciate your advising me."

"There will be time enough for that. For now, I think you need to take care. You are sometimes too trusting. Things aren't always as they appear. People disguise their true feelings."

Jasmine nodded her assent, then said, "Yet isn't disguise sometimes necessary? We all have aspects of our characters that we do best to keep hidden. Why shouldn't we commend the bigot who resists his own prejudices in the same way we commend the alcoholic who refrains from drink."

"Sometimes the alcoholic who refuses the single drink does so out of a hope of having the whole bottle later."

Jasmine again nodded in assent, saying, "I hope that God will give me the wisdom to recognize when this is the case and the strength to endure what I must."

"Speaking of enduring . . . . What I wanted to advise you about today is that there may be occasions this coming weekend when you are obliged to endure things. People may say things or do things. Or you may find instances where you feel yourself to have been slighted. But I want you to know that now would not be the time . . . . We are invited guests in someone else's home. You are probably somewhat unexpected. There's a time to make an issue of something and a time to refrain . . . ." Tina now looked at her long and searchingly, before rising and saying, "You mustn't always take things at their face value. But you also must avoid acting too hastily."

"I understand that as a guest in someone's home I have certain obligations."

"Yes, and I'm sure that even if you feel yourself provoked, you'll feel the weight of those obligations."

"If I err, I will err on the side of understanding and forgiveness."

Her aunt now looked at her with unusual tenderness, "There are limits, Jasmine, there are limits. I don't want you to be hurt. But, please remember that now is not the time."

Jasmine made note of her aunt's cautionary advice, but she considered the possibility of unhappy incidents to be remote; and as she walked out to the patio to rejoin the Hills and her cousins, thoughts of her more distant future occupied her mind. When she finished high school, she would find a job—a task she was confident she could accomplish as many girls from her school who were both weaker students and less well-mannered than she worked daily. No students from her school advanced to prestigious private colleges, but she had the good fortune to live in California, where the community college system was well established and inexpensive. She could complete her general education requirements there and advance eventually to the state university. She'd been advised that the state university system would be costly, but loans, she'd been assured, would be available. Moreover, there was the hope of scholarships, which would allow her to reduce her working hours and speed the progress of her studies. This was a long and demanding course of action, and it lacked the glamour of attending Stanford, USC, or one of the eastern colleges—the colleges that were popular among her cousins' friends—but she regarded it with that energizing combination of fear, anticipation, and excitement that defines a life adventure.

She had been considering her future education for some months, but her aunt's talk now impressed upon her the necessity of taking more definite initiative. In the past, she'd been a child, and she'd depended completely on her guardians both to make decisions about her future and to provide for her. Now, she felt a responsibility to relieve her uncle of concerns about her future education and financial support, and she resolved to inform him of her plans at her first opportunity.

Chapter 11

The Lake

The day of departure arrived, all the parties assembled in front of the Gannon house, and, once their bags were packed and the bicycles were loaded on top of the van, they began to position themselves in the three chosen vehicles. Max offered to drive for Mrs. Stubbs, and Julia, eager to be close to him, positioned herself in the other front seat of the station wagon, while Tina, Sherry, and Jasmine squeezed themselves into the back seat, Jasmine in the middle. Thomas, who had at the last minute found himself available to come along, kept Phillip company in the van, and Chrissie, after having watched Julia install herself next to Max, took her place next to Pudge in the bright red BMW. They led the way out the driveway.

Julia pulled her legs up onto the car seat, tucking her feet under her, and as she was not normally very talkative, displayed her nervousness by prattling about the heat, about what the house would be like, about how much cooler it would surely be at the lake, and then about a television commercial she had seen the previous evening that struck her as being particularly delightful. At the light just before the freeway entrance, they pulled up beside the BMW, and she dipped under her seatbelt and leaned across Max's legs to wave to Chrissie, offering Max a considerable view of her breasts which were loosely contained by a small, white spaghetti-strapped top. Chrissie looked out on Julia's animated display with mature disdain. A moment later, they were onto the freeway. Pudge sped ahead.

Julia's demeanor could quickly transform itself in the presence of an attractive young male. While she was normally a robust, athletic girl of strong will and fiery temper, the presence of a potential conquest acted like a tonic, instantly softening her face and brightening her eyes. She seemed to become more sensitized to nuances of meaning in word and gesture, and generally increased the gentleness, goodwill, and charity she displayed to her fellow beings. This reaction was so swift and so spontaneous and seemed so intrinsic to her personality that Jasmine could hardly have called it false, no matter how remarkable the transformation sometimes seemed.

Now, her original nervousness lessened, and her temporary possession of Max complete, Julia seemed to sense that her glee was too obviously showing. While she did not remove her legs from the car seat or turn to face ahead, she sat more upright, softened her voice, and listened to Max with a ladylike display of concern and interest.

With Julia's exuberance no longer filling the car and both Tina and Sherry unusually silent, Jasmine was able to observe the scenery; and, after a first half-hour of driving through burgeoning suburbs, the transformation was remarkable. The highway climbed, and the dry grass on the hillsides soon gave way to conifer forests. High mountains began to be visible in the distance. Cool, pine-scented air drifted in when Sherry lowered her window to test the outside temperature.

The highway passed two small ponds set in meadows just below the road, shot them up through a high pass, then opened up on a vast view of a rocky basin. The basin was enclosed on its farther ends by smooth granite ridges that reached above the tree line. The lower slopes were spotted with pines, growing out of a scree of white boulders. The highest ravines still held patches of snow, as smooth and irregular as the spots on a cow. The cool air and the magnificent view, especially in contrast to the heat of Arden Park and the confines of its leafy trees, filled Jasmine with a joyful exuberance. With Tina and Sherry seeming lost in their own thoughts, she bridled her enthusiasm, saying only, "Oh, how beautiful it is!" Her companions hummed polite agreement.

For a time, the road followed a perfect little river with crystal clear water and all the necessary white bars of sand, smooth rock islands, and flashing rapids. Soon after, a tree-lined, oval lake appeared below them, which Jasmine at first thought to be their destination. Another passage along an alpine river followed; then, they were driving through forest along the real lake's shore. At first, she could only glimpse the lake itself, but it seemed much bigger than she had anticipated, more a sea than a small mountain lake, and she admitted to a slight disappointment. Then the road rose up from the lake level and offered a view of the whole of its vast expanse. Looking down, it seemed she could see through its astonishingly clear waters into the blue-tinged depths of the earth. The perfect ring of mountain peaks and their nearly exact reflection on the distant reaches of the lake offered a double portion of bliss.

They soon turned, not away from the lake as she had anticipated, but towards it, and Jasmine realized they were crossing onto a peninsula. A moment later, they were parked in front of the house itself, though she could hardly have called it a house, as it seemed more a castle from a fairy tale. The walls, which seemed to rise a hundred feet above her back-tilted head, were wrought from dark, multi-hued stone, each piece a foot or more in diameter, and the innumerable turrets were roofed with steep cones of mossy slate. The cut-glass windows, some expansive and others small, unexpected, and lovely were set deep in the walls, like passages into a fortress.

While Jasmine gawked in awe, the van pulled into the driveway behind them. For the moment, even the Hills seemed overwhelmed: the doors of the cars remained closed. Then Pudge was out of the BMW, opening passenger doors and trunk lids, and lifting bags from the various compartments. Chrissie, just behind, beamed in reflected possession of this magnificence, and all began to chatter happily.

"It is really extraordinary, Jeremy," Tina said. "Your descriptions did it no justice."

"It's my mom's thing," Pudge said. "Inside, it's a real pit."

Mrs. Blunt, a slightly round woman, of Mediterranian complexion, with very dark eyes and tightly bound black hair, greeted them pleasantly. She bustled about, directing them to their rooms, and to all appearances was truly pleased with her son's interest in displaying his family. The inside was, of course, not a pit at all, but the rock construction had resisted modernizations, and the deep-set windows and high, dark ceiling beams created a cavernous impression, one which Jasmine found thrilling.

"This is the busiest weekend of the year on the lake," Mrs. Blunt said, as she directed each to an individual room. "Nothing like it is in October when we have it almost to ourselves."

"And when it'll freeze your nads off," Pudge said quietly to Max, though not so quietly that others besides his mother could not hear.

As she didn't participate in the quiet maneuvering that occurred to obtain the best view, Jasmine found herself in a downstairs room that looked out on the drive rather than the lake. The less desirable rooms, with so many others to choose from, could not have been much used; and despite a small casement window that had been cranked wide open for airing, the bedding retained a smell of damp stone. Nonetheless the dark oak floor, while scarred and worn, gleamed, reminding her of the wooden banister in her grandmother's house and flooding her with tender memories. Sparkling-fresh towels were set out for her on a simple, three-drawered dresser, which matched the bed frame and lamp table beside it. In camp style, the bed was spread only with a green wool blanket, pulled tight across the mattress. A white sheet was turned back at the top, a fluffy white pillow lay at the head, and a down duvet was fan-folded at its foot.

While the room scarcely offered space to lay out her suitcase and the design of the furniture was not at all decorative, Jasmine immediately fell in love with all of it. Not even the dampness discouraged her, blended as it was with the fresh smell of pine coming in the window, contrasted as it was with the oiled patina of the wood floors and furniture, and set off as it was by the crisp freshness of the folded towels and bed linen.

No one had told her what she should do after she'd set out her suitcase, and, once she'd located the bathroom, there was nothing really to be done. Only Sherry was on the same floor with her, and her room, which was beyond the bath, appeared quiet. Jasmine, of course, always had a book with her, and normally she would have been more than content to sit in such a charming room and read about the adventures of nineteenth-century English girls. Now, however, she was eager for a closer look at the lake. She did not wish to meet Mr. Blunt so soon, not for her own sake so much as because she wanted to spare her aunt anxiety, and she certainly didn't want to appear anywhere in the house where she was unexpected. She was tempted for a moment to squeeze through her own tiny window, but concluded that such an act, if detected, would subject her aunt to exactly the type of humiliation she most feared. Yet she very much did want to see the lake, and it seemed to her that no one could object if she walked down the hall, stepped through the living room, and went out the front door through which she'd already entered.

Her plan began well, and she broke into a run as she stepped free of the dark interior of the house. She then rounded the corner, started down a steep path of rock steps, closely guarded by a stone retaining wall on one side and tall ferns and a profusion of purple lupines on the other, only to find her path blocked by a fallen pine tree. The tangle of branches reached higher than her own head. She was looking about, both for a path around it and to view the stump from which the tree had broken off, when a bald head rose up right from the middle of the thicket. The workman, a very stout man whose round face was red and dripping with perspiration, stared out at her, and Jasmine, in her surprise, stared back with an open mouth. He was no more than a few feet from her, and he was breathing heavily.

"I was on my way down to the lake," she finally managed to say, to which the man replied, "I'm afraid you'll have to go through the yard." He pointed to a gate in the rock wall just back up the path from her.

"It's a miracle that it didn't hit anything," Jasmine said, suddenly wondering if it could have, just at this moment, landed on the man in front of her.

"Yes," the man said, "it came down during the night." He pointed up to a split and ragged gash in the pine tree overhead.

"It was only a limb, then," Jasmine said, thinking that the profusion of needles and branches before her seemed far too abundant to comprise only a single limb.

"Yes," the man said. "A big one though . . . . Some squirrels must have had a wild ride." He laughed with delight, then stretched his back and neck and said, "How do you think a branch decides what year and day to come down?"

"Was there a wind?"

"Not a breath."

"Maybe it was planning to come down to celebrate the Fourth."

"Not a very smart limb then, was it? Missing the date by a day."

Jasmine smiled at this, and the man smiled back.

"Have you come up with Jemmy?"

Jasmine was at first perplexed by this, then realized he was referring to Pudge, whose actual first name was Jeremy.

"I have. Jeremy asked us for the weekend."

The man nodded noncommittally.

"It was wonderful of him to ask us," Jasmine said. "It's so beautiful here."

"You like the lake, then?"

"Very much. And the house is something straight out of a novel."

"So you are a reader of novels," he said, nodding toward the one she was carrying under her arm.

Jasmine admitted that this was so.

"I don't care much for novels," the man replied. "There's plenty that's real to learn in the world. I don't see how people find time for made-up stories."

"I think there's a great deal to be learned from novels."

"You do?"

"Yes. It's where we learn about people. It's how we learn about their hearts and souls. It's how we learn that we're not alone in the world."

The man regarded her pleasantly, apparently content with the opportunity for rest that the interruption had provided. "Why not get straight to the point then and read philosophy or psychology?" he asked.

There was a suggestion of friendly challenge in his question, and Jasmine was pleased when just the response she wanted occurred to her. "They oversimplify," she said, at which the man laughed aloud. She smiled back, "If you needed an excuse," she went on, "you could think of reading novels as a study in geography— geography of the human soul."

"Oh, I don't think I need much of an excuse at my age."

"I don't think anyone ever needs an excuse for reading a good novel."

"Some people use books to escape. My wife does. What about you? Would you rather read a novel than look at this lake, which you say you find so lovely?"

"Oh, no," she said quickly. "I don't even know why I brought it along. Out of habit, I guess. Carrying a book has saved me a great deal of boredom in my life. But even if I did choose to read, I would still be aware that I was sitting in the most beautiful place in the world."

"*The* most beautiful, is it? Have you seen Lake Como, then? Have you been to the South Seas?"

"No," she admitted, "and it would not be fair to judge what I haven't seen. Of course, I had never seen this lake before today either . . . ." She felt herself momentarily vexed, as she did not want to betray the profound impression her first panorama of the lake had made on her. The man regarded her pleasantly until she came upon a solution. "But I think I can fairly conclude that it is at least tied for being the most beautiful place in the world."

"And how can you conclude that without having seen all the others?"

"This lake is perfect. Since there are no degrees of perfection, it can't be surpassed."

The man laughed again. He turned behind him to look out over the blue waters. "I have seen Lake Como, I have seen the

South Seas, and I have a couple of other contenders, but this *is* the most beautiful place in the world . . . that I have seen. And it is *at least tied* for being *the* most beautiful place in the world." He turned to her quickly. "But if you've never before been here, I can't keep you from it any longer. It's just as beautiful close-up as it is from here."

"Couldn't I help you?" Jasmine said, casting her eyes over the heap of branches. "I could carry limbs away."

"No, no," he said. "You need to go now while the sun is still on the water. You go up through that gate, go out through another gate just like it on the other side, and a trail will carry you down to the lake."

At this high elevation, it was still high-spring to the garden's mind, and a profusion of blooms greeted Jasmine as she entered the garden. The purple lupines predominated, but there was a remarkable array of daisies, asters, and larkspur, and the occasional well-formed tulip still lingered. She felt too much a trespasser to linger, however, and passed quickly to the far gate and down a narrow winding path toward the lake.

The lake was rimmed with white boulders, some nearly as tall as she. After she had walked to the water's edge to watch the perfectly clear water lap onto the pebbled shore, she found an ideal nest in which to sit down, a grouping of white, rounded boulders that had tilted together to form a shallow cave, with its opening looking out over the lake.

It was evening now, and the sun was dropping close to the rim of mountains across from her. A gentle breeze blew, and to her complete delight, a white sail floated smoothly around a nearby point and passed directly in front of her, not a quarter mile from where she sat.

She was musing as to whether a view so beautiful could actually provide sustenance, removing or at least alleviating the need for food, when she heard voices approaching. Happy with the prospect of reestablishing contact with her Arden Park companions, she was about to stand and announce herself, when a female voice, one that suddenly seemed just behind the rock on which she leaned, spoke in intimate tones, "You shouldn't."

There was a rustling of clothes and the sound of what Jasmine deeply hoped wasn't kissing, followed by a brief silence.

"Why shouldn't we," a male voice now said, one with a distinct theatrical depth that could only belong to Max Hill.

Chrissie's easily identifiable giggle followed, then another moment of near silence. Jasmine wanted, almost desperately, to let them know of her presence but could see no way of doing so without revealing that she had witnessed what had already transpired. She remained where she was, not moving at all and scarcely breathing.

"God," Max now said, "would I love to take you back to LA and show you off. Girls from all over the country show up there, and not one in a hundred have what you do."

"I'm too tall," Chrissie demurred.

"Tall, sweetie, is in."

"But there are so many pretty girls, and most of them go nowhere."

"Pretty girls? Sure. But you're way beyond pretty. Any director would snap you up in a minute."

Chrissie now moaned. Whether it was with pleasure at what he said or pleasure with something he did, Jasmine could not be sure.

After a silent moment had passed, there was again the sound of rustling clothes. "We can't do this now," Chrissie said.

"My lovely, *we* can do anything we want," Max now said, to which Chrissie first giggled in reply, then said, "We have to go up to dinner."

After she had heard their footsteps pass away, Jasmine wondered how soon she might leave her current hiding place. She did not want to be at fault for delaying the meal, but it seemed best that Chrissie not know she had been detected. Finally, she crept along amid the rocks to where she could emerge without it being apparent that she had overheard them. She need not have worried. The rocky shoreline and the wooded slope reaching up to the house were deserted.

Jasmine was not quite the last to arrive at the table, but the others had begun seating themselves, and she received a sharp look from her aunt. Chrissie entered shortly after her, but hers was the entrance of an honoree: through her the Arden Park and Lake Tahoe households had been linked, and she had acquired the status of a hostess. How much the flame in her cheeks resulted from the events that had transpired on the beach and how much from an appreciation of the importance of her role was impossible to know. Her bearing was regal.

Jasmine sought out Julia and found her just across from her own place. She was seated next to Max, on whose profile she gazed with a countenance nearly as brilliant as her sister's. Phillip and Sherry sat on Julia's left hand, toward the head of the table.

Jasmine now became aware that all eyes were falling on her, and Phillip, seeing her confusion, nodded toward the tail end of the table. Jasmine looked there and discovered that Mrs. Blunt was in the process of introducing her to her husband. In the confusion of her late arrival, she'd avoided a close scrutiny of the fearful figure at the table's head. As she now turned to him, Mrs. Blunt was saying, "Hal, Jasmine is Chrissie's and Julia's cousin."

"We've met," the man said rather abruptly, leaving Jasmine in momentary confusion. "We agreed on the uselessness of novels and established the relationship between perfection and beauty." The redness of his face had receded, his hair, which before had been tussled and dampened with perspiration, was now smoothly combed, and instead of an open-throated flannel shirt he wore a starched white one, but the smile which he offered immediately allowed her to identify him as the man from the garden. In the garden, he had appeared rather coarse and nearly obese. Combed and draped in his perfectly white shirt, he would have appeared handsome, except for a fleshiness of his face, which made his eyes narrow and fox-like.

Jasmine, encouraged by the smile, was able to say, "I believe, Mr. Blunt, that we *disagreed* about the uselessness of novels."

He only nodded in reply, and the others, befuddled and discomforted by the exchange, gradually drifted into other conversations. Jasmine's aunt sat to her left, Chrissie, Pudge, and Thomas on the far side of her. Tina spoke to Mrs. Blunt of the beauty of lake; then a question about the changes that occurred in various seasons led to a detailed discussion of the difficulties of maintaining two houses, especially where one was located in a cold-weather, mountain location. As Mrs. Blunt, who asked to be called Jane, proved to be an avid talker for whom no detail of household management seemed too trivial to merit her expert attention and full explication, little conversation or attention was required of Jasmine, and she was able occasionally to grasp pieces of the conversations at other parts of the table.

At one point, she heard Max saying, "Of course life isn't fair, but why should someone be punished for his good fortune," to which Phillip replied, "Or, for that matter, why should someone be punished for his poor fortune." Later, she became aware that Sherry was describing financial aspects of the movie industry to Mr. Blunt.

"I don't know many of the details, and I'm not really very much of a businesswoman. But if you wanted my advice, Mr. Blunt, I'd say steer clear. Everybody always seems to be losing gobs of money."

A cook was preparing their meal in the kitchen, but Mrs. Blunt was serving it herself. When she was taking the salad plates away, Tina's offer to assist was accepted. Jasmine stood immediately, intending to carry dishes as well, but Mrs. Blunt suggested that she remain with the younger people. Tina's protest as to Jasmine's willingness to help was dismissed. Jasmine retook her seat.

"Pudge is going to look just like his father when he gets old," Julia was saying to Max in a confidential, giggling whisper, and Max responded with a deep chortle. Farther up the table, Phillip and Mr. Blunt seemed to have continued the conversation about good fortune, and Phillip was saying, "I think we need to keep in mind that we are the products of privilege. No one can deny that being born into an affluent and educated family offers tremendous advantages that have nothing to do with merit."

Mr. Blunt did not respond to this. Instead, seeing that Jasmine was now attending to their conversation, he turned to her. "Mr. Gannon is arguing that death taxes ought to be increased rather than gotten rid of. What exactly does the young novelist think of that?"

"Sir, if I created the impression that I'm a novelist, I was in error. I'm merely a reader of novels."

Mr. Blunt laughed and said, "I'm sure you'll be writing them soon enough."

"As for taxes, I know very little about the levels of taxes and whether they are too high or too low."

"That's never stopped any politician from pronouncing judgment," Mr. Blunt said, inciting appreciative laughter from his end of the table. All now waited for her reply.

"It seems to me that two issues need to be balanced," she said, taking a deep breath. "All people have a desire to provide for their young. Wouldn't we be acting in opposition to a very basic human motivation if we tried to deny people the opportunity to pass possessions down to their children? Isn't it a good thing—even a noble thing—that parents want to provide security and opportunity for their children?"

"Absolutely," Mr. Blunt said. "No one over the age of fifty would plant a tree unless he thought his children would be allowed to enjoy it."

"On the other side," Jasmine went on, "we must allow that wealth acquired through inheritance in no way implies merit."

"Agreed," Mr. Blunt said, "but if it's my money and I want to give it to my nitwit offspring, why shouldn't I be able to?"

"Don't people sometimes, in guarding their wealth too closely, not only provide opportunities for those who inherit it but also limit opportunities for others? If wealth is so concentrated and distributed that able young people are denied educations, if it denies opportunity, then I think the injustice to those who chance to be born poor is too great."

"And can anybody really say that disadvantaged children in our worst schools have any realistic opportunity to succeed?" Phillip asked.

"How many of them would take advantage of opportunities if they existed?" Mr. Blunt queried.

Seemingly made reticent by the heat of Mr. Blunt's response, no one answered immediately, and Jasmine took it upon herself to say, "I attend one of the those 'worst' schools. My impression is that there are many who would not, but there are some who would."

"And is it impossible for them to accomplish that where they are?" Mr. Blunt asked. "I mean, isn't it as much or more a matter of the students' desires and persistence than of the quality of the school?"

"No, it isn't impossible. It is more difficult."

"How many of us would have had the independent motivation to do well in a really bad school?" Phillip asked. "If our teachers hadn't cared which classes we took or whether or not we did our homework? If our classmates had always been disrupting class? If we'd had out-of-date books? If we'd felt unsafe even when we were sitting in class? . . . ."

"Jasmine for one," Max offered, he and Julia having begun attending to the conversation.

"Yes," Sherry now said. "But Jasmine is so completely exceptional. What about more ordinary sorts like Max and me. I doubt we would have ever cracked a book."

Thomas laughed aloud at this comment, saying, "God knows, I rarely did anyway."

Mr. Blunt now looked on Jasmine in favorable appraisal, "And how many more students like you are there among your classmates?"

"I have a friend who does just as well as I do, without having had the advantages that I have. If anyone is extraordinary, she is. Her father works at the post office, her mother is a seamstress, and only a few years ago she spoke not one word of English, but all of her work is done beautifully . . . . There are others who, I believe, if their parents had encouraged them, or if they'd been able to attend a school where more was expected of them, might have done well."

"How many?" Mr. Blunt asked. "Would you guess more than five?"

"Perhaps about five," Jasmine admitted.

"A very small number," Mr. Blunt said, with some satisfaction.

"No matter how small the number," Phillip now protested, "isn't it critical that we keep the doors of opportunity open to them? All people need to feel they have opportunities to improve their lives."

"Jasmine's friend seems to have done very well," Mr. Blunt answered, turning toward her.

"Mr. Blunt, I think that to expect everyone to accomplish what Amy has would be unfair. Amy is blessed with unusual intelligence. She studies and reads five to six hours every day. There is no television in her home. Her parents are devoutly religious and very demanding. Her life is extraordinary."

"Shouldn't ordinary people have opportunities as well?" Phillip posed.

"Escaping poverty has always taken extraordinary efforts," Mr. Blunt said. "That was true for my parents, and I'm sure it was true for all your people's forebears at some time, as well. People aren't entitled to wealth. They earn it."

"Or their parents earn it for them," Phillip said, "which brings us back to the inheritance question."

Everyone laughed at this except Mr. Blunt. "I take your point," he said, "and I even agree, *to a point.* Where I disagree is when the wealth itself becomes an evil. The accumulation of capital is essential to an industrialized economy. It takes a lot of money to build a railroad."

Mr. Blunt was allowed the last word, as the ladies now interrupted them with the arrival of the main courses. Tina and Mrs. Blunt carried in overflowing platters of beef fillets, shrimp, fresh corn, twice-baked potatoes, and fresh bread, all of which Mr. Blunt greeted with cheery-faced relish. The food was simple, if abundant offerings of the freshest and most choice of the season's produce can be so described, and from the first courses to the final strawberry shortcake was relished by all.

When the last puddles of pink-tinted cream had been scooped up, Mr. Blunt proposed an after-dinner game of bridge for the older folks. His wishes could not reasonably be denied, but aside from him, his wife, and Tina, only the junior Pudge knew how to play, and it was apparent that he needed to be available to serve as host for his friends. Tina, having noticed and commented on an ivory and ebony cribbage set in the living room, proposed a game of cribbage. Mr. Blunt assented. Tina, knowing that Chrissie and Julia had more important activities on their minds than playing card games with the older generation, recruited Jasmine as the fourth player. Mrs. Blunt, however, declined to play, pleading duties in the kitchen. Max, a young man who was wise enough in the ways of the world to appreciate the value of ingratiating himself with a man as wealthy as Mr. Blunt, volunteered to take her place and followed them into the living room.

Tina Stubbs had looked forward to the weekend with that same invigorating anticipation with which a skilled businessperson, athlete, or gambler approaches a new competition. She was ambitious for her nieces, especially for Chrissie, and she prided herself on her skillful agency in those affairs in which her sister's passivity made her ineffectual. Mr. Blunt's wealth was vast; the Gannon pedigree unassailable. A Blunt-Gannon alliance would be formidable. Were Chrissie someday to marry Pudge, she would be positioned to take her place among those bejeweled ladies who catch the eyes of presidents—and her aunt, as her trusted advisor, would have their ears.

Of course, there were hazards. Pudge was not all that could have been hoped: he lacked wit; his conversation could be tedious; he would likely grow fat. On the other hand, he was attractive enough in a manly, portly sort of way; and he liked to be agreeable to Chrissie, which gave her a strong hand in directing him. There was also the difficulty of politics. Mr. Blunt was a Republican— even fiercely so; the Gannons, though moderate, had long been Democrats. Frictions would arise. Yet wasn't it possible for people of good will to overcome politics? She herself was prepared to submerge her own strongly held convictions in the interests of the young people's welfare, and she was determined to establish exactly the right tone among the others. The important thing was not to allow oneself to be drawn into debate. Appeals to eternal truths and bipartisan statesmanship would carry her through the weekend.

She would meet provocation with serenity. Good breeding and transcendent humanitarianism would prevail.

The card game, as it offered close-up opportunities for the exchange of more than pleasantries, would be especially challenging. Nonetheless, she felt herself up to the task. She entered the living room with her jaw held high—a position which had the advantage of minimizing her neck wrinkles—confident that she would be able to maintain her composure even under the most trying circumstances.

Jasmine put on a brave face as well. Her heart sank at the prospect of playing cards on the occasion of a perfect summer evening at what still seemed to her the most beautiful place in the world, but it was apparent that Mr. Blunt especially looked forward to the game. Perhaps because she had first met him on the pathway—and taken him not for the master of the house but a workman—Jasmine was not much frightened by him; nevertheless, she could not have refused a host who had been so gracious, especially as he had been quick to claim her as his partner.

The living room offered the advantage of a view of the lake, but the game presented little challenge. Tina was a competent player; but Max, who was paired with her, had not played for many years and required re-instruction in the rules. Though he was a quick study, he made amateurish errors in his counting and, no doubt, in his crib selections as well.

Jasmine had spent many hours counting cribbage hands for her Aunt Cynthia and played more than adequately, and Mr. Blunt was a skilled player, who counted his fifteens quickly and knew how to enhance or limit the possibilities in a crib. A lucky run of fives in Max's first hand kept the pegs close through the first turn, but thereafter Jasmine and Mr. Blunt's lead mounted quickly.

Mr. Blunt enjoyed winning—perhaps more than was seemly against such unskilled competition—and when Jasmine laid down a hand which he counted out to eighteen, he beamed at her with pleasure, saying, "I bet I could teach you to play bridge in an hour."

The outcome of the second game was already foregone when Mrs. Blunt, who had settled herself on the couch after finishing her chores in the kitchen, called their attention to Pudge and Chrissie. The couple were now standing out at the lake's edge, side-by-side and holding hands.

"What a lovely couple!" she said.

Tina sighed in agreement. The scene was indeed lovely, with the two young people profiled against the gleaming water, but Jasmine could not deny some correspondence between her own inner feelings and the mocking glance she now received from her partner. She could not return the look in kind, knowing that to be complicit in it would be a betrayal of not only her cousin, but her aunt and hostess as well, nor could she either feign innocence, as that would have been a lie, or disregard it, as that would have seemed a criticism of him. Instead, despite her considerable confusion, she held his eyes, managing, she hoped, not to let her mouth curl either up or down or to let her eyebrows arch even a fraction.

Mr. Blunt laughed aloud at this, causing his wife and Tina to look at him with some alarm. "The girl's a future diplomat," he said suddenly.

While it would have been preposterous ever to think of Chrissie as diplomatic, Tina was not reluctant to accept any reflection that cast her in a favorable light, and now, misunderstanding the object of Mr. Blunt's assertion, said, "Chrissie's a remarkably mature and talented girl."

Ignoring this, Mr. Blunt addressed himself to Jasmine. "Are you a Republican or Democrat?"

"Goodness, Hal!" Mrs. Blunt now said. "What kind of a question is that?"

"Jane made me promise not to discuss politics this weekend," Mr. Blunt explained, "but I'm sure Jasmine won't mind."

"I'm not yet seventeen, so I haven't registered to vote, and I'm not exactly sure how I will register. My grandmother was a Democrat, and, of course, my uncle is, so I suppose that is where I'll begin. But I would like to think that I will vote for the best person at the time, at least the one that represents the best ideas."

"That's a noble thought," Mr. Blunt said, "but it's the nature of politics that eventually you will have to vote for some bastards, so which ones will you choose?"

"Hal!" Mrs. Blunt again intoned.

Mr. Blunt disregarded her. "I'd bet my Big Bertha that when the time comes you'll be a Republican."

Tina, whose veneer of serenity had been scuffed by her loss at cards, now asked, "How could you know something like that?"

"Why she's grown up in the house of a famous Democrat, and she's had a whole cadre of party-liners to call her a traitor every time she's tried to express an intelligent thought. But she still hasn't broken. This girl thinks for herself. When the time comes, she'll make the right decision."

"I certainly hope that she will," Tina said pointedly.

There passed a moment of silence, during which Jasmine felt all eyes on her. She saw hazard, however, in meeting them. Her Aunt Tina's were likely to prove sharp and admonitory, Mr. Blunt's would be flattering and conspiratorial, and Mrs. Blunt's would be frightened. She chose, rather, to turn toward Max, whose look was surprisingly kind and approving.

"I agree entirely with Jasmine," he said. "For people of our generation, politics isn't the issue. The two parties are the same. Makes absolutely no difference one way or the other which gets elected."

"But it *does* make a difference," Mr. Blunt protested. "If nothing else, it makes a difference in how much taxes I'm going to pay."

"I'm sure when I have more to worry about from the tax man, I'll agree with you completely," Max said. "In the meantime, there's no practical difference. Either one, Tweedle Dee or Tweedle Dum, it's the same. It doesn't matter one iota which party's in power. It has no power to affect our lives."

"You think then that it is impossible for the efforts of men to guide and affect events?" Mr. Blunt queried.

"I do. It's completely out of our control."

"And do you agree with this, young miss?"

"Perhaps we can't control directly," Jasmine said, "but if the progress of the world is the sum of individual events, we can each do our own part."

"The decline of the world is not then inevitable?"

"I think it only becomes so if we submit to the idea that it is."

"Here, here," Mr. Blunt affirmed.

Max laughed good-naturedly, avowing, "I promise always to do my part. Though I admit that I can't see how that will do much good."

"I think that we always do some good," Jasmine said, "even when it isn't apparent to us."

"I wish I had as much faith as you," Max said. "Pick up any newspaper—it's all going to hell in a handbasket."

Jasmine understood that Max was speaking more for Mr. Blunt's benefit than for hers, but she felt compelled to reply nonetheless. "Isn't it possible," she suggested, "that we are all doing much more good than we think? We learn quickly of evil and ugliness; we get news of horrible events in even the most distant corners of the world. What we learn may sometimes be discouraging, but might it not also help us in finding ways to make the world better?"

This thought caused Jasmine's audience to pause and give consideration, but Mr. Blunt ended the silence with a shake of his head. "I wish it were so . . . . I truly wish it were so. But I'm afraid most human beings aren't that strong. Things they see—in movies, on television—things they hear, it becomes normal to them. They don't have the character to fight it, so they sign on. Good God, my own son brings it into the house and plays it on the record player! Have you heard that stuff? Have you seen what passes for television? Lord knows, Jeremy doesn't have the backbone to resist."

"Unfortunately, it's what entertains," Max said, "and if it entertains, people are going to have it, no matter how awful it is."

"No reason whatsoever why we should give in to it," Mr. Blunt said, now with some vehemence. "If people who know better would just speak up, we could put an end to it. Instead, whenever anybody protests, the damned liberals start calling them names, racists, or fascists, or morons. Talk a bunch of nonsense about different cultures and diversity, and keep us right on the road to . . . ."

Tina had lost at cards, and she now felt herself to be losing an argument as well. By counseling herself and practicing deep breathing she had managed to restrain herself so far. Now, the term "damned liberals" sent a shock through her whole body. She was proud to think of herself as a liberal, believed herself to have a personal understanding of hardship and misfortune, and prided herself on maintaining her views, even while living amidst wealth and privilege. She felt honor-bound to respond. She began gently enough, saying, "But don't we need to give consideration to people from different backgrounds? Aren't they entitled to their opinions?"

"Of course, they're entitled to their opinions. That doesn't mean we need to adopt them for ourselves," Mr. Blunt replied. "Because lots of people choose to be ignorant and immoral doesn't mean that we should condone stupidity and licentiousness. That's no way to run a railroad."

"And who's to decide what is immoral—or stupid and licentious for that matter?" Tina asked.

"For God's sake, woman, we are! Look at us. We're educated. We know a little bit about history. We've had some experience with managing things, learned a little bit about self-discipline. We have a certain responsibility . . . ."

"What you mean is you've been privileged."

"I have been privileged. I've been privileged to live in a country that protects individual rights, encourages science, innovation and progress, rewards hard work, maintains some kind of law and order, and offers me the opportunity to feed and house my family. I've been very privileged."

"So this country seems to you. It's not the same one all Americans experience."

"They can if they want to."

Tina looked on Mr. Blunt with near pity. "No, they can't," she said.

"So what's your alternative?" Mr. Blunt now asked. "Should some character who chants doggerel, wears his pants down around their knees, and brings the f-word to every living room in America be making policy for our country?"

"I wasn't electing anyone President," Tina said. "Besides, I said nothing of the sort. We need to understand his experience. We need to respect his culture."

"His culture is exactly the same one as mine . . . ."

"I think not."

Mr. Blunt shrugged in resignation. "Whether it's a culture or just a bunch of bad ideas, what does it matter anyway? Bad ideas are still bad ideas. We don't need to respect them. What we need to do is just the opposite. We need to treat them with the contempt they deserve."

Up until now, no one had addressed race directly, perhaps out of deference to Jasmine; but this was America, after all, where race could not stay long on the sidelines. *It was America,* where the moral high ground should, and very nearly always does, reside in racial and religious liberalism, in open-mindedness and tolerance. Here, Tina understood that she could press her advantage; and perhaps regretting her flippant remark about electing a President, said, "You seem to imply that this young man represents all African-Americans. I find that very offensive."

"Blacks are no doubt as various in their opinions as you and I, though I must say it sometimes doesn't seem like there are very many of them who want to speak up. Ask Jesse Jackson if he repudiates our gun-toting, baggy-pants. Ask your friends at the Equal Employment Opportunity Commission . . . ." Mr. Blunt now continued his rant—for the vehemence of his speech had now crossed the boundary of civil discussion, and a rant it had become—with a recounting of a process by which the shortcomings of Negro people became a demonstration of the evils of white people. "Why are so many black men in jail?" he concluded. "Because they commit too many crimes? Because they take too many drugs? Of course not. It's because white people are forcing drugs up their noses and pushing guns into their hands. Now, that's what I call a racist attitude. You'd think blacks were no more capable of controlling their own actions than alley cats."

The room was very quiet after this, and Mr. Blunt appeared for a moment even to regret his outburst, but Tina felt she must make a reply. "I think you discount too easily the effects of slavery and a hundred years of discrimination," she said, attempting to maintain her composure, though her head was nearly exploding. "Husbands and wives were sold and separated. Enterprise and hard work were rewarded only with heavier burdens. There was no upward mobility for slaves. No possibility of education. No hope of a real family. No reward for learning, hard work, and education. Only punishment. Aspirations were only handicaps." This statement gave Mr. Blunt a moment of pause, and Tina took the opportunity to continue. "And the idea that slavery ended in 1862 is absurd. Cotton farmers kept black people in de facto slavery nearly until the Civil Rights Act passed, and even that didn't end it. There were still many, many poor black people with nowhere to go."

Mr. Blunt was thoughtful. "And the result was made even worse by the selection process. Slave traders wouldn't have been able to catch the quickest and smartest. The leaders who did get caught—the most enterprising, the most intelligent—were feared and killed by their new masters."

At this, Tina's resolve to remain calm had to be foregone. "I find that type of thinking to be despicable," she said.

The harshness of her voice caused a moment of shocked silence, but Mr. Blunt, whose face was already quite red and who might have been expected now to become very angry indeed, seemed almost pleased with her reaction. He replied with a cheerful calm that suggested relish as much as actual anger. "I understand that you find it despicable, but do you find it incorrect."

"The conclusions to which that type of thinking leads are in no way correct," Tina replied. "That is precisely the despicable sort of logic people have used for thousands of years to repress others."

"I see no grounds in it for repression. I believe only that we should all be treated as individuals, regardless of race." He now glanced toward Jasmine. "For example, your niece, I assume, is partly of African heritage, but I have no doubt that she is infinitely more intelligent than our Jeremy, who, unless a milkman's sneaked into the larder, is entirely of European descent."

"Hal!" Mrs. Blunt said mournfully. "That's awful."

"It's true, dear. Jeremy has his virtues but brains is not among them."

"Jemmy doesn't test well," Mrs. Blunt explained.

"And the reason he doesn't test well is that he lacks brain power."

"Jeremy is a very bright boy," Mrs. Blunt protested. "He's just nervous about taking tests."

"So nervous that he's usually drinking beer when he should be studying for them."

"That's horrible, Hal. I won't have you saying it."

"Nonetheless it's true. I believe in calling a spade a spade. Jemmy has his virtues, and he may yet make something of himself if he ever decides to apply himself, but he'll never be a great thinker. When God was handing out brains, Jeremy was probably out having a cigar."

"I'm sure I don't believe a word of it," Tina said to Mr. Blunt. She turned toward Mrs. Blunt. "Some children simply don't test well. It's no reflection on their abilities."

"Yes, I'm sure," Mr. Blunt interposed. "Nonetheless, I imagine all of your nieces test just fine."

Mrs. Stubbs might now have recognized an opportunity to move the conversation into less controversial topics, such as the children's activities and studies, and thereby limit the damage to Chrissie's hopes, but her ears still burned and her heart was filled wrath. She could not resist this opportunity to gain further moral advantage. "It would be deeply unjust," she said, "to deny Jeremy opportunities in life simply because he isn't skilled at taking tests."

Mr. Blunt appeared to be on the verge of laughter. "On the contrary, it would be unjust to do anything else. We'll get him tutors and push on the best we can, but in the end, if Jeremy doesn't make the grade some doors will be closed to him. So be it."

"That's precisely the excuse that's been used to deny black children opportunities for decades."

"It's not an excuse. It's a reason."

"And this so-called 'reason' has been the justification for denying African-Americans access to the best universities and best jobs."

"It's been the justification for denying access to the ones who are blockheads."

A series of arguments and counter-arguments—or, rather, accusations and counter-accusations—ensued, which led to each charging the other with racial prejudice.

"You don't think blacks are capable of competing with whites," concluded Mr. Blunt. "That's the real prejudice."

"The real prejudice is that you refuse to acknowledge how privileged you are by being white, male, wealthy, and able to set all the rules," Tina answered.

While Tina had trembled with rage as she spoke, Mr. Blunt had fully regained his composure and seemed even to be taking a perverse satisfaction in having provoked his antagonist. Tina now eyed him with real malignity, while he seemed on the verge of laughter.

Hoping to forestall yet more harsh invective, Jasmine now said, "My grandmother often said that poor people have poor ways."

"Yes, they do!" Mr. Blunt said quickly, "and until they rid themselves of poor ways, they can never hope to escape poverty."

"But she did not say," Jasmine continued, "whether they were poor because they had poor ways, or they had poor ways because they were poor."

There passed another moment of silence, after which Mr. Blunt laughed aloud. "No doubt it's circular. But one thing is certain, giving people money cures nothing in the long run."

"From your perspective that may seem clear," Tina said. "But then you always had enough to eat. Money cures hunger."

Mr. Blunt paused for a moment before answering. "I fear any response I make to that will prejudice my argument in your eyes. But I confess it, I've always had enough to eat, though perhaps not with the margin of safety you suppose. Nonetheless, I think you overestimate the influence of wealth."

"That's easy to say when you've always had enough."

Mr. Blunt sighed. "So I *have* prejudiced my argument."

"I am only suggesting that for you, a white male who has lived a life of privilege, to presume that you have the answers for everyone is no longer acceptable."

"Whether something is easy for me to say or difficult and whether I am a white male or a green hermaphrodite in no way changes the truth or falsehood of the statement."

"We live in a world of multiple truths," Tina continued. "Those who have had the power to have their version of the truth enshrined in the textbooks shouldn't deceive themselves."

"Whether the textbooks tell it or not, the truth remains unaltered," Mr. Blunt replied.

Having already run aground on issues of nurture and nature, and cause and effect, the conversation now struck hard on the nature of truth, and the pair were reduced to casting recriminations, Tina at Mr. Blunt for narrow-mindedness, and he at her for lack of backbone. Even in their current frames of mind, however, both could see that they would not soon resolve this issue to the satisfaction of humanity. Their enthusiasm waned, their accusations were made with less vigor, and Mr. Blunt was willing to direct the conversation elsewhere.

"I've been able to give much more to Jeremy than my parents ever provided for me," he said, "but he's no better off for it. I give him more things, but I fail him in the more important ways."

Max, who had not spoken through all this, now interjected: "Pudge? Goodness no. You failed him nowhere. He's as good a man as you'll find anywhere."

"I understand perfectly my son's limitations," Mr. Blunt replied.

"I think it's best if we leave Jemmy alone," Mrs. Blunt suggested.

All present, even Mr. Blunt, seemed to take Mrs. Blunt's admonition to heart.

"Yes, we're not really being fair to him," Tina agreed softly, finally laying down and counting a hand which she'd already been holding for some minutes.

"I love Jeremy with all my heart," Mr. Blunt said, casting an apologetic eye on his wife. "I was only using him as an example. We need to be realistic."

Jasmine had so long played cribbage with her Aunt Cynthia that she could do it with half a mind, and her thoughts now tumbled quickly. Since the time she had lived in her grandmother's house, she had not heard anyone speak so bluntly about the condition of people of her father's race, and never before in her life had she heard a white person speak in such a manner. Yet she had not been struck so much by the offensiveness of Mr. Blunt's observations as by their familiarity: her grandmother had often spoken in very much the same tones.

Her Ganny had been a great devotee of Booker T. Washington. While she had read other writers to her grandchildren, including Frederick Douglas, whom she praised unstintingly, and, more reluctantly, W. E. B. Dubois, toward whom she harbored some resentment for his treatment of Washington, she had remained loyal to the sage of Tuskegee. Granny had cherished her copies of the magazines in which *Up From Slavery* had first been published and had regularly, reverently withdrawn them from the oil cloth in which her own mother had presented them to her. She both read to her grandchildren from the pages and preached to them over the pages, and in Jasmine's mind, the views of her grandmother and those of Mr. Washington had become so intertwined as to be inseparable. Indeed, she and William had reserved a private name for her to describe those times when she had become most impassioned about the state of her race: Granny Washington.

Consequently, though she was sadly struck by Mr. Blunt's unflattering examination of the living conditions of African-Americans, she was not offended by it. Mr. Washington himself had begun life sleeping amid filthy rags on a dirt floor; and he and Granny both had lamented the ignorance and primitive manners of freed slaves and their descendents. While it was not a culture they would have wanted to preserve, Mr. Washington and her Granny had assured her that this degradation was no shame to the Negro race; nor even could white slave holders have been long condemned. People everywhere were weak-minded. Few could separate good and evil—especially evil that profited them—when all about them mistook one for the other. It was left to the strong-minded few to end such evil institutions as slavery. That Jasmine and William would be among these few had needed no mentioning.

Jasmine's grandmother, and William and Jasmine as well, had long since been lifted up to a level equal to that of anyone, but no excess of vigilance was possible in assuring that this level was maintained. Granny Washington had been a tyrant of the toothbrush and bath, would never have allowed Jasmine to don a blouse that was missing even a single button, and insisted that she and William keep the deepest corners of their closets dust-free.

Among the other correspondences Jasmine perceived between what her grandmother had taught her and what Mr. Blunt said was a common distrust of wealth as a guarantor of success. After all, her grandmother had not been rich (in retrospect, she realized that they had been very poor indeed), but Jasmine had met no one who surpassed her in grace, dignity, and nobility of the spirit. As Granny Washington said, there was dignity in labor that no amount of wealth could confer.

Nor was Jasmine deeply troubled by Mr. Blunt's allusions to the genetic makeup of her race: first, from her biology classes she knew enough about population genetics to understand that racial statistics referred only to probabilities and guaranteed nothing about any specific individual; and second, she firmly believed in the rights of every individual to equal opportunity regardless of race. If the former was correctly understood, and the latter vigorously defended, no threat could arise from either scientific inquiry or amateur speculation.

She was, however, disturbed by a general and elusive sensation of guilt, a sense of failure on her own part and perhaps even, almost unthinkably, on Granny's. Mr. Washington's purpose in describing the dire circumstances of former slaves was to assure that others understood the magnitude of the task involved in improving their conditions and to encourage all his fellow Americans to accept their responsibilities in accomplishing this task. Thus, the battle had been fought for public schools, Negro colleges, and free libraries. The old school desks in their basement testified that her Granny had shouldered the burden for many years; yet she had withdrawn from this task. Moreover she had not emphasized to Jasmine that she must carry the mission forward.

The most cheering construction of this behavior would have been to conclude that Granny considered the task to be completed or at least to have been set inevitably on its course, but evidence would not allow Jasmine this escape: she remembered her grandmother lamenting that "people no longer want to lift themselves up" and her umbrage with people who had failed to "lift themselves up by their bootstraps."

Had her grandmother's laments been those of a weary and defeated old woman? Was a teenaged girl, especially one who had grown up with the advantages Jasmine had, perhaps not allowed such resignation? In this, her grandmother's lessons remained ambiguous: she knew that she must always be truthful and loyal; that she must always conduct herself in a way that would bring honor on her family; and that she must never shy from honest labor; but it was not clear what obligations she had to the Negro race.

Of course, she was at most one-half Negro; of course, she had lived among her Caucasian relatives; of course, situated as she was, she had so rarely been confronted with racial discrimination that making an issue of it would have been whining; of course, she always attempted to be helpful to her schoolmates . . ., of course . . ., of course . . . . Remonstrate as she might, however, Mr. Blunt was correct in observing that there were many Negroes who seemed not to have succeeded in lifting themselves up. What responsibility did she have in aiding them to do so?

Had her grandmother been allowed to visit her school she would only have experienced discouragement. The deplorable behavior of many of the Negro children, the proportion of them who could not or would not learn, their execrable grammar, and especially the ridicule those who most applied themselves suffered from their less ambitious peers would have depressed her utterly, as the thought of it now did Jasmine. What exactly was to be done?

The question disturbed her, and she could reach no satisfactory resolution; yet on one instruction from both her Granny and Mr. Washington she could rely: she must always keep a firm grip on her own bootstraps and lift herself as high as they would carry her.

Chapter 12

Mountain Trails

During breakfast, Pudge proposed a bicycle ride along a trail that led through the mountains surrounding the lake, to which Phillip eagerly assented. Thomas demurred, on the grounds of a reunion with college chums in Reno. While Max was being encouraged to ride along—there being three bikes equal to an off-road outing—it became apparent that resistance was developing among some feminine members of the party.

Except for Jasmine, none of the girls had anticipated a morning without male companions, and a silence from their sections of the table began to make itself felt. Mrs. Blunt was the first to intervene.

"Jemmy, don't you think the girls might like to ride, as well?"

"Sure, if they want," Pudge said, looking toward Chrissie.

Left to themselves, the girls would never have struck upon the idea of going for a bicycle ride. Indeed, aside from Jasmine, they had observed the loading and unloading of the bicycles with some indifference, never truly accepting that they would be expected to pedal one. None was eager to find herself sweaty, dirty, and perhaps even in some danger. Potential abandonment by the boys, however, created a more complicated set of interests.

Chrissie was the first to hit upon a line of defense. "But there aren't enough bikes," she said, with feigned dismay.

A silence ensued, after which Pudge, unable to read with complete accuracy the quick, demanding look he was receiving from his girlfriend, attempted to appease her by saying, "No problem, we could rent more bikes in town. That'd be cool."

For this, however, he received only a sharp, hostile glare.

Immediately perceiving the girls' predicament, Tina now intervened, "Is it really necessary to rent bikes?"

"Everything's so pretty," Jasmine now offered. "I think I would be just as happy to walk."

"The girls could walk the lakeshore trail, while the boys ride," Mr. Blunt suggested, but he was soon silenced by his wife's stern look.

"The mountain trail's not bad for walking," Pudge now said, looking quickly to Chrissie, whose blank look he seemed to find encouraging. "Anybody who wanted to could ride, and the rest could walk. No problem."

The rewarding smile he'd anticipated, however, did not materialize. Instead, the silence resumed.

"Riding on the trails must take a great deal of skill," Tina now suggested.

Jane Blunt concurred. "Just last month a girl hit a stick and was thrown over her handlebars. She's paralyzed."

Pudge attempted to reassure his mother, saying, "I think it would have been a log, Mom," but a weight of disapproval now hung in the air.

"How much instruction have any of you had?" Tina asked.

"Mountain biking isn't something you go out and get instruction in," Phillip suggested. "It's something you just learn."

"But isn't that dangerous?"

"Not very," Phillip said. "Besides, if it weren't a little dangerous, it wouldn't be fun."

"I've heard that they offer professional instruction at Squaw Valley," Mrs. Blunt now said.

"Really?" Tina responded. "How far away would that be?"

"Not even an hour," Mrs. Blunt answered.

"I would feel much better if the girls—especially the girls—could have a lesson or two first," Tina said.

"It's an hour there and an hour back," Pudge said, "and we don't even know if they have any classes today." Chrissie again directed a warning glare toward him. "But I guess we could call," he went on. Then, seeing her look again evolve to open hostility, he said, "Hey, maybe we all ought to just walk."

Max quickly submitted, and Phillip, outnumbered as he was, could only mumble in agreement. Jasmine could see that he was disappointed, however, and might have offered to ride with him had she not felt certain that such an offer would provoke the wrath of her cousins.

The group now resumed its cheerful breakfast. Pudge, on whom Chrissie again looked admiringly, seemed pleased with his handling of the affair, no doubt considering himself to have preserved them all from a painful misadventure. He quickly reclaimed his characteristic attitude of gentlemanly indulgence of things feminine and frivolous, and when Chrissie suggested that, since the mountain trail was steep and dusty, they might do better to walk the flat lakeside trail, he made no rebuttal.

At this point, however, Mrs. Blunt pointed out that there were several smaller trails that led off the mountain trail, one of which led to Ribbon Falls and others to spectacular views of the lake. These trails, while not suitable for riding, were delightful for hiking and likely, even on such a busy weekend, to afford the group nearly complete privacy. Julia quickly professed a deep interest in seeing either the falls or a panorama of the lake, and hearing no dissent from the other girls at the table, Pudge reversed his earlier reversal: they would go to the mountain trail, but of course no bikes would be loaded onto the cars.

Mr. Blunt's spanking new Suburban was deemed the most suitable vehicle for a rugged outing, and the young people squeezed cheerfully into the well-appointed seats. In reality, as the road to the trailhead was fully paved, the old van would have served as well. Nevertheless, the solidity of the vehicle, its high stature, and the powerful thrum of its engine provided an exhilarating sense of adventure. Pudge set the radio to blaring rock and roll music, and they were all soon singing along, while frequently upbraiding each other good-naturedly for failure to remember lyrics correctly.

A wooden sign informed them that they'd found the trailhead, but the corner that indicated the mileage to the falls had been shot away. When questioned, Pudge admitted that he had never been all the way to the falls and was unsure of the exact distance, though he felt sure it was no more than a mile or two. Phillip observed that given the steep, rocky terrain a round trip hike of four miles would prove challenging. They became aware that they had not remembered to bring drinking water, and Chrissie noted that Julia's new sandals would not be adequate for such a distance, an observation which provoked a virulent glance from Julia and an avowal that she was already completely accustomed to the leather straps on her sandals and that they never caused her any pain whatsoever.

"You'll ruin them on the rocks, though, Julia," Chrissie now said.

While the others would have been willing to modify their plans, Chrissie was now intent on arriving at the falls, and she suggested that the others begin the hike at a modest pace, while Pudge and Julia went back for water and sturdier shoes. Despite her unhappiness, Julia could find no pretext for resisting this suggestion, and she and Pudge were soon heading back down the road they'd just come up.

The trail began by passing through a flat, even slightly downward sloping, grove of pine and fir trees. Chrissie set off quickly, pulling Max after her, and Sherry and Phillip followed in turn, with Jasmine following behind. As the trail was only wide enough for a single person, conversation involving more that two people was impossible. Chrissie and Max had already advanced beyond the first curve, and Phillip performed the courtesy of discussing landmarks and vistas with Sherry. Thus, Jasmine was left to her own observations.

The trail soon opened up on a steep rocky hillside and became no more than a narrow cut in the face of the mountain. The view was breathtaking. The white granite about them set off the green of the trees and the bright colors of the wildflowers that tucked into every nook in the rocks; and, below, the limpid waters at the lake's edge extended out into vast expanses of smooth reflection and sparkling wind ripples.

After they'd crossed the hillside and again entered a more wooded area, they reached a point where they found Max and Chrissie waiting for them. Three trails diverged here. Fortunately, there was a second sign to guide them, but unfortunately, there was some ambiguity as to which trail was designated by the arrow next to Ribbon Falls. It seemed for a moment that they would all be halted until Pudge could return to guide them. Chrissie, however, felt sure that the highest trail, the one that went most directly up the mountain, led to the falls, and suggested that some might start up the trail while others remained to inform Pudge and Julia of the path they'd chosen. Jasmine, as she had been the least involved in conversation and was therefore the logical choice, offered to remain behind. Chrissie thanked her heartily and started up the trail, Max in tow behind her. Phillip and Sherry, more sensible to the awkwardness of leaving one member of their party alone, lingered. They had, Jasmine now discovered, been discussing teaching.

"It's not just that I want to help people," Phillip said, glancing quickly at Jasmine. "There's probably enough do-gooders in the world already. It's more a lucky coincidence. Discovering books was the most exciting experience of my life. Helping other people make the same discovery, being there when their eyes open to literature, sharing it with them . . . I can't think of anything I'd rather do."

"But how many of them will actually ever make that discovery?" Sherry asked. "And even if they do, won't it get boring for you? Watching kids go through the same old routines year after year . . . And being around so many really stupid people."

"They won't all be stupid. People like us have gone through schools, too. And I think the most fun part would be discovering interests and talents where you least expect them."

"I don't think you'll find very many. I'm sorry but hardly anybody really has that much interest in literature anymore. Not like you and Jasmine. You're exceptional," she said, then added with a quick smile to Jasmine, "in the best way. Both of you. And I think that's *extremely* cool. I think that's why you're always so interesting to talk to, and I really admire you for it. But most of the time, you'd just be working with a bunch of idiots like me, trying to get us to put down two consecutive sentences that make sense, when what we really want to be doing is reading a magazine or watching TV. I mean people just don't write stuff anymore. I'm not sure it's even all that necessary."

"Somebody has to write the magazines," Phillip suggested.

"Even that, computers could probably write it. It doesn't take a literary mind."

"Don't you sometimes, though, run into an article that's really cool? Something that really makes your day? Some clever thing or new way of looking at something? Somebody has to write that."

"I suppose they do," Sherry admitted. "But wouldn't it be much more interesting to own the magazine, to hire the people who can write that kind of stuff, and to make a whole lot of money off of it?" She concluded with a self-deprecating laugh, which Phillip shared, and she reached out and touched his arm. "It's an absolute disgrace that teachers are forced to live such squalid lives. God, they can hardly afford to buy a decent house. Do you think even one teacher lives in Arden Park?"

"Probably not, but money really *isn't* everything. It's important to do something you like."

"Why not do something you like that also makes money?"

"The two seem to be mutually exclusive," Phillip said.

Sherry now turned to Jasmine, asking, "Do you think there's something wrong with making money?"

Phillip interrupted. "I didn't say there was anything wrong with making money."

"Not in so many words."

"I meant that they seemed to be mutually exclusive *for me*."

Sherry again turned to Jasmine. "What about you? Would it be impossible for you to find something you love that happens to earn a reasonable income?"

"I think that an income that that could afford me a clean, safe, and warm home, in which I could surround myself with interesting books, would be reasonable."

"I know you truly mean that," Sherry said, regarding her intently. "You're such a good person . . . you're truly a good person." She now turned again to Phillip. "But most of us aren't as good as Jasmine. Not me, that's for sure. And I don't even know if you are Phillip . . . . Besides, think of how much good someone like Jasmine could do, if she did have money."

"I think you underestimate yourself," Jasmine now said. "I'm no better than you and I certainly couldn't be any better than Phillip, since if there's any good in me, more than anyone, more than anything, he's responsible for it."

Phillip guffawed, saying, "I am not."

"You are," Jasmine now said flatly. "Do you remember a frightened little girl who you discovered in your uncle's house? If not for you, almost anything might have become of her."

An embarrassing silence passed, in which Phillip seemed unable to speak and Jasmine's heart threatened to break. Sherry, who had observed this last exchange with mixed incredulity, admiration, and awe, now stood and broke this painful silence, saying, "I'll go ahead a little," but Phillip stood up as well, saying, "We can check out the beginning of the trail. Maybe it's the wrong one anyway." Sherry looked once toward Jasmine, who quickly assured her that she would be fine waiting alone. Her heart too tender to risk meeting Phillip's eyes, Jasmine didn't turn to watch them disappear up the trail above her.

Pudge and Julia, much to Julia's frustration, had been delayed at the house by Mrs. Blunt's insistence that individual, iced-water containers be supplied for each hiker, and nearly an hour elapsed before they arrived at the juncture where Jasmine sat waiting. When it became clear to him that the others had left Jasmine behind—to start up the much longer trail to Ribbon Lake, as it turned out, rather than the middle trail that led to Ribbon Falls—Pudge's anger set his jaw rigid. He set off after them at a punishing pace.

Julia's cheeks were now red with frustration. "Why would you let them leave you here?" she asked, her blue eyes vivid with anger.

Jasmine could see no way to justify herself that would not

cause Julia's wrath to affix more firmly on her sister, and said only, "They may have already discovered their mistake and turned back."

Julia said, "Oh, God," and began trudging up the dusty path. Whether Julia expected her to follow or wished to go on alone was impossible to determine. Jasmine surmised the latter.

While she was not much distressed by having yet again been left alone, Jasmine began after a time to regret that her current view was restricted and decided to climb to where she would have a vista of the lake. She had been walking for only a few minutes, however, when she began to hear the soft burbling of water and realized that off to one side of the trail, down a wooded slope, a small creek angled away from her and down the next ravine in the mountain. The banks of the creek were crowded with ferns, which, as the day was growing warm seem to offer a cool escape from the dust and sun. She was debating with herself whether or not she might dare leave the trail and risk missing the others as they descended, when she heard voices blending with the soft babbling of the water. She had moved farther up the trail, hoping to see some of her companions, when she observed through a break in the trees a rocky slide down which the tiny creek made a picturesque tumble. A moment later, Phillip began letting himself down the mossy boulders at the creek's edge, Sherry following behind him. The drop could not have measured more than twenty feet, but the footing was apparently treacherous as the two were descending with great care.

Phillip had reached the bottom, and Jasmine was about to call out to him, when a yelp arose from Sherry. She then slid precipitately down the last five feet of rock into Phillip's catching arms. They remained there holding each other, gazing into each other's eyes.

Jasmine was too delicate an ethicist to countenance spying on others, even though it might occur inadvertently, and especially not in a case where she was the spy. Indeed, she wished very much that she had not witnessed what she already had and was relieved at this moment to hear footsteps coming down the trail above her. She looked up to see Pudge leading the others down the trail.

He drew near, his face now set hard in anger. He passed by her without speaking, then turned back to ask if she had seen Phillip and Sherry.

"They're coming down along the creek," Jasmine answered.

"Tell them we're leaving," Pudge said. Then, he continued down the trail.

Chrissie passed without comment, oblivious to her, and Max only shrugged and smiled. Julia was last and she passed by with an angry look of disapproval, from which Jasmine gathered that she still blamed her for allowing Max and Chrissie to go off alone.

Jasmine now dared a glance down toward Phillip and Sherry and seeing that no further intimacies were on display called to them. Phillip looked up, she gestured to indicate that they were en route back down, and he waved and nodded in agreement. She then followed after Julia.

Once back at the car, it became apparent that Pudge had witnessed something to make him very angry. All felt this tension, and their return ride offered none of the exuberance of their ride out. Chrissie, who sat up front with Pudge, dared to turn on the radio, but he turned it off with a quick punch of his finger. Sherry commented on the cool, prettiness of the little stream, but her gentle words, spoken even as they were in her most soothing voice, did not succeed in softening the brittle air.

Only Max seemed unaffected. While Julia had contrived that he and she sit together in the far back of the Rover on the way out, Jasmine sat next to him now, Julia being too angry even to look at him.

"Good thing Pudge rescued us," he said jovially, addressing the group as a whole. "That lake was five miles away." When no one responded, he now shouted up to Pudge. "If you hadn't caught up with us, my man, we'd probably have ended up like the Donner Party. Dead along the trail, frozen in snowdrifts, eating each other."

By the quickness with which Pudge had overtaken them, it was apparent that he and Chrissie had not been making arduous progress up the trail, and no one, not even his sister, offered any response to this joke. He gave Jasmine a nudge with his elbow, toward which she turned with great reluctance, only to find him smiling and winking at her. She was immediately struck with dumb consternation, drew herself tighter together, stared down at her hands in her lap, and felt her whole body flush with shame.

"Tough crowd," Max said, at which Sherry turned back to him and said, "I think we all must be a little tired."

Max answered with an ironic smile, to which she responded with a stern, warning look.

Chapter 13

A Fine Bawcock

That afternoon, after a private conversation in his sister's room, Max announced that he'd called his agent and was needed immediately in Los Angeles. While this type of announcement would normally have provoked a flurry of questions about the type of engagement and amusing stories from Max about the likely ineptitude of the producers, he left quietly, Phillip having agreed to drive him to the airport in Reno. Jasmine passed her afternoon in reading and writing a letter to her brother while sitting in her rock nest at the lakeshore. By early evening Phillip and Thomas had both returned, and a game of Balderdash was arranged among the young people. They sat at a table in the walled yard. The sun could be seen dropping down toward the ridge on the far side of the lake, but the lake itself was hidden behind the wall.

The game required that players construct false definitions for an abstruse word; then, when one player read out the manufactured definitions along with the correct one, they guessed as to which was correct. The words tended to be Anglo Saxon, Asiatic, or aboriginal, so knowledge of Latin and Greek roots was of much less benefit than an ability to convincingly exploit purely accidental connotations. Aside from Pudge, the participants were all more clever than average, and the game began merrily enough, Sherry taking the lead in points with her wickedly convincing but completely false definitions.

When it was Jasmine's turn to pronounce the word and definitions, however, the word "bawcock" arose. Thomas began a general guffawing, until he was hushed by the others, who didn't want him to prejudice the group and influence their responses. The slips of paper were handed to Jasmine, and she read them off: "a toilet fixture" from Pudge, "a male parrot" from Julia, "a mixture of grain and straw fed to camels" from Phillip, "an archaic expression of contempt" from Chrissie, "a form of feathering on an arrow" from Sherry; "the sound of passing flatulence" from Thomas, and the real definition, "a fine fellow."

This time Julia's "a male parrot" won the vote; then, when Jasmine revealed the true definition, Thomas took up with bluster. "Pudge to a T. Here's to the bawcock who brought us here," he said, raising his glass of cola in a mock toast.

Chrissie, Julia, Sherry, and even Phillip made some ado of cheering and giggling, but Pudge's perplexed face revealed that he could not conclude whether he ought to be angry or pleased. Jasmine had a sufficiently acute appreciation of the force of a word's connotations, even when inadvertent, that she fully sympathized with him. Thomas, however, seemingly oblivious to his host's distress, persisted: "A fine bawcock our Pudge. No finer bawcock on earth."

Phillip, beginning to sense the inappropriateness of Thomas's behavior, now said, "That's redundant though. Since a bawcock is already a fine fellow by definition, I'm not sure one could be a 'fine' bawcock."

"Such a man bears redundancy," Thomas said. "Not only is he a fine bawcock, he is a fine, fine bawcock indeed."

Chrissie was sitting next to Pudge and, since Max's departure, appeared to have repaired the breech between them. She didn't dare join in the banter, but it was apparent, from a dancing of her eyes that was concealed from Pudge that she enjoyed it.

Pudge now turned to her and whispered something in her ear. She pulled away with a sharp look of distaste, saying, "Don't be an ass, Pudge." Then, recovering herself, she turned to her brother. "I think Tommy's still a little drunk from his outing with his alcoholic fraternity brothers, aren't you, Tommy?"

"A couple of beers . . . . Maybe three . . . ."

"Maybe six," Chrissie said.

Thomas shrugged a confession, but his manner suggested pride as much as shame, and he did not give up his bantering. Instead, he turned to Phillip, saying, "I only called him a fine fellow, in fact a fine, fine, super-fine fellow. What could be wrong with that?"

Instead of responding, Phillip pointed at Julia, whose turn it was to draw, and ordered, "Next word." Julia at first hesitated, as though she were not quite ready to leave the interesting interchange, then to Jasmine's relief drew the next card.

Now suffering under a constraint to maintain civility, the game lost its cheerful good humor. Pudge put little energy into his definition and then withdrew, and Thomas's eyes actually fell shut as he awaited his turn. He soon excused himself as well—to go to his room to sleep, Jasmine hoped—and the game was suspended. Chrissie went off to find Pudge, and Julia, her normal preferred companion having now departed for parts south, invited Sherry to accompany her on a drive to town. There, Jasmine guessed, she would pursue a tactical consultation on the events of the weekend.

This left only Phillip and Jasmine at the table. Both were eager to escape the confines of the garden wall, and they were soon walking the path along the lake's edge. They spoke quietly for a time about the beauty of the lake, but it was apparent that Phillip's thoughts were elsewhere, and though he spoke out of context, Jasmine was not surprised when he said, "Sherry's a lot smarter than she lets on."

Jasmine, who had a full appreciation of Sherry's natural intelligence and powers of perception, agreed.

"It's just that you never know exactly what to expect from her. I imagine some people—at first at least—think she's just a spoiled LA princess. But she's not. She's much more complex than that. She's not shallow."

"No, she isn't shallow," Jasmine said carefully.

They walked on quietly for a while, until Jasmine, willing enough to change the subject, said, "I appreciated the way you helped quiet Thomas."

"I don't think there's any permanent damage done. Pudge probably didn't even get it all."

"He felt it."

Phillip nodded his agreement. "If Tommy can come out and act decently at dinner, I think it'll blow over. Chrissie can handle Pudge. She wouldn't do anything to hurt him."

"Perhaps not intentionally," she said, though in this, she felt false. Was not deceit always hurtful at some level? Wasn't recklessness about others feelings a meanness in itself? And was not the very idea of "handling" demeaning to the handled? "Max can be very charming," she ventured to say.

"He can, but in some ways Sherry actually seems the more grown up of the two. She's wise in some ways—it's usually her taking care of him, rather than the reverse. But there's nothing fake about her. It's not like she's trying to act grown up like Chrissie and Julia sometimes do. Really, I think she's one of the more impressive girls . . . women . . . I've ever met. She has an independence and self-assurance about her. There's nothing fake about it."

His expression revealed the pleasure he took in talking about Sherry. Moreover, since he often seemed to know Jasmine's thoughts even before she did, his failure to perceive how troubled she now was revealed how consumed he was.

"She's lovely," Jasmine forced herself to say.

"She is," Phillip said, "but she's more than just that. She likes to pretend that she's just the spoiled princess, but she's not. She's really bright and insightful. She understands there's more to the world than Bel Air and Malibu, but she doesn't want to pretend she's something she's not. She understands herself, and I think that's really cool. You have to admire her for that." These words were painful to Jasmine, but she felt no right to interrupt; nor did he allow her opportunity. "Sherry appreciates nice things," he said, "and there's nothing wrong with that—we all do—but she understands that's all they are: nice things. No real sacrifices have ever been required of her. But she's strong. I'm sure she'd rise to almost any occasion." Caught up in his own thoughts, Phillip had spoken without looking at Jasmine. Now, he turned to her, and she was dismayed by the brightness in his eyes. "How weird that she wound up living right across the street," he said, "during the very same summer I'm in Arden Park!"

Jasmine could not help observing to herself that it was very weird indeed, that it might just as easily not have happened.

Chapter 14

Fireworks

Dinner on the second night was a traditional Fourth of July barbecue, with chicken, corn on the cob once again (for which Jane Blunt apologized with the excuse that it was never so good as at this time of year), freshly baked bread, once-baked potatoes, and salad—traditional except for the chicken being skinned breasts marinated and otherwise made ready by an Arden Park restaurant, the corn, tomatoes, and cucumbers for the salad having been delivered fresh that very afternoon from the valley, and the bread having been driven to the house by a local baker while it was still hot from the oven. The heat of the day had lifted, the temperature in the garden was perfect, and the food was plentiful, artistically presented, and savory, all of which caused Sherry to remark to Mrs. Blunt that, if this was not the best meal she'd ever had in her life, then the previous evening's was.

Mrs. Blunt's usual reserve gave way to a smile of girlish pleasure, and Mr. Blunt, watching his wife's discomposure, said, "Jane, we've

shown one young lady the most beautiful place on earth"—
indicating Jasmine—"and you've given another the most enjoyable
meal of her life"—indicating Sherry. "I'd call that a pretty successful
weekend, wouldn't you?"

Mrs. Blunt, flustered by the praise she'd received, and the
chorus of affirming comments, continued to beam.

"It's not just the meals," Sherry now said, "it's everything. The
house, the garden, the way you've decorated the rooms. It's just
perfect in every way. You're a marvel, Mrs. Blunt."

"Hal should get all the credit for the garden," Mrs. Blunt
managed to sputter, though nearly overcome with gratification.
All were pleased to witness her delight, as she had been a diligent
and very capable host, and a tone of pleasant, mutual appreciation
persisted throughout the meal.

No wine was served to the young people at the table, this
apparently being the policy of the Blunt household, but it was tacitly
accepted by Harold and Jane Blunt—and now Tina as well—that
Pudge and his friends drank alcoholic beverages when outside adult
observation. Thus, instead of lingering at the table, Pudge excused
himself quickly after dinner and fled to the beach, taking Thomas,
Phillip, Chrissie, and Sherry with him. Julia, who had been more
silent than normal during dinner, refused his invitation and remained
at the table, and Jasmine, sensing that any refusal to take alcohol
would be dispiriting to the others, chose to remain as well.

The idea of another cribbage game was considered and quickly
rejected by Mrs. Blunt on the grounds of the evening being far too
lovely for cards. Instead, she proposed that Mr. Blunt give a tour
of his garden. All agreed, though Julia could manage little more
than an indifferent shrug, and lagged behind the others.

Mr. Blunt was a man of strong opinions, which he was not at
all reluctant to express, but, like the experienced political operator
which he was, he did not seem to harbor resentments. Throughout
the day, he had endeavored to be cordial to Tina, and now, in
reference to an especially impressive display of pink larkspur blooms,
she attempted a small joke, "I would have thought you would
avoid pink."

Mr. Blunt gave a laugh that was perhaps more hearty than was merited and said, "I operate a bipartisan, equal-opportunity garden."

The many flowers, pink and every other color imaginable, made an impressive display that drew everyone's appreciation, but it was soon apparent that only Jasmine took a real interest in Mr. Blunt's discussion of the best varieties of high elevation plants and how they responded to cold snaps and heavy snow cover. She was especially delighted to discover a long, deep row of rhubarb that ran along one wall, providing a backdrop for a low bed of sweet violets.

"You like rhubarb?" Mr. Blunt asked, with obvious delight. "I like it myself. You should take home a trunkfull."

"My grandmother made a strawberry-rhubarb pie that my brother and I just loved—and sometimes rhubarb tarts."

"It's possible to get good strawberries again. Jane finds them some damn place or another. For years, you could only get vine-ripened cardboard."

Tina observed that the growers were Cambodian families that had set up small farms and begun growing traditional varieties.

"It was the Japs who grew them when I was a kid. The ones now I think are just about as good. You couldn't do much better than them for a pie. Myself, I'm just about as happy with a straight bowl of rhubarb."

"Aunt Cynthia let me start a row along the back fence in Arden Park, but it faded away in a year or two."

They discussed for a while rhubarb's aversion to hot weather and speculated about its need for winter chilling.

"A Swede neighbor once told me if I buried the plants in snow for a few weeks during the winter, they would do just fine even in the valley," Mr. Blunt said. "It seemed easier just to grow it here. I could bring you snow if you wanted to try it out."

Jasmine did not respond to this, for while the offer was kind and almost certainly sincere, it was not reasonable to expect the majority stockholder of a billion dollar company to transport snow for the sake of her rhubarb.

"In any case," he said, perhaps realizing himself the extravagance of his offer, "we've got plenty of the white stuff here in the winter. You can come and get some anytime you want, and while you're at it you can spend a day or two in the 'most beautiful place in the world.'"

"The garden was the one place where my grandmother allowed us to go without shoes," Jasmine reflected. "In some ways, Mr. Blunt, you resemble my grandmother."

"Really, Jasmine!" Tina said quickly. "I'm sure you were too little to remember anything about her." She then added, relevant to nothing, "I'm sure she would never have called a Japanese person a Jap."

Though Jasmine was not as certain as her aunt that she had not heard her grandmother use the term Jap in teaching about the war—she had been surprised to learn that the term "hymie" was impolite—she too had found Mr. Blunt's usage jarring. He was the CEO and largest stockholder of a substantial corporation: How could he not know that "Jap" was no longer considered a proper term? Was it possible that no one around him—not his wife, son, or subordinates—ever dared to correct or chastise him?

"I mean no offense," Mr. Blunt said.

"Many people find that type of reference *very* offensive," Tina said.

"If so, I'm afraid the prejudice is in their minds, because I assure you there's none in mine . . . . I'm a half-mick, half-Polack, half-what-have-you and don't care who says so."

"Do you think you would feel the same if you were Mexican or African-American, or even Italian?"

"I don't see why not," Mr. Blunt said quickly, then, after considering, added, "Anyway, I hope I would. I think we make too much of these things."

Jasmine had often given consideration to the range of connotations in even minor variations of speech and was impelled to do so again now. Sometimes distinctions seemed no more significant than those between shades of socks—"a Jew" versus "Jewish"; an "Oriental" versus an "Asian; "black people" versus "blacks" versus "Negroes" versus "colored" versus "coloreds" versus "colored people" versus "people of color" versus "African-Americans." ("African-American people" sounded ridiculous.) It would have been impossible to unravel the full range of subtle connotations, much less to explain them to an alien, but just as a man who wore brown socks with black shoes told a different story than if he'd selected black ones, so each term told a slightly different story about the teller.

She now recalled an incident from Thomas's last year of high school. She had ridden with Tina to pick him up from a swimming practice and while they were waiting had gone to use the bathroom. Boys were dressing in the adjoining dressing room, and she had overheard repeated use of the term "nigger lips" in a laughing, nearly shouted conversation. After she had left the restroom, she watched the door to the boys' room, but no black boys exited; nor did she believe there were any Negro boys on Thomas's team. Negro boys at her own school sometimes taunted each other with similar language, and such a comment would never likely be directed at her personally as her lips were thin; nonetheless, recollection of this event never failed to make her shudder with pain and humiliation.

"I agree that we make too much of terminology," Jasmine said, her recollection having put a tremble of anger in her voice, "but I very much would not like to be called 'half-nigger' and I certainly would never describe myself and my brother as such."

Mr. Blunt was visibly abashed. He now spoke apologetically, saying, "But that's my point. We need to take some of the sting out of such terms. Sticks and stones and all that . . . ."

Mrs. Blunt now pointed out two stacks of firewood that sat in perfectly even rows under the cover of the back stairs. "Harold's wood," she said. "We come up here to relax for a weekend, and he spends the entire time with his chainsaw and splitting maul."

"Hard work never hurt anyone," Mr. Blunt said.

"Tell that to a coal miner," Tina replied.

Mr. Blunt laughed good-naturedly. "*A little* hard work never hurt anyone," he corrected.

Tina could not help being pleased with her unusual success at repartee, and she permitted herself a guilty smile.

Approaching darkness warned them that fireworks would soon begin, and as Mrs. Blunt had allowed her cook a holiday, the women began carrying dishes up into the kitchen. Julia, unable to accept the ignominy of doing housework that her sister had avoided, escaped to her room after carrying up her own plate. Even so, with Jasmine doing the carrying and the two older women sharing tasks in the kitchen, the job went quickly, especially since Mrs. Blunt had been tidy in her preparation. Jasmine found herself with nearly a half-hour of time to be alone in her room.

Jasmine had often been alone in her childhood, and time for reflection had become almost a necessity to her. The events of the day—Chrissie's and Max's deception of Julia and Pudge; Sherry's attentions to Phillip; the shameful ridicule of their young host; even her exchanges with Mr. Blunt—these were all disturbing in some ways, especially as she did not feel herself always to have behaved exactly as she should. It was not that she felt she should have reported on Max and Chrissie—it was not her position to do so, nor would either Pudge or Julia have thanked her for it. Indeed, any revelation would likely have incurred the wrath of all four in perpetuity. Nor could she have permitted herself to speak critically of Sherry; her own emotions were too assertive for her to make any impartial judgments. In the matter of Pudge's ridicule, however, she admonished herself. A kind comment from her, or even a suggestion that the game move on, might have saved him embarrassment.

As for Mr. Blunt, it was not completely true that he meant no offense by using unpopular ethnic terms, for he took obvious enjoyment in "knocking the chip" from her aunt's shoulder. Moreover, the attention he paid to her, a mere teenager, seemed somewhat exaggerated. If he was proffering this kindness as evidence of his lack of personal prejudice, his conduct was too calculated for a gathering of friends—or, at a minimum, a too-ready submission to convenience. Nonetheless, he had made her feel welcome, had flattered her with his conversation, and had even shared private jokes and reminiscences with her. While she could not as yet fully comprehend his motives, she could believe that she would someday come to like him.

A rolling boom out over the lake signaled the beginning of the fireworks, and Jasmine now found a sweater and hurried down toward the beach. The young people sat in the sand, in a line facing the water: Chrissie sat next to Pudge, Phillip's shoulder was against Sherry's, and Julia sat a little apart from them next to her brother. The elders took places farther up the beach, distant enough that the young people might talk without being overheard, and Jasmine, after a moment's pause, sat down slightly behind the other young people, placing herself between the two groups.

The first of the fireworks already blossomed overhead, producing far too much noise to permit conversation beyond oohs and ahs, and brief expressions of appreciation. The raft from which the rockets were being launched was not far offshore, and the blue and white darts seemed not only to fill the sky overhead and lake below but also to illuminate the beach and nearby trees.

When a longer than usual pause came, Mr. Blunt said, "To think, this is happening all over the country tonight—'through every Middlesex village and farm.'"

Pudge turned back and clapped gently and said, "Bravo. Here's to Middlesex."

Jasmine had been acquainted with patriotic oration since her childhood, as her grandmother had been inclined to sermonizing, not only on Independence Day, but on every other holiday, including New Year's Day (when she commemorated the emancipation of slaves) and Labor Day (on which she celebrated the dignity of labor). Moreover, knowing herself to be a descendant of slaves, she'd thought often about the nature of freedom and how it had been lost to her ancestors.

She turned back to look at Mr. Blunt, and recited softly:

> So through the night rode Paul Revere;
> And so through the night went his cry of alarm
> To every Middlesex village and farm—
> A cry of defiance and not of fear,
> A voice in the darkness, a knock at the door,
> And a word that shall echo for evermore!

There was a moment of silence. "Here, here," Mr. Blunt said. When the last embers of the furious final blasts had fallen from the sky, Mr. Blunt recited again: "'We hold these truths to be self-evident, that all men are created equal, that they are endowed by their Creator with certain unalienable Rights, that among these are Life, Liberty and the pursuit of Happiness.'" Then, with a dip of his head to Jasmine, he added, "And that includes *all young women* as well."

"And what of those who are no longer so young?" Tina asked, though her tone was not sharp.

"All men *and* women, young and old," Mr. Blunt conceded. The row of young people had now begun to chatter among themselves. "My own son probably doesn't know where those words come from," Mr. Blunt observed.

Pudge looked back over his shoulder. "Of course I do: The Constitution of the United States of America." The blustering tone of his voice, and the way in which Chrissie held his arm to keep him from falling as he turned, suggested inebriation.

"Right country anyway," Mr. Blunt said.

During all this time, Julia had been sipping steadily from a large plastic cup, and now, in one of the flashes of light, she could be seen to tip over onto her side. Her brother, in a gesture of filial affection unusual for him, pulled her back up and leaned her against his shoulder.

Chapter 15

André of Mexico Visits Thomas

It was a quiet and subdued party that returned home on the fifth to encounter an irritatingly animated and demanding Cynthia. Dr. Gannon had called and announced that he would be home for a short stay in only four days. As always happened on his returns, adjustments were made in the household; albeit, as it was never openly acknowledged that any changes occurred in his absence, they were accomplished quietly. Cars began to be parked in a more orderly manner in the garage and drive; the television Cynthia had installed in their bedroom was packed away; beauty magazines and popular novels were removed from the family room to the girls' bedrooms; no one entered the house while still wet from swimming; T-shirts began to be worn over bikini tops; potato chips and other snacks ceased to be eaten from bags; dishes were put into the dishwasher, instead of being left on the counter for Esmeralda; radios and tape and CD players were muted; crude language all but disappeared; and numerous other adjustments were made, many without the consciousness of those making them. Finally, on the night of the seventh, Cynthia asked Esmeralda to set dinner in the dining room in order that no one would be tempted to suggest that it had not been used at all in his absence.

For Cynthia, Dr. Gannon's presence was more valued than a hundred televisions, but the others—though they all respected him, loved him each in his or her own way, and were proud of his position and the influence it brought—could not help resenting this intrusion into their summer idyll. As Julia was heard to say when ordered by her mother to turn off the television and clean her room, "When Dad comes home, things just, like, get too bizarre."

Max had returned to Arden Park only a day after the Gannons. One night during this period of preparations, after having left the Gannons' before midnight—an hour earlier than was normal—he commented on these changes to his sister, saying, "I'd say we were pretty well kicked out of the house."

"We were not."

"The former Miss Arden Park"—for such they'd begun to call Cynthia in their private conversations—"made it pretty clear it was time for us to hit the road."

"They're all a little on edge," Sherry admitted.

"This Dr. Gannon must be quite a character," Max said, pouring himself a glass of his grandfather's brandy. "He's got everybody jumping all over the place and he's not even due home for two days."

"It's like when a guy is having an affair," Sherry observed, "he breaks up with his mistress before he tells his wife."

Max chuckled at this. "So they're breaking up with us."

"I'm sure it's only temporary."

Max took a seat on the couch. His sister remained standing, leaning against the doorway to the hallway. "Jasmine's not sweating it," he observed.

"She wouldn't be."

"She's interesting."

"And rather exotic looking," Sherry said, raising inquiring eyebrows.

"I don't find her really beautiful. Close, but not. On the verge maybe."

"*Virg*inal, you might say."

"You might . . . . Do you think I could get her to fall in love with me?"

"No."

"I think I could."

Sherry groaned aloud. "I think you should leave her alone."

"And why exactly is that?"

"She's sixteen. She's nice."

"I agree with you. She is a nice girl. She's a wonderful girl. You sound like you think there's something wrong with me."

"There's plenty wrong with you," she said with a smile, "though I have to admit that you're a real cutie."

"You always accuse me of going through girlfriends too quickly. Maybe it's just that I've been going out with the wrong types. Maybe Jasmine *is* my type."

"You are definitely not hers."

"I can change. I can convince her that she's changed me. She's young. She's influenceable."

"Probably not as influenceable as you think . . . . She loves Phillip."

"He's her cousin . . . ."

"Actually, he isn't."

He sat up on the edge of the couch. "If that's true, I'd be doing you a service by getting her out of the way."

"I wouldn't want to see her manipulated in that way. She's far too decent . . . and young."

"I'm offended," he said, again sitting back. "I have no intention of manipulating her or taking advantage of her . . . ."

"Or *seducing* her?"

"Especially not seducing her."

Sherry guffawed.

"That's the absolute truth. I have far too much respect for her for that."

"Well this *is* a change."

"I don't know exactly what it is. There's something wonderful about her. When she's there with you, it's like she's all right there . . . ."

"I doubt that you have any idea of how much isn't there. There's a lot more going on in Jasmine than people think."

"I don't mean that she's shallow. Just the opposite. I don't know how to explain it."

"I think the word you're looking for is 'character.'"

"Really? . . . Maybe it is."

"Things like honesty, self-discipline, fairness, respect . . . ."

"Things you think I wouldn't know much about."

"I don't think you're completely *dis*honest."

"Thank you for that."

"Don't act snippy with me. You know exactly what I mean. She's honest in ways none of the rest of us are."

"Maybe she's just old-fashioned. Maybe that's what I've been looking for all along, an old-fashioned girl."

"Spare me," Sherry said. "Besides, I doubt if the world *ever* made many people like Jasmine."

As though to mock the family's preparations, a legislative crisis forced the cancellation of Dr. Gannon's visit. The TV went back into Cynthia's room, the Hills renewed their late-night vigils, and the wraps came off the girls' bikinis. Thomas, however, soon informed them that they would have a different visitor. After a long, late-night telephone conversation conducted in his father's closed-up office, he announced that a fraternity brother would be arriving to stay with them. The young man's father, a Mexican national, had been placed in charge of the European divisions of his company and had relocated to Belgium. Rather than return home to an empty house in Mexico for the summer, the young man had arranged to spend time with various of his schoolmates.

"From Mexico?" Cynthia asked, concern apparent in her voice.

"I know what you're thinking," Thomas replied, "a little brown gardener. But that's not André . . . . That's really not André."

"That's not what I was thinking at all," Cynthia said truthfully. She had instinctively recoiled from this prospect of a disruption in her schedule and the words "From Mexico?" had been merely a mechanical reply. Admittedly, if given more time, she might have experienced particular misgivings about a Mexican visitor. Forewarned as she was, however, she now said, "It's broadening to have friends from different places in the world."

Thomas hid a smirk by saying, "Anyway, he's only going to be here a couple of nights, and then he's out of here."

"A couple of nights?" Cynthia said.

"One or two. Three at the most. His dad's going to be in New York for a while, and André's going back there. He's just waiting on some money."

"What kind of company is his father associated with?"

"Mining. Cement maybe. Something industrial anyway."

"Have you made plans of what you'll do? Any activities?"

Thomas shook his head. "It's not a tourist trip. He's in here for a couple of days, then he's on his way. He'll probably spend his time hanging out by the pool."

"We'll have to provide some hospitality. I'll need to inform Esmeralda."

"Sure," Thomas said, but he seemed reluctant to say more.

"And he will need a place to sleep," Cynthia noted.

They now discussed where he would be housed. Dr. Gannon's office was considered and rejected, though more out of respect to Dr. Gannon, whose existence had recently been made more real to them, than because of any of the impracticalities that were put forward. The guest house, which was located off the pool, across from Jasmine's wing of the house, was not even considered. It had been built with the expectation that it would house visiting dignitaries, but, in practice, had been used almost exclusively by Tina. Since Dr. Gannon's departure, she had taken full possession.

"It's safer to put him in my room with me, anyway," Thomas said.

On the occasions during the summer when Thomas had been home, he and Phillip had shared his room without difficulty. With Thomas's frequent comings and goings there had been only a few nights when they'd actually slept in the same room, and a spare mattress that had resided under the bed since the days of grammar school sleepovers had served. The idea of having three nearly grown men in the same room, however, one of whom was unrelated, suggested unseemly disarray and the odor of dirty socks.

"Why don't Julia and Chrissie move in together?" Thomas asked. "Phillip could move into one of their rooms."

Neither Chrissie nor Julia would have willingly moved under normal circumstances, and they had been on especially chilly terms since the trip to the lake. The suggestion was met with frozen looks and obdurate silence.

"Since you two hate each other," Thomas said, "what if Jasmine moved in with one of you? Then Phillip could go downstairs."

This suggestion, one which likely would never have been made prior to the arrival of the Hills and the consequent softening of the social lines between Jasmine and her cousins, provoked no outburst of protest.

"That might be the best solution," Cynthia said.

"Chrissie's room is bigger," Julia quickly offered.

"It is not."

"It's got more space!" Julia protested. "Besides, you're not even here most of the year."

Chrissie was capable of arguing any point indefinitely, but now, to the surprise of all, she chose the moral high ground, saying. "God, it's only a couple of days. What's the big deal?"

The move, while welcomed by none, presented the most difficulties for Jasmine. First, she had long been allowed to regard her wing of the house as a private sanctuary. While this held the disadvantage of distancing her from normal household play and intimacy, it had had the advantage of sparing her both involvement in many household intrigues and exposure to innumerable incidents of backbiting and gossip. Had it not been Phillip moving into her room, she might even have dared to argue against it; but there existed a certain pleasure in sharing her space with him. Nonetheless, she would not have wanted the move to lead to something more permanent. She hoped never to be expected to move upstairs, not even when both Chrissie's and Thomas's rooms were again empty.

Knowing how difficult it would have been for her to share her own room, she vowed to be especially considerate of Chrissie's. Of course, she would have to sleep and dress there, but she could transfer other activities—her reading and writing and even some of her grooming—to the living room, which was usually abandoned in any case. She stayed up late, clearing a drawer in her dresser for Phillip, planning and organizing her clothing so that she would not be obliged to invade his privacy as long as he remained in her room, and trying to imagine what their visitor would be like.

Most of the Mexicans encountered in Arden Park were gardeners or housecleaners, and as Thomas had suggested, the first image the term Mexican presented to her was one of a domestic worker. She attended school, however, with many ethnically Mexican students, and in her Spanish class she had learned that Mexico, like the United States, was a nation of mixed races. Taking into account that the boy's name was more French than Spanish, that he attended a prestigious, expensive, American university, that his father was a successful businessman, and that Thomas, who was inclined to snobbery, had befriended him, she realized that her immediate expectations were likely to be in error. She looked forward to having them overthrown.

Competing with her school track team had offered Jasmine the added advantage of building her endurance to where she could accompany Phillip on his easier training runs. She was up early the next morning, expecting to join him in a run before the day grew too warm; but Cynthia called her into the garden, and Phillip, thinking her still asleep, had gone on without her. Jasmine and her aunt were still in the yard making selections for their bouquets, when a yellow taxi advanced along the road in front of the house. A taxi was an unusual sight in Arden Park, where they usually only appeared in the dark hours of the morning when someone needed to catch an early airline flight, and Jasmine and her aunt both paused to watch it pass. To their surprise, it pulled into the Gannon driveway.

They watched, fully expecting the car to back and turn around, but the driver opened the back door, pulled out a large green duffle bag, then reached in to wake a sleeping passenger. A gangling young man in baggy jeans, with a misshapen mop of dark curly hair and acned cheeks hidden by a thin, fuzzy beard, slowly pulled himself out.

"I wonder who that could be?" Cynthia asked, and Jasmine, not quite as bewildered as her aunt, replied, "I believe it will be Thomas's friend."

"From Mexico?"

"Yes, I believe so."

"Really!"

Jasmine followed her aunt out to the drive to greet him and discovered a very bleary-eyed, somewhat bewildered figure.

"Is this the Rock's house," he asked.

"The Rock?" Cynthia asked.

"Tommy the Rock. Thomas Gannon."

"It is," Cynthia said, "though we didn't know that he was called 'the Rock.'"

"The Rock is what we call him at school, because he keeps saying how all the girls want a piece of him."

Cynthia, having the good sense to ignore this, reached out her hand and said, "You must be André." Then, after receiving a confirming if curiously doubtful nod, said, "I'm Mrs. Gannon."

The boy, who looked no more than eighteen, stood slack-jawed and remained to all appearances completely unaware of Cynthia's extended hand.

"You're Mrs. Gannon?" he said, in a voice of pure wonder.

Cynthia nodded.

"Tommy's mother?"

She nodded again.

"Whoa! You seem way too young!" His face showed real consternation.

That a friend of Thomas's should be so cognizant of her aunt's appearance—or, more precisely, that he should admit that he was—seemed remarkably forward to Jasmine. Cynthia, however, despite having to drop her untaken hand, answered with an affirming nod and one of her dazzling smiles. The boy seemed so delighted by this that he suddenly hugged her, saying, "Tommy the Rock's mother! Amazing!"

André had not as yet acknowledged Jasmine in any way, and Cynthia, noticeably flustered by the surprise hug, failed to introduce her now. Despite the boy's humble appearance, Jasmine wondered if he mistook her for servant. She reasoned that he'd grown up in Mexico where servants were more common, and she was holding garden shears in one hand and broken flower stems in the other, and, of course, her skin was dark. Moreover, it was nearly unthinkable that Thomas would have spoken to him of her, since from the time she was a small child he'd taken no more notice of her than of his mother's dogs, just as he would have taken no notice of his sisters had they not occasionally inserted themselves between his feet.

Now, not wanting André to face future embarrassment, Jasmine was about to introduce herself, when he began to praise the many trees and beautiful gardens of Arden Park.

"Wow! What great trees! Do they grow here, like, naturally?"

"They have to be planted," Cynthia said.

"Bummer. They're really cool anyway, though. I mean, I've never seen so many trees . . . . Not in one spot anyway."

Arden Park did have a very pleasant growth of trees, especially sycamores, but Jasmine did not believe it was as breathtaking as André's open-mouthed stare upward seemed to imply.

"Let's see what we can do about finding Thomas," Cynthia said, and they all started for the house.

André and Cynthia walked ahead. "It gets hot here though, doesn't it?" he was saying. "Like how hot will it get here? Ninety? Or a hundred? A hundred and ten? A hundred and twenty?"

"Most days are in the nineties, but we always get some stretches when it's over a hundred."

"A hundred degrees," André said in wonder. "That's hot."

"I would think that being from Mexico you would be accustomed to warm weather."

"You would, huh?" he said, not disagreeing with her; then he suddenly sighed very deeply and audibly. "But you know we've moved around so much I've never gotten used to Fahrenheit and Celsius and all that. Fahrenheit makes it seem so much hotter. You know what I mean?"

As he followed them to the house, Jasmine had the opportunity to consider the effect of expectations on human relations. Thomas had charged Cynthia with expecting "a little brown gardener." Whether she actually had or not, it was very unlikely that she had expected the André who now walked beside her. After thoughtful consideration, Jasmine herself had begun to anticipate one of the aristocratic *rubios grandes* pictured in her textbook. While this boy was rather tall, he did not appear very aristocratic, his hair was dark, and, while there was a suggestion of impediment in the slowness of his speech, nothing about his accent suggested Spanish. Moreover, his hair had an un-Hispanic curl and an ungainly lopsided pouf. His pants were too long and bagged about his untied and rather dirty sneakers; his poor complexion was sullied by the film of downy beard; his conversation was witless; and he'd arrived twelve hours before he was expected.

He was, she admitted to herself, a disappointment; and for this, she chastised herself. If it was a common, almost ubiquitous fault to be overly influenced by one's expectations, it was also an error to rely too heavily on first impressions. Indeed, both were common human tendencies—her own grandmother had been quick to judge other women by their decisions regarding hats—but commonness of an error in others was no excuse for an error of one's own. Thomas and his fraternity brothers had given the young man the opportunity to display deeper levels of his character that had induced them to invite him into their brotherhood. Surely she could offer him the courtesy of reserving her judgment, especially considering both the cultural differences that might be influencing her perceptions and the young man's fatigue.

Jasmine was sent upstairs to wake Thomas, who made his bleary-eyed descent in gym shorts and a T-shirt. He took one look at André and hurried him upstairs to his room. A half-hour later, when Cynthia sent Jasmine up to inquire about breakfast, Thomas let himself out of his room through a half-opened door and joined them at the table.

"Should I tell Esmeralda to expect André?" Tina asked.

"He's asleep," Thomas said. "He'll probably sleep all day."

"Sleep all day?" Cynthia said.

Thomas did not reply to this; instead, he spooned cereal into his mouth and read the sports page of the newspaper.

"He arrived earlier than expected," Cynthia said.

"I guess something came up," Thomas said, not raising his head to look at her.

"Do you think he'll be hungry?" Cynthia asked.

Thomas now allowed his mother the courtesy of looking at her. "Hey, don't worry about André," he said. "If he misses breakfast, that's his problem."

"When he's in my house, Thomas, I'm afraid that also becomes my problem."

"If you're worried give him a Coke and a bag of potato chips. I'm telling you, it's not something you need to worry about. He's just crashing here for a couple of days."

"Crashing here?" Cynthia said, to which Thomas's reply was a nod. "This is not some kind of a crash pad," Cynthia said.

Thomas looked up. "It's just a figure of speech. I'm just saying you don't have to treat it like some kind of formal visit. He puts up here for a couple of days, and he's gone."

Phillip now came in from his morning run, and there followed some discussion between him and his aunt as to how he was to get his clothes without waking their visitor.

Thomas finally interrupted, turning to his mother, "Give it up, Mom." He then turned to Phillip. "Just go in. Moza's dead to the world . . . . Of course, there's always a chance that he is dead."

"Thomas!" Cynthia said.

Thomas chuckled. "Frat-boy humor, Mom."

"I don't think we need it in this house."

Thomas shrugged and resumed eating.

"His name is André," Jasmine now said, "but you called him something else."

"'Moza.' It's his nickname. It's a frat thing."

"Like 'Tommy the Rock'?" Cynthia asked accusingly.

Thomas shrugged without looking up.

"He also told us why they call you that."

Thomas stopped eating suddenly.

"Though I'm sure it's a lie," Cynthia went on, walking over to tussle his hair, "because I can't imagine why any girl would want a *piece* of a boy who is as bad-mannered to his mother as you are . . . . Should we call him Moza or André?"

"André will do fine."

"I'll move my clothes," Jasmine said.

From her new upstairs vantage point, Jasmine was able to observe a curious evolution in her cousins' attitudes toward their new visitor. Neither his appearance nor his manner were prepossessing, and the girls were at first inconvenienced and annoyed. When two days had passed and he was still among them, they were indignant, and they privately told their brother so. When he'd been with them for a full week, however, they'd begun to discover unexpected talents. First, he brought powerful possessions with him, a remarkable collection of rare musical discs, some of which contained unknown recordings by the most fashionable groups. He also displayed an uncanny ability to uncover the esoteric and bizarre on the internet. These discoveries were often viewed behind firmly and pointedly closed doors and caused wild eruptions of laughter. Nor did it hurt that he demonstrated a good-hearted admiration for the beauty of the young women who surrounded him, a total lack of self-conscious pride, and a cheerful bluntness in speech, which in anyone more socially ambitious would have seemed offensive. Permission to like André was discreetly spread.

Jasmine's approval was not sought, and had she been asked, she would have been perplexed as to how to reply. Despite André's good-hearted openness, Jasmine could not approve of him. He introduced to the house a level of crudeness and lazy deportment that she felt demeaned them all. Moreover, the license the others displayed in their treatment of him was at times shameful. All found him amusing, but in both Chrissie and Julia, this amusement held more than a suggestion of ridicule. The two sisters treated him like a talented but remarkably ugly pet, like a mutt puppy Jasmine had seen on Spanish-speaking television that had danced on its hind legs and done flips.

As is only natural, Jasmine was now exposed to more of her cousins' conversation than ever before—more perhaps than she would have liked to hear. One afternoon, Thomas, Max, and Moza chatted in the hallway. Thomas was explaining, with much amusement, the circumstances of André's arrival in Arden Park. Apparently, he had left his previous location, the San Francisco home of another fraternity brother, in the middle of the night, at the insistence of the head of the household, by being placed in a taxi and having his two-hundred-dollar fare to Sacramento paid for him.

"It was a very cold thing," André said.

"What'd you do to make his old man so mad?" Thomas asked, his voice betraying some amusement.

"No big deal. Just the usual."

Max laughed aloud. "Think of it this way. He thought so much of you that he hired you a private driver."

"Better than a *migra* bus to Tijuana, huh?" Thomas suggested. He laughed harder at this than André, asking through his own laughter. "What did Ted say?"

"He didn't say nothing, bro. His dad said I was either out the door or he was calling the cops."

"And Ted pointed the way?"

"It was cold," André repeated, which again incited Thomas to open laughter. "His little sister liked me though."

"Now we're getting there," Thomas said.

"No, man, that was completely okay."

"What did you do? Offer her some candy?"

"She was sixteen," André said in protest, "but she looked like she was about twenty, and she was knowledgeable . . . . I'm telling you she was truly knowledgeable. I mean she knew more about dope and stuff than I do. She taught *me* things."

"Moza, nobody could teach you things about dope so it must have been about stuff."

"Kids," André said incredulously, "they're way ahead of where we were at their age."

"I'm sure that's a source of deep concern for you."

"I worry about things," André protested, the whining of his voice momentarily sincere.

"Like what, Moza? The trade deficit?"

"Maybe not the trade deficit . . . . Things . . . . You want to do one?"

"Why not?" Thomas answered, and the door across the hall was firmly shut.

A few minutes later, steps sounded in the hall. There was a knock at the closed door, and it was Julia who said, "Open up, you _____s." The door was opened and again shut tight.

Chrissie soon came upstairs as well. She installed herself on her bed and began buffing her nails.

After a moment, she said, "They're smoking dope in there, aren't they?"

"I'm not sure," Jasmine replied, though she knew the odor of marijuana from her schoolyard and would have been hard-pressed to find another explanation for the fragrance that had escaped into the hall.

Chrissie sniffed the air in their room, walked into the hall and sniffed again, then returned and sniffed again. "Shit," she finally concluded. She sat back down on her bed in a huff, got up again, walked to the door, then sat down once again. "Kids at your school probably smoke dope all the time," she said.

"Some do," Jasmine admitted.

"It just seems like such a sleazeball, loser thing to do."

Jasmine didn't respond to this, though she would have agreed that many of the least ambitious students were among the most frequent users.

"Max is in there, huh?"

"I believe so. He was here earlier."

"Maybe it's not so bad, huh?"

Jasmine sought to construct an answer. She inwardly weighed the negative qualities she associated with regular marijuana users—a laziness of manner, a tendency to forego normal courtesies, a capacity to find mundane ideas and artworks enthralling, and neglect of personal grooming—against its reported calming, beneficent qualities, including enhancement of empathetic capacities.

"Used in moderation, it doesn't seem harmful," she said, "but there seems to be a risk of habituation."

"Oh, no," Chrissie said quickly, "it isn't addictive. But the people who use it are such freaks."

"I see people who make a habit of its use," Jasmine said, thinking of the groups of students who lingered just off the school grounds and came onto campus bleary-eyed and loopy— *every* day. She was intending to add her assessment that even a single use incurred some risk of future habituation, just as even one drink could be fatal for a person who was predisposed to alcoholism. Before she could do so, Chrissie reached her own conclusion.

"At least, it's not like heroin where people can't quit. Anybody can quit smoking dope anytime they want."

"Yes, I think that's true . . .," Jasmine said, observing to herself that there no doubt existed infinite variations of addiction, habituation, and even appreciation, and that to consider them to be fixed categories perhaps conferred false security. "But they must want to," she now said, intending to suggest that a drug that so inspired its own appreciation as to make someone want to use it daily and *never* to want to quit using it, whether or not its physical effects were harsh, was a very powerful drug indeed.

Chrissie, however, who never really sought counsel so much as endorsement of her own views, had already reached her own conclusion. "If he ever brought crack or needles into this house, I'd kill him. That stuff is so ghetto."

Thomas now spent more of his time sealed up in his room with Moza, listening to music. On occasions, Max Hill was admitted to their company as well, and from time to time all of them would venture out to the patio. Undisguised alcohol consumption had progressed from a single glass at dinner, to a second and sometimes even third glass at the table, to unfinished glasses being carried away out to the patio, followed by unfinished bottles, and finally to a general consumption of all types of alcoholic beverages throughout the house. Chrissie, Sherry, and Julia, who on one occasion had been known to throw up behind the rose bushes, all took part, though generally more sparingly.

The young men's appearances on the patio were occasions for unconstrained consumption of beer and wine, in addition to a great deal of laughter; and it soon became apparent that marijuana was being smoked at the far edges of the garden, and eventually, when Mrs. Gannon and her sister were known to be away, on the patio itself.

Chapter 16

The Young People Plan a Party

Once it had become apparent that he would be unable to return home as planned, Dr. Gannon began encouraging his wife to make a trip to Washington to be with him. Neither the monuments of Washington, nor its politics and society held any deep attraction for Cynthia, who loved above all being at peace in her own home, but she was deeply fond of her husband. Thus, she overcame her instinctive reluctance insofar as to mention a trip as a possibility to her sister. Tina, eager to meet the prominent and powerful in the nation's capital, immediately seized on the necessity of such a trip and recommended herself as a traveling companion.

"I'm sure there's not room in David's apartment, so I'll just get a hotel near the Capitol. I might even take the shuttle to New York for a few days," she suggested, in order that her presence might not seem too great a constraint on the long-separated spouses.

Cynthia, however, who had little modesty about her affection for her husband, foresaw no hindrance from her sister's company— at least no hindrance that couldn't be overcome by the convenience of having her travel plans made for her. Thus, a trip was planned for late July.

The children were invited to accompany. None could find time in their schedules. Thus, the young people were to be left alone for a week at the end of the month. A party immediately began to be planned.

Whether out of habit or because they anticipated her disapproval, Jasmine was not immediately included in these plans. Late one afternoon, however, she went with her book to the stoop outside her former bedroom, a place that would be apart from the frequent hubbub around the pool, only to discover Thomas and André there ahead of her. They were encompassed by a fragrant cloud of marijuana smoke.

"Jaz-MEEN," André said, greeting her with the nickname he had assigned to her. "Would you care for a little smoke?"

Jasmine shook her head, saying nothing, and began quickly to back in the direction from which she had come. André stopped her.

"Do you know anybody from Animal Nature?" he asked her.

Animal Nature was a local band of some renown. Though one of the musicians had been in her tenth grade geometry class, she couldn't claim really to know him. She shook her head.

"Tommy said they were from your school."

"They are . . . or one is. But I don't really know him."

"They're the only people from around here anybody's ever heard of. Do you know anybody who could talk to him for us?"

Jasmine could answer in complete honesty that she did not.

"We'll just have to find another way," André said pleasantly. "Hey, it's going to be blasting. I mean, this is one great place for a party. If we get Animal Nature, it's going to rock."

Thomas regarded André with bemusement. "You'll never get Animal Nature."

"We might. I hear those guys love to party. If we can show them how many ladies are going to be here and how righteous the dope will be, it can happen . . . . But, wow, hey maybe there's a better way. The Maxter's got to know some people from LA," he said, referring to Max Hill. "We promise them some northland exposure, fly 'em up, then party bigtime. What could be wrong with that?"

While Jasmine could see a number of things that might be wrong with that, the question was directed to Thomas. He voiced no reservations.

"Yeah, that's probably the way to go," André said. "Animal Nature's not that hot anyway . . . . Are you sure you don't know anybody at all?"

"I'm sorry I can't be of help," Jasmine said, immediately regretting her phrasing, for in fact she was not sorry; rather, she had considered herself fortunate that she could avoid involvement with an honest and inoffensive answer.

"No problem. Don't worry about it," André said. "There's a way. There's always a way."

Thomas now chuckled and directed himself to Jasmine. "Moza once got Bite to show up at a party."

"I could probably get them again," Moza said, momentarily brightening.

"I think they're on an Australian tour," Thomas said.

"Yeah, and, man, last time they didn't even bring guitars. How much did that suck?"

"I imagine Animal Nature is considerably less in demand than Bite."

Moza remained in dismay at his memories. "Guys who don't even bring their guitars . . . how long can somebody like that last? Animal Nature is righteous, man. It could be us who put them over the top."

"Absolutely," Thomas said, his voice mocking, though Moza seemed not to be aware of this.

"We could promise them a good time, let 'em know how the Maxter can help them out with the studio guys in LA . . . . Hey, maybe even promise them a song placement in some movie. That'd work."

"It would work, if we had even the slightest chance of getting them into a movie."

"We do, man, we do. Maxter's big in LA. His dad's a movie producer. That's juice. That's something we can use."

Jasmine was not familiar with the group called Bite—indeed, had Animal Nature not had a representative at her school, she would not have known of them either—and when the two continued to discuss bands—in that illogical and contradictory mode that Jasmine had come to associate with marijuana smoking—she resumed her attempt to back away. Moza, however, was not quite ready to let her go. "This guy from Animal Nature, is he cool?" he asked.

"I hardly know him."

"I mean do you think he'd be up for a party? It's his home town. It seems like he'd show a little loyalty."

"I have no way of knowing."

"Yeah, he's probably got big eyes by now. Probably thinks he's going to be hanging with MTV." He looked at Jasmine questioningly.

"I don't know."

"He could be cool, though," André said, seemingly encouraged by this answer. "Like there is this snowboarder dude who won't go to any of the big competitions or anything, even though he's like the best in the world. That's righteous. That's integrity. Like the Marines, you know, *semper fidelis*. Hard core. Faithful to his roots. I know Animal

Nature okayed some stuff to give away on MP3. So they aren't in it for the bucks. Not yet anyway. They might be cool."

André now began a rambling account of the future of music distribution on the internet, with many more digressions, sentence fragments, reversals in logic, inherent contradictions, likes, and other colloquial forms of speech that you, gracious reader, will be allowed to escape.

Jasmine likewise took this opportunity to make her exit, retreating to the quiet of the living room, where she was allowed to ponder her dilemma in solitude. It was apparent that her aunts had not heard of the party plans, for if they had by some lapse of judgment granted permission, Tina could not have resisted taking an active role in organization. Therefore, it seemed all but certain that the party was being planned for the time period when they would be away. Opportunity still availed itself for Thomas to inform his mother of his plans, but Jasmine suspected that he had no intention of doing so, even though he must have understood that the secret could not be kept, especially not in the aftermath. His course seemed impossibly foolhardy, but Thomas had become indifferent to parental approval and seemed often to take amusement in consternation and upset in the Gannon household. It was not that he sought actively to injure or torment anyone; rather he never deigned to modify his own behavior for the welfare of others or to foresee and forestall brooding troubles. He seemed to regard Arden Park as a temporary bivouac. He observed its trials and tribulations from a distance and took amusement where he could.

Thus, Jasmine would have seen no technical betrayal of confidence in informing her aunts of his plans—Cynthia's attitude would have been a matter of indifference to Thomas; any resulting uproar an entertainment—and Jasmine *did* see many potential hazards in the proposed party. First, André and Thomas seemed to be proposing an open affair; there seemed to be no hope that any guest list would be constructed. Dr. Gannon, who valued the privacy and security of his home to the extent of being a reluctant and infrequent entertainer, would certainly have demanded to see such a list before giving his approval, would have vetted each name, and would have set requirements for the maximum number of invitees. Given the number of minors likely to attend, he certainly would not have allowed alcohol; yet Jasmine had learned enough of unchaperoned teenage parties to know that alcohol would surely be present in abundance, as well as marijuana and samplings of stronger drugs. The vagaries of mob behavior to which teenaged party-goers were known to be especially susceptible, the inflammatory nature of the music that was likely to be played, and the alcohol- and drug-impaired judgment of the attendees portended a myriad of calamities. Accidents and legal entanglements were real possibilities.

Yet, in opposition to all these considerations was Jasmine's unwillingness to snitch. Attending school as she did among children of very different backgrounds and economic positions, Jasmine had developed a highly sensitized awareness of the differences in norms and values between social groups. While she had been living upstairs, she had become aware of the existence of a tacit understanding that certain subjects of conversation from the upper rooms were not to be shared below. While she had heard of this party on her own stoop, the discussion rightfully belonged to the province of the upper rooms, and short of a conviction that a real and imminent danger of bodily harm existed, she would not have felt justified in conveying this type of information to her aunts. Parties, she reasoned, went on every weekend, and seldom did serious injury result. If this party seemed to her to bode no good, this was perhaps only because of her own inexperience and habitual fretfulness. Thomas was not concerned; why should she be? After all, he was the eldest and the greatest responsibility resided with him. For her to assume responsibility would be presumptuous.

Nonetheless, over the next few days, she was not able to free herself of her unease, in part because the duties of loyalty and respect urged her to disclose to her aunts what she knew, and in part because she could not overcome forebodings of real, sinister harm. Her worry only increased when she learned first that Chrissie and Julia were taking a part in the planning, then that Sherry and Max Hill had joined the forces. Then, her agitation was deepened yet further when she was allowed to observe a conversation between her cousins, which occurred one morning after breakfast, while she was clearing the dishes into the dishwasher.

"Phillip still isn't going for it," Chrissie said, looking about her to assure that her mother and aunt had left the room.

"He doesn't have to go for it," Julia replied.

Chrissie gave her sister a brief disparaging look.

"What's the big deal? We're having a party. So what?"

It was a measure of Phillip's continuing influence in the household that silence was again an adequate answer.

"He'll go for it if Sherry wants him to," Julia continued. "We'll get *her* to talk to him. We can even say that the party is for her and Max. There's no way he'd diss her by sitting out her party."

Julia judged her own plan so flawless that she departed immediately, without waiting for Chrissie's approval; and, in truth, though it made her heart ache to admit it was so, Jasmine feared she would succeed. There was much to admire in Sherry Hill, both in her appearance and her quickness of spirit, and Phillip had continued to display signs of enthrallment. Not the least of these was his inability to perceive or correctly interpret Jasmine's reticence in speaking of her.

In principle, Jasmine did not believe in speaking ill of anyone about whom she lacked definite knowledge of incorrect conduct; among people with whom she associated, whether at home or at school, she required personal knowledge of such conduct before allowing herself to draw conclusions. Aside from sipping glasses of wine—and she was moderate in this—nothing Sherry Hill had done could be judged as improper, especially given the evolving mores of the household. Other actions which gave her pause—a certain flirtatiousness; a casual, possibly inadvertent lack of modesty; a certain freeness in speech and conduct; her occasional luxuriant puff at her brothers' cigarettes— were part and parcel of her undeniable charm. Moreover, Jasmine had long since admonished herself to take special care in any judgments or criticisms where Sherry Hill was concerned, for she recognized that she was far from impartial.

Jealousy is a useful and blameless emotion only when it applies to someone on whom one has a legitimate claim. Jasmine judged herself to have no such claim on Phillip. Neither she nor he had ever spoken of any obligations, romantic or filial, between them which might have constrained either of them from pursuit of a chosen mate. Under these circumstances, any expression of wounded feelings on her part could only be injurious and ignoble. Moreover, she was obliged before speaking or acting to consider what effects her own unexpressed and unjustified feelings might have on her judgment and to take actions to suppress their influence.

Thus, through reason and self-awareness, she was able to moderate her antipathy; when that failed, she disguised her feelings, reserved her criticisms, and repressed her suspicions. It was in accord with this mode of conduct that she now denied herself the privilege of speaking directly with Phillip about her apprehensions.

She fretted for two days; then, quite suddenly, the worst of her worries were over. Phillip, it seemed, had agreed to the party, but had insisted that Cynthia and Tina be informed. The others had importuned that he himself be the bearer of this information. The task had been completed, and while the women had reserved their decision, Jasmine had no doubt but that they would insist that the party be cancelled.

How wrong she was! Fate intervened. First, Dr. Gannon was required at a conference in Switzerland during the planned time of his wife's trip. The visit to Washington was cancelled. Then, to Jasmine's consternation, her aunts, instead of insisting on canceling the party, encouraged and supported it.

"You're having a party with them here?" Thomas inquired of Chrissie.

"I don't see why not."

"You're kidding."

"I'm not kidding. They'll just stay in the living room, and Mom can't stay awake after ten o'clock anyway."

Thomas allowed his disdainful smile and said, "Whatever."

Two planning centers now quickly established themselves, an official one that met most frequently in the kitchen, and an unofficial one that met in the smoke-filled air of Jasmine's stoop. Tina led the official planning. She contacted caterers, set the girls to constructing guest lists, booked the services of Esmeralda and

two of her nieces for the evening, scheduled gardening and pool
cleaning, hired a firm to install outdoor torches for lighting the
full extent of the yard, rented additional glassware and linen,
contacted the neighbors, and debated the merits of hiring valets to
park the cars, all amid a myriad of more trivial concerns, such as
assuring that the housecleaners scrubbed all the lawn furniture
and washed every window in the house.

André led the planning sessions on the stoop with a diligence
that may have surpassed even Tina's, while Thomas stood by as a
bemused assistant. A location for the kegs was determined (they
would go exactly here, on the stairs, where Tina and Cynthia were
most unlikely to venture); the merits of various bands were debated;
and strategies for procuring the best one possible were advanced.
André, however, stayed curiously aloof from the band discussions,
leaving the others to suppose he had a surprise planned for them.

The girls, Chrissie, Julia, and Sherry, had footing in both camps.
Sherry, who was not directly a member of the household, usually
limited herself to enthusiastic approval in the kitchen and amused
observation out on the stoop. Julia took responsibility for passing
intelligence from the kitchen camp to the boys, information which
was received with disdain, incredulity, or amusement, and typically
followed by an all-encompassing, "Whatever."

Chapter 17

Phillip Uses His Influence and Jasmine Uses Hers

Jasmine, while finding it impossible to avoid knowledge of the
goings on, endeavored to remain free from direct involvement. Her
room now being occupied by Phillip and her stoop occupied by
the boys, her sole refuge became the living room. With the party

only a week away, Phillip came there one afternoon to seek her out. They had been spending less time together in recent weeks, as much of his time was taken up with Sherry Hill. Even their training runs, the times when she was surest to have him alone, had been neglected.

He began not quite as she had expected, by saying, "Your room is really hot, isn't it?"

"I've never been much bothered by heat. I think it's because I was accustomed to it as a little girl."

"Hardly any air comes out of the duct, and even that's not very cool . . . .," he said, thinking out loud. "It's probably cold in the winter too, huh?"

"I believe it's a little cooler than the rest of the house in winter, and a little warmer in summer."

"A *little* warmer. Around five o'clock it's a sauna in there."

"The delta breeze is almost always up by eight or nine. If you open the windows, it moves right over the bed."

"Yeah, but for the next two hours the sheets feel like they just came out of an oven and by midnight they're drenched in sweat . . . . It shouldn't be like that. I think it's something Cynthia should be informed about."

During her childhood days in her grandmother's house, Jasmine had developed an ability to manage discomforts primarily by accommodating herself to them. Whether it was by placing pots in the attic under a leaking roof, adding an additional quilt to her bed, propping a falling fence, or learning to disregard peeling paint, Granny had instilled in her a sense that only obvious and simple measures might be taken to increase comfort. Any inconveniences caused by the inadequacy of these measures were regarded as trivial. More extreme and more costly measures were not to be considered.

This proclivity for treating the symptoms rather than the cause was in part an exigency of poverty and in part the result of feminine ignorance of household mechanics. In any case, Jasmine had adopted it as her general mode of approaching household and logistical problems: if her room was too hot, she opened the window or sat on the stoop; if it was too cold, she wore socks to bed; if the noise of the washing machine intruded, she imagined ocean waves; even her clothing, if it did not quite suit, could be darned, patched, or modified. As this make-do approach to problem-solving was now reinforced by a habitual effort to minimize the inconvenience and costs she imposed on her caretakers, she replied with uncharacteristic vehemence to Phillip's proposal.

"I love my room just the way it is. I wouldn't want one thing in it to be changed."

Phillip saw in this reply no complex psychology; rather he dismissed it as the type of attachment a small child might hold for a familiar but particularly objectionable blanket. The virtue of "making do" was not much in his character. He had grown up in a household with more than adequate capital and had been instructed in the importance of properly repairing what malfunctioned and replacing anything shoddy. Thus, workmen were hired to repair the roof before water could enter; the house was repainted before it began to peel; a permanent masonry wall was built to replace a sound but water-streaked fence; and rooms were installed with individual thermostats to insure the comfort of each inhabitant according to his wishes. Moreover, while the honesty and integrity of tradesworkers was always considered, the cost was rarely disputed. Tradespeople needed to make a living like anyone else. The Gannons would take unfair advantage of no one.

Nonetheless, Phillip was willing enough to abide uncomfortable conditions for himself, especially since he had now been to a New England college where he'd been obliged to harden himself to a drafty dormitory, noisy, steamy radiators, plugged sinks and showers in the lavatories, and occasional squalor in the other public rooms. He was caught now between two conflicting impulses: he was not willing to accept these circumstances for Jasmine, toward whom he still felt a strong protective obligation, but he so respected her that he would not act directly against her wishes, even when he believed them to be ill-founded or childish. He decided to let the matter pass for now, and to await an opportunity to inform his aunts of the malfunction in an entirely quiet and inconspicuous manner.

"This is why you've always spent so much time out on the stair," he speculated aloud.

"It may be why I went there first. But it's also quiet and shady, and I have the leaves to look up into."

"Do you remember that day when you were little and I found you out there crying?"

Jasmine acknowledged that she did.

"It seems like only yesterday."

"It seems a very long time ago to me."

"I guess it would . . . . You were so little."

"I always felt myself the correct size." Jasmine could not herself have explained what she meant by this, and she joined in Phillip's amused laughter.

As is natural for someone who has cared for, nurtured, and mentored another, Phillip held tender feelings for his beneficiary, and not solely because her happiness reflected well on him. Now, however, these gratifying sensations of pride and affection were vitiated by knowledge that he was dissembling. He knew that he was delaying the true purpose of his coming to see her, which made his actions distasteful to him. Thus, rather than proceed with the hope that some occasion would arise for him to introduce the subject into his conversation naturally, he chose now forthrightly to announce its purpose. Nor did he allow himself the comfort of blaming others for sending him on his current mission, though in fact Sherry had prevailed upon him to approach her.

"I came here," he now said, forcing himself to meet her eyes, "to ask your help in getting Animal Nature for the party."

Jasmine assumed that quiet condition of her face—eyes diverted, chin slightly lifted, facial expression blank—which to others often signaled detachment, but which Phillip knew to be the mask she used to disguise wounded feelings. For nearly the very first time in his life, he experienced exasperation with her.

"Jasmine, it's only a band. The party has Cynthia's and Tina's complete approval. It's not like you'd be involving yourself in a crime."

"I don't really know anyone . . . ."

"Moza doesn't know them at all. The only thing he has figured to do is to go through their agent, and he says that's certain death. He says it has to be a personal contact. There's no other way."

"Isn't it their agent who is supposed to set up their engagements?"

"Yes, but Moza says we have to get them because they *want* to come. Their agent is only going to be concerned with how much money they'll make. We can't pay them anything like what a club would; in fact, Moza says if we work it right we shouldn't have to pay them at all . . . . The thing is, we've got to find a way to talk directly to someone from the band. Preferably the lead guy. Who's the one you know?"

"A boy named Drew Tyler sat behind me in geometry . . . ."

"He's the guy," Phillip said excitedly. "He's the lead singer."

"But that was two years ago," Jasmine continued. "After that we did little more than nod to each other in the corridors, and he left school last year."

Phillip was given pause here. It was not in his nature to impose on friendships, much less mere acquaintances, and he sympathized with Jasmine's position; nevertheless, under the influence of his desire to please Sherry, he had been willing to speak with Jasmine, and, had he been ever so remotely acquainted with Drew Tyler, would have called him himself.

"Sometimes, Jasmine, I think both you and I are too reserved. I mean we sit back too much. We don't want to impose. Sometimes we need to push ourselves a little. We need to assert ourselves more."

"I'm concerned that the party may not turn out exactly as you hope," she replied.

"I know. We've all heard so many stories about parties that go crazy that we think it happens all the time. But it doesn't have to. Tina and Cynthia will both be here. What could go wrong? I mean in the worst case, Cynthia can just send everybody home."

Jasmine, having attended a high school where disregard of school authorities' wishes was endemic, had less confidence than Phillip in Tina's and Cynthia's abilities to disperse troublemakers.

"The party's going to happen anyway, Jasmine. I'd just like you to talk to this Tyler guy. I'd appreciate it if you would do it as a favor to me."

"I will see if I can find a way to reach him," she said, "though I can't at the moment think exactly how."

"I'll bet, if you want him to, Moza can get his home number."

"I think I would prefer to try it another way."

"That's cool," Phillip said, "however you want . . . . And don't worry. It's going to be okay. People have parties every day. The world doesn't fall apart."

She did not say what she was thinking, that sometimes it did very much seem to fall apart.

Jasmine had understated her acquaintance with Drew Tyler, partly to avoid giving encouragement, partly out of a reluctance to exaggerate, and partly because she had forgotten much of the substance of their past exchanges. Moreover, she understood that people often respond as much to feelings of personal obligation— and want of courage in refusing personal appeals—as to logic or fairness. Such proved to be the case with Drew Tyler. Though neither Amy Shi nor Jasmine could have been described as "well-connected" in their school community, they were connected enough—and respected enough—that within forty-eight hours of Jasmine's telling Amy of her wish to speak with Drew, he had heard of it from five different sources. Only one such call would have been necessary to induce him to telephone her—because she was a classmate, because she had always treated him in a kind and considerate manner, and because she had on several occasions explained geometric principles to him in simple, uncondescending language and thereby opened a window of understanding that, though it was shortly to seal shut again from lack of use, enhanced not only his grade to a passing status but also his perception of his own intelligence and abilities. He had not forgotten Jasmine Johnson.

"Is this Jasmine?" he asked in response to her hello.

"Yes, it is."

"Hey, cool. This is Drew. Drew Tyler. Do you remember me?"

His voice, though deeper than it had been, recalled the

gentleness with which he had communicated with her in class. She assured him that she remembered him perfectly well.

"I understand you're looking for a band."

Jasmine explained the circumstances of the party, her friends' and cousins' high opinion of his music, and their desire that he might agree to perform. "Of course, I realize you have many engagements, and if you weren't able to do it, we would all understand. It's very nice that you were so considerate as to call me."

"I have one," he now said.

"An engagement?"

"No, I have a band . . . . I think it would be cool to play at your party."

"You do?"

"Sure. Yeah. I think it would be fun."

"I hope that it would be," Jasmine answered.

Then, when she did not continue, he asked, "So, will you let us do it?"

"I don't want to take too much of your time."

"Our agent would like to have people think we're really busy, like 'maybe we can get you a date in September as a special favor,' but it's not really like that."

Any further temporizing would exceed the bounds of courtesy: Jasmine accepted the offer.

"I hear that you live in Arden Park."

She admitted that she did.

"I never knew that. That's cool though."

There passed another moment of silence, during which Jasmine realized she had not discussed payment. "How much do you charge?" she asked.

"It's a private party?" he asked. "Just you and your friends?"

"And my cousins' friends."

She waited, hoping, despite the embarrassment that this would create, that the fee would be much too high.

"About twenty dollars?" he finally said. "Just to put gas in our truck."

"Goodness," Jasmine said, "that's certainly very kind."

"Hey, we're like fellow dragons, you know," he said, referring to their school mascot. "You got me through geometry . . . . In Arden Park. Amazing."

They then made arrangements for him to come to the house and plan when and where to set up their equipment.

"Cool. Jasmine Johnson from 3rd period Geometry. I hope your friends like us."

"I'm sure they will."

"Rock on then. Arden Park . . . that's outstanding."

While this conversation was in every way agreeable, Jasmine's foreboding was only increased by it, as it added to her sense of responsibility for the party's outcome. She could not in fairness blame Drew for this, however, and, once she was able to recognize, in the short-haired young man who appeared at the Gannons' door, the long-haired boy she had known in school, she was able to greet him with cheer and gratitude. The boy she remembered had worn his hair in a silky smooth brown curtain that fell away from a center part nearly to his shoulders. In class, it had usually hung down about his face, and his deep-lashed, gentle and rather beautiful brown eyes had only been revealed when he occasionally tucked the strands of his hair behind his ears. His hair now had been cut to a normal length, perhaps even a little shorter, and, while his eyes were still enchanting, his face had broadened and grown more masculine. The overall result was to replace an adorable boy with a likable young man. His smile, however, remained spontaneous, full of wonder, and innocent of guile. He seemed not to have lost that good-natured humility that had made her especially want to be of help to him.

Unfortunately, this first, reassuring impression was counteracted by the arrival of a fellow band member, a drummer who went by the name of Satin and projected a more sinister appearance. Satin wore a sweatshirt with a hood that shielded much of his face—this despite their arrival time of 1:30 in the afternoon on a day that promised temperatures that would exceed 100°.

"Satin's our new drummer," Drew said. "Gavin was . . . before. You remember Gavin?"

Jasmine indicated that she did not.

"Yeah, he didn't really come to school a lot," Drew said, with a glance toward Satin, who had hidden even further back behind his hood and seemed not to be paying them any attention. "But our agent found us Satin, which is cool, because Satin is really, really good. He's really added energy."

Drew and Satin were soon introduced to Moza and Thomas. Moza immediately went into a monologue of praise for various Animal Nature songs, exhibiting knowledge of guitar sequences, lyrics, and performance venues that marked him as an aficionado. Drew happily pursued this line of conversation and extended it to other musical groups and to other kinds of music and their influences, all of which Satin seemed to regard with contempt.

After some minutes, he interrupted with the first words he'd spoken since arriving at the house. "So where we gonna play?"

This led to a tour of the backyard, where several potential locations for the band equipment were surveyed and found wanting. Electrical outlets were much in want, there was some concern about blowing circuits, and a general shaking of heads ensued. Satin, who had prowled silently until now, grunted and snorted. He had removed his sweatshirt, under which he wore nothing, to reveal a perfectly bald head and a highly muscular torso that was tanned to a reddish bronze. A series of intricate tattoos ran up his arms and across his shoulders. Gold, pirate loops hung from his ears. "We'll go around the box," he said.

As no one, not even Drew, seemed to know exactly what he was speaking about, he went on, though with obvious reluctance. "I'll wire it at the service. They got four hundred amps coming in here. We can take juice off the pool heaters."

He'd spoken with such assurance that all were reluctant to reply. Drew finally said, "I think, you know, we can make do with some extension cords and stuff. It's just a house. We can't really use the big amps anyway."

"We aren't dragging _____ cords all over the _____ place, and I'm not doing this _____ thing unplugged," Satin said, lacing his speech with profanities. He now began wandering through a shady flower bed, pushing azalea bushes aside and fracturing a number of ferns.

Though removing his sweatshirt had made him appear shorter in stature, none of the bellicosity of Satin's demeanor had fallen away with it. He held his arms apart from his body as though ready to fight, he fixed his small, blue eyes on his listeners as though challenging them, and a perpetual sneer indicated his contempt for all that he heard. The impression created was that he wished to be regarded as at least dangerous and possibly criminal, and while she understood that first impressions could be deceiving, Jasmine saw no reason to believe that he dissembled.

As they were preparing to leave, Drew lingered behind to speak with Jasmine.

"Sorry about Satin. It's kind of like his act, you know? I think . . . . It's like his image . . . . Edgy."

"Then he's only pretending."

"Sort of, yeah. I think. Maybe not. I mean, he's kind of new. Gav just left two weeks ago. We've only practiced with him a couple of times."

"And he's not always like this?'

"Yeah . . . . I mean, no, he is always like this . . . so far. But it's an act. Or it's partly an act. Our agent says we need to start thinking more professional. A total package kind of a thing."

Jasmine's success in procuring the services of Animal Nature earned her the gratitude and praise of her housemates, but this only served to increase her apprehension. She was consulted on two occasions concerning the planning: as to whether a dancing platform ought to be constructed, an idea which was rejected on the grounds that dancing could proceed nearly as well on the grass; and as to the advisability of assigning a monitor to assure that no inebriated drivers damaged parked cars, about which it was decided that all should remain observant and report questionable cases to Pudge. In neither case had she expressed an opinion, as she was as yet unable to contemplate accommodations and half-measures when her real hope was that some event would occur to make the entire party disappear. She was sure that if she could only disclose the full extent of her worries to Phillip, he would provide comforting counsel. His time, however, was now occupied with Sherry Hill, and no good opportunity had offered itself. She retreated more and more often to the quiet living room, to the company of her books and the shining piano.

Chapter 18

Max Hill Shows Attention to Jasmine

Whereas the living room was isolated and not on the way to anywhere else in the house, it was a public room, and one evening while Jasmine sat reading, Max Hill presented himself there. He was pleased to arrive undetected, for he was afforded an opportunity to observe Jasmine at her ease. She sat on the couch with her legs curled under her, one elbow perched on the armrest. Her chin rested on her thumb and her four fingers lay gently against her cheek. Her white running shoes sat on the floor beside the couch, neatly placed side-by-side.

She read with an intense concentration and slightly parted lips that suggested childlike labor at her reading and innocent wonder at the story she was contemplating. The morning sun worked its way through a row of camellia bushes just outside the chintz covered bank of tall windows, and the effect of the dappled light on the white carpeting and her bronze, perfectly soft and smooth skin made her seem to glow with health and goodness.

Of course, Max knew perfectly well that Jasmine read with great facility, and had he considered the issue objectively, he would have realized that, in most respects, she had led a less protected life than her cousins. Nonetheless, in her presence he had begun to feel a sensation of regard for purity and innocence. As this sensation led him to think especially well of himself, he did not attempt to overthrow it, but instead extended it and vowed silently to guide, protect, and serve her.

"Hello, Jasmine," he said softly, still standing in the doorway.

She looked up, alarmed at first, then offered him a gentle smile, which he accepted with real gratitude.

"You look so peaceful there," he said. "I almost hate to interrupt you . . . . What are you reading?"

She was reading *Shogun*, and she turned the cover of the book toward him. He stepped forward to read it saying, "Wow! That's a lot of book."

"I only wish it were longer."

"It's about Japan, isn't it?"

She confirmed that it was.

"You always seem to be reading," he said gently.

"I do enjoy it, but I hope that I don't do too much of it. Reading, I think, should enrich one's own experience not become an escape from it."

It occurred to him that *being around* someone who read as much as Jasmine might also serve to enrich one's life, without the bother of having to do the actual reading.

"I see little danger of your turning into a bookworm," he said.

"Oh, no," she said, "I *am* a bookworm."

He leaned against the piano. "The house is very quiet this morning."

"I think that Julia has gone out to the store for cereal," Jasmine said. It had been apparent at breakfast that her brand of cereal had been used up, and she'd earlier heard the Mustang go out of the driveway.

He shrugged and settled himself on the piano bench. "I'd just as soon talk with you anyway."

Jasmine made no reply to this, and after a moment, he said, "You're not so happy with this party thing, are you?"

"I have little to judge by," she said.

Jasmine's demeanor now recalled to him certain moral crises he had experienced as a boy, concerning trivial things such as keeping up with his schoolwork, copying homework, and kissing a girl named Jody. All these seemed trivial to him now, but he was curiously pleased to remember the hours of torment he had felt about them at the time. Now, he was also gratified to experience in himself a male protective instinct.

"You really don't need to worry," he said. "It's only a party. People have them every day. Your aunts are okay with it."

"My concern is that my aunts don't understand exactly what they have approved."

"That's in the nature of things, isn't it? Sometimes the older generation needs us young people to push them along."

"I don't think my Uncle David would like feeling pushed."

"He won't be there, though, will he? What he doesn't know about isn't going to hurt him."

Jasmine did not reply to this, and, in fact, she appeared struck dumb by it. Max concluded that his logic was working its effect.

"As I understand it, he'll be somewhere in Bangkok at the very time our party is going on," he said, adding gently, "By the time he hears about it, it'll all be water under the bridge."

"I wouldn't want to feel that I was in any way deceiving him."

"There's a big difference between deceiving someone and not informing them of what they don't need to know. You don't tell him about every detail of your private life, do you? Your boyfriends, your arguments with your friends . . . ."

"I would tell him if I felt it was in any way likely to become a concern of his."

"Well, there you go."

"But he has every right to expect to be informed of what happens in his own house."

"Of course, it's his home, but its Thomas's, Chrissie's, and Julia's home, too. Shouldn't they have some say?"

"He has always allowed what he thought was in their best interests."

"And you don't think this is in their best interests?"

"I don't believe that Uncle David would think so."

"But he won't know!" Max said.

"I'm sure my aunts will at some time inform him, but whether . . . ."

"Yes, and when they inform him, it will all be happily concluded, and he won't have one second of worry about anything."

"Whether or not he knows," Jasmine said, continuing the thought he had interrupted, "there will have been a deception."

"I don't see how there can be a deception when nobody's told any lies about anything."

Her eyes, which had moved searchingly across his face while he spoke, and then had fallen in disappointment, suggested a vast gulf between them, one that Max felt with unexpected poignancy.

"Jasmine," he said softly. "I admire you for thinking so respectfully of your uncle. Of course, you would. He's been good to you. And I would never suggest to you that you should be disloyal. But I think you're making far too much of this. It's only a party. It's not something to worry about. It's just a chance to have some fun. College students work very hard. On weekends they have parties to blow off steam. It's not a big deal. In fact, it's one of the really great things about college . . . . Do you like to dance?"

Aside from a lunch-hour ballroom dancing class that had been held at her middle school, which she had enjoyed but which had been attended only by girls, Jasmine had danced publicly on only one occasion: between events at a track meet, girls from her team had drawn her into a stepping and clapping routine, an activity in which she had not performed well. She had observed much dancing at her school—it went on more or less perpetually between classes—and, while she admired the skills of some of the dancers, she was appalled at the frequent body thrusting and breast shaking. It was true, however, that in the sacrosanct privacy of her room, when she felt herself absolutely sure not to be interrupted, she sometimes danced quite enjoyably, albeit in her own syncretic form derived from her ballroom lessons, ballets she'd viewed on television, and some of the steps she'd observed at school. Remembering this, she could not now answer with a simple "no" and found herself blushing.

Max leaned closer. "So you do like to dance!" he said. The well-intended delight and glee in his voice was so apparent that Jasmine could not resist a smile.

"I have no skills as a dancer," she said. "I do enjoy music, and I can imagine enjoying dancing."

"You won't just enjoy it," Max said quickly, "You'll love it."

"I very much doubt if I will dance at all."

"You most certainly will, because you'll dance with me."

"I would not make a very enjoyable partner."

"You'll make a fabulous partner."

Max had no recommendations as a dancer other than an understanding that successful rock and roll dancing was more a matter of attitude than of skill: any movements undertaken with an attitude of supreme confidence were presumed self-expressive and therefore immune to criticism, whether it was standing in a trance or thrashing dangerously about the room. Nonetheless, he felt no compunctions about offering himself as Jasmine's teacher.

"We'll rock the night away," he concluded. "You're going to love it."

This date established, however, and believing himself successfully to have done a good deed in breaching her resistance to the party and easing her through an episode of youthful emotional pangs, he did not wish to leave the room. He found both this quiet, deserted wing of the house and Jasmine's presence very pleasing.

"You look perfect there," he said, and, in fact, seated as she was in the broken morning sunlight, she appeared very well. "You're like something out of a French movie."

Jasmine now drew her lips thin, clasped her book tightly to her stomach, and stared down at her own arms. Max tried to explain himself.

"There's a whole genre of French movies—they always feature girls about your age. The girls always have incredibly interesting faces, and, like you, they have their own ways of seeing things. Really, it's what the films are about. I think if a French director could see you here, he'd want to do a new movie on the spot. Have you ever thought about acting?"

She shook her head minutely.

"Never?" he questioned. "Not even between you and your pillow at night."

She now raised her eyes to look at him. "Of course, like other girls I have fantasies and dreams, of being a dancer, of being a princess, even of being an actress, but I don't believe that to be the same as 'thinking about' being an actress. I've thought about it only insofar as to realize it is not something to which I should aspire."

"And what do you aspire to?"

"I hope to be a teacher. I've had the good fortune to have several teachers in my life who have increased my understanding, and, really, in many ways, improved me as a person. While I can imagine that that may sound silly to you, it's something that I would very much like to be able to do for others."

"It doesn't sound silly at all," he said quickly. "I was only thinking that perhaps a person with your talents would find more fulfilling work among adults."

"I like children."

"I'm sure any child would be very lucky to have you for a teacher . . . . You'll have every little boy falling in love with you."

"I'll be too strict," she said.

Max now suppressed both a laugh and an off-color comment, and instead said, "Strict or not, you'll having them clinging to your skirt."

"They can cling if they like, but they'll still need to do their work. It's more important for a teacher to be respected than to be liked."

"Now I'm wondering if I should pity your students."

"You will only need to pity those who would be happier in ignorance."

Max laughed, saying, "Don't you think, in the long run, you might find teaching tiresome? After a while you know . . . drumming the same old facts into little kids who'd rather be out on the playground."

"I may," Jasmine said seriously. "I know that my grandmother eventually grew discouraged with teaching. I can't be certain that the same won't happen to me. Even so, isn't it of some use to be a good teacher even if it's only for a time?"

"I don't see why not . . . . But there is the financial angle to consider."

"A teacher's salary would be enough," she said. Then, gesturing to the genteel grandeur of the room around her, she continued, "I would like to be able in some way to repay the Gannons for their goodness to me. Were I to acquire the riches of Solomon, though, I doubt that I could ever accomplish that."

"I'm sure they expect no repayment."

"That in no way makes them less deserving of it."

"No, it doesn't," Max said.

"On the contrary," Jasmine went on, "it makes them more deserving."

"I'm sure they enjoy doing things for you. I'll bet it would offend them ever to hear you speak of repayment."

Jasmine considered this more seriously even than Max had intended. "It is true, I think, that by being too proud, a person can devalue someone else's kindness, but their goodness to me has been so thorough and extensive that I don't think any small measures I could take would detract from it."

"They probably feel like they've been more than paid back already. I know Cynthia relies on you for all kinds of things."

"They require very little of me."

"You do twice as much as Chrissie and Julia combined."

"I'm more often at home."

"You're also a lot less lazy."

"I'm hardly imposed upon," Jasmine said. "I enjoy helping Cynthia."

"And I know she enjoys having your help. More than that, she's completely dependent on it."

"I think you overestimate my importance. But it's kind of you nonetheless."

He laughed yet again, thinking as he did that Jasmine, despite her delightful innocence, was in some ways more the grown-up than her aunt.

Prior to meeting Jasmine, Max Hill had encountered people of integrity only in books. He had reached the conclusion that they were primarily a literary convention, and that for real people, integrity was something one put on to create an effect, like a pair of tasseled shoes. While he had admired how charmingly integrity fitted Jasmine, he had at first felt certain that he would soon enough catch her with her shoes off. Now, he realized that it was perhaps he who had been deluded all his life: Jasmine was a real thing. And what a delightful thing it was! Of course, he understood that she was little more than a child and that such ideals as hers could not stand the test of adult society, but he experienced a deep, almost intoxicating desire to protect her from such adult corruptions as long as such might be possible. Indeed, he had begun to suspect that this was perhaps the single thing in life to which he was best suited.

Chapter 19

Phillip and Sherry Hill Drive Out to a Farm

Jasmine would soon rise and pleading duties in her room escape Max's presence; yet even while this conversation was concluding, another was being conducted in Phillip's Porsche. He and Sherry had gone out on a ride along the river road in search of a peach orchard where Tina had been assured that they would find ripe peaches of particularly nice flavor. Sherry was driving, as was the custom when they went out together, because she had not previously learned how to drive a car with a manual transmission, and Phillip was teaching her. The road, which was both narrow and curving, ran atop the levee, with the orchards filing by down below on one side and the decline to the river on the other. Sherry, who in fact had already learned how to shift proficiently, exhibited no lack of confidence in her driving. She accelerated aggressively, pushed the shift lever authoritatively, and worked her way through the curves with an absence of the use of brakes that demonstrated a natural feel for both the handling of the automobile and the minimal banking of the curves.

While under normal circumstances Phillip would have considered this driving reckless, he was so exhilarated by the speed at which the car handled the curves, the cool morning air blowing over their heads, and, of course, by being in Sherry's presence that his heart raced with joy, excitement, and admiration for the adept and daring girl at the wheel. Not that he wasn't afraid, especially when they passed near the water and he imagined them flying out over it, nose-diving, and sinking into the green depths. But danger placed before the young attracts as often as it repels, and all things considered, it seemed to him a wonderful morning to be out and about.

Tina had sent them on this mission to locate a sure source of superior produce for the party, for which she was planning to make fruit ices. The idea of fruit ices was, of course, ridiculous in the context of the party that was actually likely to take place. First, while no one could deny that fruit ices were delicious, the effort and expense required to produce them was vastly out of proportion to the attention they would receive from the party-goers, who would for the most part be just as happy with cherry-flavored snow cones. In the early hours, some of the boys, especially those who were using marijuana, would be interested in food, which they would want to be plentiful and greasy. Most of the girls, would consume only diet soft drinks, with the exception of those with sufficient experience to take solid foods as a preventative of acute alcohol poisoning.

Sherry and Phillip both understood this in their own ways, yet they proceeded with their task happily, as any pretext for going out alone together was welcome. Fortunately, the orchard to which Tina had directed them was rather far, allowing them ample time for conversation even at the high speeds at which Sherry drove. As was surprisingly common between them, the conversation turned to Jasmine.

"Max has a thing for her," Sherry said.

"Max?" Phillip said, with genuine surprise.

"Haven't you noticed how he's been acting with her?"

"With Jasmine?"

"Yes, with Jasmine."

"I've seen him talking with her . . . ."

Sherry chuckled. "His eyes are on her the minute she comes into a room, and the first chance he gets he works her into a corner."

Phillip now experienced that perceptual and emotional revolution that occurs when an older brother discovers that his eternally childish little sister has attracted a suitor. A multitude of thoughts merged with the rush of wind over his head, and an upheaval of emotions added to the twists each road curve set off in his stomach. Too young? Too inexperienced? Too innocent? Yes, but . . . . Was he worthy of her? Would he be kind to her and respectful of her? Yes, but . . . . Would he hurt her? Could he be *sure* that he wouldn't hurt her?

"Do you think that he's serious?" he asked.

"Majorly. All he does when we get home is talk about her. He remembers the things she says word-for-word. He keeps telling me how great she is . . . . And I've never seen him be so considerate and thoughtful. Not just to Jasmine—you'd expect him to be good with her—but with me too. With everybody. Haven't you noticed how he's offered to help with everything for the party? How he's always trying to mediate things between Julia and Chrissie? That's all Jasmine."

Some time passed before Phillip said, "You know, I think that's terrific."

"You do?"

"I do."

"You're sure?"

"Yes, I'm sure. Though I have to admit that I'm surprised. I would have imagined Max with somebody a little bit more . . . a little bit more . . . .

"More slutty," Sherry suggested.

"No," Phillip said quickly, though not without an

understanding wince, "somebody more adventurous. More out there in the fast lane. Even somebody more like Julia."

They rode through several curves, considering the issues of Julia and sluttiness, the wind still blowing about their ears, and then Phillip said, "It seems like that whole thing with Julia's cooled off."

She nodded and said, "Because he was spending too much time flirting with Chrissie."

"Was he?"

Sherry laughed aloud. "Earth to Phillip. It was more-or-less continual."

"With Pudge around?"

"When they thought they could get away with it."

"And that was what made Julia so touchy?"

She acknowledged that it was.

"But that's over too, isn't it? Or am I missing something else?"

"It's over with them both. That's the kind of thing Max knows how to handle . . . when he wants to. And I think Jasmine made him want to." She turned to look at him and her shining hair whipped at the tip of her nose. "Sometimes something happens in Max that makes him want to cause trouble. Jasmine makes him *not* want to cause trouble. And I think that's just what he needs. Plus, you know, he wants her to like him. He knows Jasmine wouldn't have anything to do with him if he and Julia were any kind of an item."

"You think Jasmine was jealous?"

"No, but a girl like Jasmine would never let herself in for a situation where she'd have to be jealous. Any guy who wanted to have a chance with her would have to be completely free and totally committed."

It was remarkable to Phillip, who thought he knew Jasmine better than anyone else in the world, that he could be taught new things about her, especially by someone like Sherry, who had only known her for a few weeks. Yet it was true: Jasmine was a girl who would demand—and deserve—much from any boyfriend or future spouse.

Sherry's discernment increased Phillip's admiration for her, and the implications of it reassured him in his happiness for Jasmine. Jasmine was a deeply good girl who was turning into a strong-minded and level-headed woman. She deserved someone with Max's social graces. Max could introduce her to a society where her virtues would shine and multiply. He could offer her enough money to be secure. And, if there was some question about his past behaviors, there was no doubt that a girl like Jasmine could make anyone better. A hundred times—a thousand times—she had by her very presence impelled Phillip to call up his own better nature. Why couldn't she do the same for Max? It was an unexpected match and couldn't have been predicted, but it had an attractive symmetry. As much as Phillip loved Jasmine as she was right now, she still had growing up to do. Max would help her grow out of her closed-in, Arden Park self and to blossom; and she would make him better. That she could succeed was already apparent by how much he admired her.

Yet, a small, nagging worry persisted. Couldn't anybody, anybody at all, get lost in an infatuation? Weren't all girls, even ones who were much older and much more experienced than Jasmine, subject to being swept off their feet and having their judgments upended? And couldn't a young man, mesmerized by a girl, convince himself that the spell would last forever? Yes, yes, and yes—for *almost* any girl or boy. But Jasmine was Jasmine. And Max was Sherry's brother. Deep down, Max shared his sister's instinctive insight, her knowledge of right behavior, and her goodness. It was impossible to believe that all would not work out for the best.

"I'm glad you think this is a good thing for Jasmine," Sherry was saying. "I think it may be the best thing that ever happened to Max. I mean that. Really. *The best thing that could possibly happen to him.* Max can get bored. He can be cynical. He hasn't always been as good as he can be. Jasmine's changed him—in ways I didn't know were even possible. It's almost like she's saved his life. And he knows it. He knows it, and I know it too. Jasmine could turn Max's whole life around."

They found the sign indicating "Lazy Oaks Orchards," turned down the dirt lane that angled off the levee, scattered a trio of indignant chickens, and parked in the shade of three magnificent valley oaks. The dirt yard was so carpeted with leaves as not to be dusty; the low, tin-roofed fruit-sorting shed was stacked high with antique ladders and buckets; and a larger, mansard-roofed barn sat out beyond the shade in the bright morning sun. The scene was further decorated by two large, sleepy mongrels that wandered out to greet them, their tails wagging affably.

The effect was one of having gone back in time fifty years, and Phillip was charmed to silence. Sherry, however, as no proprietor was in sight, gave the car horn two long blasts, sending the chickens—which were searching the car tracks for plunder— scurrying and squawking, causing the dogs to give several half- hearted barks, and inducing a peacock, which sat in a lower branch of one of the oaks, to wail. Still, no one came.

Rather than listen to the horn again, Phillip urged Sherry out of the car. The dogs sniffed them thoroughly, then retreated to the shelter of the fruit shed.

"Do you believe this place?" Phillip asked.

Sherry shrugged.

"This is wonderful," Phillip said, trying again to draw a response from her.

"It's kind of cool," Sherry said, though her enthusiasm seemed perfunctory, "like, old fashioned."

"Like something out of the 1930's," Phillip suggested. "Like something out of Steinbeck. If *East of Eden* had been in the Central Valley, this is where it would have been."

He began wandering the yard, and Sherry followed. First, they made a short, cautious circuit of the yard, looking into the fruit shed where they found several wooden fruit sorting tables as well as a treasure of other very dusty, very long unused, and mostly mysterious farm paraphernalia. Then they made a wider circuit, out to the barn and beyond, where they discovered a cottage that was built of the same bare wood as the barn but so small that it could not possibly have contained more than two rooms. It had no particular charm other than its small size, the great oak that ensconced it, and a displaying peacock on its roof, but Phillip immediately felt some connection with this location and tried to express it to Sherry.

"I could live here," he said.

"You're kidding."

"No, I'm not. I could. I'm not going to, but if something happened, if I had to, I could. I could be happy here. I could take the money my parents are spending to send me to school, and I could do something like this, and maybe never need another penny. Not the whole orchard, maybe, but it would be enough to start."

"You'd live here for about two weeks and then you'd be going out of your skull with boredom."

It was a measure of Phillip's ignorance of the world of manual laborers that he could now say, "If I got bored, I could always read books."

"There aren't enough books in the world," Sherry replied.

Phillip, who had experienced many episodes of near despair that there existed so many good books that there was no hope of his ever reading them all, did not answer this now. Instead, he climbed up the single wooden step to the door and knocked. Receiving no answer, they turned back to the yard.

The view on their return was of the brightly shining Porsche, sitting under the overarching trees with a chicken walking about on its hood. The quaint fruit shed provided background. That the immaculate car was old suggested reverence for the past, and the quietness of this pastoral scene had a poignancy not even Sherry could deny.

"It looks like something out of a Ralph Lauren ad," she said.

In fact, it did. Had the designer himself been there to see it, he might have been inspired to create a whole new Lazy Oaks line of clothing. This observation, however, was not particularly welcome to Phillip, who now found himself obliged to acknowledge that the interest he took in this scene might no more stand the test of time than deliberately wrinkled shirts.

This disillusionment was compounded when the proprietor arrived from a far distant part of the orchard in a blaring, unmuffled dune buggy. The young driver skidded the vehicle to a stop, managing in spite of the cover of leaves to put up a cloud of dust, then revved the engine several times before turning it off. While he waited for the dust to pass and the noise to fall away, Phillip perused the back of the dune buggy. It was loaded with several sorts of unpleasant items, including a chemical sprayer, a chainsaw, varmint traps, at least a dozen beer cans, and a shotgun.

The young man inquired as to their needs and then sold them a box of peaches, but could not resist nearly continuous staring at Sherry. He repeatedly asked Phillip the price he'd paid for his car, then, getting no answer, resorted to asking about its racing qualities. Phillip was obliged to admit that it was never raced and that he knew almost nothing about the horsepower of its engine or the gear ratios of its transmission.

"If I had a car like that . . .," the boy concluded, with a dismissive shake of his head that implied that things would be very different.

"That's a first-rate paint job, though," he said, as they were preparing to drive away. He rubbed his hand over the surface of the hood. "It'd look a lot better with some metal flake."

Phillip cradled the box of peaches in his lap, as Sherry drove home. If anything, she negotiated the curves at even greater speed than she had on their way out. No one under the age of twenty will find it remarkable that they arrived home safely.

Chapter 20

What Happened on the Day of the Party

The morning of the party arrived, and the house was consumed with preparation. The pool was being cleaned, Esmeralda was busy in the kitchen, with Tina constantly in and out directing her activities, and the gardener was mowing. Added to this was the periodic banging of a hammer, as Satin, his bare back, bald head, and tattooed and muscled torso all gleaming with sweat, pounded together a set of risers to create a platform for the band. The platform had not quite fit on the grass, and he had been obliged to extend it into a bed of azaleas, where he'd smashed down several, in addition to cutting down a small Japanese maple tree. Japanese maples were a favorite of Dr. Gannon, and his children had known it would be missed by him, but they'd reasoned that they would have ample time to find a replacement and that they might, in any case, explain that it had died of natural causes.

None of this noise, however, not even the noxious, heart-stopping racket of the gardener's leaf blower—which Dr. Gannon had banished as an unfair imposition on his neighbors, but which had been readmitted in his absence—disturbed the robust group of young people that loitered about the pool. All were here, even Jasmine, who had been driven from the living room when Esmeralda had been detailed to a final vacuuming.

Relations seemed to have been patched up between Chrissie and Julia, between Chrissie and Pudge, and even between Julia and Max. Max's temporary retreat to Los Angeles had signaled to Chrissie that she must avoid an open break with Pudge, and once the girl had set her mind to this task, it had been easily accomplished. Pudge was really very fond of Chrissie, took ridiculous pride in the ribbings his rugby teammates gave him about her voluptuousness, and instinctively considered her his superior. Moreover, he was kind-hearted and could not bear to have her either unhappy or peeved with him. As a result, he was predisposed to accept any explanation of her behavior she was likely to give. When she expressed disappointment with him for his immature behavior in regard to Max, explaining that she knew exactly how to handle his type, he quickly retreated from his strong pose. Though it was he who had seen her kissing Max Hill, it was he who apologized. She relented, though begrudgingly, and they were again united.

Julia, too, had forsaken any claim to Max. She felt herself to have been scorned and had been, for a time, blazingly angry. She was somewhat appeased when Max departed the lake, much mollified when, on his return to Arden Park, he kept a distance from Chrissie, and finally, when he again began whispering witticisms in her ear, she forgave him (though she maintained to herself that nothing less than abject begging would ever induce her to take an interest in him again). Once these private asides from Max would have consisted primarily of disparagements of Pudge, but Max was sufficiently astute to recognize that Julia might now feel some sympathy for the other wounded party. Instead, he now turned his scornful comments on André.

As for Chrissie, she was happy to have the contretemps behind her, especially as she felt herself to have handled things well. She and Pudge weren't married after all: every woman had a right, even a responsibility, to pursue the best for herself and her future life. If an opportunity presented itself that seemed to offer more happiness, more romance, how could she not pursue it? Besides, Pudge could at times be agonizingly boring. Some girls might trade dullness for wealth, but she would not. She was better than that.

That she was obliged to conceal these sound arguments from Pudge troubled her not. Chrissie lacked the strength of mind to evaluate self-serving judgments with the extra rigor that a spirit of fairness requires. Her instincts and her convenience told her that a girl had a right to play the game of love selfishly; her logic fell in line with her instincts, telling her the same. Besides, she did like Pudge most of the time. It was convenient to have him around the pool and available to take her places; and she was wise enough to see that, as a girl got older, the luster of romance faded in comparison with the gleam of wealth. Her hopes for Max were not completely abandoned, but they must be set aside for the time being. In the event that they never fully materialized, Pudge remained the perfect safety.

The blaring of the leaf-blower now stopped, and Moza, who was often restless and now was pacing at the edge of the pool, resumed an earlier discourse on the future of rock-and-roll music. Except for Thomas, who continued to indulge him with ironic smirks and smiles, all had tired of Moza and were looking forward to his departure. No one, not even Thomas, paid attention to what he now said. Except for the peripatetic Moza, all the young people appeared completely idle and devoid of purpose. Of course, they were not.

Forgive us, dear reader, if we fail to convey the full complexity of this scene, if we provide a mere glimpse of the human drama that lies hidden. Sherry and Phillip sit a little apart from the umbrella-covered table; the others, except for Moza, are arrayed around it, in calibrated spacing. Chrissie sits next to Pudge, though not intimately close. Julia sits across the table from them. Max is placed exactly half-way between the two sisters, but his attention is on neither. He is watching Jasmine, where she stands at the edge of the patio. He is willing her eyes to come to his so that he can offer her a seat beside him. Thomas, reclines in a lawn chair, his eyes closed, and with what appears to be a smile perpetually on his lips.

Here, fires that once blazed have been beaten back; hidden embers still smolder, even in breasts that would not admit to harboring them; scars are still fresh and bright, even on young, fast-healing hearts. Such a scene, the complexity of feelings it presents, the myriad of hopes and plottings, the private exchanges that occur (both those observed and unobserved), the subtle meanings of looks accepted an instant too long and those rejected an instant too soon, all this is the province of literary masters, and all such masters are long dead. Such masters, my friend, could have conveyed the full complexity of this scene as easily as you or I might flip an omelet, but we are relegated to calling on your imagination: for example, as to each young woman's calculations concerning the exact amount of which piece of flesh her outfit for the evening ought to expose or suggest, and as to the depth of carnality of each young man's fantasies and his degree of confidence that they will be fulfilled.

This quiet drama was interrupted as Moza, who stopped his pacing, slapped his hands to his head, and said, "Hey, I got it! They need to cover some Blister songs." The antecedent to the "they" was apparent to none, none had previously heard a group called Blister, yet none sought clarification. Moza resumed his thoughtful meander.

Alas, dear reader, already again we must ask your indulgence for we find ourselves unable to describe the panoply of consternation, disappointment, mischievous glee, and fear that now freezes our young people in place. Dr. David Gannon, garment bag over his arm, has emerged around the corner of the house.

It was Julia who first threw off her paralysis. "Daddy!" she exclaimed, while leaping to her feet. She edged away from the table, somewhat cautiously at first, then more quickly and kissed him on the cheek. Dr. Gannon returned the hug, then turned to his older daughter, who, having taken her sister's cue, now presented herself to be kissed. Patiently and giving his full attention to each, despite holding in his hand a slip of paper the presentation of which was obviously imminent, Dr. Gannon now kissed Jasmine and shook his nephew's hand and Pudge's. He then turned his gaze to Thomas, who, while he had risen to a sitting position and opened his eyes, had not been able to bring himself to his feet. Thomas answered his look with a wave, saying, "Hey, Dad."

Dr. Gannon was far too well brought up to ignore guests in his home, even if those guests were young and he distracted. He was soon introduced to the Hills who made proper how-do-you-do's, noted what a wonderful summer they had had in Arden Park, and thanked him sincerely for the considerable part his family had played in making it so enjoyable. Moza's introduction was less successful, as he pumped Dr. Gannon's hand a bit too vigorously and familiarly, saying dubiously, "Dr. Gannon, the man of the house, cool," all the while looking around to assess the reactions of Thomas and his sisters. Satin, as he was working several paces away and was to all appearances a workman, required no introduction; however, when he now again began pounding at a riser, he drew the doctor's attention. All saw his eyes land on the dismal little maple tree where it lay wilting in the sun.

"What in the world . . . ?" he began, in amazement, then strode forward to examine the chopped off trunk. "You, young man, what in the world do you think you're doing?"

Satin glanced up at him, but apparently finding this question unworthy of an answer, advanced to another corner of the risers, crushing yet another azalea bush en route. He resumed his hammering.

"Stop that immediately!" Dr. Gannon said.

"Go _____ _____," Satin said, using the most grotesque of oaths.

All were momentarily stunned. The doctor himself was first to recover from his paralysis. "Go," he said, his face white with anger, "go now." He pointed around the side of the house. "I want you out of my yard and off my property."

"Chill, man," Moza said. "Everything's cool."

"Everything very much is not cool," Dr. Gannon said.

Satin now rose up, still holding the heavy sledge. His usual smirk had been replaced with a glare of cold malevolence. He spread his legs in a boxer's stance, his hands tightened on the wooden handle, and he jerked his hands forward as though to throw the sledge in the doctor's face. He laughed when the older man flinched.

Pudge, whose eyebrows proudly displayed no less than six rugby scars, certainly did not lack physical courage, and he was the first to intercede. He took a place between Satin and Dr. Gannon and locked his hands in front of him like a nightclub doorman. Phillip was soon in action as well. He moved up to Satin and gentled his own arm around his shoulders. This succeeded in redirecting Satin's anger toward Phillip, an event that nearly drove Pudge to direct assault. Even Thomas was now induced to come forward. The three of them attempted to shepherd Satin around the end of the pool, but he would have none of it. Instead, he shrugged them off and slammed the sledge down onto the surface of his newly built platform, from which it rebounded in lopsided, end-over-end loops all the way into the pool—an event so curious that it seemed even to distract Satin momentarily. He recovered quickly, however, issued several more oaths in Dr. Gannon's direction, and stalked off toward the front yard, brushing Dr. Gannon as he passed. Pudge followed as far as the corner of the house and looked after him, then returned and announced his departure.

Dr. Gannon turned to Thomas. "Explain," he demanded.

"That's where the band was going to be," Thomas replied.

"Yeah, we've got Animal Nature," Moza now offered. "They're really cool. They're going to set up there and we'll be pulling the power off the main box on the garage . . . ."

"We won't be pulling power off of anything," Dr. Gannon now said.

"But it's all worked out, man."

Max, like all the Gannon relatives, already understood that the party would not now occur, and he pulled Moza aside and quieted him. Dr. Gannon again turned his attention to his family members. He seemed for a moment to have been stunned by Satin's and Moza's conduct, but when he discovered the forgotten piece of paper in his hand, his face reignited with anger. "I suppose this is the explanation for *this*," he said, waving the paper in the air. "I have here a bill for two kegs of beer, not one keg of beer but two, that a man was just trying to deliver to our house. I told him that he had to be mistaken, that they couldn't possibly be coming here, but now that I look at this I see the name at the bottom is Thomas Gannon . . . ."

Thomas fidgeted.

"I take it you're the one responsible for all of it then," Dr. Gannon said, moving a step forward and clutching the paper in front of him.

Thomas only shrugged in response, and the veins in Dr. Gannon's forehead began to throb. It was now necessary to consider not only the prospect of violence but that of stroke as well. Again, Phillip intervened.

"We're all responsible," Phillip said, "and, for that, I can only say that I am extremely sorry."

"We were just planning to have a party with our friends," Julia now intoned, tears in her voice.

Her father glared at her with unnatural harshness, but he had never been able to maintain the same sternness with his daughters that he did with his son, especially in the face of tears, and he looked away without comment.

"There will be no party," he said.

"There's got to be a party," Moza interjected, breaking free of Max's hold on his shoulder. "We got Animal Nature. We got the beer. _____, man."

Though his concluding obscenity was not directed at Dr. Gannon, but intended only to express general dismay, Dr. Gannon's expression evolved from incredulous to grim. "I suggest that you, young man, follow your friend and leave here immediately."

"But I'm staying here," Moza said, as though wounded by his impoliteness.

When Thomas acknowledged with a shrug that this was true, Dr. Gannon turned again to Moza. "You were staying here. You have five minutes to pick up your possessions and leave."

"Cool off, man. I don't have any money," Moza protested, but Max now had him firmly by the shoulders.

"We'll dispose of him," Max said knowingly to Dr. Gannon, indicating to Sherry that she too should take this opportunity to exit. He succeeded in turning Moza in the direction of the front yard, but Moza was not yet ready to be taken away.

"You need to chill, man," he shot back over his shoulder. "I don't have any money. I can't go anywhere."

Dr. Gannon responded to this by removing several bills from his wallet and handing them to Sherry.

"You have five minutes to remove your possessions from this house. I believe this young lady will be kind enough to call a cab to take you to the bus station. You'll want to wait for it out in the street in front of the house."

Moza, acceding to the finality of this statement and the others' refusal to protest, now pulled free from Max and marched with wounded dignity into the house. Max and Sherry followed, and Dr. Gannon turned again to Thomas. He handed him the bill he had been clutching in his hand. "See that this is paid. You will also need to offer my apologies to the driver. I mistook my own ignorance for his." He turned to Chrissie. "Please ask your mother to come out here. And you, Thomas, when you've made sure that young man has cleared the house, you will come out here and remove *that*"—he now pointed to the risers—"from our flowerbed."

Thomas was eager to follow at least one of Dr. Gannon's directives, as Moza's penchant for thievery required monitoring; and, as it was apparent that Dr. Gannon did not now wish further discussion with the young people, the rest retreated to the house as well. Jasmine knew that she had behaved badly in contacting Drew and otherwise abetting preparations, and she felt truly sorry that Dr. Gannon, who had no doubt expected a joyous homecoming, should meet such disappointment. The stunned look on his face when his eyes had fallen on the broken-off maple tree had filled her with shame. She could have forgiven herself her mistakes if she had acted in accordance with her beliefs. She had not. She had disregarded her own better judgment out of a desire to be agreeable to the other young people. She was as responsible as the rest. Now, she could only aid in restoring the pride, joy, and tranquillity he ought to have found in his own home, and hope someday to win his forgiveness and regain his trust.

Chrissie was quick to warn her mother of her father's current disposition, though she need hardly have done so, for as soon as she became aware of his presence, even Cynthia saw the folly of all they had done. Her first reaction was panic—This was a crisis! A horrible crisis!—and she took herself off to her bathroom and cried a brief torrent of tears. She then wiped her eyes and cheeks, looked at herself in the mirror, and began her evaluation. As she was already dressed in attractive white shorts and small pink top that revealed an appealing but not irresponsible amount of cleavage, she saw no need to change, but she did apply lipstick and, after carefully drying her eyes, fresh mascara. She ran a quick brush through her hair, before throwing it back again with her hands. The result was favorable. She had tanned beautifully over the summer, her hair had lovely highlights, and her figure showed well. Her husband might have encountered younger women in Washington, but she was quite sure he had not found better. Now, the only thing to do was to go to him and admit her failure. He'd left the children in her care, and she'd been too weak to control them. For weeks, she'd known deep-down that things were not right. Now, everything would be put back as it should be.

She found him on the patio, where he had seated himself while waiting. She recognized from his upright posture, his controlled breathing, and folded hands that he was very angry indeed, and therefore, as she had anticipated, too far gone for treatment with mere joy and affection—perhaps even too far gone for abject contrition. When he was this angry, nothing but time would allow him to make even the tiniest concession. Even remorse, which might have appeared well on the children, would only make him disgusted with her. Everything depended on his continuing appreciation of her value.

What he needed, and as quickly as possible, was to be given the feeling that he was again in control of his household. This became her mission.

"David," she began. Then, seeing his ravaged look, added, "What a terrible thing to come home to."

"Yes," he said.

"What do we do now?"

"I've told the children that the party is canceled."

"Of course you have."

"You're in agreement with that then."

"Of course."

"I assume Thomas is behind it all."

"I assume so," she said, then, feeling guilty at allowing so much of the blame to be passed to her son, added, "I should have supervised."

"He's grown now. We should have been able to trust him. His failings are no longer those of a teenager. They aren't forgivable in the same way. He needs to become aware of that . . . . We've been too lenient with him."

"A young man has to learn some things for himself."

"Some people seem destined to learn the hard way. But to do something like this, something actually criminal, supplying alcohol to teenagers . . . ." He allowed his wife to consider the implications of an arrest, not only on her son's future but her husband's political position as well.

"It could have been a catastrophe," she admitted.

"Yes."

"But it has been avoided?"

"I hope so."

"What else is there we can do?"

"They will have to contact everyone possible to tell them that the party is canceled. Then, someone will have to wait out front to send away anyone who hasn't gotten the message. We'll have to take this away . . .," he said, pointing to the risers.

"I can call Francisco," she said, referring to the gardener. "He was just here this morning. I'm sure we can get him back."

"Thomas should do it himself."

"Yes," Cynthia agreed, but she went no further as she doubted her ability to get Thomas to do anything promptly.

"I told that friend of Thomas's that he would have to leave."

"Good," she said. "He's already stayed much longer than he should have. I've been trying to think of a way to get rid of him . . . . His father was supposed to be someone . . . someone in some company or something. But now I don't think he is at all."

David Gannon was very angry with his wife, but he'd learned from long experience that expressing his anger to Cynthia yielded little good. Yes, it caused her remorse, but her remorse was soon forgotten. Yes, it caused her pain, but her pain was his suffering. Containing his anger, he now said, "I hope I wasn't too harsh."

"You did exactly right, I'm sure."

"There was something about the wiring."

"I'll call an electrician right this minute."

Dr. Gannon said nothing more, and Cynthia now ventured to touch his arm. "Why don't you go in and get changed. Give us an hour and we'll have this place looking like home again. I'm so sorry that you had to be subjected to this. It was my responsibility, and I just wasn't forceful enough." She wrung her hands.

While Dr. Gannon, like most husbands, was capable of feeling deep anger at his wife, he was not capable of staying angry with her for long. When she had first arrived on the patio, any demonstration of his affection, given his extreme anger, would have been hypocritical. But he already regretted having had to forego the joyful kiss and greeting he had anticipated, and was now able to respond to her touch with a gentle squeeze of her shoulder and even a brief nuzzle next to her ear. The smell of her perfume had a further tranquilizing effect, and had Tina not chosen this moment to appear on the patio, the party might have been temporarily forgotten.

Tina, however, had turned livid on receiving the news of the cancellation, and had answered Chrissie with the words, "It certainly will not be cancelled." Indeed, she was so incensed that she had not yet fully marshaled her own emotions by the time she reached the patio.

"David," she said, her voice pinched, "what a wonderful surprise."

Dr. Gannon rose and gave his sister-in-law a careful hug. "There's a cyclone in Malaysia. I used the excuse of being a few hours closer to Asia to wait it out here."

"Well, we're all grateful to that cyclone . . . . You've heard of the young people's party?"

"I have."

"You understand that it's been very long in the planning. And it's in honor of our neighbors, the Hills, who will only be with us for a few more weeks. Their father is a movie producer."

"There will be no party."

"That's impossible," Tina said.

This comment was regarded with mute horror by Cynthia.

"It is not only possible," Dr. Gannon said, "but certain."

"You've taken no role in the management of this household," Tina said. "You have no idea of the amount of hard work that's gone into preparation for this evening, or how disappointed your children will be. This business about the beer was unfortunate, but that's now fully resolved. It's much too late to change plans. I have to remain firm about this."

Dr. Gannon's face turned impassive. He now repeated his earlier words one at a time, "There will be no party," with a deliberate articulation and steadiness of gaze that could not be misunderstood. Yet, to Cynthia's horror, her sister persisted!

"You have been away through all this," she now said, "and you know so little of all the preparations we've made . . . . This about the beer—it was entirely wrong—and I'm so glad you put an end to it. Cynthia and I certainly didn't know a thing about it."

"It never occurred to me that you would have. Thomas had probably planned to hide it somewhere, though how he could have imagined you wouldn't find out, I don't know. Then again maybe he didn't care."

"But with the issue of the alcohol resolved and all of the catering contracted . . . ."

"Damn it, woman, it's off," Dr. Gannon said.

With a lift of her chin, Tina turned and marched back into the kitchen. Cynthia patted her husband's arm and soothed him. After perhaps a minute had passed, she said, "There may be a useful lesson in this for the children."

"Perhaps for all of us," Dr. Gannon said. He then proceeded to follow his wife's suggestion and began his retreat towards his own room.

Alas, reminders of his unhappiness were all about—in flower displays, food preparations, decorated tables, even the presence of Esmeralda. Worse yet, when he reached his room, he discovered that the power had gone out, leaving his room uncomfortably hot and making it impossible for him to use his electric shaver, which he had hoped to do in anticipation of rubbing cheeks with his wife. He might have liked to swim but wished never again to see the platform in the flower bed.

Every day in Washington, he encountered disorder, pique, vindictiveness, obstruction, obfuscation, and defiance. His directives were sometimes arbitrarily overturned; he had even on one occasion suffered reproof. None of these had dispirited him so much as this assault on his own home. Nonetheless, as he began his unpacking, he found a few thoughts to reassure him. The visitors—the Hills— had behaved well; his children, by their acquiescence, had seemed to acknowledge their error; and his wife had failed more from her habitual indolence than bad judgment. This final recognition incited a surge of sharp anger at Tina Stubbs, and her words, "I have to remain firm," replayed themselves in his head. He slammed his suitcase shut so hard that it slid from the bed.

Even before he was in the shower, hammers began to pound in the distance, accompanied by the sharp squeaking of nails being pulled from lumber. The process of restoration had begun. With this, he must be satisfied.

A drive to return all things to normal as quickly as possible now possessed the entire household. Even Thomas, who could be found out in the street in front of the house with Moza, felt this exigency. While he was teasing his friend about leaving in exactly the same manner he had arrived, and conducting a close negotiation concerning various quantities of three different types of drugs that were to be exchanged for the balance of his air fare to Los Angeles, he was making absolutely certain that Moza made no attempt to re-enter the house.

Phillip also felt the necessity of normalizing arrangements, and he began secreting his possessions out of Jasmine's room and back up to Thomas's. He encouraged Jasmine to move as well, a suggestion which she received with great relief, as it offered her, in an admittedly unsubstantial way, an opportunity to begin making amends to her uncle.

Thus it was that they found themselves alone in Jasmine's room. Where there had once been only openness and mutual wishes for each other's happiness, there had now entered some constraint, on Phillip's side because he sensed some disapproval from her, and on Jasmine's because she disapproved without feeling any right to do so.

"Did you see his eyes when he saw his tree?" Phillip asked.

She had.

"It was terrible," he said.

She could only agree.

"The things that guy said to him . . .," he went on, shaking his head in disbelief. "Why did he have to choose this moment to come home?"

"It may be a good thing that he did," Jasmine said.

Phillip, to his credit, immediately took the meaning of this and replied, "You really think it would have gotten out of hand?"

"If you mean that worse would have happened than having our uncle's flowerbed ruined, then yes. If you mean that something catastrophic might have occurred, a fire, a drowning, the police, an accident, real damage to the house, I can't say. I can say that we went too far in creating the possibility."

"I think Satin was mostly just an act."

"What if he wasn't acting?"

"It's part of their show. They think they have to do that kind of stuff to create an image."

"Shouldn't we do him the justice of believing what he says, or at least believing in the image he portrays?"

"That's a deeply complicated and very Jasmine-like statement," Phillip said, his smile kind but weary. Then, after stuffing the last of his socks into a gym bag, he resumed. "But to answer your question, yes, we should." He then carried the last armful of his belongings out the door.

Mrs. Gannon, cool drinks in hand, awaited Dr. Gannon when he had finished his shower. They passed a pleasant interlude during which Cynthia made no complaint about his cheeks' scratchings, and he, having been awake for most of the past twenty-four hours, then napped. During this time, Tina made herself very useful, seeing that the last remnants of the band platform were taken away, decorations were disassembled, and food was sent away to a charity. An electrician was called, the power was soon put to rights, and in the middle of his nap, Dr. Gannon was obliged to slip himself under the cover of a blanket to protect himself from the cold air flowing down from the ceiling.

When Dr. Gannon was distressed, Mrs. Gannon's ministrations often set him right, and this case proved no exception. It was perhaps a weakness, but the comfort of his own bed, his wife's affection, and the quiet shade of his own garden increased his feeling of well being, turned him philosophical, and regenerated his faith that the affairs of his family, though they might not proceed exactly according to his wishes or expectations, would turn out well enough. After all, each of his children would eventually need to find his or her own way in life. He could use his experience and wisdom to guide them, but he could no more dictate to them their own interests and dreams than he could control the events of the world and nation.

With the major alterations to the household undone, non-family members departed, and his children humbled and quieted, they were able to enjoy a tranquil, if subdued, family meal. As they were finishing their chocolate cake, a bakery-supplied confection of mouth-watering richness which Cynthia had dared to extract from the general sacking of party fare, the phone rang. Dr. Gannon had been granted a reprieve. Instead of blowing out as expected, the cyclone in Asia had persisted, growing stronger and wider, causing much damage, and forcing the total cancellation of Dr. Gannon's meetings. It is an ill wind that blows no good, and this turn of the weather, unfortunate as it was for those many thousands of people living many thousands of miles away, afforded Dr. Gannon the opportunity to extend his stay.

Dr. Gannon was to have three additional days. This he saw as fortuitous. He had neglected the young people of the family for too long. Only by good luck had they escaped disaster. Now, he would reaffirm his position in the household and set it on a right footing. He would begin first thing in the morning by having private conversations with each of the children.

Exercise is a palliative to guilt, and while moving their belongings, Phillip and Jasmine had made plans to share an early morning run. Thus, it was Jasmine Dr. Gannon first encountered in the kitchen. She had just taken the orange juice from the refrigerator and still held the open door, when he appeared at the door. She set the carton back on the shelf.

"Jasmine, you understand that I was very disappointed yesterday."

"I do," she said.

"When I am in Washington, it's very important to my peace of mind that I can feel confident that things are going well at home. Yesterday left me feeling anything but confident." It was apparent in his manner that he had prepared this much of his speech in advance, yet he stopped here as though searching for the right words. "I had hoped to come home to . . . ." He stopped again. "I do not want you to think that I am . . . ." He stopped yet again and regarded her with a concentrated frown. Whether his look suggested more of anger, frustration, or injury she could not divine.

"I am sure you hoped to come home to a peaceful and secure household, where you could find time for quiet rest, in the company of your family," she said. "It is what you had every right to expect, and I am deeply sorry that we failed you. I know that I must accept my share of the blame, and I can only hope that you will forgive me and that you will accept my promise never to act in such a way again."

"Yes," Dr. Gannon said with a nod, though he seemed to remain at a lack for words, and could now only repeat himself. "Yes, of course. I was disappointed."

"I behaved badly, and I am sorry."

"Cynthia mentioned . . . I did understand . . . that it was you who suggested the musical group."

"A member of the group was in my class at school. I contacted him, and it was because of me that he agreed to play."

"I would have expected it to be one of the others."

At this, Jasmine could only bow her head in shame.

After a moment, Dr. Gannon seemed to take pity on her downcast head. "But you've apologized now, and you've assured me that you won't repeat the incident. I don't suppose there's much more than that I can ask from you. After all, no real harm was done."

"Yes," Jasmine now said, "but I understand that real harm might have been done, and I would never want to bring that on this household. I hope you will always understand how much I appreciate what you and my aunts have done for me and how much I love Arden Park."

"Yes," Dr. Gannon said, an actual tear sparkling in his eye, "I think I do know . . . and about that Jasmine, I wonder, how much have you been thinking about your future?"

"I have considered it, sir. Aunt Tina has encouraged me to do so, and I've made plans that I've been intending to communicate with you and that I hope will meet your approval."

"You have?"

"I will be eighteen next year, and I feel I should no longer impose on your kindness. I believe that if I attend community college and take a job, I should be able to support myself."

"Jasmine, you have always been a member of the family, and none of us has ever thought of you as an imposition."

"I know that, and I could not be more grateful, yet my position is necessarily slightly different, and I feel a very real need to achieve greater independence."

"We haven't expected that type of independence from any of the other children."

"How much of this is a matter of my different position and how much a matter of my own personality, I do not know, but I do feel that for me independence is better."

"But you wouldn't leave our house?"

"I love Arden Park and a part of me would never want to leave; yet I know that I must grow up someday. I will need to make my own life."

"Someday, yes. Fortunately, not just as yet . . . . Speaking of growing up, Cynthia tells me you've caught the eye of a certain young man."

For an instant, Jasmine thought he might be referring to Phillip, and this was the source of the extreme brightness that now glossed her face. Her uncle soon made his meaning more clear.

"I'm told that you're the reason he's nearly abandoned Los Angeles."

"No," Jasmine said, "that's not the case."

"You know, Jasmine, there's nothing wrong in that. He's a little older, I realize."

"Sir, I don't believe that he's stayed here because of me, and if it were true, he should not have."

The slight smile that had begun on Dr. Gannon's face now disappeared. "I guess he's not what you girls would call handsome. He isn't very tall, is he?"

"I don't dislike his appearance."

"I take it that you don't really like it either . . . ."

"Many girls I'm sure would find him very handsome. I hardly have an opinion one way or the other."

Her faint praise having convinced him that he had correctly guessed the reason for her coolness, Dr. Gannon now said, "Looks aren't everything, you know. There's much more to think about in a relationship than how someone looks. Max is intelligent, well-mannered, and if my guess is right, a very level-headed young man. He's well-started in his career, and I'd say he has all the makings of a success." He reclaimed his earlier smile. "And, perhaps most importantly of all, he's taken with you. That in itself speaks well for him."

"I don't believe that he truly is taken with me. If he is, I wish that he weren't."

"He may seem older now, but it's not unusual for a girl to take an interest in someone a little older."

"He does seem older to me. If I felt that he had any real interest in me or that I might ever feel any in him, his age might be a concern. Now, I hardly think of it."

"I understand that he in fact does have an interest in you—a *very real* interest."

"I think there is a misunderstanding."

"Jasmine, there is no misunderstanding. I didn't think I was telling you anything you didn't know. If so, now you do know."

"I've done nothing to encourage him."

At this, Dr. Gannon laughed, saying, "That I can believe!" Then, he continued, "Jasmine, I hope you will give this some thought. Sometimes a girl gets an idea in her head of what the perfect boy looks like, and before she understands how wrong she's been, she's let her best chance go by. You need to give people a chance. Sometimes it takes time to see people as they really are. I understand that Max comes from a different background than ours. Some things he says or does may not seem familiar or even quite right. But things were very different here than they were in Tennessee, weren't they? Yet we didn't turn out to be all that bad, did we? Sometimes differences that at first seem like obstacles turn out to be superficial. Deeper down, we're all very much alike. We need to stay open to possibilities." Dr. Gannon now looked at Jasmine from under his eyebrow. "Do you understand what I'm saying?"

"That I should not let prejudice affect my judgment."

"Good," Dr. Gannon continued. "Now, I hope you will give this boy a chance. He may not be all you've been looking for, but then there aren't as many princes as there used to be, are there? I'm not asking that you fall in love with him, or anything so serious. I only hope that you will keep an open mind. Is that too much to ask?"

Jasmine's mind had been resolutely shut for some time, and what he asked might have been too much if it had come from anyone else. Dr. Gannon she could not refuse. "I will keep an open mind," she said.

"And you will be fair?"

"I try always to be."

"That's all that I can ask."

Phillip, having seen the two in conversation, had signaled to Jasmine and taken his run alone—much to Jasmine's regret. He now arrived back in the kitchen and made humble, manly apologies. These Dr. Gannon accepted, and when the two young people had left—Phillip for the shower and Jasmine for the sidewalks—it seemed to David that the morning had gone well. He was not even much troubled when he failed to elicit such satisfying statements from his own children. He caught Chrissie and Julia together as they were on their way out. They assured him that they'd known that "the whole idea sucked from the start," that they "were just trying to be nice" to Thomas's friend André, who was "a real loser," and that they were "really sorry things got so messed up." They did not, however, have time at the moment to listen to the lecture he had intended for them, and he had to be satisfied with this. As for Thomas, he washed his hands of the matter with the observation that he had "only been home a couple of days all summer" and could hardly be expected to keep up with what his little sisters were doing. As for André, he was "flaky," and he would never have allowed him in the house if he hadn't felt sorry for him.

While Cynthia observed that all the children had expressed regret and a laudable compassion for the hapless André, Dr. Gannon could not yet be satisfied. He demanded that all the family reserve a time in the afternoon, when they could meet together. The meeting was set for 1:00. Thomas was the last to arrive at 1:40, and Dr. Gannon was just preparing to address them, when the Hills arrived at the front door. They were ushered into the living room, and introductions were re-made, this time more formally. Cynthia suggested refreshments, Julia and Chrissie, happy with this escape, helped Jasmine serve, and the original intent of the meeting was forgotten.

Julia and Chrissie served drinks graciously. Thomas offered no excuse for escape, instead chatting amiably with his aunt. The Hills appeared remarkably mature and agreeable, and Sherry, in conversing with Phillip, demonstrated a rapt attention and sparkle to match the best of Washington hostesses. His household again seemed happy and orderly, and David Gannon began to regret his ogre-like arrival. All the young people were well-mannered, intelligent, healthy, and remarkably attractive. Nothing terrible had happened. All had expressed remorse at letting things progress so far; no doubt they had sufficient foresight and good judgment to have staved off any truly harmful incidents; given time, they well might have canceled the party on their own.

David Gannon was perhaps too much a politician in that he considered uncontrolled anger always to be an error, even when it was justified and efficacious. In this case, his original wrath might have persisted longer had he known that the young people the night before had stood at the street corner and turned away no less than one hundred cars full of insistent and sometimes inebriated teenagers. But he knew nothing of this, and he was now sorry to have humiliated his children by appearing dictatorial and abusive and wished to make amends.

"Perhaps we could have a party, after all," he suggested to his wife. "Nothing so big of course: the Hills, the Blunts, Mr. and Mrs. Lee, of course. And all of us. That's enough to make a party, isn't it?"

Cynthia thought the idea wonderful and presented it to the group on his behalf. His own children were at first doubtful, but Max Hill joined the campaign, thereby both carrying the issue with the other young people and enhancing the already considerable esteem with which Dr. Gannon regarded him.

"We old folks can sit out on the patio," Dr. Gannon said, "and you younger people can have your night of dancing in the living room. Of course, there won't be any live music . . . ."

"A band doesn't make much sense really, anyway," Max said, "when you can have whatever music you want by whomever you want played out of speakers. The whole idea was wrong from the start."

Jasmine blushed upon hearing this said, for Dr. Gannon had been made aware that she'd taken a part in contracting the band's services, but Max was quick to see his error and immediately sought to relieve her distress.

"You should know, Dr. Gannon, that Jasmine certainly would never have had anything to do with that band it if we hadn't pressured her into it."

"Yes . . . . I'm sure . . .," he said, regarding Jasmine dubiously. He did not believe for a moment that Max Hill in using the term "we" was doing anything other than covering up for his son and daughters, but he remained perplexed at Jasmine's role. It was, of course, completely unlike her to have displayed such poor judgment, but it was also unprecedented for her to have attracted the attention of a young man of such grace, distinction, and maturity as Max. "In any case, I think it's something best put behind us now," he said.

Max, eager to accommodate Dr. Gannon's suggestion, now walked briskly to the piano bench where Jasmine sat. "Play something for us," he said, in an admiring voice.

"I just play for fun," Jasmine said honestly. "It's nothing for an audience."

"I don't believe that for a minute," Max said. "Everything you do you do beautifully."

"I assure you, mine is not a case of false modesty. I play for my own amusement and I'm not the least bit good at it even when I play alone. I'm sure having an audience would completely paralyze my fingers."

"But we all know that you play for Phillip," Max said.

Phillip, realizing that he would have been every bit as reluctant to play for an audience as Jasmine, now intervened, saying, "We don't play the piano, we just play *at it*. Neither one of us has ever had any lessons, so we just put up with each other's mistakes."

"That may be so," Dr. Gannon said, but I've heard a few things coming out of this room that have not sounded bad at all. I think you may have improved quite a lot more than you let on. Why don't you just give us a small sample?"

While Jasmine might have refused the others until kingdom come, she could not refuse her uncle. Fortunately, she had before her a piece that she had played many times, a piece of Bach that had been transcribed for intermediate level students. She was able to get through it without error, but with considerably less élan than she displayed in private, unguarded moments, and anyone with a real interest in classical music would have known at once that this was a child's version of the original.

Nonetheless, Max clapped long and loud, and the others followed his lead. When Max's last bravo had faded away, Sherry called on Phillip to take the bench. Phillip decidedly declined then turned to Sherry. "But I know you play, Sherry, and, from what Max says, you play very well."

"I haven't touched a piano in three years," she said.

"Jasmine did her part," Dr. Gannon now said, "I'm afraid you're going to have to face the music yourself."

All laughed at this, and Sherry good-naturedly took a place at the piano, all the while holding Jasmine's arm so that she could not escape the bench. She then did a quick version of Chopsticks, which caused everyone to laugh, followed by a rendition of Heart and Soul, which she merged seamlessly into a medley of old-fashioned show tunes that she played with remarkable facility, injecting light-hearted personality into each note. She made errors, of course, but they seemed only to add to the joyous recital. She ended with a flourish, stood up, and said, "That's all. That's all I remember."

The satirical wit with which she'd played the tunes, which were all fun and familiar, seemed to have perfectly updated them, and the applause this time was from all.

Dr. Gannon immediately suggested a sing-along at the next-day's party. His own children would normally have abhorred such an old-fashioned suggestion, but Sherry's playing had been delightful, and they were more eager than usual to please their father.

"That'd be cool," Julia said.

"Yeah, if we knew any of the words," Chrissie suggested.

"We could get some sheet music," Dr. Gannon suggested. "Thomas could go down to the store this afternoon and pick something up."

Thomas shrugged his agreement, but Sherry now said, "I'm so out of practice."

Max dismissed her, saying, "It's a great idea!" and then suggested that she and Jasmine prepare a duet.

Jasmine, who understood perfectly that her skills were no match for Sherry's, immediately refused this invitation. Then, when Max began to plead, she managed to escape by offering him a confidential shake of her head. He, though he had misperceived her performance to be truly superior and didn't understand why she would not want to play, was so flattered by receiving this private com-munication from her that he relented and changed the subject to the types of songs they would sing. This consideration did not go unnoted, and Jasmine resolved to express her thanks to him at the first opportunity.

A discussion of Sherry's musical knowledge ensued. She had been in many musical comedies in her high school years, both in her school and with an independent theater, and the list of songs with which she was familiar, both vocally and at the keyboard, was comprehensive. She also suggested some Beatles tunes, though it was concluded that purchasing music for them would be unnecessary.

All of this delighted Dr. Gannon as a sing-along would be a family activity that could be enjoyed by people across generations, including the elderly Hills, because it suggested a degree of refinement of interests (without obliging him to listen to classical music which he found dull), and especially since it had been embraced by the young people themselves. He was aware, of course, that they were at this point eager to please him and that their actions were somewhat affected, but he was under the impression that the Hills were introducing more mature attitudes to the household, ones which he heartily approved. He saw no harm in his children's efforts to be agreeable. Perhaps discovering fun in an unexpected place would expand their horizons and temper their disdain for all things unfashionable.

As they were leaving, Dr. Gannon asked Jasmine to stay behind for a moment.

"In all of yesterday's doings, I forgot to tell you about something very important. Just before I left Washington, I had a visitor. Your brother came to my office. He asked me to carry his love for you." He bent and kissed her on the forehead. "And a kiss as well."

This was the single subject on which Jasmine could not restrain herself, not even when confronting the august figure of her uncle, and not even his kiss—the most tender she believed herself ever to have received—could distract her now from a single-minded sleuthing for all details about her brother's appearance and character. The momentous news in all this was that he had recently been promoted and expected to be posted to a Middle Eastern region.

"Will he be in much danger?"

"Some, yes. But you need to keep in mind that there are very, very many soldiers in the Army and comparatively few casualties. I can't deny that he will be in some danger, but I think it much less dangerous than people commonly suppose."

While this would have given little reassurance to most people, Jasmine was of the type of rational temperament that could take such counsel to heart. William was a soldier, and as such he could not shy from dangerous assignments, nor could she imagine that it would be in his nature to do so.

Dr. Gannon concluded by assuring her that her brother had hoped to get to California to see her before his new assignment, but that orders had precluded a visit. "He's really a very handsome and likable young man. It was an honor for me to be able to introduce him to my colleagues. You have every reason to be very proud of him." With this, he left her to her tears.

Thomas would not have been capable of buying sheet music on his own, nor was it in his nature to take more than a passive interest in any family activity. Dr. Gannon had, however, designated him as the music man, and therefore, as he was more familiar with the geography of Arden Park than Sherry, it was he who drove her to the store. For several reasons, the relationship between him and Sherry had remained more distant than it had between the others. Thomas seldom felt the necessity to make himself agreeable, and was not adept at polite or playful conversation. Except when he was drinking, he often appeared haughty and disdainful. By him, only women of remarkable beauty could be taken seriously, yet he was far too proud to court actively and thereby risk rejection. As a result, his experience was limited to girls who had unambiguously thrown themselves at him and to those whom he felt free to treat with contempt. As a result, he had come to see women in general as calculating, ambitious, and untrustworthy.

While Sherry had recognized in him the callousness of an unsentimental player of the games of love, she held no strong prejudice against him. She was as adept at handling such players as anyone, considered herself capable of manipulating such a situation to her advantage, and welcomed a challenge. Nonetheless, she had held back from Thomas. He was often away, and playing games with an absent partner held little promise; and she had perceived better opportunities with Phillip.

The drive to the store was the first time they'd spent significant time alone, however, and she was happy to recognize an amusing plaything. Up until now, he had seemed to look upon her in the same manner he might a very attractive friend of his younger sister: she was a case that bore watching but held no immediate interest. She made quick work of dispensing with this perception.

"So, Mr. Thomas Gannon," she said, "are you swamped with fortune-seekers at school?"

"There are a few," he said, giving her the surprised side-glance she had anticipated.

"I'll bet," she said, causing him to chuckle.

"Are you a future quadrabillionaire?"

"You never know," he said.

"I don't figure you for an engineer, so you must be a business major."

"Sociology," he said.

"You're not."

"It's not what you know," he said, "it's who you know, and sociology is the fast-track to a quick exit. There are about ten sociology papers in the whole world and they just keep getting recycled. I've got all ten of them."

"Does this mean you're going to work for the welfare department?" she asked.

"Venture capital. I already have an internship."

"Don't you need a business degree?"

"If you can deliver the cash, Federico's College of Beauty will do just fine. I'll have a full-time job two weeks after graduation. Then it'll get interesting."

"Megabucks," she suggested.

"Giga," he replied.

Whether or not Thomas understood that it was not his abilities so much as the Gannon name and influence that his employers wished to exploit she did not attempt to determine—even the most feckless of the rich and famous were likely to believe that their advancement was due to their savvy and charm—nor was she offended. His was a practical attitude.

"I like money," she said.

"Which only goes to show you have half a brain."

"Everything else being equal, more money is certainly better than less."

"What else is there to be equal?"

The refreshing frankness of this query caused Sherry to laugh aloud. Nonetheless, she was prepared with a reply. "Good looks," she said.

"Money," Thomas said, shaking his head in dismissal.

"For a man maybe. Money has a way of making any man look good. But it's not the same for girls. A girl with good looks can find a way to get money, but all the money in the world can't buy a girl good looks."

"It can get her a lot of help. Tucks and lifts and a little shaping up and down here and there . . . . No problem."

"Yeah, it helps, but I think you can always tell. A girl can anyway. I imagine a guy can too. I've heard there's a trampoline effect."

"You know how sometimes water balloons bounce and sometimes they break? . . . You're always afraid they're going to break."

Sherry was not offended—even recognized in herself an odd weakness for male vulgarity. She enjoyed being treated as a fellow realist, though she knew if he took it too much further, she would have to cut him off. Otherwise, he'd be over on her side of the seat.

"Tommy the Rock wasn't it?" she now asked, remembering the nickname that André had used for him. "What is 'the Rock' for? Somehow I doubt it has to do with Saint Peter."

"Just one of those frat-boy things."

"Is it because you're such a tough and mean guy?"

"It is."

"No."

"Yes."

"No. It isn't. It's because that sounds better than 'Tommy the Toot.'"

"Who told you that?"

"Moza."

"You can't believe anything you hear from Moza."

"I don't believe it because he said it. I believe it because you put up with him. What other use would you have for a roach like him." When Thomas failed to answer, she went on, saying, "Crack is very addictive and you shouldn't do it. Plus, it's ghetto."

"I don't do crack."

"You don't do it *anymore* you mean?"

He shrugged.

"You do a little blow though . . . . I've seen you sniffling."

"Not much of that either."

"If you don't have an addictive personality, you can probably handle that."

"I don't have an addictive personality."

"Do you think every addict in the world believes that?"

"I don't know. It's true with me. I can take it or leave it." They rode quietly for a while; then he said, "Moza left me a few lines. Want to do 'em?"

"Not in the least."

Thomas chuckled, and began even while driving to turn a dollar bill into a narrow funnel. He poured some white powder into it and handed it to her. He rolled another bill into a straw.

She held the bill for him, and he used the straw to draw the powder up into his nose.

"I hear they do a lot of this in LA," he said.

"Actually, it's passé. Now, it's all about family values."

"Really?"

"Don't be ridiculous. But people don't do as much cocaine as they used to. That may be because the true believers are already dead. It's definitely not the party drug anymore."

"What is?"

"Alcohol."

"The kegger lives on."

"Martinis actually . . . . I love martinis."

"We could stop in and have a couple somewhere."

She shook her head. "No thanks."

"Suit yourself."

Probably as a result of the stimulant, Thomas now grew more talkative. The effect this had on Sherry was paradoxical. While he spoke more confidently and with an inclination to be domineering in his speech, she felt herself increasingly to be his superior. She had considerable experience with people in his current state of intoxication, understood its delusional effects, and felt she knew how to manipulate them to her advantage. He spoke with confidence of his future in venture capital, with some disdain of his fellow students, who seemed not to understand where "the real money was."

"There's not that much difference between a million dollar deal and a hundred million dollar deal. But the hundred million dollar deal earns you a hundred times as much . . . Bigger bills fly off the table."

"But aren't you venture capital guys supposed to be putting up the money?"

He shook his head. "We just put the deal together. For that, we get our fees and we get a piece of the equity. So, if something goes diamond-cutter, we're there for the whole shebang. If it gets squishy, we take our fees and walk away."

A multitude of thoughts and observations influenced Sherry's present calculations: for example, that Thomas was indeed likely to make a great deal of money; that, while it was perhaps less glamorous to provide financing than genius, it was more sure; that Thomas was no genius; that there might exist for him in the not so distant future a tailspin of drug use and dissolution; that before anything so dire happened, he was likely to go through wads of money and provide considerable entertainment; that if he survived the drug thing, he might be a steady provider, though his tendency to be domineering could get in the way. She did not, however, experience any need to voice her observations or otherwise to encourage his conversation with feminine attention. The cocaine had rendered him gush and so confident of the world's admiration as to make flattery superfluous.

She was also aware that he was pleasant to look at. His skin was clear, and his regular facial features suggested a greater pleasantness of character than he possessed. He was tall enough to be a basketball player, carried himself well, was neither fat nor thin, and completely lacked Pudge's unpleasant hairiness. She might have shortened the swept-back, sun-streaked waves of his hair, as they hinted at homosexuality—completely misleadingly, she believed—but she might not even have done that. His blue eyes were another matter. In unguarded moments, they could be devilishly handsome, and they no doubt would appeal to many girls, especially those who grew weak-kneed in the presence of masculine disdain. They did not appeal to her. The arrogance which occasionally escaped them, especially when paired with the smirk that he wore almost habitually when among his sisters, might be a useful tool for dispensing with siblings, but if he ever dared to cast such a look on her, she would have to cut him off at the knees.

In spite of these reservations, however, Sherry was enjoying herself. Thomas's size in itself was sexy, and even if it was drug-induced, his confidence created a degree of masculine charisma. With Phillip it was always a matter of him carefully proposing some activity and her carefully responding in such a way as to indicate her preferences without injuring his feelings.

With Thomas there would be none of that. He would tell her what they were going to do, or at least ask in such a way that it was completely clear what he wanted to do, then she could proceed to manipulate the outcome. It would be something of a relief.

Sherry could not help observing that, in direct comparison to Phillip, Thomas matched up well. He was older certainly, and that was part of it, but he was also temperamentally more forceful. Just as Phillip's runner's physique seemed to shrink in Thomas's presence, his less assertive personality seemed to grow annoyingly inconsequential in the face of Thomas's bluster. What was it with all his agonizing over the environment, politics, and ethics! After a while, it was annoying.

Add to this Thomas's more mature outlook about money— they would all—*all!*—see the essential importance of wealth eventually—and Sherry found it rather refreshing to be in his presence.

"Let's have that martini, after all," she said.

"Good girl," Thomas said, and while this term of address would not do in the long run, she found it amusing in the present moment.

Chapter 21

Dr. Gannon's Party

While Dr. Gannon's original motivation in suggesting a party had been to make amends for his abrupt cancellation of the more adventuresome project, his chief delight now resided in the possibility that Jasmine's relationship with Max might be advanced. He had for some time been aware of Jasmine's improved appearance, first in a general, scarcely acknowledged way, then more specifically in the male manner which her age and his fatherly relationship to her obliged him to suppress, at least to the extent that it went beyond an acknowledgement that she was "growing up" and becoming "a lovely young woman." Now, after a three month's absence, the transformation was too striking to be ignored.

He was proud of Jasmine, as we all are of the good results of our own good deeds. Moreover, he was appreciative that she had never created by any misbehavior an ethical dilemma in which he might be tempted to disown her. Indeed, there were times, far too many in his opinion, when he would have preferred to claim her as his genetic heir than any one of the rightful three.

Max's interest in her therefore was auspicious. First, the young man's appreciation of her attractiveness confirmed that his own awareness of her was not unnatural. Moreover, it presented an opportunity to express his pride, appreciation, and affection for her in a manner that would avoid confusion about the wholesomeness of his motivations. Max Hill was a young man of intelligence, pleasant appearance, and good breeding. His family was financially secure, his conversation mature and entertaining, and his manners extraordinary. And what could recommend him more highly than his appreciation of Jasmine? What could show more nobility of character than his refusal to let either race or family history deter him? Therefore, he was not at all displeased when on the night of the party, he happened to look across from the patio to see Max and Jasmine standing before a living room window, him smiling and leaning close, and she, her hands folded in front of her, casting her eyes down and basking in his attention (for who would not bask in the light of such an adoring gaze?).

He returned to the patio table, still smiling with pleasure at the scene he'd witnessed.

"Your grandson is a very fine young man," he said, speaking to Mr. Lee.

Mr. Lee, whose hearing was somewhat impaired, accepted this with a thoughtful nod, but Mrs. Lee, to whom praise of her grandchildren, especially from prominent men, was the sweetest music, could not resist an opportunity to propose Sherry for similar recognition. "And Sherry has always been an absolute jewel," she said, lowering her forehead and batting her eyes.

Dr. Gannon, while disconcerted by the intimate tone of her voice, was far too much the politician not to compliment and flatter, where he saw compliment and flattery to be deserved, and he now lavished honest praise on the two young people's maturity and good judgment.

"And they are such a handsome pair, as well," Mrs. Lee said, nearly gushing over with pleasure.

Dr. Gannon who was loath to comment on the appearance of any person who was not a movie star or model, or who otherwise directly exploited good appearance for financial gain, did go so far as to say, "It certainly is a blessing to combine such good appearance with integrity and manners. For some reason, some young people seem to have gotten the impression that rudeness is a sign of distinction."

"Sherry looks almost the perfect image of her mother at her age, and people used to think that she and I were sisters. Sometimes we were even taken for twins!"

"Sherry does remarkably resemble you," Dr. Gannon said, relinquishing his habitual honesty in deference to what he perceived to be a degree of senility.

"She has exactly my figure," Mrs. Lee said.

"Too bad she never made any good use of it," Mr. Lee replied, directing his comment to the other men at the table. Mrs. Lee gave him an openly hostile look, to which he replied with a harrumph. Dr. Gannon and Mr. Blunt exchanged a look, which, well-mannered people that they were, they did not allow to develop into any detectable expression of meaning, but which they understood to reveal that they had taken the same meaning: yes, a man in his eighties might still harbor resentments over withheld affections.

All but Cynthia saw that it was better not to encourage the Lees further at this juncture. She, however, having experienced a remarkably trouble-free and satisfying marital life, mistook his meaning and said, "Oh, Mr. Lee, I think Yvette has absolutely lovely taste in clothing."

"Taste maybe," Mr. Lee grumbled, "but no taste *for it* . . . . It's probably better for the young boys now with the pill and all. A woman can't always be pleading about getting preggers or one thing or another. Not that it would have done any good in my case anyway."

Even Cynthia caught his meaning, and, expecting Mrs. Lee to be crushed by this public airing of laundry and in need of some comforting, she turned a kindly eye to her. The senility which had released their inhibitions in speech, however, seemed also to have fitted them with selective hearing. She beamed at her husband in a kindly way.

"And her _____ name's not Yvette, and never was," Mr. Lee said. "Never acted like an Yvette either."

"That's perfectly true," Mrs. Lee now said. "It's quite an interesting story how I acquired that name, and it involved a beau who Jimmy always resented."

"What a bunch of hooey. The guy was a decorator. Wrecked our old house and made it unlivable. Still haven't gotten rid of all the crapola she bought from him. Light in the loafers, too . . . ."

"His name was Armand. He was very artistic, and Jimmy always disliked him for that. He gave me the name Yvette because he said I had such a tiny waist. You see my real name is Eva, and Yvette means little Eva. The moment he called me that I knew that was the name I was really meant to have."

"You certainly have maintained your lovely waist," Cynthia said.

"When I was a girl, Jimmy could fit his two hands around my waist. Of course, his hands aren't what they used to be."

Mr. Lee grunted aloud at this, but apparently considered it not sufficiently important to make reply and said to Mr. Blunt, "Our son-in-law is in the movie business. A real bloomer-button, that one . . . . A thief, too."

"Jimmy, he is not a thief."

"When you take other people's money and spend it on five dollar cups of coffee and bottled water, and then cook the books so you don't show a profit and don't pay anybody back . . . . I don't know what you call it, but I call it theft."

"Jimmy put a little money into a movie venture," Mrs. Lee explained, "and the movie wasn't a success."

"Wasn't a success? It grossed over a hundred million dollars."

"The movie business is very complicated," Mrs. Lee offered. "Our son-in-law is a financial genius."

"Yeah, it's complicated. About as complicated as a mugging."

"Oh, Jimmy . . . . Don't pay any attention to him. He's just getting senile. Our daughter is married to a very influential man in Hollywood, and he couldn't possibly be the success he is if he weren't fair and square in everything he did. Of course, he's shrewd. He has to be. But everybody knows that some movies just aren't successful. It's a very risky business. Even those fine old Jewish fellows didn't always make money."

Up until now, the Gannons had known the Lees only as a quiet, pleasant couple who lived across the street. Of course, they were all interested to discover this streak of eccentricity and, except for Tina, amused by it. Any expression of concern for finances, however, unless it was expressed in the same offhand manner in which one might discuss the outcome of a sporting event, was a source of concern. The Lees' house was showing signs of deferred maintenance: the shaded north side of the roof was mossy, vines had overgrown the fences, and the entire exterior would have benefited from a fresh coat of paint. Gardeners, of course, kept the yard mowed, and there was nothing really disreputable in its appearance—at least, not yet. Might they be so poor that they would be forced to forego even basic maintenance? Such concerns were not uncommon in Arden Park, however, and usually came to nothing, especially as any family in true financial distress soon moved. Moreover, allowances were made for the elderly, and their eccentricities were indulged with atypical forgiveness.

Nonetheless, Mr. Hill's next comment brought relief and reassurance. "Hell, I knew I was going to lose the money. A man would have to be complete damn fool not to know. I only did it for Crystal's sake—you want to show your kids that you support them, even if they are on their third marriage. In our day, we didn't split up like that . . . ." Then, as he was wont to do, he again changed the subject. "Blue chips. That's what I say. And bonds. Gives a man a reason to watch the ticker every day."

As there were limits in Arden Park to the acceptable degree of household neglect, there were also limits to acceptable conversation. Women's ears were no longer treated as delicate, and some (Mr. Blunt was one of these) occasionally spoke crudely in their presence, but the coarsest of conversation was reserved for male company. Dr. Gannon was one of the few who defied this double standard. As his rigid sense of right behavior would have caused him to feel hypocritical in hiding one side of his personality from the other gender, he eschewed harsh language at all times. He was liberal enough in his views, however, to accept that other men might see advantages in supporting different codes of behavior for solely male and mixed company; and, in fact, despite his delicacy, he to some degree enjoyed the frankness and raw humor that sprang up among males. For example, in male company, a man might lament a lack of ardor on his wife's part, and be appreciated for his candor and sympathized with for his misfortune. Moreover, he would likely find other sufferers of the same fate. To raise the subject in mixed company, however, where feminine loyalty and spousal ire were likely to conspire to produce hours of domestic strife, was certainly taboo. In Mr. Lee's case this transgression had been amusing for all, but it had been excusable only because of his advanced age. Nor would it be safe to let it persist.

Even Harold Blunt, who was himself inclined to test the boundaries of acceptable conversation, appreciated this situation. It was he who redirected the conversation—by questioning Mr. Lee about his line of business.

"Hardware wholesaler. Great business," Mr. Lee replied. "Not one glamorous thing about it. It's not like the movies where people are willing to throw their money away to get into some starlet's panties."

They discussed for a while the economics of cabinet hinges, drawer pulls, and towel racks, but this was of little interest even to Mr. Lee, who professed to have forgotten almost everything about it, and then managed to recall details of the physical traits of young women who had worked for him fifty years previously.

If his purpose was to taunt his wife, he failed, as she paid him no attention whatsoever. Instead, she sought to engage the other three women in a discussion of her high blood pressure medication. The women's inattention encouraged the men to take more glee in Mr. Lee's appraisals than was discreet. In this, they were observed by Tina, who had tired of Mrs. Lee and had no interest in blood pressure in any case.

Tina had been fortunate in her sister's choice of a brother-in-law for her, as his habitually proper conduct seldom exposed her to masculine bonhomie, something which invariably provoked her ire. Now, the men's laughter, which to her both sounded and appeared smug, rushed a wave of anger right out the top of her skull, and before she'd had time to consider, it had carried with it the words, "Aren't you boys cute?"

In the silence that ensued, several events occurred simultaneously. First, Harold Blunt's past differences with Tina developed into a dislike that verged on detestation. Dr. Gannon felt an instant wave of shame, followed by embarrassment on behalf of the other men. A spark of irritation toward Tina then set to smoldering a coal bed of resentment toward her, and the words "I have to remain firm" again rose up to provoke him. Mrs. Blunt experienced a brief exhilaration at Tina's courage, then, casting a wary eye at her husband, said, "Boys will be boys." Mr. Blunt seemed about to reply when Mrs. Lee interrupted, saying, "I've never understood why boys act so silly, but you know, dear, it all works to our advantage in the end."

Exactly how this worked to women's advantage was sufficiently interesting a question—to the men because their instinctive paranoia about feminine exploitation had long led them to suspect this was true; to the women because it provided a perversely empowering view of their own positions—to forestall a cascade of emotion and rhetoric, one that might have caused a real breach. No final resolution of the issue occurred, of course, but Mrs. Lee's interjection had allowed the men to view themselves as the vigorous young men they'd once been, and the women to take pride in their maturity and gender-specific wisdom. In this, there was enough advantage to both sides to permit a temporary truce.

While it was a pleasant evening, with a gentle delta breeze offering an almost tropical comfort, dinner had been planned for the dining room as a precaution against hot weather. The different generations now assembled there, and Dr. Gannon was soon able to see that his hopes for the evening were well on the way to being realized. The young people's conversation was happy and animated, and Jasmine's flushed expression showed that even she was highly exhilarated. He gave Max Hill an encouraging look and, amid the general joy, directed a lively discussion at the table. The Lees had been under the influence of pre-dinner gin and tonics earlier and now had tired. Only they and Jasmine were quiet.

Dr. Gannon, attributing Jasmine's silence to her private joy, would have allowed her to escape his attempts at keeping all parties involved and everything lively. Max, however, was dogged in seeking her opinion and shifting the subject of conversation to her accomplishments.

"Did you all know," he asked, "that Jasmine is a National Merit Semi-Finalist?" He had elicited this information from her by asking her about her school, about her college plans, and then about her test scores. He had made the calculation himself that her test results were good enough to win the award, had received a confirmation from her that this was correct, and had gushed with delight at the discovery. "And she's a shoo-in for a finalist award. Sherry and I *combined* didn't score what she did."

"How could I not have heard of this?" Dr. Gannon exclaimed. "Jasmine, that's absolutely wonderful. Why didn't you tell me, Cynthia?"

"I didn't know," Cynthia answered, beaming with joy, and in the process appearing remarkably beautiful. "Though I do know that she gets letters every day from the best colleges. I think she's gotten at least ten from Harvard."

Because she had known that Phillip had been a finalist (he had been too wealthy to receive an actual scholarship), Jasmine had taken particular pleasure in being notified that she would receive consideration. She had not commented on it to her family, however, because the finalists would not be determined for some months, and she didn't wish to make too much of being only in contention for an award. As for the letters from colleges, she now understood that she was receiving special attention because of her mixed race. While none of the Gannon children had been unusually ambitious about their educations, some of their friends had sought admission to prestigious colleges with a passion that verged on the hysterical. Most had suffered disappointment. To make much of her preferment would have been as politic as gloating about the shape of her nose.

Phillip, who had not previously known himself to be jealous of his close connection with Jasmine, now found himself deeply pleased for her, but also surprised and perplexed that someone else had learned of it before he. Nonetheless, he gathered himself to say, "To receive such an award, especially considering the high school she goes to—if it was anybody but Jasmine, it would be totally unbelievable."

"My friend, Amy Shi, scored even better."

The restrictive commas between which she placed her friend's name were now apparent to Phillip, and he experienced a moment of angry regret that she might have experienced a school life so isolated from her real peers.

"I think she must be a very remarkable girl," Dr. Gannon said, "very remarkable indeed, and I know Cynthia and I would very much like to meet her someday."

"Have I met her already?" Cynthia now asked.

"You did. At my middle school graduation."

"I remember," Cynthia said, with amazement. "She was a very sweet and pretty girl. Weren't her parents . . . immigrants, weren't they?"

"They came from Taiwan when Amy was nine."

"Yes, I do remember," Cynthia said. "They were extremely nice. We really need to have them over sometime, David."

"And we shall."

Jasmine did not doubt the sincerity of either her aunt's or her uncle's intentions: Cynthia associated almost exclusively with people of her own social class and race, but this was very nearly entirely a matter of convenience rather than prejudice; and Dr. Gannon was resolutely liberal in all such matters. She herself foresaw some difficulties in a dinner with the Shis, however. The Shis were a very private family and maintained Chinese traditions that made social engagement challenging both for them and their hosts. For example, Amy had always felt obliged to reciprocate even the tiniest gesture from Jasmine, such as a sharpened pencil, with a gift. An obligation to respond proportionately to a dinner invitation in Arden Park could place a burden on their finances, which Jasmine surmised to be little more than adequate. Consequently, Jasmine did nothing to encourage her aunt and uncle further.

After this exchange, Jasmine hoped that the conversation would now turn to others' activities, but Max was determined that this should not happen.

"Did you know," he now asked the table, "that Jasmine placed second in her league in the 3200-meter run?"

"I certainly knew that she was a very fast runner," Cynthia said.

"And she was only a junior. She'll probably win it by a hundred yards next year. And knowing Jasmine, we'll probably see her in the Olympics a year or two after that."

Given that success in their sport is measured by a ruthless and ineluctable stopwatch, both Jasmine and Phillip knew how truly fulsome this praise was. She had indeed become a good runner, much better than the average girl on the street, but there is a vast difference between high school success and international stardom. Both understood exactly how insuperable that difference was.

"I enjoy running," she now said, glancing toward Phillip, "but I have no intention of continuing competitively after high school. There are many, many runners vastly better than I am, and I have no realistic hope of catching them."

"Listen to her," Max said, his adoring tone implying how admirable her modesty was, and how untrustworthy it made her words.

"I think I will do better to concentrate on a career."

"And have you decided what that will be, Jasmine?" Dr. Gannon asked.

"I would like to be a teacher."

"Teachers are the very future of the country," Dr. Gannon said.

"They're truly unsung heroes," Mrs. Blunt echoed, to which Cynthia added, "Every person has to find the thing that they like best."

"Like lying around the pool," Julia muttered to Sherry.

"Like taking care of a household and four children," Dr. Gannon said sharply, having overheard his daughter.

"Just kidding, Dad."

"You could make a helluva lot more money in business," Mr. Blunt said, ignoring Julia and directing himself to Jasmine.

"I don't think Jasmine is motivated by money," Max now offered.

"I know that I have to earn enough money to take care of myself, and I would like not to have to worry about my financial future; but I believe I can be content with less than I have now."

"For a while you could," Sherry said quickly, "but how long do you think it would stay like that?"

"I don't know," Jasmine answered honestly.

"If you want to be a teacher, I know you wouldn't let some old blowhard like me discourage you," Mr. Blunt said, "but I hope you'll consider that it's possible to do good in business just as it is in public service."

"Businesses are for making money," Pudge said, "it's not the same."

"They are for making money, and in the process they do a lot of good. They put roofs over people's heads, food in their mouths, medicine in their stomachs, and . . ."

" . . . every kind of trash on their televisions," Tina interjected.

This brought a cheerful laugh from all, and even a good-natured snicker from Mr. Blunt. "Television may not be business's proudest moment," he said, "but you can't deny that it puts on what most people want to see. If most people are idiots, there isn't much to be done about it."

"Maybe we ought to see to it that people see things that will lift them up instead of dragging them down into the gutter."

"Who exactly are *we*?" Mr. Blunt asked.

This was a conversation that held little promise for happy fellowship, especially considering previous tensions that had surfaced between Tina and Mr. Blunt, and Dr. Gannon, himself still irritated with his sister-in-law, sought to cut it short by saying, "And I thought I was coming home to escape politics . . . ."

This, too, was met with general laughter.

"Yes," Cynthia said, "we need to allow David a break from all that."

"We do, I'm sure," Mr. Blunt said, then added with a wry smile, "though I would like to know what your president is thinking about the trade agreement with Mexico."

This again generated laughter as Mr. Blunt had clearly not expected an answer, but, seeing an opportunity for agreement, Dr. Gannon answered, "My take is that he'll do everything he can to get it through."

"He'll have to fight the unions."

"Maybe not as much as you think."

"And the unions will try to convince everybody that it's a tool to oppress the poor."

"To some extent."

"Why is it that it's okay to treat people in poor nations like charity cases, but it's not okay to make them employees or business partners?"

"I agree with you that anti-trade ideology serves poor nations badly, but there is the reality of exploitation to consider," Dr. Gannon said, though it was apparent that his enthusiasm for the topic had waned. He turned quickly to Pudge. "And how about you Jeremy? What are your plans for next year?"

"Just to keep on keeping on, Dr. Gannon."

"And to pick up his grades, we hope," Mr. Blunt added.

Pudge, who had only just managed to graduate with his high school class, now planned to pass a year at a private preparatory college, which had as its purpose—in addition to earning a considerable profit for its owners—advancing its students to prestigious four-year universities. If his year there went well, he would be accepted, if perhaps not by one of the nation's first-tier universities, by one safely in the second tier, and this inauspicious beginning would be forgotten.

Dr. Gannon, now reminded of these less than glorious circumstances, thought it best not to reply directly to Mr. Blunt's statement. "Will you keep up your rugby?" he asked.

"Only club," Jeremy said, for his new school, wishing to avoid publicity, sponsored only intramural athletics.

"It was a terrific thing you boys did," Dr. Gannon said, by which all knew that he was referring to a state tournament which Pudge's team had won.

"It was cool," Jeremy affirmed.

"Very," Dr. Gannon replied.

There were murmurs of approval from all, then Cynthia asked, "Whatever happened with those Samoan boys?" The question referred to a much talked-about incident that had occurred during the past season. Jeremy's team had gotten into a brawl with a rival public school team comprised exclusively of boys of Samoan-heritage. While this incident might best have been forgotten, Cynthia had meant well. Pudge seemed often to be overlooked in conversation, and she had wanted to keep him a little longer at the center of attention.

Pudge shrugged. "Sometimes things get a little rough in the scrum. It's a rough sport."

"There was a little more gouging than was absolutely necessary," Mr. Blunt said, "and kicking you know where."

"*They* were horrible. They . . .," Chrissie began, but her father stopped her before she could begin detailing the offenses of her boyfriend's opposition

"Rugby sounds a lot like politics. A lot of gouging and nasty talk goes on in the scrum, but when it's over you have to forget about it."

Pudge nodded his agreement. "The thing is they were thinking we were all rich, white kids, and they hate losing to rich, white kids. But we didn't want them to think that just because we went to a private school, we were a bunch of wusses."

"We wouldn't have wanted them to think that, would we?" Tina said.

"Well, no," Dr. Gannon said, "we wouldn't have wanted them to think that Pudge and his teammates were quitters or that they were cowardly, and I think that's what he meant."

"Jeremy's team wasn't all white," Mrs. Blunt observed. "There were boys of every race and color."

"What's that got to do with anything anyway?" Mr. Blunt said.

The answer to this was so exceedingly complex that no one, not even Tina, could advance an answer. Pudge now continued, saying, "We played again before the season was over, and it was cool. They knew we weren't going to back off, and we knew they could play. We respected each other. It was all cool."

"Which is how it should be," Mr. Blunt offered.

Pudge having been given his time in the spotlight, the conversation was now turned to the Hills. Since Sherry's activities were restricted to social engagements and a rudimentary plan for attending university sometime in the future, the conversation quickly focused on Max's acting career.

While acting could not be considered a wise career choice, Dr. Gannon was in a charitable frame of mind, and found himself impressed with the maturity and professionalism with which the boy had chosen to pursue it.

"A famous name, of course, would make everything much easier," Max said.

"That's so unfair . . .," Julia began.

"Unfair or not, I understand it," Max continued. "Actors are hired to sell tickets. A famous name sells tickets. I don't have that, so I have to take it another direction. I have two other very useful things working for me. First, my stepfather's in the business, so that gets me in the door. Second, God gave me a great set of pipes. So I can always get voice-over work."

There was some discussion of "voice-over" work and what it entailed—primarily narrating television commercials, documentaries, and non-broadcast industrial films. Max was admirably reluctant to over-glamorize his roles, describing them as "bread-and-butter work." "Sometimes a radio spot will require a little acting," he said, "but for the most part it's just a matter of having a voice and being literate."

"I'm sure there's much more to it than that," Dr. Gannon said.

Max shook his head. "How many famous speaking voices are there?" he asked.

The group struggled to name three, and even these were known for acting roles as well.

"But how many famous actors are there?"

There were, of course, dozens, even hundreds.

"And how many of those have great speaking voices?"

This was a question that none had considered, so Max made the final point for them. "Voice isn't that important. It's the combination that matters, the look and voice together that create the whole gestalt . . . . So, voice-over is just a way of keeping in the hunt for acting roles. And from there I'd eventually like to go on to directing and producing."

"God, you'd be *so* good in movies," Julia said.

All were inclined to agree with this sentiment, even Dr. Gannon, who said, "And I thought politics was a tough business . . . . But if anybody can make a success of it, I'm sure you can, and I look forward to turning on the television one day and saying, 'There's that grandchild of the Lees who spent that summer with us.'"

"There are never any guarantees in the business," Max said. "In fact, do you know who would be the closest to a sure thing of anyone?"

No one knew exactly to what he was referring, and the query was met with blank looks.

"Jasmine!" he answered, causing everyone to laugh, because his answer so transparently betrayed the subject to which his mind was compelled to return. "I'm completely serious," he said. "Her face is the perfect distillation of . . . of . . . goodness. Though 'goodness' isn't a big enough word to describe it. It's truth. It's beauty. It's kindness. It's all there. In Jasmine's face. One look and you know it."

None could deny that Jasmine now seemed to project a luminescence, not only from her light eyes but also from her skin, which had developed a Poussin-like, deep, rosy under-glow. Her hair, which remained obsidian-dark and shining, she pulled back tightly from her forehead, giving her face an open and ingenuous quality, which was especially appealing when she was overtaken by spontaneous emotion, whether a laugh, a frown, or even a brown study. This irresistible prettiness was in part a matter of her being at a lovely age—she had developed the physical beauty of a woman but retained the facial expressions of a girl—it was in part a matter of her being Jasmine.

Now, she was deeply embarrassed, and, despite the compliment, miffed. This caused her skin to brighten further and her eyes to flash, and induced her to raise her head slightly in that almost regal pose with which she had learned to meet the indignities boys at her school hurled about.

"If she spoke French," Max continued. "Rohmer would snap her up in a heartbeat as his latest ingenue. It wouldn't matter that nothing ever happens in his movies. He could just put the camera on Jasmine. Her face says, 'This is exquisite, perfect. This is what's good in the world.'"

"Even if what you say were true," Jasmine now said, "which I know perfectly well it isn't, I should never want to be judged on my appearance alone."

The severity of her speech, which was not at all modulated by her normal gentleness of tone, momentarily quieted everyone. So consumed was Max, however, that his enthusiasm soon pushed him to speak out again.

"But it's exactly because your appearance reflects exactly what you are that it's so perfect! There's not one false thing in how you look or who you are. They're perfect reflections of each other. That's why it's so . . . just . . . wonderful!"

Max's uncharacteristic lack for words provoked a strong burst of laughter from Sherry, Thomas, Pudge, and Phillip. The adults, especially Cynthia, who so deeply felt the significance of Jasmine's triumph that she was near to tears, shared their delight. Julia's and Chrissie's smiles were less spontaneous. Both had for a time felt a claim to Max's affections. Neither had ever considered Jasmine to be a rival in anything whatsoever. That she might be a competitor in something as deeply their purview as romance did not yet so much incite their competitive instincts as it perplexed them. This whole performance might, they reasoned, be a tactic of Max's, a deliberate charade designed to incite their jealousy, or perhaps to win the favor of their parents. He appeared sincere, of course, even to the point of fluster, but then he was a trained actor and was supposed to be good at dissembling.

Unfortunately, this explanation, gratifying as it would have been to either, failed to be completely convincing, primarily because, if Max was acting, he was acting too well. Consequently, in order to preserve happy images of themselves, they independently reached similar conclusions: that Max had been taken by an embarrassingly childish infatuation. This event obliged them to reduce their opinion of him and consider themselves lucky not to have gotten more deeply involved with him than they had.

Their thoughts had followed such similar patterns that they were now able to exchange a private look of awed derisiveness that was understood by both immediately; and Julia was so forward as to say aloud: "Isn't *that* just peachy."

The situation was regarded by many in the group to be "peachy" indeed, and they greeted Julia's witty insight with approving laughter rather than the disapproving silence it deserved. Chrissie understood the thrust of her sister's remark perfectly, yet she laughed as well, albeit with a different pitch.

Jasmine was not unaware of her cousins' more subtle methods of one-upmanship. When she discovered Julia's and Chrissie's haughtiness directed at herself, it could be easily enough ignored. Now, when she saw it directed at Max, the single person she would have considered most unlikely to be targeted in the past, she felt a moment of sympathy for him. After all, he had spoken without concern for appearances. He had been willing to sacrifice his pride and to face the contempt of his peers in order to make his point, one which, objectively taken, had to be considered highly flattering to her. Moreover, to all appearances he had acted more sincerely and more directly from the heart than she had ever known him to act before. If he had acted out of character, he had chosen a new character that in many ways was to be preferred to the old. Of course, she could not forget incidents she had witnessed in the past. To do so, would be folly. But might she in some way have misinterpreted? And if she hadn't been mistaken was she not obliged to be forgiving? She felt no affection for Max and did not believe that she ever could, yet she could feel sympathy. She had promised her uncle that she would treat him with more kindness, and this she would do.

As for Max, never before had he experienced himself to be so intensely motivated. The only subject of conversation that interested him was Jasmine. No view pleased him unless she was in the foreground. Her voice intoxicated him. He could feel the loveliness of her skin and eyes in his stomach. Yet there was nothing ignoble or wrong in any of this. Yes, he wanted to be close to her. Yes, he wanted to be special to her. Yes, he wanted to have her exclusive attention and for her to want his. But that was enough. To be close to her, special to her, to have her to keep and cherish, this was what he now most wanted in the world. And because she was good, so very good, and because he wanted only for her happiness and success, it followed that he must be good as well. She was making him a better person—indeed, he already felt himself changed. He was convinced of it. It only remained for him to prove to her that it was so.

The idea of the group sing had lost luster with a day's consideration and was dropped; nor were the young people of Arden Park much inclined to dance, at least not without the protection of a large crowd and the stimulant of alcohol. Max would have liked very much to teach Jasmine to dance, both because the position of mentor appealed to him and because he would have liked touching her hands, arms, and hips. Instead, he had to be satisfied with finding a place on the couch next to her and lavishing questions upon her about her likes and dislikes, about her plans for her future, and finally—because his sister had advised him of her very strong affection for William—about her brother.

"He is in the army now," she said of her brother. "He's already received promotions, so I know that he's doing very well, but he says that his advancement will be limited unless he attends college. He's wanted to attend the academy, but in his last letter he didn't write of that, and I worry that he may be losing hope."

"I'm sure he'd make an ideal candidate."

"I'm not certain how you could know that without having met him, but I thank you for saying so, especially since I agree with you."

"I know because your uncle has told me about him, and he's never said anything but great things. But I also know because he's your brother, and any brother of yours has to be a fantastic person."

"Oh, no. You shouldn't compare him to me. He's a much stronger and more mature person than I am. I had the good fortune to grow up here with the Gannons, while he's been nearly completely on his own since he was fifteen years old. Yet he hasn't changed. He's still kind and considerate, and he hasn't become at all bitter or resentful. I can only wish that under the same circumstances I would have done as well."

"You would have," he said, touching her knee. "In your own way, you've done every bit as well."

"He's done everything so completely on his own, while I've always had my aunts and uncle and cousins to support me. And, of course, Phillip has always been as kind as any brother. I can't imagine how it would have been had I been so alone."

Max listened carefully and admiringly to this statement, then began to question her further about William, asking not only about him generally, but desiring to know specific details as well, such as his past stations, his current rank, his birth date, his present address, and even his military serial number. This curiosity would have seemed more queer had Jasmine not seen his questioning as an effort to demonstrate his interest and concern. She saw no harm in answering, and as William remained her favorite subject of conversation, she was happy even to go to her room to find for him a picture, one which, to her surprise, he asked to borrow.

The day after the party, Dr. Gannon was obliged again to leave for Washington. While she had never ceased being a little afraid of her uncle and could not avoid feeling some relief at his departure, Jasmine was not insensible to the kindnesses he had done her during his visit, and she expressed her good-byes with tender feelings.

Dr. Gannon's parting was a real sorrow to his wife, who enjoyed his presence and was increasingly aware of the advantages of his advice and wisdom over her sister's. His children, who had not completely forgiven him for canceling the party, were absent at his departure.

It was now well into August, when the heat of Arden Park grew most wearisome. The young people began plotting escape. Surprisingly, Max Hill was the first to leave. He called a cab to take him to the airport, hinted to his sister that he might be going so far as to visit his mother and stepfather, and offered Jasmine such a tender good-bye that she took some hope it would be a final one. Then, at the very last minute, when the weather turned beastly hot, Sherry decided that she would accompany her brother to Los Angeles.

Thomas also wished to depart for Southern California. He would need a car there and was obliged to drive. As the trip required nearly ten hours, he was eager for company and invited Phillip to ride with him. Phillip, having college acquaintances near Los Angeles who had offered invitations for the summer, agreed. It was debated whether it would be more enjoyable to travel in Phillip's Porsche, which lacked air conditioning, or in Thomas's less sporty but more comfortable Volkswagen. In a fit of youthful, devil-may-care exuberance, the sports car was chosen.

Jasmine found opportunity for one additional conversation with Phillip before he left, as they went running together the morning before his departure. While the two sat on the front step and performed their pre-run rituals of smoothing socks, lacing shoes, and light exercise, she asked how long he would be in Los Angeles.

"A week or so. It depends." Then, as though sensing this were not explanation enough, he went on. "It depends on what my friends are doing. And on what Sherry and Max have planned. I've never spent much time in LA. I doubt that I'll like it."

"If the company is good, I'm sure you will."

"Yes," Phillip said, turning to Jasmine, "and Sherry and Max always keep things interesting, don't they?"

"They do."

"We were lucky to have them here." He turned to observe her response, but this required no answer, and Jasmine made none. He turned back again. "Sherry's told me that Max really likes you." Jasmine again made no answer. "I know he's not Prince Charming exactly . . . ."

"He looks every bit as nice as any person needs to."

Phillip smiled at this, taking it as an encouragement. "And he seems to be a pretty charming guy."

"Certainly he is to many people."

"And he's working very hard at being charming to you."

"Is he?"

"Yeah, he is."

"If I've done anything to encourage him, it wasn't intentional."

"I'm not sure you have done anything. You've treated him like . . . well, you haven't exactly treated him very well."

"I haven't meant to be rude."

"No, but you haven't exactly been very friendly either."

"I'm not sure I wish him to be a friend."

"Sure you do. Max is a pretty decent guy. He's done interesting things. He knows interesting people . . . . Besides that, he can hardly go five minutes without asking some question about you or making some comment about how smart and good you are. Why not give him a chance?"

For one brief moment, Jasmine was tempted to describe what she had heard on the shore of Lake Tahoe, but she very soon realized how far beyond the two of them the ramifications might extend. Phillip could hardly welcome the news as it would create a constraint between himself and Sherry. Moreover, if Julia were somehow to find out, the rift between her and Chrissie might reopen. In no case, could the revelation earn her any goodwill from her housemates. And all of this would be for the sake of an encounter that to all appearances had been relegated to the distant past. Wasn't it better to allow people to correct their errors privately? Didn't we all at times benefit by not having our indiscretions observed and reported?

"I know he may not always have behaved exactly the way you think he should have," Phillip now went on to say, "but you know, Jasmine, your standards are pretty high. Sometimes, as you get older, you may find out that you have to think about things a little differently."

"You're advising me that I need to grow up," Jasmine said, without resentment, for she had been troubled over just this possibility—that her feelings were immature.

"No . . . I'm advising that you *will* grow up. Circumstances change, and things that seem bad now won't. Like the party, the way we did it, that was wrong, but it didn't have to be. There isn't anything wrong with fun."

"I could never have fun knowing that I was deceiving Uncle David."

"Of course you couldn't, and that's part of what we all admire so much about you. But people are sometimes stronger than you give them credit for. They aren't hurt as easily as you think."

"I felt that David was hurt."

"He was, but he's going to get over it, and probably sooner than you think." Here Phillip paused for a moment; then, no doubt feeling the lack of respect in this statement, he continued. "We didn't foresee how things might turn out, not the rest of us. But you recognized the danger ahead of time. That's the way you are. You look ahead . . . and you think of others. And because of that, you make us all better. I know Max feels the same way as I do. That's one of the reasons he's so impressed with you. He wants to be a better person. You could make him one."

That there was room for improvement in Max Hill's character was beyond question, but Jasmine resisted a temptation to criticize. "He and I have had very different histories," she said. "He's older and more experienced in the world. It's natural that we would see things differently."

"And it's natural that as time passes and you understand each other better, you will begin to see things more alike . . . . He's fascinated with you, you know. He wants to understand what makes you tick. And I know that the more he understands, the more impressed he will be."

Jasmine gave no answer to this.

"His and Sherry's home life hasn't always been ideal, you know. His mother's remarried several times. His current stepfather isn't very good to her, and Sherry says he treats Max more like a frat brother than a father. She thinks that's had a very bad influence. At times, it's made him disrespectful. Since he's met you, though, that's completely reversed. She says he's much more considerate of everyone, even their grandparents."

"I hope that he is, but I'm sure I've had nothing to do with it."

"People do change. They really do," Phillip said, perhaps in anticipation of a skeptical reaction from her or perhaps to forestall one of his own. "Sherry thinks coming here is the best thing that ever happened to him."

Jasmine for a second time suppressed an observation that the Hills' arrival was perhaps not equally fortuitous for all; nor did she voice her opinion that temporary changes in character outnumbered permanent ones by ten to one. Instead, their pre-run preparations already having been over-extended, she set out towards the sidewalk.

To Jasmine's surprise, Phillip now suggested that they run past her school. The campus being in a neighborhood that lacked trees and other esthetic qualities, they had never before run there, and it being in a neighborhood to which Arden Park residents rarely ventured, Phillip had never previously visited there. Jasmine cautioned him that there was not a great deal to see, that the school was much like any other public school, littered and poorly painted, with weedy, unedged lawns trampled mostly to bare dirt, yet Phillip insisted.

The pace they ran was an easy one for both, and as they started off, Phillip was cheerful and talkative. He soon grew more somber. The street crossed a set of railroad tracks, then passed under a freeway overpass. While the distance was only a little more than a mile, the transition was striking. The houses along the street began now to be fenced with woven wire tough enough for a prison yard, the sidewalks and the grass strips along the curbing having been abandoned to the street. Whereas in Arden Park the streets were lined with tall sycamores and elms, here all but a few of the trees had died, and those that remained were parched and dying. Drifts of litter clogged the gutters.

After a few blocks, the houses gave way to an occasional small shopping arcade. Most of the shops were closed. Many had boarded-up windows. Then, finally, just near the school, they passed a corner grocery, outside of which—already at eight in the morning— a group of black men sat smoking and drinking. As they passed by, the men smiled at them admiringly, and not unkindly, then hooted and laughed aloud.

"And how do you get here every day?" Phillip asked.

"I bike," Jasmine said. "Or if it's raining I walk."

"No one gives you a ride?"

"Someone would if I asked. I like walking."

"But you get all wet."

Jasmine laughed. "Have you ever heard of a raincoat? I like walking in the rain best."

"Just the same, you shouldn't walk here. It isn't safe."

Jasmine could not argue that it was safe. Though hundreds of other students walked to school every day as well, safety is always a relative concept, and walking near the school was not nearly so safe as walking in Arden Park. Indeed, Jasmine would never have chosen on her own to run past the school or into the neighborhoods surrounding it.

"I do understand that I need to be careful," she said, "but there are always other students on the streets. I might not want to walk here alone at night, but during school hours it isn't overly dangerous."

"As if other students would protect you," Phillip said quietly.

"Some of them would," Jasmine answered.

"And some of them are probably exactly who you need to fear most."

She couldn't deny this.

"Has anything ever happened? Have you ever been threatened or harassed in any way?"

As they were passing the exact hedge from which Jasmine had once been obliged to extract both herself and her bicycle, she could not in good conscience fail to report the event now.

"Once when I was on my bicycle, I was forced off the road by a man in a pickup," she said, "but I wasn't injured in any way. I think, though, that it was a random incident that might as easily have occurred anywhere else. I don't know that the neighborhood had anything to do with it."

"You weren't hurt?"

"No, and your bicycle wasn't even damaged."

"Did you tell Cynthia or David?"

She admitted that she hadn't, explaining, "I wasn't injured. Nothing like it has ever happened since."

"They should never have made you come here," Phillip said, his face now gaunt with anger. "Cynthia and David had no business making you come here."

"I would not have chosen to go anywhere else," Jasmine protested.

They were now approaching the school grounds, and Phillip slowed to a walk. The breezeways were dusty, the corners cluttered with windblown litter, the lawns mostly dirt. The buildings were decorated with spray-painted graffiti, which was not without an artistic touch, a sort of exotic quality of design, and if it weren't for a striking smell of urine, they might have stopped.

"It isn't the buildings that make the school," Jasmine explained. "What's important is that you're able to learn what you need to learn."

"Are you able to do that?"

"Yes," she said, but reflection forced a more honest response from her. "Mostly, I am."

While there were a few other diligent students and a number of classmates who would have done well had they made an effort, Jasmine was aware that she and Amy were by a considerable margin the two best students in her school. Chrissie and Julia, in contrast, were better than average but far from spectacular performers among their peers. Nevertheless, when Jasmine scanned their texts, it was apparent that the level of material they were covering was more advanced in every subject.

"I think that I'm learning enough," Jasmine now said. "Of course, it's not exactly the same as a private school. I may have some catching up to do later on. But I am learning other things."

"What sorts of things?"

"About getting along with other people. Learning that what I accomplish will be up to me in the end."

Dr. David Gannon believed himself, with considerable justification, to have accomplished what he had through hard work; John Gannon, Phillip's father, had inherited much greater wealth and could not deny that he was a product of the opportunities that money affords. The not uncommon result was that, despite both being nominal Democrats, John Gannon's was considerably the more liberal household. Thus, if he questioned the rewards of daily interaction with boors and criminals, Phillip could not dismiss the liberal truism that encountering different types of people is a useful educational experience. Instead, he challenged Jasmine's second assertion.

"Do you mean that your teachers don't challenge you?" he asked.

"They try to. They want to."

"But they don't."

It would have sounded vain for her to explain to him that, had more advanced classes been offered or if more had been demanded of students in classes, only she and Amy would have benefited. Instead, she didn't reply.

"So you're saying that your teachers do the best they can under the circumstances, which consist of broken-down equipment, old or missing books, broken windows, and all this . . . mess."

"They usually get the windows fixed quickly," Jasmine said; then in reply to Phillip's chortle, she went on, "but poor classrooms and old books are only an inconvenience. Anyone who wants to learn can."

This statement denied another liberal truism which Phillip had often heard voiced in his home: that all children, if given the opportunity, want to learn. He tried now to reconcile her statement with that view, saying, "Isn't it more a matter of their not having been given a fair opportunity?" He then gestured again to his surroundings, "I mean, look at this."

"Some students may not have the foresight to recognize that education would benefit them and some don't believe themselves able to do schoolwork, but our teachers always tell them otherwise. I think many students choose not to believe them. They don't like to study, and they don't want to be in school."

"But isn't that the school's fault?"

"The school doesn't require students to skip classes, sleep in class, call each other names, take drugs, or fight with each other. Our teachers plead with them not to."

"But look at this place!"

"Abraham Lincoln learned his letters by writing on a shovel with a piece of charcoal."

Phillip laughed. "I wouldn't put too much faith in that story."

Jasmine, who had treasured this story since her grandmother had read an account of it to her when she was a small child, realized for the first time that there might be an element of myth in it. "If it's a myth," she now said, feeling somewhat abashed, "I think it's a useful one."

They resumed their run, looping back into Arden Park, immediately feeling the relief of the quieter—and cooler—tree-lined streets and their relative safety and tranquillity.

Nearly seventeen, Jasmine would soon be a year past the minimum age to drive, and Phillip now said, "At least, you can start driving to school. You can't walk through that neighborhood anymore."

"Thank you for thinking of me," Jasmine said, "but I love riding my bike"

That evening they were eating pizza in front of the television—something that never would have happened had Dr. Gannon been home—when Phillip began describing his morning run to his aunts. Though both women often criticized the violence and inanity of television programming, either could quickly become engrossed, and they now answered distractedly, giving perfunctory moans of distress at the details Phillip recounted, while at the same time watching a situation comedy featuring sex and poop jokes. When he concluded, however, by saying, "Jasmine has to have a car to drive," they immediately turned their full attention to him. Tina's eyes momentarily flashed anger at her sister's nephew; then remembering whom she was speaking to, she caught herself.

"Of course, it would be lovely if there were some way for Jasmine to have a car," she said, "but Dr. Gannon felt—and I have to agree with him—that it isn't quite practical."

"You've discussed it with him?" Phillip asked.

"Maybe not is so many words, but yes, we have discussed the issue of cars many time, and . . ."

"I think if he knew . . . I *know* that if he knew what it was like there—the neighborhood that Jasmine has to walk through—he'd agree with me." Tina looked to her sister for support, but Cynthia appeared astonished and speechless. Phillip continued, "It's not safe for Jasmine to walk in that neighborhood. A group of men hooted at her today, even when I was with her. I'm afraid to think of what happens when nobody's with her."

Tina turned to Jasmine. "Is it really so awful, Jasmine?"

"I think it appears more dangerous to Phillip than it really is," Jasmine said. "It's possible to avoid situations . . . ." She intended to explain how she crossed the street to avoid passing through loitering groups, how she waited to be sure other students were near and watching before she passed certain corners, and how she never left the main route, but Phillip interrupted.

"But why should she have to worry about it? Even if nothing ever happens, it's not worth it. Just walking through that neighborhood puts you on your guard. She shouldn't have to do that. She should be studying or daydreaming or talking with her friends, not thinking about how to avoid getting . . . mugged or something. You know that she was once run off the road when she was bicycling to school?" Cynthia's baffled look revealed that she did not know. "You didn't know," he went on, "just like you don't know what it's like to go to that school."

"I'm sure if it couldn't have been all that serious," Tina said, with a glance toward Jasmine, "or we would have heard some word of it."

"How can being run off the road by a truck not be serious?"

"A truck!" Cynthia exclaimed.

"It was only a pickup," Jasmine now said, "and I don't believe his intent was to hit me. He probably just saw it as some kind of a prank."

"The kind of prank that gets people killed," Phillip said.

"Isn't that a little extreme, Phillip?" Tina said. "She wasn't injured after all . . . . You weren't injured were you, Jasmine?"

Jasmine confirmed that she wasn't.

"She may not have been hurt the last time," Phillip said, "but that doesn't mean she won't be the next. It just can't go on. You can't let her walk or bike over there. It's irresponsible."

The word "irresponsible" was, no doubt, too inflammatory, and, had it been spoken by anyone else, it's unlikely that Tina would have been able to refrain from voicing the anger that so brightly colored her face. Instead, she said, "I think that's unfair to your aunt," with the dignified but remonstrative lift of her chin which her nieces and nephews well understood to indicate that she felt herself to have been injured.

"I apologize," Phillip said, "but I know that if you saw the situation as I do, you would agree with me. Jasmine needs a car. Julia and Chrissie both had cars as soon as they were sixteen, and they had much less need of them than Jasmine."

Both Tina's mounting hostility and her Aunt Cynthia's distress were apparent, but Jasmine struggled to find words to relieve them. She began to explain that only a tiny percentage of her schoolmates had cars to drive, despite facing the same circumstances as she, but then realized that this would appear to be a plea for sympathy.

"Phillip, I appreciate your concern," she finally said, casting a steady look toward him. "I really am grateful. But I've never for a moment experienced any real need for a car or any particular desire to have one. I'm quite content with things exactly as they are."

"That's just the problem," Phillip said, anger still causing his voice to tremble. "You're too content."

Cynthia now appeared lost, as though she had walked in on a conversation in progress and could not quite take hold of its subject. Jasmine took pity on her.

"How could I be anything but content?" she said. "I live in a lovely home in a beautiful neighborhood, I'm well provided for, and I live among people who love and care for me. Surely I'm the luckiest orphan who ever lived."

Even a thousand past incidents of indolence, vanity, and self-absorption could not subvert the warmth and tenderness that appeared in Cynthia's smile once her sympathies were aroused. Now, stirred by the word "orphan," one she could never really attach to her Jasmine, and feeling the kindness of both her niece's words and her nephew's nobility in trying to protect her, she cast her most proud and grateful smile on them.

"Phillip, I would never, ever want to put Jasmine in danger. If I thought . . ."

"I know that, Cynthia. That's why I've told you."

"And we *will* do something," Cynthia now said.

Had the Gannon family van been available, she would surely have offered it for Jasmine's use now; but car maintenance having been neglected in Dr. Gannon's absence, the van had suffered major engine failure just after the trip home from the lake. To the satisfaction of the children, it had been towed off to a charity.

"She'll drive the Volvo," Cynthia announced. "I seldom go out anyway." It was true that Cynthia liked staying at home and that on many days Dr. Gannon's Volvo went unused, but the suggestion was wildly impractical. No adult woman in Arden Park—much less the wife of Dr. Gannon—could be marooned for eight hours a day with no car. Perhaps seeing her folly, she went on, "I fully intend to look into this. I'm going to drive over to that school and see exactly what you're talking about. And if necessary, I'll talk to the principal, even the school board or the police, if it comes to that. I promise you that we will not allow Jasmine to be endangered in any way."

"Absolutely not," Tina echoed. She got up now and moved off towards the kitchen, saying, "To think that anyone could suspect us of being callous about Jasmine's safety"

Cynthia now smiled calmly, the issue to her mind being fully resolved. "Jasmine is a treasure to us. And, of course, it was Tina who went all the way to Tennessee to bring her back to us." To her dismay, her nephew persisted.

"I don't see how talking to the principal or school board, or even the police, will accomplish anything," he said, "but I do believe there is a solution."

"A solution?"

"Yes, I've decided to give Jasmine my car."

Cynthia sat up quickly and looked desperately toward the kitchen.

"To give Jasmine your car?" she said.

"Not I guess literally to give her the car, but to give it to her to use. I can't take it with me to Providence. Mom and dad are gone and have no use for it anyway. Really, Jasmine would be doing me a favor to keep it running."

"To keep it running?" Cynthia repeated.

"It's not good for a car to sit unused. And this way Jasmine will have a car to use. It's absolutely no inconvenience to me to let her use it. In fact, I'd feel good about having the opportunity to do something useful for her."

"Well, I don't know," Cynthia mumbled, while looking desperately towards the kitchen. "Of course, it's very kind of you to offer. You've always been so considerate of Jasmine. But automobiles are such a big responsibility."

Tina could now be seen through the doorway, and Cynthia quickly called to her. She recounted the nature of Phillip's offer, concluding, "Of course, it's very kind of him to offer, and isn't it just like Phillip to be so thoughtful? But isn't it . . . cars and all . . . accidents, repairs, and whatnot . . . isn't it all . . . wouldn't it all be rather complicated?"

"Impossible," Tina said.

"Why do you think so?" Phillip asked slowly, a steely constraint not quite containing the anger in his voice. "It's my car, after all. I know that my father would have no objection—it was his originally. It seems like this would be the best possible use for it."

"The insurance alone would be ghastly," Tina said. "Not to mention repairs, gasoline . . . . Where would we park it?" When photographed or displayed in a soft light, Tina's angular face could be nearly as attractive as her sister's. Now, as she glared toward Jasmine, perhaps picturing the size of the Gannons' driveway, which could park a cavalcade of limousines, a slight jutting of her jaw and a narrowing of her eyes, turned her face far from pretty. "Jasmine doesn't have a license," she finally said, "which makes it out of the question."

"I don't see why I couldn't teach her to drive," Phillip replied.

"I'm sure Dr. Gannon would never agree to such a thing," Tina said.

"Driving school then," Phillip said. "Chrissie and Julia managed it well enough, I'm sure Jasmine can get through too."

"Driving schools aren't free you know," Tina enjoined.

"But if the cost could somehow be managed . . . ?"

"Insurance is abominable . . . . It's impossible."

Phillip now turned to Cynthia. "I know we can find a way to manage the costs. And I can guarantee you, dangerous as cars may be, Jasmine will be much safer driving to school than walking through that neighborhood. I feel sure that if Uncle David had seen what I did he would agree with me. Would you please discuss it with him?"

"Certainly I can talk with him about it, but . . . ."

"The insurance couldn't be managed in any case," Tina said.

"I'm sure my father would be more than happy . . . ."

"We just couldn't allow that," Tina said, "and we haven't even discussed the cost of driving school."

Some days earlier, when they had made a visit to the family's athletic club, Phillip and Jasmine had seen a sign advertising a babysitting position. Jasmine's good manners and quiet demeanor, especially as bolstered by her family connection and her improving appearance, had won the trust, confidence, and good will of club members and staff alike. Jasmine had noted to Phillip that it was a job she might like to have, and Phillip had assured her it was a job she likely could get.

"If it couldn't be managed otherwise," he now said, "I'm sure Jasmine could get the child care job at the club. That sign's already been up for three weeks."

"I'm sure she could," Cynthia said. "Everyone at the club says such lovely things about her." She cast one of her bright, always heartening, smiles on Jasmine.

"There may be age requirements . . .," Tina said.

"Sixteen," Phillip said. "It was posted on the flyer."

"Or other requirements," Tina concluded.

Phillip turned to Cynthia. "You will talk to Dr. Gannon?"

"Certainly."

"Tonight?"

"Yes, tonight."

"I have your promise, Aunt Cynthia."

"I will talk to him."

Pressed as she was by her promise, Cynthia spoke with her husband that evening. To her surprise, he agreed readily to Phillip's proposal, even insisting that Cynthia use the family account to pay for both the insurance and the lessons, concluding, "My goodness, Jasmine's sixteen now. It's hard to believe."

As for the babysitting job, Cynthia quietly advised that the job ought to go to someone more needy—that Jasmine's taking it might be resented by some of the less affluent parents in the club. Jasmine had used a nearly identical argument to justify withdrawing from the summer program for minority students three years earlier, and she could hardly object now.

Chapter 22

William Discovers a Lost Uncle

Jasmine was relieved to have Max away and to be spared his attentions; and as she was generally content with keeping her own company, she would have suffered no hardship had the exodus not taken Phillip with it as well. As it was, she could resist neither wondering about Phillip's activities and the extent of Sherry's involvement nor chastising herself for taking a meddling interest.

Happily, only a few days after Phillip's and Thomas's departure, a new development interrupted her speculations. For a number of years, William had been attempting to trace their grandmother's and grandfather's ancestries. Now, through the internet, he had made contact with a California man who seemed to be a near relative of their great grandfather. Evidence suggested that the grandfather of a Mr. Reginald Johnson of Northern California had been their own great grandfather's younger brother, making Mr. Johnson their second cousin, once removed. William had contacted the gentleman, who was a retired railroad man, and whom he described as being polite and welcoming, if perhaps somewhat elderly. All evidence of family connection, including not only the old man's memories but also dates and locations of birth, had proved encouraging, and Reginald Johnson had generously invited both of them to visit him in his home. Best of all, he lived within a day's drive of Arden Park.

Five years had now passed since her grandmother's death, and Jasmine's memories of her had grown more distant and dreamlike; but she continued to experience moments of deep longing for her. Indeed, in some respects, her fading memories made the ache more intense, as she could not always identify its source or recall consoling moments. Of course, she understood that no actual blood relation existed between Mr. Johnson and her Granny, but she could not prevent herself from hoping that he would help her reclaim memories.

His military position allowed William to board a flight quickly and to rent a car despite being two years below the normal age limit, and it was only a matter of forty-eight hours between the time Jasmine learned of her brother's discovery of Mr. Johnson's existence and William's arrival in Arden Park. The joy of seeing him would have been quite enough to permit her to cast aside other cares, but combined with the prospect of a trip to visit lost family, it made her positively jubilant. She ran out to meet the small car, and when William emerged, cast herself upon him so forcefully that he was obliged for a moment to carry her. William was not unusually tall, only just six feet, but he seemed both tall and strong to his sister. His green eyes might at first appraisal have seemed cold to some, but to Jasmine, they were full of the warmth of love. His hair was cropped short in the military fashion, his bearing was soldierly, and his skin, a little darker than her own, suggested robust good health. Best of all, the fullness of his lips and softness of his smile reminded her of Granny.

While Jasmine thought her brother remarkably handsome and would have liked to display him to the entire household, Tina had gone out shopping with her nieces. It was Cynthia to whom she most wanted to show him off, however, and she was gratified that her aunt greeted him with one of her warmest smiles. William noted once again that Cynthia reminded him of their mother. Jasmine knew that Cynthia loved her, that she always endeavored to understand her, and that she was slow to take offense. Thus, they could plead William's short leave and resist invitations to rest, dine, or swim. William took time only to change his uniform, which he was required to wear while traveling, and they were off on their adventure.

In her excitement, Jasmine had not fully appreciated the extent of their drive (they would be a full five hours on the road); yet, when she did, she was made only more jubilant. She would have William completely to herself! For five hours! Such joy!

The highway led directly north up the great Sacramento Valley. Early on, they sailed between fields of golden grain or tall green rice, and later past orchards, but these soon gave way to completely brown fields. In the winter and spring, this land would have been green and full of wild flowers or grazing cattle; but now the cattle were gone and the pastures had been reduced to dust and weeds. There was little to recommend this scenery, but neither of the Johnsons had passed this way before, and both were exhilarated to be in each other's company. They spoke admiringly of the grandeur of the mountains which could just be seen in the distance through a hazy pall of smog and smoke, of the vast stretches of unpopulated land, and of the remarkable, astonishing intensity of the sun.

They arrived at the small town where their relation resided and set out to follow the directions he had given. After turning down several narrow streets, they realized that all the people along the streets, including several small children who played quietly in their yards under the very hot sun, were brown-skinned. They passed one corner lot where the house sat on bare dirt, had a single cinderblock for a step, and a sagging screen door from which all the screening had been removed. Most of the houses were much better kept, but the nicer yards, the ones that offered flowers, mowed grass, and fruit trees, were surrounded by woven wire fencing that created an unfortunate industrial appearance.

Dismayed but not disheartened, they parked themselves in front of their uncle's home—for they had decided they ought to call him "Uncle" in deference to his age. This house, Jasmine surmised, had once been one of the nicest in the neighborhood, perhaps the very nicest of all. Its pretty gables were trimmed in bric-a-brac, and it was surrounded by the remnants of a white picket fence. Now, however, the porch was overgrown by privet bushes, and the leaf-clogged gutters overhead had sprouted a crop of annual grasses, which the summer heat had turned to dry tinder.

They studied the house, digesting the story told by its neglected garden and peeling paint, before lifting the gate, which seemed to be attached to the fence by nothing more than an overgrowth of jasmine vines. The wooden porch itself, though worn and worrisome, did not give way under their feet, and after a short wait, their knock was answered by a dim figure who opened the door a few inches and squinted past a safety chain.

William politely explained who they were, after which the door shut, the chain rattled as it was unhooked, and they were ushered into the surprising cool of a dark living room. They were very eager to see their uncle's face, as they wondered if they would discover a family resemblance in him, but the dim light at first allowed them only to detect that the room was small and much cluttered with shelves and stacks of books. Their uncle, in a voice much deeper and fuller than they would have expected from his small stature, now invited them to sit down. They took a place on a couch, and Mr. Johnson, after adjusting the blinds to admit more light, took a seat in the rocking chair.

"Now, let me get a look at you," he said.

This was their great grandfather's brother's son, which meant one-sixteenth of their own blood line matched only half of his, yet perhaps as much because they wished it as because it was true, glimpses of resemblance could be found. His skin was darker than theirs, his face more narrow and angular, but there was perhaps a shape to his forehead, a certain gentleness to his eyes, even a tilt of his chin that just hinted at familiarity.

After observing them for a moment, he smiled and said, "Well I guess you better get up and give your old uncle a hug then."

This Jasmine and William were both happy to do, especially as it gave them great pleasure to see a degree of mirth enter his previously wary eyes. He patted William on the back and hugged Jasmine gently and tenderly. The apparent feebleness of his grasp, which his strong voice had belied, struck tears to Jasmine's eyes, and, as they sat again, it was plain that the old man, too, wished a moment to compose himself.

Fortunately, William was able to perceive this turn of events, and, more able to contain his emotions than the other two, he began to discuss the circumstances which had allowed him to locate his uncle.

"I think," he concluded, "that you may be our last living relative."

Mr. Johnson seemed to consider this for a moment, before saying, "I am and I'm not . . . . You see I have children. I *had* children. Whether they're dead or alive, though, that's another matter. I couldn't really say." He shrugged in dismissal, implying that this was as much of the story that needed to be told, and Jasmine and William, though very curious, acceded to his apparent wishes and changed the subject.

"Did you move here then directly from Tennessee?"

"I did not. I went first to Chicago."

"I've heard Chicago is a very exciting place," William said.

"I didn't care for it. Didn't care for it at all. Seemed to me that just everybody was looking for trouble. I heard about a job with the railroad. I came out to Los Angeles, and then the railroad set me down here."

"There was a train station here?"

"Still is. Only freight trains now though. I was a porter, of course, that being the job that was usually reserved for colored men."

While Mr. Johnson spoke willingly of his younger life, even providing details about the egg-collecting and cow-herding chores he had been obliged to perform as early as the age of five, his recollection of more current events was clouded, and whenever the subject of his wife and children arose he turned silent and morose. They were already more than an hour into their conversation when the idea of refreshments first occurred to Mr. Johnson.

"I suppose you might be wanting something to drink," he said. They protested that they were completely happy in their current condition, and it was in fact several more minutes before he arose without excusing himself and exited to what they assumed was the kitchen. They waited quietly for some minutes, before they determined that the informality of his conduct suggested it would be acceptable to follow him. The kitchen was small, old in every possible way, and tidy, but it held no Mr. Johnson. After a few moments searching, however, they saw the wavering branches of a tree through a back window and soon realized that Mr. Johnson had mounted a ladder to pick lemons.

They hurried out to help him with this task and discovered amid tall weeds at least a dozen fruit trees of various varieties.

"Lemons will keep on a tree for months," Mr. Johnson informed them. "I thought we might have some lemonade."

As the tree was quite full of lemons and only a few were needed for their purpose, the picking was soon done, and William offered his hand to help Mr. Johnson down from the ladder. "Normally, you would want to clip them off the tree," Mr. Johnson said, taking obvious pleasure in finding the fruit suitable, "but we'll be using them so soon, picking them off will be satisfactory."

The trip to the garden seemed to have invigorated the old man. The three of them had an agreeable and comparatively lively time boiling water, sugar, and a pinch of salt to make a syrup, squeezing the lemons—which while soft with age were fresh and wholesome inside—and then pouring the whole hot mixture over ice that crackled and popped. The resulting drink was just slightly tart and remarkably cool and refreshing.

"Imagine that, walking out into your own back yard and finding it full of lemons and oranges and all those good things," he said with glee.

He now talked of the goodness of providence in moving him to California. "I was never meant to work a farm . . . or in a factory either. The railroad was good to me. It was steady work. The pay was good. I bought my own home. Who'd have imagined any of that when I was a bare-footed boy out filling the mule barrel?" He soon seemed to tire, however, and the peculiar gloom that had seemed to overtake him whenever he spoke of his family again asserted itself. "Was there something wrong with that?" he said, as though to dare them to say so. "Now, tell me, what was there wrong in that?"

William and Jasmine, though unsure of his specific reference, assured him that they saw no wrong in any of what he had related.

"People don't believe in work anymore," he said. "The children in this neighborhood—don't go to school most of the time, all kinds of drugs and alcohol, late-night carousing, disrespect for everyone and everything, out-of-wedlock children, and welfare—they all on welfare." He looked at them now, a gleam of pride and defiance in his eyes. "They've got nothing, and that's what they're always going to have. They'd like to have mine if they could get it. But they aren't going to. I worked too hard all my life to let that happen." Before either William or Jasmine could compose a response to this vitriol, the challenging fire in his eyes receded. He continued in a softer tone. "They was three things my daddy said slavery did to the Negroes, three things that were the worst of it. Yeah, they beat on people and chained them up and put bits in their mouths and fed them slop, but that wasn't the worst of it. Three things worse: One, they denied us an education, couldn't read, couldn't write, had only to believe what we were told. Two, they took our families away. A man and a woman couldn't get married, no matter how they loved each other, couldn't raise their own children, couldn't bring them up the way they saw fit. And three, they wouldn't let us have property. They wouldn't let us claim our own things. Not a house, not a mule, not a chicken. Not even our own clothes. And what have our children done? Can't make 'em go to school. Girls having babies and not even sure who the father is. Own their own houses?" He shook his head. "A body would have to *work* for that."

This reflection recalled vividly to both Jasmine and William lessons from their Granny, and they now exchanged a look of near astonishment. Earlier there had been a desire to detect a family connection between themselves and their uncle; and in the warmth of her uncle's first embrace Jasmine had felt a dizzying sensation of kinship, but she could not be certain whether this was as much imagination as reality. In this statement of her uncle's there was no ambiguity. Many times as a child, she had heard almost identical recantations of these three evils of slavery: denial of education, of marriage, and of ownership of property.

"Slaves were also denied baptism," Jasmine said, because this had been another frequent lesson from her grandmother. Baptism, she had explained to them, would have made slaves children of God, precluding them from being treated like animals.

Mr. Johnson, however, was less insistent on this point than their Granny had been. Churchgoing, he admitted, had been his wife's concern. It had been a constant source of unhappiness between her and him and between her and the children as well. "I wasn't much of a churchgoer myself, never went in for all that, but I supported Joetta when it came to the children. We always supported each other because that's what a man and a wife do . . . though, of course, no woman should try to tell a man how he's supposed to be."

Jasmine was not a superstitious person—her Granny had taught her to disdain theories about such things as black cats, propped ladders, and spilled salt; but she did have strong religious feelings, and these were not untinged with superstition. Had she been raised a Catholic, she might now have genuflected and whispered a Hail Mary, as she could not help suspecting that the source of Mr. Johnson's grief lay in the family rift caused by his rejection of the church. Instead, she promised herself that she would read an extra chapter of her Bible each night, work harder to understand all of Jesus' teachings, and apply them more faithfully in her own life.

Mr. Johnson's house was small, and while they'd not ventured down the hallway off the living room, he'd made no suggestions about housing them for the night; nor had they encountered any evidence of his having made preparations. Thus, it was no surprise to Jasmine when William politely suggested that it was time that they leave, making excuses of a plane he had to catch the following day, a long drive, and a wish not to disturb the Gannons with a very late arrival. Jasmine was not disappointed by this: while meeting their uncle had been interesting and had enriched her understanding of her Tennessee family, she feared that housing them might put the man under some strain, and, after all, their kinship was slight.

She was curious, however, as to how the old man would react, and she now watched him carefully for expressions of protest, disappointment, or relief. To her surprise, he reacted not at all, seeming even not to have heard, though they were sitting no more than three feet apart, and it was impossible that he would not have. Instead he stared past them out the front window of the house without moving so much as an eyelash.

William, too, had noted this lack of reaction, and he now began repeating his previous statements, mumbling and changing his wording sufficiently to avoid offending the man if he had indeed heard and was only biding his time in answering. When the man still did not react in any way, William began to stand, as though to leave. It was then that Mr. Johnson began to tilt to the side.

They began, first cautiously then with increasing urgency, to assess his condition. Jasmine gently shook his arm. "Mr. Johnson, are you all right?"

There was no response to this, and William now urgently touched his fingers to the side of his neck. While he did, Mr. Johnson turned once toward Jasmine, giving her a look of complete loss and confusion.

"He has a pulse," William said. He placed his ear just in front of his nose. "And he's breathing . . . . Do you think he's had a stroke?"

Mr. Johnson's head was perched at an odd angle, and they now made efforts to lay him down on the couch. He looked up at them with live but uncomprehending and incomprehensible eyes.

"We could put him in the car," Jasmine said doubtfully, her first fright now giving way to sympathy for her poor, bewildered uncle. "But where would we take him?"

There were several moments of scurrying about in search of a telephone, of which they found none. William ran across the street to a neighbor's house to call. Jasmine feared for a moment to be alone with her uncle—almost to the point of paralysis—but once she'd reached out and stroked his forehead, her panic eased. William returned in less than a minute.

"She wouldn't let me in," he said, "but she promised she'd call."

They now had a few minutes to give their full attention to their uncle. Jasmine sat, holding his head in her lap, smoothing his forehead, and attempting to hold back the anxiety that she could feel in her voice. "Help is on the way," she heard herself say. "I'm sure you're going to be fine, just fine." He looked up at her and his lips moved, but no words came out. "Just rest now. There's nothing to worry about." This of course was completely untrue, and Jasmine, being Jasmine, suffered to lie even in such a circumstance. Thus, when he again seemed to struggle, she said, "You're in God's hands. Rest. God's peace . . . ." She did not know exactly what she had intended to say about God's peace, and for a moment, she deeply wished that she could remember some useful verses of scripture. Instead, she again smoothed his brow, and seeing his arm begin to tremble, she placed a hand on his wrist and gently petted it.

A siren sounded in the distance. "They're on their way," William said. "It can't be more than a minute or two now."

Perhaps it was not even so long, but minutes can seem very long indeed when someone is suffering, perhaps at risk of dying, and one lacks the knowledge and tools to help. All Jasmine could do was pet and comfort; yet, as she saw that her efforts seemed to have some good effect, she did so with a surety and confidence that surprised even herself. She looked down in his eyes, smoothed his brow, and felt not fear so much as a deep, overwhelming sympathy, something not unlike love. It was a blessing that he had someone to comfort him, almost a joy that it was she, and a God-send they had a good, strong man like William standing over them. It was as though she were now being given an opportunity previously denied—an opportunity to offer comfort and love to her parents—and even a way to make amends to her Granny for having been so frightened in her time of need. Yet the feeling transcended these three individuals. It was as though she could now comfort the generations of their forebears—the generations of all humanity—who had suffered without a hand or voice of love beside them. That is to say, Jasmine had the pure heart of a caregiver, and like all who give comfort, she relinquished fear and revulsion and thought not of her own safety, her own ignorance, or even her own goodness, but only of bringing peace to another's heart, soul, and body.

No sentient being could fail to respond to the tenderness in Jasmine's voice and eyes; and even before the ambulance arrived Mr. Johnson proved himself to still have faculties of perception, as he began responding to her reassurances by squeezing her arm and nodding his head. Jasmine was much encouraged by this and showed her joy by squeezing back and assuring him he was already well on his way to recovery.

By the time the ambulance arrived, Mr. Johnson was trying to sit up. The attendants, a man and woman who were not much older than Jasmine, insisted that he remain on the couch and, after determining that he was still unable to speak, prepared to strap him on their gurney. He waved his arms, shook his head, and otherwise remonstrated so vociferously that Jasmine feared he would relapse into his previous condition. The attendants, though not unkindly, were firm and professional and would not relent. Still, Mr. Johnson resisted.

Jasmine, with the permission of the technicians, managed to calm him, and by giving reassurances that she and William would accompany him to the hospital, secured his cooperation. Still, as they were about to slide him into the ambulance, he again began to struggle. Jasmine was called on again, and Mr. Johnson drew her close. He managed now to speak the words, "Come with me," by which it was understood that he wished that she might accompany him in the ambulance. Whether it was because they thought her a close relation or because it seemed the most practical strategy, the attendants agreed. Thus, Jasmine held Mr. Johnson's hand on the way to the hospital, during which time his faculties of speech rapidly returned. William followed behind in the rented automobile.

During this interval it had become apparent that the attendants believed that Mr. Johnson had suffered a stroke, a diagnosis which confirmed Jasmine's own fears. What she had not known, however, was how very beneficial it was that he was being taken to the hospital so soon after its occurrence. Within seconds of his arrival at the emergency room door, he was wheeled into a treatment room, a needle was inserted in his arm, and a medicine for dissolving blood clots was flowing toward his brain.

This medicine seemed miraculously to restore him. He still spoke with a light slur and at moments appeared confused and disoriented, but understood who Jasmine was, the circumstances of her being with him, and the reason for his presence in the hospital. He was able even to produce health insurance information from his wallet, a relief to his niece and nephew, who, feeling sufficiently reassured about his recovery, had begun to be concerned with finances.

"Railroad always had a good union," he explained. "Insurance, I got that."

The doctors remained concerned, however. His recovery, it seemed, had been too quick and complete to credit the medication, and this suggested that hemorrhage was the cause of the incident. If such was the case, the medication he had been given would actually have done harm, for he would now be at extreme risk for reoccurrence. Nor could they resolve to take counteraction against it, for a possibility remained that the original diagnosis had been correct.

After private consultation, the doctors returned, prescribing a regimen of complete rest, to the point of absolute immobility. Conversation was to be minimal. No excitation whatever could be allowed for a period of twenty-four hours. Mr. Johnson began to protest—"It wasn't anything more than a dizzy spell"—and tried even to rise up from his bed. The looks of real fear with which the doctor's greeted this movement and the hostile manner in which Mr. Johnson responded to their protests propelled Jasmine to action. She pressed her uncle's shoulders back, promised to stay with him through every moment, and assured him that it would be only a very short while before they were back on Hardy Street drinking lemonade. She placed a hand behind his neck, and he allowed her to ease his head back onto the pillow.

To everyone's relief, the night passed without further incident. The doctors' worst fears were removed, and given Mr. Johnson's lucidity, they went so far as to judge that he could return home. Thus, William, who had spent the night sleeping on Mr. Johnson's couch and protecting his belongings, was able to take them home shortly after lunch. Now, however, William found himself obliged to hurry to catch his plane as he would risk being absent without leave. There could be no question of Jasmine leaving with him, as Mr. Johnson was still very unstable and completely unable to care for himself.

"I wish I could stay a little longer," William said as he stepped out onto the porch. "Even if it was only for an hour or two, you could at least have a nap. As it is, I'll have to drive directly to the airport. If I missed the flight, I could be in real trouble."

Jasmine was appalled at the possibility of anything sullying her brother's military record. She assured him that she'd had more than enough sleep, and she implored him to leave immediately. He agreed regretfully, but refused to depart before he had moved one of the larger chairs into Mr. Johnson's bedroom. Jasmine then followed her brother out to the curb and watched his car turn the corner at the end of the street.

She stood for a moment, her heart heavy, then took possession of herself and quickly returned to Mr. Johnson's room. There he lay quietly. He opened his eyes to greet her, smiled narrowly, and closed them again.

Jasmine assumed that he would sleep much of the day, as the nurses had awakened him hourly during the night to check his speech and comprehension. Seated as she had been just beside his bed, Jasmine had awakened for each of these assessments as well, and despite the claims she'd made to her brother, she had not slept for more than an hour or two. Seeing Mr. Johnson at rest, however, she settled into the chair at the foot of his bed and allowed her own eyes to close. She puzzled for a few moments over the sequence of events that had placed her where she was, wondered if Providence had not played a hand, and troubled herself over how she might eventually be returned to her home. The last image she recalled was that of William's car passing into the distance. The memory of it filled her with a sense of loss and abandonment. With this weight on her heart, she fell into a deep, sweltering sleep.

Mr. Johnson's convalescence began well enough. His humility and gentle conduct indicated that he had been frightened by his episode and that he now was grateful to be alive. Nor did he fail to appreciate the assistance he had received from his niece and nephew. For much of two days, he lay in bed, greeting Jasmine with tender smiles and accepting with humble expressions of gratitude the bowls of soup, glasses of juice, and sandwiches she offered.

It is not in the nature of human beings to be long content with merely being alive, however, nor, as Jasmine was soon to discover, was Mr. Johnson by nature a congenial person. Moreover, the doctor had warned her that what he called "cerebral incidents" often resulted in episodes of emotional depression.

Mr. Johnson's irritability first demonstrated itself in his weariness with the food being served. It began by his refusing to eat, then by his asking if she couldn't please bring something else, and progressed to his complaining that she apparently did not know how to cook "real food" and was in that way typical of all the spoiled young people of her generation.

Jasmine reminded herself that much needed to be forgiven because of Mr. Johnson's age and condition. In her own defense, she only went so far as to point out that there was little food to be had in the house, that she did not know where the nearest market was, and that she had in any case been reluctant to leave him alone.

To this he replied that he was perfectly well enough for her to leave the house, that there was a market no more than a mile away (though that might seem a little far to people of her generation), and that all she had to do was "get off her butt and walk" and they would soon have "fresh provisions," instead of the canned dishwater and green lunchmeat they'd been consuming.

Had there been any justice in this harangue, Jasmine might have been wounded. As it was, his arrows missed their mark, especially as she welcomed an opportunity to escape the house. He had been calling to her so frequently—for more water or ice, for rubbing of his aching neck, for a stable arm to lead him to the bathroom, for adjustment of his bed or pillow, or even for a shave—that she had scarcely found time to step out onto the porch. Now that he had proposed the departure, she was only too happy to go out, especially as it would allow her to purchase stamps and send a note to the Gannons.

There was, however, a question of money. Despite her apparent maturity, Jasmine was only a teenager, and she was as likely to be carrying twenty cents in her purse as twenty dollars. Now, she possessed more money than was usual for her, a cache of nine dollars and some pennies. She was far too wary of Mr. Johnson's temper to consider asking him for money. Thus, she started out along the directions he gave her, devising ways that she might extract from her small cache at least two meals of more interesting fare, as well as a stamp or two.

The store was large and modern. She gathered six eggs, a quart of milk, a loaf of bread, two tomatoes, and four plums, leaving her with just under two dollars to spend. If she could find a piece of meat for a dollar, she would be able to buy three stamps. This proved impossible. She returned the milk, reasoning that older people seldom drank milk in any case, leaving her enough money to purchase a package of two very small pork chops and a single stamp.

That evening, she fed Mr. Johnson a meal of a pork chop, two plums, and a potato that she'd found in his cupboard. While he seemed to relish the food, he complained of the lack of greens, and Jasmine was obliged to admit that she had been constrained by a lack of money. While he regarded this statement with some suspicion, she was much relieved that he did not accuse her of lying, as she already felt some guilt at having withheld the cost of the stamp, an amount which would have permitted her to buy a small bundle of the desired greens.

After she had eaten, she sat down to compose a note to her aunt. In it she dutifully informed her family that she was well, expressed her hopes that they were also, and described the condition of her uncle and the symptoms of dizziness and occasional disorientation which made it impossible for her to leave.

"I am hoping that a neighbor will be able to inform me of the addresses of his children, as he refuses even to speak their names," she wrote. "I feel sure that they would want to know of his illness and to be reunited with him."

She did not write of her uncle's contentiousness or the humble circumstances in which she now found herself, but she did express a wish to be quickly returned to Arden Park. "One benefit of my being here, besides the great blessing that someone was present to help my uncle, is that I realize now even more than before how kind all of you have been to me and how much I treasure my home in Arden Park."

The next day at breakfast, Mr. Johnson complained that scrambled eggs without bacon were no better than cold mush.

Jasmine took this opportunity to observe that there was no bacon to be found in the refrigerator.

"Why didn't you buy some, then?"

"I hadn't enough money."

"Not enough money to buy a little bacon?"

She shook her head.

He observed her disapprovingly for a moment, then asked, "How old are you, girl?"

"Sixteen, though I'll be seventeen soon."

"Is that the truth?" he asked, continuing to observe her with piercing eyes.

"I would have no reason to deceive you, Mr. Johnson, nor would I do so if I did."

He considered this for a moment, before motioning towards the door. "Leave the room," he said, "and don't come back until I tell you."

Jasmine did as she was asked, but her exile proved much shorter than she had expected. Hardly a minute had passed before he was calling her back. He held a small object out to her that on closer observation proved to be a bank debit card.

"You get what money you need and only what you need, and you bring me the receipt. The bank's right down from the store." He then told her the code she would need to enter into the computer in order to withdraw money. "I'm putting my trust in you, child—more than I probably should. But a man's got to eat."

While Mr. Johnson was not squalid in his habits, he had developed the ways of a bachelor, and even the not-so-distant corners of his house had suffered from a lack of regular housekeeping. Having been given the resources to obtain cleaning materials, Jasmine assumed these tasks. In the early morning hours, she opened the doors and curtains and began transferring decades of dust from inside to out. As she was able even to clear one shelf of the bookcase, she permitted herself to remove all the unshelved books from tables and chairs in order that they too might be tidied and dusted up. More even than the cleaning, the entry of the morning light dispelled the perpetual gloom of the house. She felt cheered.

To her relief, she had learned that Mr. Johnson was far from indigent. In his checking account alone, the balance of which was displayed each time she drew twenty dollars from the bank, he held more than $10,000. Of course, this gave her no excuse for spending his money profligately, nor could she have without incurring his wrath, as he not only studied the balance on each bank receipt but also each line of her grocery bills—all with a magnifying glass, as his sight had been affected by his illness.

Though he had done no more than look into the kitchen, Mr. Johnson was by the end of the week getting out of bed, dressing, and moving to his chair in the living room. She had begun to hope that he would be well enough soon to take care of himself when there was a setback: he fell while attempting the step down into his back yard. Jasmine, who had been washing out clothes in the bathroom, heard the fall and found him lying at the base of the stair. She feared for a moment that he was dead, but as she moved her face close to listen for breathing, his eyes opened. A few moments later, something resembling consciousness appeared in them, and he was able to respond to inquiries about injury. After considerable questioning, testing, and prodding, she determined that he was badly bruised but otherwise unhurt. She helped him to his feet and returned him to his bed.

Jasmine's hopes of imminent departure were dashed. She began entreaties to his neighbors. Neither of the adjacent neighbors had been on speaking terms with Mr. Johnson. Both disclaimed any knowledge of his children. An older gentleman who passed on the street admitted that Mr. Johnson had not said so much as a word to him in fifteen years, despite his passing daily on the sidewalk.

Jasmine thought next to try across the street, where she had seen a woman with a heavy, Afro-style of hair sometimes watching them from her porch. She climbed up the tidy steps, but before she'd had time to knock, the door was opened. From up close, she could see that the woman was much older than she had thought, possibly as old as Mr. Johnson himself. She had been misled by her thick, shapely hair, which even from close up gleamed and showed only a speckling of gray.

After apologizing for troubling her, Jasmine introduced herself as Mr. Johnson's niece, learned that the woman's name was Mrs. Madeline Atkinson, and explained that Mr. Johnson had taken ill. Did she know anything of his family or their circumstances?

"Joetta died when the children were still in school. The man as good as killed her."

"I've gotten the impression that his children are perhaps dead as well."

"He tell you they were dead? That was just a lie. They're alive all right. Why wouldn't they be?"

"Do you think there would be some way of contacting them?"

She thought only a moment, then shook her head. "I wouldn't wish him on them if I did know. He's a tightfisted, mean old man, and that's all there is to it. A man reaps what he sows, and all that man ever sowed was meanness and selfishness."

"He hasn't been completely unkindly to me," Jasmine said in his defense. "I was hoping to bring about a reconciliation."

"Oh, he can be kind to strangers, all right. Or if you've got something he needs. If you're rich or white as you maybe . . . ."

"I see," Jasmine said. "Do you see no possibility that his children would like to see him again?"

Mrs. Atkinson shook her head.

"Not even if I could convince him that he should ask them . . . and get him to promise that he will be good to them?"

"Some things don't change," the woman said, shaking her head. "Send him to the welfare," the woman said. "They *have to* take him."

"I had hoped that wouldn't be necessary . . . . If you are able to think of anything, of anyone who might know how to contact his children, I would be very grateful if you could tell me."

"There ain't no one," the woman said adamantly, "not since Joetta died."

Nonetheless, later that afternoon there was a knock at the door. Jasmine answered, and Mrs. Atkinson beckoned her outside. She handed her a slip of paper with an address in one of the smaller industrial cities near San Francisco.

"I called my daughter. She says that Rochelle was there once, but that was at least five years ago." She shook her head. "You know how young people move about . . . . I'm sorry, but that's the best I can do." She started to leave. "He's not being mean with you?"

"I won't say that he isn't difficult, but I know that he appreciates everything that people do for him."

"Maybe he has changed," she said. "We all give up on him years ago. Lord knows, that ain't right, though, is it?"

"I'm sure that you did everything you could," Jasmine said, clutching the paper in front. "I thank you with all my heart . . . And it must have been you who called the ambulance?"

"I'm sorry I couldn't let that young man in," she said, "but these days, you never know."

"You did everything that was needed. Thank you so much."

The woman smiled at this, then as she walked away, called back over her shoulder, "If you need something—to use the telephone or anything—you can come on over." She began walking away again, then stopped once more. "Was that young man your brother?" Jasmine nodded. "Whew!" she said. "That's one fine looking boy . . . . He in the military or something?"

"He is."

"I thought so, the way he says 'yes, ma'am' and acts so polite and everything."

Jasmine now shared a gleeful smile with the woman, before thanking her one last time and turning into the house. She smoothed the paper out on the table. It was her one fragment of hope that she might soon go home.

Chapter 23

Goings and Comings for All But Jasmine

Jasmine's note found Cynthia Gannon and her sister in a house that was very quiet indeed, especially as the sole remaining teenage resident, Julia, was in such a state of temper that she would not speak to anyone. On the day Jasmine and William had departed Arden Park to see their uncle, information had arrived from the south indicating that all the young people were having a wonderful time, and the suggestion was made that Chrissie join them. Cynthia expressed some reluctance: Phillip and Thomas were staying with friends, but Chrissie would stay at the Hills' home in Bel Air. The issue of chaperoning was ambiguous. Chrissie, however, recruited her aunt as an advocate. It was pointed out that she was completely on her own at college and that she would be entirely among friends. Reassured by her sister, Cynthia had relented—and thereby invoked the wrath of Julia, whose misery had loved having her sister's for company.

"How odd," Cynthia said, as she set the letter down on the patio table, "to think of our Jasmine as having another family."

Tina, who for more than a decade had made efforts to remind her sister of this fact, did not consider it odd at all. "It's perfectly natural that she would want to make a stronger connection with her father's family. After all, she spent a good part of her childhood with them."

"But all that seems so long ago . . . Not that it isn't natural, of course. Anybody would be curious. How could she not be? But I am so pleased that she hasn't forgotten us . . . ."

"I don't suppose she decently could, could she?"

"No, but young people . . . they can be so forgetful . . . thoughtless I guess is what I mean . . . . I do hope her uncle is all right."

"I'm sure he is. There's always a tendency to exaggerate these things."

There passed an interval during which Cynthia buffed her nails, and Tina considered a telephone call she'd received earlier from her favorite niece. There'd been a small incident, nothing really, but something that needed to be presented to her mother "just right, so she didn't get all upset." Chrissie had received a citation for using a false identity card to buy liquor. "It was nothing," she had assured her aunt. The problem was how to present it to Cynthia? Was it possible they could keep it completely secret?

"It doesn't seem the same without Jasmine here, though, does it?" Cynthia was saying. "She's usually so quiet that you'd think you'd never miss her, but now that she's gone . . . it's like . . . it's like when Pom's at the vet's." As she said her name, Pom, who was lying on the shady grass beside them, stretched and looked up, and Cynthia offered her a smile and a whispered, "Sweet little Pom."

"Nothing seems quite right without Jasmine," Cynthia continued. "It's all just a little too . . . empty."

"I forgot to mention," Tina said, "Chrissie received some sort of ticket, a citation I think she said."

"Was she driving too fast?" Cynthia asked.

"No. It's much too silly even to talk about. I feel like I'm meddling even mentioning it. It had something to do with an identity card. They were going to a restaurant—a nightclub sort of place. Whatever the case, there was an age limit, and she'd borrowed a driver's license from another girl . . . . She showed the license, and some fool of a bartender—I'm sure he was just trying to make himself seem important—decided to make a fuss and took possession of it. There was an incident and she received a citation."

"Oh, my!" Cynthia said.

"It's ironic, really. We teach them how to behave in a mature and intelligent manner, and then it's all undermined by this kind of ridiculous thing. If it weren't so annoying, it would be too silly to talk about."

"Silly?"

"Yes. It was all so unnecessary."

"Unnecessary?"

"I'm sure there were many more useful things the police could have been doing."

"The police were called?"

"It *is* policemen who issue citations."

"Oh, dear. Will she . . . Will *we* have to go *to court?*" she asked, saying this last in a whisper.

"She's nineteen so . . . ."

"I don't see how we could let her go in alone."

Tina laughed at this. "I know that it's hard to believe that your little girl is grown up, but I'm sure she's perfectly capable of handling a thing like this."

"You do?"

"Of course. It's really not that much different from a speeding ticket."

"A speeding ticket?"

"Yes. Someone at the restaurant showed some very bad judgment and went a little overboard. I don't think we should read anything more into it than that."

"And it's nothing more than a speeding ticket?"

"Less really. More like a parking ticket. There isn't much danger of her injuring herself in a restaurant."

Cynthia agreed that there wasn't. "And you think we should let her handle it on her own?"

"I'm sure she'll handle it fine. If there were any difficulty at all, the Hills have a lawyer who would help, but I'm sure he won't be needed. All in all, it might prove to be a good experience for her."

"A good experience?"

"As much as we may not like to admit it, all three of them have had very protected childhoods. They're going to need to toughen up a little and get a little wiser. I think this was a case where Chrissie's innocence got her in trouble—she wanted too badly to accommodate her friends. She'll need to learn to be a little shrewder and more selfish in her decision-making."

"But wasn't it Chrissie who borrowed the identification?"

"Yes, but it was only because she didn't want to inconvenience her friends. They would have had to leave if she hadn't presented some type of ID."

"They are very good children, aren't they?" Cynthia said, though her eyes still admitted an element of doubt.

"They are. But that can be a handicap sometimes. Their own innocence can put them at risk."

Cynthia had begun by assuming that David would have to be involved, and that had been her foremost concern. Now, seeing that the incident was hardly anything more than a parking ticket, it was apparent that they should not let it become a distraction to him. After all, he was a very busy man with responsibilities that affected the entire country—even the world. A man in his position needed especially strong support at home.

"So," she said to her sister, "it may be better to let her resolve this on her own."

"I'm sure of it."

"It's something of a learning experience for her, isn't it? If she works through this herself, the lesson will be reinforced more strongly."

"She does need to learn how to negotiate the politics of this type of thing."

"And to avoid anything like it in the future."

Tina nodded her agreement. "She's a Gannon and always will be. There will always be people who want to blow things up into something scandalous."

"Scandalous?" Cynthia asked, feeling real alarm.

"Not this time, of course," Tina said, her voice calm and dismissive, "but you know how people are. A famous name. Some reporter could spot it somewhere and decide to make an issue of it."

"Do you think something might appear in the papers?"

"Oh, no," Tina said, though Chrissie had mentioned a bystander who had seemed disturbingly curious. "I was speaking generally. Reporters being reporters, and the Gannon name being what it is, it's the type of thing that could occur sometime. In a way, it seems almost inevitable. It's one of the prices we have to pay."

"But there's no chance of *this* appearing in the newspapers?" Cynthia said, thinking that she very much did not want David to learn of it there.

"Absolutely not," Tina said, then added, "Oh, possibly in a list sort of thing—one of those statistics things that they publish. But, even if there were, I don't see how anyone could possibly be sure it was our Chrissie. After all, Los Angeles has twenty million people. Even a name like Chrissie Gannon—it's not exactly common maybe—but it's not unique either, not in a population of twenty million. No one could be sure. Oh, no, I don't think there's anything to worry about in that regard."

Cynthia had experienced a strong sensation of relief at Tina's original "Absolutely not." Not liking to dwell long on upsetting problems—and having the capacity not to hear what she did not want to hear—she had listened with only half-consciousness to the caveats that had followed, instead turning her attention to sorting the rest of the mail. To her surprise, a second envelope had arrived from Los Angeles.

This proved to be a note from Max Hill. Cynthia feared that it would contain additional information about Chrissie's mishap; however, he made no mention of it. Instead, he inquired of their health, going so far as to mention his wishes that Pom not be suffering from the heat, expressed his delight with having the Gannon family members in Los Angeles, where he was enjoying taking them to all the sights, which he felt like he was seeing again for the first time. He mentioned that he had had several days of work on a nature documentary. Then, after noting that he had learned of Jasmine's departure from Chrissie, he concluded by asking for her address.

"I have something extremely important to tell her. I'm sure you'll find out about it soon, but I'd like to tell her first if you don't mind."

Cynthia experienced a brief and not totally unpleasant shock as she imagined that the boy might be speaking of matrimony. She read the letter again and realized that not even so confident a young man as Max could have said "tell" when he meant "ask"— unless, of course, something was already understood between them. If this was the case with Jasmine, she had certainly hidden it, but then Jasmine was so often inscrutable. She herself had been exactly Jasmine's age when she'd determined that she would someday marry David. It was not to be spoken aloud—not in so many words—for years afterwards, but the two of them had known.

In a way, it would be just too wonderful! Nevertheless, she could not let herself be so consumed by excitement. If it were true, it would have to be forestalled, if not stopped. Jasmine was too young, but, beyond that, there was a disturbing difference in ages. She and David had only been a year apart. They were able to wait together. She'd been a step ahead of him, as nice teenaged girls always are a step ahead of nice teenaged boys. She'd known how to keep it interesting and him interested. Jasmine would lack such skills; nor would Max be as content to wait. He was already in his twenties, and—though he was wonderful, of course—he wasn't nice in the same way David had been or Phillip was. He was . . . he was . . . he was more like Thomas.

Cynthia would normally have shared these types of ruminations with Tina, but her sister had never been so charmed with Max's infatuation with Jasmine as she was, and she had sometimes felt that her sister was inclined to be too severe with Jasmine. Not that she doubted that Tina meant well—she spoke often of the necessity of building the children's self-reliance, of insisting that they take responsibility for their own affairs, and of the importance of raising children who were not oversensitive—but it did seem to Cynthia that she was more scrupulous in enforcing her standards of conduct with Jasmine than with any of the Gannon children. She tried setting the letter aside inconspicuously, but she'd never been much good at hiding anything from anyone, least of all from her sister.

"Is that a letter from the girls?" she asked.

"It's just a sweet, little note from Max."

"Is there any news about Chrissie?"

"Nothing really," Cynthia replied, then catching Tina's demanding gaze added, "He'd like Jasmine's address. He probably wants to send her some little *billet doux* . . . ."

"*Billet doux?*" Tina said, adopting her sister's habit of repeating. Her tone, however, was stinging.

"No, of course not, nothing exactly quite like that . . .," Cynthia said quickly, "I was being silly." Then, in her own defense, she added, "But it is very thoughtful of him, to consider that she might be lonely."

"Cynthia," Tina said, inclining her head, her voice admonitory, "it's completely ridiculous. And besides that, it's inappropriate. He's six years older than she. She's hardly more than a child. He may think that it's all sweet and fun, but that girl is likely to have her feelings very badly wounded. I dare say we could have a real emotional crisis on our hands. Jasmine may sometimes appear to be strong, but she's actually very immature. She's much too innocent and childish for this sort of thing. She lacks the necessary sophistication."

"I've always thought of Jasmine as being unusually steady."

"I know you have. Everybody does. But all she really has is that childish, do-good-and-daddy-will-love-you sort of attitude. It won't hold up in the real world. People are going to run right over her."

Cynthia could not readily imagine anyone running right over Jasmine. Of course, she was unusually accommodating and thoughtful, and she was always willing to help in any situation, but that was just her nature, just as being truthful and steadfast were. It was impossible to imagine her groveling for anything. Unlike her own children, who had begged incessantly for every toy and piece of candy they wanted, Jasmine had never whined about anything.

"She's not nearly as assertive as she should be," Tina said, "especially considering the prejudice she will encounter."

"Prejudice?"

"Yes, prejudice. You are *so* naïve about some things. Jasmine is black. She will face all kinds of obstacles because of her skin color, and unless she's prepared to go out and fight for what she wants, she won't get anywhere in the real world. Things won't come easily for her. She'll have to fight for everything she gets."

"Our Jasmine?"

"Wake up, Cynthia. Sometimes I think you live in a cocoon."

"She seems so much like anybody else. It just doesn't seem possible."

"It's not just possible, it's certain, and unless she gets a whole lot wiser to the ways of the world, she's going to cause us nothing but trouble. Right now, a boy could tell her anything and she'd follow him like a puppy."

"Max Hill?"

"Not Max I suppose. I don't imagine she'd be worth the trouble to him . . . . But this is all so preposterous and it's gone on so long that I'm not even sure of him. You'd think a young man with his experience would know better. How he could give such a child more than ten minutes of his time is a complete mystery to me. Maybe there's something wrong with him."

"Jasmine does have her own charms you know. I can imagine a boy finding her very pretty."

"A boy, possibly. But certainly not a grown man like Max. It's scandalous of him to keep it up, and I have a mind to tell him so. I certainly wouldn't send him that address."

"Really? I don't see how I could refuse."

"What's so complicated? You just don't send it."

"How would I explain that to him?"

"You're a grown-up, sis. That means you don't have to explain."

"I suppose not," she said. Cynthia usually acted on Tina's advice, as she recognized that her own judgment was not always sound; and, had Tina been somewhat more diplomatic or less vehement in their current exchange, she would likely have ended by doing so in this case. However, while comparing Jasmine's affair with Max with her own romance with David, she'd developed a deep sympathy for the young lovers. The idea of secret love notes passing between Max and Jasmine charmed her, as did the possibility of aiding their romance. Moreover, love was the one area in which she herself had operated with particular success. In the ways of love, her instincts might even be more trustworthy than Tina's! She resolved that she would send the address and did—though she could not quite muster the courage to inform her sister.

As the days passed, Mr. Johnson grew more stable on his feet and was able to move about the house and yard, albeit very slowly; his emotional and cognitive states, however, showed signs of deterioration. What had begun as a lament over the lack of success of his children had evolved into an almost continual berating of their perfidies and laziness. Most disturbing of all, he seemed at times now to confuse Jasmine with his own daughter.

Late one morning, while she was listening for the mailman to arrive, hoping for the letter that would free her, he began to complain of a lack of sugar in his iced tea. He had never wanted sugar before, being content with sending her out to pick a lemon, but now it had become essential. It took her some time to find the sugar bowl, then as it was empty, longer still to find the cupboard where the bag was stored.

When she returned, he eyed her malevolently.

"'He's just an old man,'" he mocked. "'What does it matter if he gets his tea or not?' That's what you were thinking. I'm surprised you come back at all."

"I had some difficulty finding your supply of sugar," Jasmine explained.

"You never did think of anyone but yourself," the man went on, "your own mouth, your own comfort, your own pretty face."

"Mr. Johnson!" Jasmine replied, too alarmed to be angry. "I think you must be confusing me with someone else." After a moment's perplexity, his face again softened, and he drank his tea in silence. But only a moment later, he looked up and harrumphed derisively.

Jasmine had found that she could sometimes distract him when he was in such dark moods by encouraging him to talk about his childhood. This had the advantage of helping her to learn more about her own ancestry, which had been her original intent in traveling here, and she now attempted this again. "You say you raised guinea hens, Mr. Johnson. Why was it guinea hens and not chickens?"

"Oh, we had chickens, too. I can't remember what brought us to keep guinea hens, other than that they were very good at taking care of themselves. Once you had them, they just kept coming of their own. I don't remember that we fed them like we did the chickens." These types of reminiscences seemed to be comforting to him, and after they'd discussed also the quantity of milk they got from their cow and the frequency with which they had eaten cornbread, he began to look tired. Jasmine allowed the conversation to lag, and he soon fell asleep in his chair.

It was shortly thereafter that she heard the mailman arrive on the porch. Each day, her heart seemed to pause at his arrival, and she felt almost dizzy as she stepped out into the hot sunlight. The top of the stack brought a bitter disappointment. The letter to Mr. Johnson's daughter had been returned undelivered with the information that she was no longer at the address given and had left no forwarding address.

She was too disappointed to look through the remainder of the mail, and she sagged onto the couch and let the stack sit on her lap. Her uncle was not improving. None of his neighbors was likely to offer any assistance, nor was there any reason to think that they should. He was sometimes a bitter and mean-spirited man. He had, no doubt, offered his neighbors nothing but ridicule and nastiness for many years. Why should they be expected to respond sympathetically now? No one would. There was only she. Unless she was willing to spend weeks, months, or even years here, she would have to "turn him over to the welfare." But how could she have the poor man removed from his home?

While there was more than a little justification to these laments, Jasmine was not one to linger long in self-pity, and when Mr. Johnson now moaned in his sleep, she upbraided herself. He was a sick and lonely man. He'd lost his wife. He'd labored hard and been a good provider for his family, yet they'd left him. He'd suffered many disappointments. While it was regrettable that he could not have kept a more optimistic view of his life, he deserved her forgiveness and sympathy, just as any other human being did.

With these thoughts in mind, she resolved to return to the project of restoring the back yard, which she'd begun several days before. As she stood up, however, she noticed that there was a second letter addressed to her. She sat back down and was deeply surprised to discover Max Hill's name on the return address line. Jasmine's exile had now lasted for nearly two weeks; except on days when she went to the market, she spoke to no one but her uncle. The brief moment of regret she felt upon seeing Max's name on the letter, and the flash of resentment and anger that passed over her in realization that the letter was not from Phillip or even her aunt, swiftly gave way to appreciation of Max's consideration. Shame quickly followed. For some time, his behavior to her had been in no way blameworthy, yet she had continued to treat him very coldly.

Max wrote that he was well and hoped that her uncle and she were also. His time in Los Angeles had been busy with work and too full of activities to be dull, but it had lacked what he called the "sweetness" of Arden Park, primarily, he suggested, "because there was no Jasmine there." The most startling revelation came last. He had very important news to give her, such important news that he wished to deliver it in person. Though Thomas, Phillip, and Chrissie were staying on in Los Angeles with Sherry, he was returning to Arden Park immediately. "I'd like to come up and visit as soon as I get back," he wrote. "This is really awesome news." He had added a postscript. "I hope your uncle is doing better. I wouldn't want to do anything to set him back. Just let me know that he'll be okay with a visit, and I'll be right there."

The knowledge that Phillip would be remaining in Los Angeles was hardly comforting, especially considering that she had received no letters from him, but the prospect of receiving a visitor proved a helpful antidote to brooding. Max Hill would have been her last choice in a visitor, but she was eager for news of her family and very nearly desperate for a break to her tedium. Moreover, she was aware that Max was the sole person who had chosen to make the long drive from Arden Park. She could not yet place any deep trust in Max, but she was grateful to him and now felt confident he would treat her with respect and kindness.

There was, however, the question of her present circumstances and her uncle's behavior. The house was hot, small, poor, and unlike anything in Max Hill's experience. Might he find it intolerable? Moreover, she doubted that her uncle would greet any stranger congenially. Would Max be able to maintain his sympathy and understanding under such provocations? Had Max's letter arrived a week earlier, these considerations might have precluded offering him an invitation, but Jasmine's solicitousness to her uncle's wishes was now influenced by an understanding that his mental state was impaired. She had begun to resort to subterfuges and outright deceptions in order to mollify him. There was, for example, the matter of her wardrobe.

If it were not for social considerations, clothing would be necessary during summers in California's Central Valley only for protection against the sun. Jasmine made daily use of the washbasin in Mr. Johnson's bathroom, and as her most formal activity was walking to the grocery store, she did not suffer materially by her lack of wardrobe. She did, however, require some items to wear while her laundry was drying. She had purchased underwear, athletic shorts, a shirt, and a pair of rubber sandals, all of which required her to draw less than twenty dollars from Mr. Johnson's account. When Mr. Johnson asked her to explain these purchases, however, he had become very angry and had accused her of treachery and deceit. After careful soul-searching, she could find no fault of her own and attributed his outburst to his illness. When her small packet of toiletries had been exhausted, rather than face a similar episode, she began replenishing them one item at a time and answering when queried about items on the bill by naming a similarly priced food item. As Mr. Johnson was unable to read the small print on the receipts, this served to avoid confrontation. Similarly, when he complained of the food, whether the menu or cost, she now invoked "doctor's orders" as explanation for her selections.

She now reasoned that, despite his not wanting additional company, visitors would benefit her uncle by encouraging him to cease brooding and look outward. Moreover, having an automobile at their disposal would allow her to take care of certain chores, such as seeing that her uncle had his hair cut and that his utility bills were paid.

Of course, she herself was much in need of fellowship: life under such constrained circumstances, especially as she had been accustomed to such freedom and abundance, threatened to make her querulous. She did not fear that she would speak sharply to her uncle—she was too well self-disciplined for that—but she admitted an increasing inner dissatisfaction with him. A visit from a friend, she felt, would refresh her perspective and restore her sympathy.

She did, therefore, send the letter of invitation, along with a list of items that her aunt might pack for her and a suggestion that the house was too small for any overnight visitors. She thanked Max sincerely for his interest, remarked her eagerness to hear news of her family, and attempted to convey the sense of relief and expectation his letter had created.

"I do feel far from my home in Arden Park and have missed the company of my friends and family. The effect your letter had on me was something like a breath of cool air. Did I mention that Mr. Johnson's house is often very hot?"

Chapter 24

Los Angeles

At the time of his departure for Los Angeles, Julia had been very unhappy with Max Hill, and she had told herself that nothing short of abject wooing could redeem him in her eyes. She was yet more deeply wounded when Chrissie was invited to Los Angeles and she was not. Chrissie was closer to Sherry Hill's age, and Tina offered this an explanation for her having received the invitation, but Julia knew this was not the real reason. Sherry had always treated them equally. The real reason had to do with Max. Julia suspected treachery.

Chrissie, despite her disavowals of interest in Max, had remained open-minded. Their brief and limited intimacies had been stimulating for her, and, she was certain, for him as well. His decision to remain aloof was no doubt a tactic to put Pudge off the scent. A reversal would surely occur on the first occasion when they found themselves safely alone.

She had been certain enough of him that she anticipated his meeting her at the airport. She had worn a silky top over minimal undergarments in anticipation of this meeting at the gate and was vexed not to find him there, though this could be explained by her plane having arrived a few minutes early. She progressed to the baggage area and was further dismayed not to find him waiting there. After several minutes of waiting at the curb outside, she cursed aloud, causing an elderly lady to look at her in astonishment and Chrissie to offer her a look of regal scorn.

While she waited among hordes of what she took to be tourists and celebrity-seekers, she resolved that she would put Max firmly in his place as soon as he arrived. For several minutes she attempted to construct comments that would reflect the full extent of her ire, but as those minutes passed, she realized that any complaint might seem ridiculous to him, and she concluded that regal silence, which would signal her disappointment without making her appear petulant, was her best approach. Besides, haughtiness looked well on her.

A few moments later, it was Sherry and Phillip who hailed to her from farther down the curb. With them, she could not resist comment, saying, "God, you guys, I've been waiting out there for like an hour."

As this could not possibly be true (the flight had *taken off* only a little more than an hour before), and as they were accustomed to Chrissie's piques, they did not answer. Instead, they drove in silence, while she disparaged the smoggy air, the heavy traffic, the cramped seat in the plane—"Why couldn't Mom let me take first class?"— and the ridiculous old crone at the curb who had insulted her. Worse yet, the car, while a Jaguar, was not all she might have wished. The leather seats were cracked, the inside dusty, and the exterior paint along the curves of the roof actually appeared faded.

The air conditioning did work well, however, and after a few minutes, the cool air and spaciousness of the vehicle began to take their effect. She was, after all, in Los Angeles, looking gorgeous, and riding in a Jaguar, which, if it might not bear close inspection, would appear fine to passing cars and pedestrians. She signaled that her temper had abated by saying, "God, I'm glad all that's over," and Phillip and Sherry again felt free to engage her in conversation.

Max was on a video shoot in Hollywood and, to his credit, sent his apologies. Sherry, Phillip, and Thomas had been going to a lot of parties and clubs and having a great time, but Max had seemed preoccupied with other things.

"He's up to something," Sherry said. "Very hush-hush, and all that. He even talked about going to see our mother for a while, but he gave that up when she didn't want to buy him a ticket."

"But he *is* staying at home?" Chrissie asked.

"He is when he's here," Sherry answered. "He went to Washington for two days—somehow he got together the money for that. He said he was going to see your father while he was there, but we haven't seen him since he got back. Now, he's gone off somewhere else. I think he'll be home tonight though. At least, that's what I think he said . . . . But right now the important thing isn't Max. The important thing is that you've made it. And we're going to a party tonight I think you're going to love. It's over in Malibu. There'll be some very interesting people."

Actually, the important thing to Chrissie *had been* Max, and she now regretted both her questions about him and the silk top she was wearing. They might have slipped by Phillip—boys always noticed cleavage and short skirts, but they didn't always look for the reason behind them—and her questions about Max and the reason she was angry might have gone right past him; but Sherry would have got it right away. She was mad at herself for letting it show, and she decided she really didn't like Max at all and wasn't going to let him affect her in one way or the other in the future.

"Geez, I'm really ready for a party," she now said. "Arden Park is like so incredibly boring."

They asked about Pudge.

"He's the same," she said. "Always the same. I think we need a break from each other."

"We all need a vacation once in a while," Sherry said. "If only to meet some new people."

God, how true! Chrissie thought. Pudge's stolid loyalty was so dull! She also realized, quite suddenly, that she had no interest in Max Hill and was irritated at herself for even having thought of him. What she really wanted was to meet some new and exciting people, something different from the humdrum boys of Arden Park.

"Cool," Chrissie said. "Let's party."

Sherry, despite being at the wheel, turned her head and gave her a wide smile. Phillip pointed out to her that she was veering out of her lane, and he had even begun to reach for the wheel before Sherry turned and jerked the car back in line.

"I do that all the time," Sherry said. "It's okay. I always catch myself in time."

Phillip began to speak, stopped, then began again, saying, "No harm done."

Then they all laughed aloud.

Chrissie would have been yet more miffed if she'd known that even as they talked, Max Hill was 500 miles away, driving at ninety miles per hour up the Sacramento Valley. Jasmine had secretly hoped that he would be bringing Phillip with him, but such did not prove to be the case. It was Max and no one else who emerged from the Gannon's Volvo wagon. He carried with him a vase of flowers.

Jasmine had taken the precaution of warning Mr. Johnson that a friend would be arriving with a supply of clothing, but he had greeted this news with such indifference that she had doubted whether he fully comprehended. She stepped out to the porch with the idea of forewarning Max of her uncle's temperament, but was immediately overtaken with anticipation of the news he would bring and with joy at seeing not only the big, plain car, which seemed to symbolize the security she'd had the good fortune to experience throughout her childhood, but also his familiar, smiling face. Max insisted that she accept a hug from him, one which he gave by wrapping the vase around to her back and giving a polite squeeze, and she returned it with scarcely more constraint. By the time they'd completed these greetings, Mr. Johnson had already emerged onto the porch, and Jasmine had neglected to provide Max with any word of warning.

Her uncle regarded her with skepticism while she made introductions. He accepted Max's handshake, but offered only a brief, piercing look to accompany it. Max, to Jasmine's great relief, responded neither with sardonicism nor disdain. Instead, he asked about Mr. Johnson's health, and having received only a grunt in response, proceeded to make complimentary and observant comments on her uncle's house and yard.

This might have seemed mere flattery to Mr. Johnson had not Jasmine's mowing, trimming, watering, and hauling greatly improved his yard's tidiness and had his perception of his home not corresponded more closely to its condition forty year earlier than to its current state. His mind's eye continued to hold the image of a well-kept residence, designed with an interest in simple charm of structure and natural beauty.

"What a beautiful trellis," Max said, indicating the once-white trellis work that surrounded the porch posts and which was adorned with oval windows, the frames of which still held flakes of lavender paint.

Mr. Johnson observed this trellis with some interest, as well he might since it had been completely obscured by a tangled mix of dead and dying jasmine vines only three weeks earlier.

"My wife enjoyed pretty things," Mr. Johnson said. "Why put up a plain post when you could put up something that would give a person pleasure to look at?"

Max also noted the scrollwork fascia that fronted the porch and the scalloped shingles that sided the gable end of the house overhead. It was, he asserted, a type of craftsmanship that was rarely seen anymore.

"It's a small house, and nothing fancy, but it's ours. It's where we live, and there's no reason we can't have it how we want it, is there?" Mr. Johnson said, brightening in a way that he had not in more than a week.

"No reason at all," Max agreed, "and you give pleasure to everybody else who passes by in the process. Nothing wrong with that at all."

Jasmine now felt confident that Max could be admitted into the house, and even dared to leave them alone while she prepared iced tea. She hurried back with the glasses and a bowl of sugar, but discovered she need not have worried. They were now complaining about the suburbs.

"You can build those houses just as big as you want and put in fancy fixtures and all, but they have no real soul to them," Mr. Johnson said. "It's about like living in a hotel."

"Of course, I don't have a house of my own . . . ."

"You will, in time."

"But if I did I'd much prefer to have a house with personality to it—one like this one—over a cookie-cutter type of place . . . . Don't you think, Jasmine?"

Jasmine, thinking now of her Granny's house, agreed. Max beamed at her for a moment, then turned to Mr. Johnson. "I don't know if you've had enough time to become fully aware of it, sir, but you have a very remarkable niece. A lot of people *talk* about being good, but for most people it's just talk. It's second nature to Jasmine. I don't think I've ever met anyone else who wears goodness so gracefully."

"She's been good to me," the old man replied. "I don't know what I would have done without her."

This was the first real compliment or thanks Jasmine had received from Mr. Johnson since his attack, and she was deeply touched by it. She was also thankful to Max for having elicited it.

"You're very lucky to have a niece like her. I don't think there are many girls of her age who would have given up their summer vacations and pool parties and trips to the mall to take care of someone else. It's unusual, *very* unusual."

Jasmine now had further reason to be grateful to Max for it was not clear to her either that Mr. Johnson understood how very much he demanded of her or that he recognized that she might have had another life before arriving at his home. Now, however, he was smiling at her and saying, "I believe it . . . . I know that very well . . ." and making other acknowledgements of her assistance.

They spoke for some time longer about the house and how long he'd lived there, and about the railroad; and, while at one point Jasmine was obliged to steer Max away from questions about Mr. Johnson's

family, her uncle appeared content to talk. Eventually, however, he
tired, excused himself, and shuffled off to his bedroom to nap.

Jasmine took this opportunity to invite Max out to the garden,
where they were soon busy propping the picket fence in the front
yard and assessing what materials would be needed to repair it properly.
There was little they could do without new fence pieces, and Max,
though willing, was of little use. They soon proceeded to the far back
yard, where Jasmine wanted to show him a profusion of boysenberries
that hung on the back fence. Whether it was by accident or because
they enjoyed those berries that grew on their own side of the fence,
Mr. Johnson's neighbors had been watering and feeding the vines, as
was evident from their robust good health and a large crop of plump,
dark berries. The combination of ample water and very hot weather
had bestowed upon the berries an intense sweetness

"It's amazing," Max said. "Everything's all neglected and gone
to pieces, but in this one little corner there are these berries that
have to be the very best there are anywhere in the world."

"They certainly are sweet, aren't they?"

"My God, they're amazing!" The world is always sweeter when
one is in love, and Max's perceptions were no doubt impaired, but
no one could have denied that the berries were a delight. "That's
one of the most amazing things about you," he continued. "No
matter where it is, you find something like this. You make the
most average things beautiful."

"My Granny used to say it's the little things that make a life
rich."

"I suppose that's true, isn't it?" Max said thoughtfully. "No
matter how much money you make, if you can't enjoy the simple
and good things, your life won't be very happy."

"And no matter how small and insignificant the joys of your
life might seem to others, if you appreciate them, you can be happy.
After all, ordinary activities occupy the greater part of our hours."

They picked and ate berries vine-to-mouth for a while, the
juice staining Max's fingers dark red and Jasmine's darker skin nearly
purple; and she then gathered a basket for Mr. Johnson, who had
consumed her previous pickings avidly, even while he complained

of the seeds sticking beneath his dentures. When he had eaten enough for the initial sweetness to seem to have diminished, however, Max stopped and gently spoke her name.

"There's something I came here to tell you," he continued, after gaining her full attention. "It affects Mr. Johnson, too, but I wanted to tell you first."

Jasmine's heart thumped at this news, for she could imagine no deeply significant, personal communication between them that would give her pleasure.

When he had her full attention, he said, "You remember you talked to me earlier about William and how he's tried to get into West Point. And I talked with him about it, too, when he was here. When I heard he'd been turned down, I couldn't believe it. I've never met a nicer guy than him. He's like you . . . I mean if you were a boy that's what you would be like. I know he's smart, and it's just a complete rip that people with more pull have gotten in ahead of him . . . ."

"I'm sure whoever got in . . .," Jasmine began.

"I know what you're going to say, that whoever got in probably deserved it just as much as he did, but I know a little bit about how these things work and I can tell you there's no chance. Sure, sometimes good guys get in, but it's political too. If you know the right people, you're going to be able to bump the guy ahead of you. That's how it works."

Jasmine, of course, had no way of knowing whether or not what he said was true, but he spoke with such assurance that she did not now contradict him. Besides, she was eager to hear any news of William, even from such an unexpected source.

"Believe it or not, jerk that he is, Jerry—he's my step-dad— has this friend who's a Congressman. The guy's pretty much of a sleazeball, but that doesn't matter. What's important is that he owes Jerry some big favors for some publicity things he pulled off during the election, and Jerry owes me a couple of favors for pieces of information that I haven't spread around to my mother . . . ." He stopped suddenly. Having seen the stricken look on Jasmine's face, he realized his error, and he waved his hands in the air in front of him and shook his head as though to erase what had gone before. "None of this matters . . . . None of it matters at all. What matters is that he's arranged to get William what he deserves. William will join the next class of plebes."

This was very nearly too much for Jasmine to absorb, that such a brilliant joy could be wrapped in such a sordid package . . . . How could it possibly be true?

"You are sure of this?"

"Absolutely," he said, again beaming at her.

"Your Congressman is reliable?"

"Oh, no! He's absolutely not reliable. But about this, I'm perfectly sure. He won't change on this."

"But doesn't that mean that William has stolen someone else's position?"

"Of course not. It only means that he's taken back the position that belonged to him anyway."

"We have no way of knowing that."

"Maybe not for sure. But, Jasmine, it's true. It's how these things get done. The army wants something from a politician, the politician wants something from somebody else. So they make a deal. That's how the world works . . . . But that's not the important thing. The important thing is that William will be in the Academy."

"I don't think that he will be."

"He will. I'm sure. There's no doubt."

"I mean that I'm not sure he will accept under such circumstances."

Max now looked at her with undisguised awe. "Of course he'll accept."

"I don't know that he would believe that it was right to do so."

"But there's nothing wrong with this," Max said, "not really. He hasn't done anything wrong. And there's absolutely no reason he needs to know what I've done."

Jasmine was familiar with the aphorism "What he doesn't know won't hurt him," having heard it more than occasionally from one or another of her cousins, but never had she been so tempted to accept its validity. If William did not know that underhanded means had been used to secure his nomination, if indeed these machinations only corrected past injustices, if his honor could in no way be compromised, if political maneuvering were common in such cases . . . . "If, if, if . . .," she kept repeating to herself, but no amount of temporizing could change the final result: someone else would be denied admission by this Congressman's intervention.

"I think that William would consider such an appointment dishonorable."

"Dishonorable!" Max said, now with some exasperation. "Are you kidding me?"

"He has lived a military life for a long time, and military men value honor very highly."

"I'm sure there's no more honor in the military than anywhere else . . . . Besides, it can't be dishonorable if he doesn't know."

Jasmine did not answer this. He intuited her meaning and said, "You're not planning on telling him?"

"I would be deceiving him if I did not."

"If you think that you'd being doing him a favor by telling him, you're wrong."

"No . . .," she agreed, "perhaps not a favor."

"Absolutely not a favor. You'd be keeping him out of the academy."

"Isn't there hope that he still might find another way?"

"They only let in a handful of enlisted men. We had to pull some strings. There was a problem with his age. Another year, and we couldn't have pulled it off."

"It would be horrible to know that the 'pulling of strings' earned his position for him."

"It didn't. Really, it didn't," Max said, regretting the boastful impulse that had driven him to take credit. "His record is exemplary. He's done everything he needs to do to get admitted. Nobody's denying that. He just needed to have someone on the other side of the door who was on his side, somebody who could make people give him a fair chance."

"What of the people who didn't have someone on the other side?"

"What of them?"

"Won't they be victims of an injustice?"

"Victims? Victims?" he repeated incredulously. "William was the victim. We just got him what was fair."

Jasmine didn't answer this with words, but her grim look told him that his comment had not had the desired effect. He took a deep breath to calm himself.

"Jasmine, I wish it didn't have to be this way, but sometimes you just have to be willing to play the game," he continued. "You have to make some compromises. I wondered for a while if I should even tell you, but I decided I had to, because I never ever wanted you to have any reason to distrust me."

He paused for a moment, looking down at his stained hands, and Jasmine felt a moment of compassion for him. "I do appreciate what you have done," she said. "I know it required a great deal of effort, and it was enormously thoughtful, but . . . ."

He interrupted her with an exasperated sigh, obliging Jasmine to search her own actions for an error on her part. The facts were, however, that he had initiated his efforts without consulting her and had failed rightly to anticipate her reactions. For these events she could accept no blame.

He took her hand between his own now, and despite the deep discomfort it caused her, she let him keep it. He gazed into her eyes.

"There was another thing . . . something I hoped I wouldn't have to bring up. Something that I did that I had no right to do." He paused, looked away, and gripped her hand more tightly, as though in anguish at having to tell her. Though she said nothing to encourage him, he soon resumed. "It isn't the work I did. That isn't important. And it's not the expense either. I would have spent ten times as much and worked ten times as hard if I'd needed to. The thing is . . . ." He broke off and began again. "The thing is that I wasn't really supposed to tell you . . . . All this, it was in strict confidence. I really shouldn't have told you. It was just that I thought it would make you so happy, I wanted to be the one to tell you."

"But William will eventually have to know in any case."

"I don't see why. Really, he didn't have anything to do with it.

It was told to me in confidence, and, technically, I was telling you it in confidence, too."

"William and I have never kept any secrets from each other."

"*You've* never kept any from *him* maybe," he said. Then, seeing how this wounded her, he went on quickly, "It's not keeping a secret. It's keeping a confidence. Besides, some things it's better not to talk about. Why say something if it's just going to upset somebody? I'm sure he doesn't tell you about all his girlfriends and all the crummy stuff that happened at his school and in the army. And you don't tell him about every little thing that happens to you at school."

"I don't feel that this is a little thing."

"I know you don't, and I admire you for that, but as you get older you'll see how common this type of thing is. It really isn't that big a deal. No one would ever criticize William for it. Besides, I don't see how anyone could ever find out."

"We would know."

"And you would know that absolutely nothing improper was done. He received an appointment from a Congressman, just like everyone else. And he was deserving in every way. There's absolutely nothing wrong with that. That's how it's done. That's how everybody gets in."

Jasmine had for a few minutes been hearing noises at the kitchen window, where Mr. Johnson, who seemed always to wake from his naps thirsty, was probably trying to get ice for himself, something which he could accomplish only with some difficulty. Now, since they both knew perfectly well that the Congressman referred to had not nominated William on his merits and had probably never considered them, Jasmine chose not to revisit the issue, instead saying, "My uncle is awake. I think we need to go in."

They started for the kitchen, but before they could reach the door, Max stopped. "Mr. Johnson's daughter," he said quickly, "you said he had a daughter."

"I wasn't able to find her."

"What did you try?"

"I sent a letter to an old address a neighbor gave me, but it came back."

"Do you have the envelope?"

She showed it to him, and he took it from her hand and put it into his pocket. "And please don't write to William about any of this. Promise me you won't."

This Jasmine could not promise.

"At least wait. Wait until you've talked with your Uncle David . . . . If you still feel you have to then, okay. But promise me you'll get his advice first."

This she could have promised, but Max, to his credit, was well satisfied with her nod of assent.

After remarkably gracious and polite good-byes to her uncle, during which he remembered to thank Mr. Johnson not only for the tea but for the berries as well, to compliment him once again on the individuality displayed in his household, and to wish him good health, Max took his leave. Jasmine could accompany him only as far as the front door, as Mr. Johnson had taken it upon himself to visit the berry patch, which he could not be allowed to attempt without assistance.

"It's too late now anyway," Max said. "The appointment can't be reversed, not without William getting into a lot of trouble." Then, as he took his departure, he added, "This Congressman has a snowball's chance in hell of getting re-elected. Let him do this one decent thing before they toss them out."

Chapter 25

Jasmine Receives Alarming News About Thomas

For Jasmine, the days that followed proceeded much like those prior to Max's visit; although, as Mr. Johnson's condition did not worsen and she'd gained more trust in his stability, she allowed herself to take her shopping trips at a more leisurely pace. She spoke on two occasions with the woman who lived across the street, discovered that she was now cordial and considerate in all respects, and concluded that Mr. Johnson must have given very serious provocations to incite her animosity. The woman recounted to Jasmine a story of a poorly neighbor who had been taken away by "the welfare." "They would have let his neighbors take care of him just as long as they would, but he didn't have any money, and they didn't have much either. That's what the welfare is for. They take care of people when there's nobody else." While such a fate for Mr. Johnson still seemed unbearably lonely, it was a measure of Jasmine's increasing anxiety that she no longer saw malice in the woman's suggestion. Rather, she now understood her to be acting out of kindness.

Jasmine had mentioned to Max during his visit how much she had appreciated his letter, and he had apparently taken this to heart, as on the Monday that followed, she received a second letter from him. It reminded her of her promise to speak with Dr. Gannon before sending news of the appointment to her brother. "I went to see Dr. Gannon when I was in Washington, and he was all in favor. He said he was planning something himself, but he was relieved because this was a much better way. I'm sure you'll understand when you've had a chance to talk with him." The letter proceeded to give news of Chrissie and Sherry. "They're all having a great time in LA, but none of that interests me anymore."

Jasmine observed to herself that he ought not speak too much of changes in himself before he had time to discover if they were lasting. Yet, at the same time, she was obliged to acknowledge the kindness of his having taken such a long drive to visit her, of the extremity of his efforts to aid William, and of the divine grace that allowed even the most wicked to mend past ways and receive forgiveness. Moreover, if she was disturbed by the ethical implications of his actions, she could not deny that her discomfort could in part be a result of her own lack of worldly sophistication. Did not many of the ideas she'd first brought with her to Arden Park now seem childish and ridiculous? She was reminded of how her conscience had troubled her over the use of her aunt's stamps to write to William. Wasn't it Phillip who had shown her that she need not worry? Might this not turn out much the same? If so, it would be a pity to make William suffer over her childish worries. More importantly, if Dr. Gannon himself approved, how could she object?

He closed with "Love," but since "love" was a term frequently bandied about among the young people, she could discount its meaning to little more than a "How do you do" or a "Yours truly."

He made no mention of the envelope she had given him, which caused her mixed emotions. She longed to return to Arden Park—she had come to realize more than ever before how important it was to her—and could not prevent herself from hoping that Max would find a solution to her predicament. On the other hand, she did not wish to find herself further indebted to him. She had already detected a sense of personal grievance in his reactions to her discomfort. It was as though she were being ungrateful—as though she were not fulfilling her part of an obligation. None of this had been directly stated, and it was possible that she had only imagined that he harbored such feelings; nonetheless, she was reluctant to incur further obligations. He had already been very, very good to her, acting at considerable personal sacrifice and expense. If he did have special feelings for her, feelings which she could not reciprocate, it would be wrong either to encourage him or to exploit him by allowing him to act on her behalf.

Should she, she wondered, write him immediately and insist that he not take any action regarding Mr. Johnson's daughter? Despite the risk of delaying resolution of her current circumstances, she would do so in a moment to prevent an improper entanglement; but she could not conclude that anything improper had yet occurred or even predict with certainty that any impropriety was likely to ensue. He had always treated her respectfully. His admiration had seemed to her to be excessive, but this could be excused as a product of his upbringing in the movie world, where overstated emotions were the norm. Indeed, for her to infer more from his actions than a noble desire to aid a friend would have be presumptuous as to the extent of her own attractions. Until he declared his intentions more openly—if he indeed held such intentions—she could hardly discourage him more strongly than she already had. A letter from her demanding that he not act on her behalf would certainly seem ungracious and would suggest an exaggerated perception of her own position. Besides, she did want very much to return to Arden Park.

A longer letter, this one from Phillip, arrived the next day. She saved it until Mr. Johnson was sleeping and carried it out to the back yard, where she sat under the shade of a fig tree and read it slowly, extending the pleasure of seeing his handwriting. He described a whirlwind of activities in Los Angeles, a series of parties, trips to nightclubs, outings to the beach, and late morning breakfasts with aspiring actors and directors. "It's all very exciting," he wrote, "and at first you feel like you're part of the most wonderful life imaginable. After a while, though, you begin to realize that almost no one is really doing anything. Instead, they are planning, proposing, and auditioning. I suppose that's just the nature of the movie business. Nothing happens for a long time, and then suddenly everyone is very busy. But I really can't imagine living this way for very long. You wake up in the morning with no more important task than figuring out how best to entertain yourself, and after a while you begin to feel like a real slob.

"Sherry grew up with it, and it doesn't seem to faze her. It's remarkable to see her with her friends. You can tell in a minute that she's really respected by all of them, and since she's so level-headed and has the best mind of the bunch, they all turn to her for advice. She's really in her element. She has such a natural grace that she's able to fly right over all the jealousy and pettiness and see people for who they really are. That's probably why they admire her so much. I think, if she wanted to, she could probably be a very successful agent or even run a studio someday.

"You probably heard about Chrissie's problem. The guys she was with are some friends of Max. Sherry says that they're really okay, just a little wild at times. She thinks it's all pretty funny and that I make too big a deal of it, but then she doesn't know Uncle

David like we do. I think it was mostly a case of Chrissie's being with new people and sort of suspending her own judgment and letting them take over. In any case, I think she's learned her lesson (at least, I hope she has) and will play it a little cooler from now on, because it certainly wouldn't be cool if David found out."

He concluded by expressing his wishes that Mr. Johnson might recover quickly and that she would be home in Arden Park when he returned. "I don't know how long we'll stay down here, but I can't keep it up much longer. With all the late hours, I haven't done a morning run in two weeks. I'm going to be really out of shape, and we'll need to do some serious running when I get back." He used the same closing he had since he was a small boy: "Your cousin, Phillip."

While any letter from Phillip was a joy, she could not be happy that he was spending so much time with Sherry in Los Angeles or that he seemed to be enjoying himself. She was also concerned for Chrissie. This was the first she had heard of any incident, but she was aware that Chrissie could at times act impulsively, especially when angry. She suspected from the attention that Phillip gave to the matter that it was at least potentially serious in nature, and she was unable to understand why he had not counseled Chrissie to return immediately to Arden Park and receive her mother's advice.

As for Dr. Gannon, she understood the motivation for protecting him. His peace of mind was dependent on the feeling that his household was being run in an orderly and exemplary manner. As long as he was secure in this feeling, he could apply himself fully to his work, which they all understood to be of great importance. He could not be consulted on every minor crisis that arose, and Phillip judged this incident not to require their uncle's intervention. In this, Jasmine could only trust her cousin's judgment.

Multiplying blessings! The very next day, she received a third letter, this one from Sherry Hill. Sherry began by writing of how much she missed their quiet conversations in Arden Park. "I haven't had many 'girl' friends in my life, and I think it's because so few girls are as smart as you. I think I like talking with boys more because they're not so interested in petty stuff and are willing to talk about serious subjects. But with you I have the best of both: you're never petty or back-stabbing, but you're a girl. I'm so honored to be able to call you a friend.

"It's been fun with everyone here—a real blast and all that— but I think life in Arden Park has spoiled me. I can't help seeing how greedy and ambitious everybody is. And how jealous everybody is! Not just boy-girl things, but everything! Jobs, cars, who's found the best restaurant, who's gone to the neatest party, everything! Not that I don't at least partially understand the attraction. I know I'm not half as good as you are at seeing past superficial things to what's important. But I must be getting better because all the stuff that used to seem so important to me doesn't mean much anymore. Most of it just seems too ridiculous! Like one girl I know was agonizing over the shape or her earlobes! Of course, it's still fun, and it gives us all something to talk about. And if I didn't at least get invited to the best parties, I'd have to strangle somebody. But it's not the same.

"What I think we all need is the scent of Jasmine. (Sorry!) You're so good at showing us how to appreciate things that I'm sure you could raise the level of conversation for all of us. Really! I love you, Sherry."

Jasmine had only two days to review all this news before she received yet a fourth letter. This one contained alarming news.

"Thomas has some illness," her Aunt Cynthia wrote. "We don't know yet exactly what the problem is, but he's run a fever, he never wakes up, and his tests aren't good. He's been in the hospital, and his doctors have mentioned things about blood infections and his liver. David will soon be home to explain it all to me, and I'm sure he'll get it sorted out quickly and get him on the right medications, but the waiting is just awful.

"Jasmine, I want you home. I've missed you and know that everything will be better again when we are all together here in Arden Park. I feel sorry for your poor uncle, but you've already been gone a very long time, and we now need you here. After all, we're your family, too."

"P.S. Phillip has been staying with Thomas and has been at his side every minute. We were so lucky he was in Los Angeles when all this started. It makes me feel so much better to know that whenever Thomas opens his eyes, a familiar face is there to greet him. I know this may sound selfish, but now I want to have you here when I wake up. It's just too horrible when I realize this isn't a bad dream.

"Love, Cynthia."

While there was a suggestion in the letter that she had been callous, Jasmine was not troubled by it. She had long understood that her aunt was a self-centered woman. So preoccupied with her own emotional and physical states was she that she often appeared to be indifferent to those of others. In fact, however, she did not lack sympathy for others, only attentiveness. Once apprised of others' misfortunes, she was quick to show sympathy and kindness and made material efforts to give assistance. Had Jasmine informed her of her want for money, for example, Cynthia would have been quick to send it.

Jasmine loved her aunt, and she loved her even more because she now expressed so strong a wish to have her with her. She was deeply worried about Thomas, especially as his debauched habits put him at risk for serious diseases, and she was concerned for her aunt, as honesty required her to acknowledge that she was ill-equipped to manage mishap and crisis. She might have wished that her aunt had explored her circumstances deeply enough to understand that her uncle could not yet be left alone, that absolutely no one else was prepared to take care of him, and that, had she felt free to do so, she had neither a vehicle to carry her home nor the money to purchase a bus ticket. She might have wished that Cynthia understood how lonesome she had been, how isolated she had felt, and how often she had longed to be back in Arden Park. She must accept, however, that it was not in her aunt's nature to appreciate such things without prompting, and with Phillip in Los Angeles, it was unlikely that anyone in the house would do the prompting. She also understood that only a brief note from herself would be required to invoke her aunt's sympathy and assistance. How best was she to do this? Mr. Johnson remained forgetful, was unsteady on his feet, and presented a hazard not only to himself, but, when left alone in his kitchen, to the entire neighborhood as well. Even had he been well enough, there remained the problem of money. No one else would fault her for taking bus money from Mr. Johnson's account, but her own conscience would object. She pondered these questions for some time and concluded that she must somehow find a solution to her uncle's dilemma that did not include herself as caretaker—and that she must have the necessary money on hand to return home immediately when a solution was found.

She composed a letter in which she stated her uncle's circumstances, requested fifty dollars for bus fare, and urged her aunt to remain hopeful. "Thomas is young and strong, and Uncle David is the finest physician in the world. No doubt all that can be done is being done, and the results will soon bring happiness and relief.

"I have too often neglected my prayers, but it will be impossible to do so now as I know that Thomas is in need of God's strength, and we are all in need of his peace. I long to be with you all at this very moment, and promise to catch the very first bus when I believe it is safe to leave my uncle's home. He is not stable on his feet and cannot take care of himself. If I were to leave, no one would remain to watch over him. I console myself by knowing that Thomas has a household of loved ones to keep watch over him.

"Love, Jasmine."

After posting this letter, Jasmine braced herself for a conversation with Mr. Johnson. He had money enough to hire a caretaker; Jasmine could be of use in finding him one, perhaps even from within his own neighborhood.

Need we report the result of this conversation? Let it be sufficient to say that Jasmine suffered recriminations including betrayal, spying (on his finances), selfishness, and sundry other crimes. Unfortunately, he did not also send her from his house. In near despair, she began a second round of inquiries to their neighbors. She was now received more patiently, as her presence in

Mr. Johnson's house had come to be accepted and she'd done nothing to make enemies, but the prejudice against her uncle was very deep—deeper than mere bad temper could explain. Finally, in desperation, she returned to the woman across the street. Her advice was again that she call the welfare department.

"You just call them up and tell them you're leaving. Then, it'll be their butts on the line. If he kills himself or burns his house down, you can sue them. That's what welfare's for. It's their job."

"I don't see how I can leave him even for one night. If something were to happen to him . . . ."

"Listen, child, he's a grown man. He's built his own nest. If something was to happen to him, it would be nobody's fault but his own. You can't waste your life taking care of him, just like his own children couldn't. You've got your own life to live. Besides, you aren't even sure that man's your uncle. From the looks of you, I'd say he as likely isn't as is, and it seems darn near impossible for a girl with as sweet a disposition as you to be any type of kin to a man like that."

Jasmine could only agree that the physical resemblance between herself and Mr. Johnson was slight, but she recognized unsettling correspondences between his character, her grandmother's, and even her own. Her grandmother's strong views had obliged her to remove herself from society, just as Mr. Johnson's had, and she knew herself to be in her own way as dogmatic in her opinions as either of them. The difference was that she was far too deferential even to consider imposing her views on her family, neighbors, or schoolmates. While this was no doubt a virtue in a young woman, Jasmine foresaw that it would not always be so in every circumstance; moreover, given her grandmother's history and Mr. Johnson's, she was obliged to acknowledge a hereditary risk of becoming contrary and argumentative with age. To abandon Mr. Johnson now, she feared, would be tantamount to abandoning herself in her old age.

"Let him go to the welfare," her neighbor now concluded. "He's been acting superior and fussing people about being on the welfare for years. Let him find out what it feels like. He'll see it isn't any picnic."

Jasmine did go so far as to make telephone inquiries the next time she went for groceries, but it soon became apparent that Mr. Johnson's financial resources would make him ineligible for public assistance. The only alternative for her would be to have him declared incompetent to manage his own affairs and have a court-appointed guardian use his money to hire a caretaker for him. This was an action that would require the intervention of a judge, and something which Jasmine was certain her uncle would resist. It would likely require the assistance of an attorney, whom she would have no way of paying, and was sure to take weeks, if not months. The immediate crisis and her own sense of urgency precluded her viewing this type of guardianship as any type of solution whatsoever.

Chapter 26

Max Plots Jasmine's Escape

The hours that followed were long and trying for Jasmine, especially as her uncle had observed her talks with their neighbors. He now very nearly continuously spoke to her with inexcusable vitriol. If, however, you will agree to accept Jasmine Johnson's aching need to be home and the feelings of complete helplessness that fate had imposed on her, we will spare you, faithful reader, a full recantation of her frustration, boredom, and anxiety. Instead, we will jump forward one full day, at which time a car arrived in front of the house. The driver of this car was Max Hill.

Jasmine welcomed him in much the same way a starving woman would welcome the sight of a dead cow, with joy and thanksgiving. She hurried out to the street, where he hugged her with an intimacy only slightly more fervent than seemed proper, then held her away from him and looked at her. His eyes dwelled on her face so searchingly that she felt compelled to drop her own gaze and turn toward the house. He stopped her. "I have so much news," he said. "Some of it I'd rather not share with your uncle, at least not right away."

Jasmine knew perfectly well that Mr. Johnson would be watching from a window. Nonetheless, she agreed to walk with him a short distance down the street.

"First," he said, "Thomas's condition is stable. It's still critical, but it no longer seems to be deteriorating. There's reason to hope."

Jasmine was much more alarmed than reassured by this news, as she had expected to hear that his symptoms had disappeared. "He is very sick then?"

"I'm afraid so. His immune system seems to be compromised in some way, and they've been worried about pneumonia. That seems to have passed now, but the source of all his problems hasn't. Until they know what's causing it, or until he recovers, no one knows . . . Then there's the other stuff." He broke off and looked toward her as though she would understand what he implied. She tried for a moment to read a message in the exact tone and phrasing of his words, but nothing was clear to her, and she could only shake her head in ignorance. "There are some drug related issues," he finally said.

While she understood that Thomas experimented with drugs, the idea that he could use them to the point of self-injury was a shocking blow. She would never have believed so wretched a thing possible in the Gannon house.

"He's become a heavy user?" she asked, the words a grief to her.

"Well, yes . . . . No, not really . . . . No more than anybody else. Lots of people I know use a lot more drugs than Thomas and have never gone through anything like this. As far as that goes, I think it's just bad luck. But he went sort of comatose. They're kind of thinking he might have o-d'ed or gotten some tainted stuff. They're still worried about his liver. His skin looks really bad. He has a funny color."

Jasmine wanted to ask more, but Max now stopped abruptly, nodded toward a car parked a few steps down the street from them, and began leading her toward it. As they approached, a woman rose from behind the steering wheel and stood beside the car door.

"Check this out," he said under-his-breath to Jasmine, but not without some pride in his voice. "It's the daughter."

Jasmine was shocked, first at the stupendous news, then at the woman's appearance. From the bitterness of her uncle's regrets, she had come to anticipate that his children had fallen at least into poverty and dissipation, if not prison or the grave. This woman stood beside a silver Mercedes. She was dressed from head to foot in a dashiki cloth wrap, which she wore with the regal bearing of a model. As they drew nearer, the woman offered them a queer, diffident smile, and it became apparent that, while she was certainly very attractive, she was both too old and a little too round to be a model. Her skin was very nearly of the same tone as her father's, and she resembled him every bit as much as a daughter should.

Out of her dither of anticipation, Jasmine reached to take her cousin's hand—learning as she did that her name was Jolene—and accepted her bright, open, lovely smile.

"I didn't know I had any cousins at all," Jolene said.

"My brother is quite sure it's true," Jasmine replied, "and from speaking with your father it seems impossible that it could not be."

"Give me a hug, then," the woman now said, spreading her arms. Jasmine again allowed herself to be folded into another's arms, this being the second time it had happened to her in a matter of minutes; and finding that she enjoyed the perfumed, crispness of her cousin's dress, she lingered there longer than she might normally have, long enough even to leave a tear on the woman's shoulder.

When they had separated, not without a lingering brush of hands across each other's arms, the woman said, "I suppose we're not all that closely related after all, but somehow it feels good to find a relative anyway."

"It does," Jasmine said, with real feeling. "It's been a real honor to meet your father. I am reminded by him every day of my grandmother in Tennessee."

"Are you?" Jolene said, with evident skepticism.

"He's been through a very trying time, but he's obviously a

very capable and intelligent person . . . . Granny was also a woman of strong views."

"One of his strong views is that he never wanted to see any of his children again," Jolene said, looking from Jasmine to Max.

There was a moment of confused silence before Max said, "Jasmine has a terrific rapport with him. I thought if she were to introduce the idea that you were coming and to set it up properly . . . ."

"Has he said anything about me to you?" Jolene asked warily, directing her question to Jasmine.

"He's unhappy now," Jasmine replied, "and I think that he says many things he doesn't really mean."

"I told you so," Jolene said to Max. "It was a waste of time coming here."

"Jasmine," Max said, taking her hand, "there's got to be something we can do. You can't stay here forever, we all know that. Even more important, though, Mr. Johnson shouldn't remain separated from his family—I mean his real family, his close family. Isn't there some way you could get him to agree to a reconciliation?"

Jasmine now exchanged a look with Jolene, and it was apparent that they both understood the degree of Mr. Johnson's intransigence better than Max Hill. Nonetheless, as her situation was desperate, she now agreed to make an attempt.

"Your father is human just like the rest of us," she said, in part to brace her own courage. "You should know that there are times when he speaks of you very tenderly . . . . And he's just gotten up from his nap. He's always most reasonable when he first awakes."

Jolene sighed, saying, "Try if you want, but I don't think it's going to do any good."

Jasmine wanted very much to try, though she was no more certain of success than Jolene, yet she hesitated to act. As much as she yearned to return home, she could not do so if the price was anguish for her newly discovered cousin. "I won't," Jasmine now volunteered, "if seeing him would cause you too much unhappiness."

Jolene considered this for a moment, then said, "I'm the one who should take care of my father, not you. Max has told me about your cousin, and I know that you have to get yourself home."

"Yes, but there is always some other solution."

"No," Jolene said. "It's time to get this over with. This was a happy neighborhood when I was a little girl, and that house down there was a happy house. I can't go on letting it be all bad and nasty if it doesn't have to be. I won't rest easy until I've tried."

This seemed a laudable intent to Jasmine, and, while no direct mention of Mr. Johnson had been made, Jolene's tone left no doubt of the sincerity of her conviction.

"I think it would be best if I were to warn him that you're coming," Jasmine said.

"He probably wouldn't know me anyway, without you telling him, as long as it's been."

"So, if you were to wait here for a few minutes . . . ."

"I'm not going anywhere," Jolene said.

Jasmine remained unsure of how she would proceed, and she now turned toward Max in search of direction. "I can go with you," he offered. "Maybe I can put in a word of support."

Had Jasmine established any plan of her own, perhaps she would have urged him to stay behind with her newfound cousin, but in truth she felt the need of support. They approached the porch, where they found Mr. Johnson still at the window. As standing was difficult for him, this could be taken for a sign that he had seen enough to interest him.

"You'll have to be firm," Max said. "You can't let him bully you."

Jasmine did not disagree with this, though as she approached the door, she continued to hope that logic and moral persuasion would prevail.

"You again," Mr. Johnson said upon seeing Max in the doorway, though he did accept Max's extended hand and give it a weary shake.

"Yes," Jasmine said, "he's come back, and he's brought news of some importance." She urged him to sit down, and he regarded her warily. When she and Max had both taken chairs, however, he settled himself on the edge of a couch cushion. Jasmine sensed that this placed her and Max too directly in opposition to her uncle, and she shifted to a cushion beside him.

"Max has brought us news," she said, "better news than perhaps either you or I had thought possible." She turned her gaze to Max Hill.

"Jasmine's told me, Mr. Johnson, that you've been out of contact with your family for some time."

"I don't have any family."

"You have a daughter and a son both."

Mr. Johnson made no reply.

"Not only do you have a daughter and son, you have quite a distinguished son and daughter."

Mr. Johnson harrumphed, saying. "You don't know anything about anything."

"I was able to reach your daughter and speak with her. She a vice-president for an insurance company and has a very nice home."

"You're talking about somebody else."

"The woman I spoke with is named Jolene McCray now, but she was Jolene Johnson before."

"You've got some other Jolene."

"The woman I spoke to grew up in this town, and, in fact, I happen to know that she grew up in this house."

Mr. Johnson again harrumphed in disdain.

Max paused for a moment. "I also know that she wants very much to see you again."

"I don't want to see her."

Max now looked to Jasmine for help. Jasmine's grandmother had once told her that when in doubt, she should always just say or do the truest thing she knew. Now, with so much at stake and herself so very much in doubt, she braced herself by remembering this advice.

"Mr. Johnson," she began, "*Uncle* Johnson, I'm afraid I've been unfair to you. Out of concern for your health, I've avoided explaining certain circumstances that have arisen, circumstances that require me to return to my home at the first opportunity . . . ."

"Circumstances that require you to abandon an old man who

can't even get his own meals and bring that woman who's out there into my house to rob me blind."

"That woman?"

"Yes, that welfare women, or caretaker, or whatever she is."

"She is none of those."

Mr. Johnson made no reply to this, from which Jasmine inferred that he very well knew who the woman outside was.

"You can rest assured, Mr. Johnson, that I have no intention of abandoning you," Jasmine continued. "In fact, I have been working these past weeks to assure that would not happen. But, as it happens, I have a cousin at home who is ill as well, a cousin with whom I have lived since I was a small child. My aunt has requested that I return home to be with her—and him—and I confess that I very much want to go home, as being apart from them causes me much worry." The old man apparently experienced some inkling of sympathy, as his expression now evolved away from hostility toward bewilderment. Jasmine sought to reassure him. "It is true that you are not yet well enough to take care of yourself," she went on, "though I am sure that you soon will be; nor do I have any intention of abandoning you. The happy truth is that through Max's hard work and God's benevolence this very difficult situation may prove to be a blessing. Mr. Johnson, your daughter wishes to be reunited with you. I know from the many mementos about this house that you once loved her. I know from the confessions you have made to me in your most tender moments that you still love her. Could you not give reconciliation a chance? It would be a tragedy if you were to live in estrangement from each other over past incidents that long ago might have been forgiven."

There now appeared a tear in Mr. Johnson's eye. "There are things that you don't know," he said.

This Jasmine could not deny. "I would never want to intrude on your privacy," she said, "but there are many things that I already do know. For example, I know that you are an unusually proud and capable man, and I know that your daughter is proud and capable as well. I know that it will be hard for either of you to admit wrong, to offer forgiveness, or to accept forgiveness . . . ."

"It's not me who did anything wrong . . . ."

"Mr. Johnson, we all do some things wrong, even if it is only insisting too strongly on what we believe to be right. But I was not going to suggest that either of you admit wrong or that you grant forgiveness. While that may be something that could be hoped for in the future, in this case, it perhaps goes beyond what is possible. I am suggesting only that you start anew. Regard the past as past. Approach each other as strangers if you must. After all, you were willing to invite me into your house, though for all you knew I might have been guilty of far worse than your daughter. People do change with time, as you can confirm by analyzing your own life. They may change for the better or worse, but it is our Christian duty to allow everyone a hope of redemption."

Jasmine had noticed in the past that invoking God had unpredictable effects on Mr. Johnson. He might fly into a rage at the perfidy and hypocrisy of the church ladies who had attempted *to help* him after his wife's death; or he might be sobered by memories of his wife's faith and patience. She had risked it now, only because she felt she must speak the truth: if reconciliation was morally superior to steadfast retribution, as she believed it was, her authority for saying so was her own faith.

"Your daughter is a very good person," she continued. "You have an abundance of reasons to be proud of her, especially as she has shown the strength of character to put past grievances aside. I understand that the two of you have been estranged for some time; nonetheless, you were together for her childhood years, years that she describes with great tenderness. Cannot some portion of this past happiness be reclaimed now?"

Mr. Johnson remained mute. Max, with an approving nod, encouraged Jasmine to continue.

"I have recently had reason to appreciate how deeply important to me my family is," she now said, "and to recount the infinite ways in which my loved ones make my life rich and happy. I cannot tell you how serious a mistake you would be making if you were to deprive yourself of this opportunity. Mr. Johnson, I implore you to give your daughter a chance, to give yourself a chance. You have many years remaining to you. They need not be bitter and full of retribution. I don't know the full circumstances of your separation, nor do I want or need to know, but as I have said, you need not forgive, you need not ask forgiveness, you need not forget, you need only put the past in the hands of God. He is, after all, the final arbiter of all rights and wrongs. The world may accept any number of things as true—people will think as they do—but only God knows the truth."

Mr. Johnson sat with his face turned away from them and had so long remained motionless during her discourse that Jasmine now began to fear that she had caused him to suffer a recurrence of his stroke. Now, she was relieved to see him shift forward to stare at the floor between his feet. He neither met her eyes nor spoke, however, and she looked to Max for further guidance. He gestured to her that she should stand and follow him outside, which she did reluctantly, looking back toward her uncle in hopes of receiving some positive response before passing out the door. None came. When they'd moved beyond her uncle's hearing, it was soon apparent that Max was more than willing to treat Mr. Johnson's non-response as acquiescence.

"We'll sit them down, and while they're still hugging each other, we're out the door," he said.

"But isn't that trickery?" Jasmine said.

Max stopped for a moment. "Sometimes people need to be pushed a little before they can do the right thing," he said as he moved away, then added, "Besides, Mr. Johnson isn't the type of person to remain silent if he's not convinced."

There was enough truth to this statement to give Jasmine pause, and Max took this opportunity to be quickly off and away. Moments later the Mercedes pulled to a stop in front of the house. Max led the way through the gate, and Jolene followed a few steps behind.

"You're sure he said he wanted to see me?" she was saying.

"I'm sure he wants to see you. Jasmine absolutely convinced him."

"He's changed then."

"Absolutely."

"Is that true?" Jolene asked, turning to Jasmine.

"Of course, we are not privy to the deepest secrets of his heart," Jasmine said. "He's not inclined to display his most tender emotions."

"He does want to see me though?"

Jasmine hesitated.

"Of course he does," Max said.

She turned to Jasmine for confirmation, and she was again compelled to remember her grandmother's advice. "I believe that he does, just as any parent wishes to see his child. But it is true that he hasn't said so, not in exact words, and while I think it unlikely, there is some possibility that we misunderstand him."

"Of course, he hasn't said so," Max said quickly. "He wasn't able to talk for three days, and he still has difficulty expressing himself. When we told him about you, he was so overcome, he lost his ability to speak, but I could see in his eyes how important you are to him."

Jolene looked warily to Jasmine.

"I believe that he wants—at least with a part of himself—to see you very much."

"With what part though?"

"With the very best of himself," Jasmine said. "His best nature has long remained smothered here—closed up inside this house— but I'm certain that it hasn't been extinguished. With the very best part of himself, the part you saw when he was a compassionate, loving, and perhaps sometimes overzealous father, the part that provides his only hope for a happy and productive old age, with that part he wants very much to see you. That part of him has languished, but a spark of it remains. Perhaps it was God's will that Max and I might be here to keep it alive, and even more I believe it is God's will that you should come to care for him, for without that, I think it cannot stay alive very much longer."

Jolene considered this quietly; then, growing impatient, Max said, "If you don't go see him now, you're going to hear someday that he's kicked off, and you'll wish you had. And without somebody to take care of him it could happen soon. Jasmine tells me he's got money—lots of it—and the neighbors probably know it. Somebody could break in . . . ."

Jolene looked to Jasmine, and she affirmed with a modest nod that this was not without some truth.

"Besides," Max continued, "what have you got to lose? If he throws us out the door, he throws us out the door. At least you'll know that you tried."

The word "money" had now been spoken, and perhaps it should not have been; nor was there any evidence that it influenced Jolene's decision to lower her head and mount the steps to the door.

Jasmine had seen her uncle watching them from the window, but he had resumed his inanimate position on the couch when they entered. Nonetheless, he could not prevent himself from sneaking a look at his daughter as she approached. She now stood across from him and gazed down on his bent head. Neither seemed willing to speak a first word.

"Is your home as you remember it?" Jasmine asked.

This caused Jolene to break out of her trance and look about the room. "Momma didn't like clutter . . .," she said.

"It's not clutter . . .," Mr. Johnson intervened.

"But it's not much different. It's gotten smaller over the years," she said with a bright, little laugh.

"Same size it always was," Mr. Johnson, now looking at her.

"I only meant that it seems smaller. You know how a child inflates everything up in size. It's like the kitchen is 'way over there' and the garden 'oh way so far out there.' I used to think it was *a hike* out to the boysenberry patch. Plus, there was a nasty old snake lizard that lived out there that I didn't care for one little bit."

"He's been gone for years," Mr. Johnson said.

"I can't say as I'm disappointed to hear that," Jolene said. She was still looking about the room and noticed the photos on the shelf. She picked them up one-by-one while her father watched her.

"Look how much hair Larry had! He's almost bald now, Daddy. You probably wouldn't even know him."

Mr. Johnson made no reply to this.

"He's working for the phone company now."

"Putting in phone lines?" Mr. Johnson asked.

"He used to. Not any more. I don't know exactly what he does now. Something where he has to wear a coat and tie to work. Nadine, says he doesn't like it as much, but she likes the money. Nadine's his wife."

"A man's got to take a better job when he's got the chance."

"You only got one life though, Daddy."

"So you ought not to waste it."

"Don't you worry about Larry. He's got a nice house, a nice wife, and two kids . . . . His wife, she's white," she said, glancing guiltily toward Max and Jasmine. "His kids look just about like her," she added, indicating Jasmine.

"Who cares what color she is?"

"You do. You were always toadying up to white people."

Mr. Johnson harrumphed. "You act like there's something wrong with being polite and decent. Like if you did what the teacher said you were toadying up. Cut off your nose to spite your own face is what you did."

"And talk about cutting off your own nose, you wouldn't even let us borrow sugar from a neighbor . . . ."

"That's different."

How it was different was to remain a mystery as there now was a knock at the screened door, the first to be heard in the house in a month. Standing on the porch, holding a plate of cookies, was the woman from across the street. Jolene now went out to her, hugged her, and they spoke for a few moments in laughing and animated voices. During this time, Mr. Johnson sat staring at the floor, and Max and Jasmine regarded each other questioningly. The lady did not come inside, however, and Jolene re-entered shortly, the plate in hand.

"Mrs. Atkinson sent some cookies," Jolene said.

Mr. Johnson looked up and said nothing.

"It was she who gave me your previous address," Jasmine offered. "It was how Max was able to find you."

"She was always very nice," Jolene offered. "After Momma died, *she* was the one always wanting to borrow sugar." She directed a mischievous grin at her father, who could not restrain a narrow smile.

"*Borrow sugar*," he said, contemptuously. "What she wanted to borrow was my checkbook."

"I don't know, Daddy, you were some kind of handsome man." She looked at him with a smile. "Still are, I guess, though you act nasty as a polecat."

He looked at her for a moment, neither smiling nor scowling, then put out his hand and said, "Help me up. I want to show you something." Their hands touched in what Jasmine felt to be a poignant moment, and he rose up from the couch and said, "In the bedroom, I got something I need to show you."

This seemed a private moment, and Jasmine was not inclined to follow. Max said to the departing pair, "We'll be going then," in a voice that may or may not have been audible, and, when the father and daughter were far enough down the hall to be out of view, he took Jasmine's arm. "Let's get out of here," he whispered.

Jasmine regarded him with stunned surprise.

"They need to be left alone, Jasmine."

Impossible as it sounded, there was undeniable logic to this. "I need at least to say good-bye."

"Send a note."

"My clothes are in my room."

The voices she heard upon entering the hallway suggested neither violence nor malevolence, and upon exiting her small room with her very small bundle cradled in her arms, she believed that she heard laughter; yet she still hesitated to pass out the front door. Max tugged at her.

"You can send them a letter," he said, and with this thought she climbed into Max's car.

For several minutes they traveled down the road, Jasmine concerned and Max smiling, until Jasmine said, "I hadn't dared to hope it would go so well."

"It was the money that did it," Max said with a chuckle. "She found out he had some, and he saw her Mercedes."

Stung by this observation, which she could not categorically rule out, Jasmine gave a brief, involuntary gasp.

"That, and what you said," Max said quickly. "They're family. They ought to try to get back together. They've got some things to work out, but they need each other. You saw how they were together. They argued maybe, but deep down you could see there was still a bond between them . . . . You and I, we've done a good deed here. We have every reason to feel good about it."

Jasmine reasoned thusly to herself: "They are now in God's hands"; then, with a brief prayer of Thanksgiving, she turned her thoughts to the problems of Arden Park.

"And how will I find Thomas?" she asked.

Max would have preferred to glory a little longer in their good deed and Jasmine's rescue and escape, but this was, after all, Jasmine, and such could not be expected. "I'm afraid the news there isn't so good," he said. "There's been a turn for the worse."

Chapter 27

Home At Last!

Max, who under more normal circumstances would certainly have joined in the family reunion, abandoned Jasmine at the doorstep. No radios, no running feet, no giggling, not even the sound of the air conditioning, greeted her as she set her bundle of clothes at the foot of the staircase. After a moment of mounting anxiety, she heard a door close softly up the stairs. Charged by her many fears, her strong legs vaulted her up the steps two-at-a-time, silently absorbing the shock of each tread. She stopped at the top, and there, down the dim hallway, outside Thomas's room, a female figure stood with her face cupped in her hands. The woman dropped her hands and, her eyes still closed, rolled her face upward, as though to beseech God. The strangeness of this figure and her own momentary shortness of breath fixed Jasmine in place, until she understood that this woman, disheveled and distraught as she was, was her Aunt Cynthia.

"Aunt Cynthia," she said simply, but all her fear for her cousin, all her anguish over her forced separation, and her crushing sympathy for her aunt found its way into her voice. Cynthia looked up to see her, the tension seemed to go out of her body, and Jasmine rushed forward to catch her in her arms.

Jasmine spoke consoling words while she patted Cynthia's hair and allowed her to cry on her shoulder. When her sobs had diminished, Cynthia began trying to speak through them. "Oh, Jasmine, I have so wanted you home . . . . I've missed you so terribly . . . . But it's all going to be all right now . . . . I know that it is . . . . Everything's going to get better now."

"Let me fix you some tea," Jasmine now said, and her aunt, with a heartfelt murmur of consent, allowed herself to be led down to the kitchen.

While she prepared the tea and they sat sipping it, the story came out. It had all been handled miserably. First, because they had suspected his illness to be the result of an unfortunate combination of alcohol and other stimulants, Thomas's companions had been slow to resort to a doctor, instead hoping that his strange disorientation would disappear with a good night's sleep. Fortunately, one of them had had the good judgment to check on him the next morning, and had found him very difficult to awaken and hot with fever. They had then driven him to a hospital. The other boy involved had had the good judgment to contact the Gannons, but whether affected by wishful thinking or through a misguided intent to avoid disclosure of Thomas's indiscretions, he had made no mention of Thomas's semi-comatose condition, leading them to believe that he was suffering from the flu.

As many physicians do, Dr. Gannon held greater faith in the recuperative powers of the young than he did in the application of medicine. He dismissed these first reports, reassuring his wife that the flu posed no significant risk to the young and generally healthy, that taking him to the hospital had probably been over-cautious, and that all doctors were capable of treating the symptoms of influenza. He now admitted that he should have assumed immediate care of his son and was extremely angry that he had not been promptly and accurately informed of the severity of his condition. According to Cynthia, he now alternated from guilt to deep anger—at the incompetence of Thomas's doctors, at the ignorance and callousness of Thomas's friends, and at the foolishness of his own family in withholding information from him. Cynthia continued at some length bemoaning her husband's unhappiness, noting that he had acted perfectly correctly in all ways and admitting that if anyone was to blame she was.

Not wishing to interrupt, Jasmine was long in coming to understand the subsequent course of Thomas's illness. He had contracted a meningococcal disease. This had resulted in an inflammation of his brain, and within twelve hours of being delivered to the hospital he had fallen into a coma.

There followed a discourse concerning the likelihood of Thomas having contracted the disease through illicit activity, during which her aunt assured her, while sharing drugs and weakening the immune system with poor diet or lack of sleep could be contributing factors, it was completely possible to contract the disease by something as simple as sharing a canned soft drink, a much too common occurrence around the Gannon house.

There had been a period in which they all feared for Thomas's life; and even when the fever had broken and the worst seemed to have passed, his coma had persisted. It was impossible to describe how stressful the waiting had been. Finally, he had opened his eyes, and though he had been slow to speak, it was apparent that he had recognized Phillip and his siblings. He had begun to eat, and it was possible to hire an ambulance to transport him the four hundred miles north and move him into his own room in Arden Park.

"He's recovering," Cynthia now said, the false cheer in her voice alarming Jasmine every bit as much as anything she had said previously. "Your uncle assures me that he is recovering. Nothing is set in stone. Especially with someone so young and healthy." Here, she again broke off into tears, and Jasmine, now very much worried, walked around the table to kneel beside her and wrap an arm around her shoulders. "He is improving," her aunt continued. "I see it. Every day, I see it. But, oh, it's so slow!" She again burst into tears, and Jasmine patted her softly until she could resume. "He can't . . . he can't remember things . . . . There's some question of how much he ever will remember." This last came from her throat in a squeal of tears.

When her sobs had again subsided, Jasmine sought to reassure her, "I'm sure David wouldn't deceive us. I'm sure that he *is* getting better. And much can be accomplished through our care and faith in him. I'm sure he will soon be very much better."

Cynthia now managed a thin smile. "I think I believe that. I do believe that," she said. "Now, that you've returned to us, everything is going to be okay again. He'll get better and things will return to normal . . . . Oh, how I've missed you! Oh, how we've needed you! How could you have stayed away so long?"

"I wanted always to come home, and once I heard of Thomas's illness I was desperate to return . . . . But enough of that. I'm home now, and I won't go anywhere."

Cynthia managed again to brighten and even to sip at her tea.

"He's receiving the very best care that it is humanly possible for him to have. Sometimes it seems that every doctor in the country is eager to offer his assistance out of friendship for David. And Phillip! Phillip has been an absolute God-send. I don't think he's slept a wink in weeks, but he's always cheerful, always helping, and always there when Thomas awakes. He's been our savior."

"Is he with him now?"

"Yes, and I know he will be as happy to see you as I am."

Cynthia began by urging her to go upstairs to visit them, but she soon remembered that there was a requirement that she receive an immunization shot before entering his room. "Although they say that the risk of infection left with the fever . . . . Still, it's an important precaution. I don't know if I could bear another illness . . . . It will only be a few hours. Your uncle will be home then, and I know he always has some of the medicine here."

It seemed to Jasmine that her aunt had aged years in the weeks she had been away. In part, it was a result of her not wearing make-up—and her blouse, which she wore over jeans, was so wrinkled that Jasmine wondered if she had slept in it—but the lines in her face seemed deeper too, and her eyes had lost their luster.

In order that her aunt might not notice how closely she was observing her, she turned to the vase of wilted and browning zinnias on the table. Though it was a hopeless task since all the blooms had faded at least a little, she began picking off the most wilted. "There must be some fresh blooms in the garden," she suggested, and was rewarded with a burst of near-enthusiasm from Cynthia.

"Oh, let's pick flowers! Why don't we?" She then offered Jasmine a trembling, tearful smile. "I just know that everything is going to be fine again now that you're home."

The garden had been neglected, which meant that there were many aging blooms to be discarded, but they found more than enough bright, fresh blossoms to fill four vases for the downstairs rooms. Jasmine's uncle arrived as she was arranging a fifth vase to take up to her cousin. Though his manner, like that of her aunt, was subdued, he greeted her with real tenderness, giving her a brief but heartfelt hug, and observing with uncharacteristic lyricism that she seemed "a ray of sunshine on a gloomy day—a gloomy week perhaps I should say." He then led her into his office. "I won't require you to take the shot," he said, settling in behind his desk. "After all, Thomas contracted the disease in Los Angeles, and any bacteria have long since been eliminated."

"What would you *advise*?" Jasmine asked, having noted an emphasis on the word "require."

Dr. Gannon sighed. "There is some risk from the shot, you understand. One in a million or so react badly, and there's no immediate medical reason for having it. But I would advise you— let me say that I would request of you—that you consider taking it. It gives great reassurance to your aunt to know that everyone has been vaccinated—more no doubt than it should—but the psychological element in these public health things is a legitimate concern. It comforts Cynthia, and I can only surmise that it will offer some reassurance to our neighbors and your schoolmates as well."

"I think I would like to have the immunization," Jasmine said, for his concern for her aunt was apparent, and Jasmine was eager to do anything that might comfort her.

"Thank you," her uncle said with real feeling. "I knew you would agree." He then proceeded to draw the necessary medicines from his desk drawer and administered the injection into her shoulder.

"Will I see Thomas much changed?" Jasmine now asked.

Dr. Gannon regarded her carefully. "You're nearly grown now, aren't you?"

"I don't anticipate that I will grow very much taller."

Her uncle chuckled at this. "I was referring to your emotional development," he said. "You are an unusually mature girl, mature beyond your years."

"I'm not yet seventeen," Jasmine replied. "I suppose that I feel about exactly that age, though sometimes perhaps I feel a little younger."

Dr. Gannon again smiled. "Thomas suffered a very high fever for an extended period of time. That is what caused his coma. There are still residual effects—memory loss, disorientation. He is likely to have trouble resuming his studies. Concentration will be difficult for him. Some of these functions will return to him with time and therapy. Whether or not all of them will, we don't yet know."

"But there is reason for hope?"

"There is. But I want to avoid raising hopes too high. There's a great deal we don't know about how the brain functions. Lost function in one area can be compensated for by improved function in another. But there's no question that there has been some damage. Therapy will help. Hard work will too. But there is a physical reality to these things as well. As doctors, we have done all we can.

Even with the best of therapy, a possibility remains that he will never recover fully."

"If there is anything we can do, any possible way that we can help, I know that we will all give every minute of our time to assist."

"For the moment, everything that can be done is being done. He needs sleep, of course. Rest is a great healer. But he will also need stimulation—mental stimulation and physical exercise as well. Phillip has been wonderful. He sat with him nearly every minute while we were still waiting for him to regain consciousness, and he was there when Thomas first opened his eyes. I wouldn't have thought it possible, but since then he's done even more—talking with him, reading to him, gently urging him to take an interest in his old activities. But Thomas's function is much slowed, and I know that it must be very tedious for him. Sometimes, it isn't clear how much he understands of what is read. I would have expected him to be interested in music, but he seems to find it unbearable. He prefers quiet. He's not willing to undertake anything beyond very simple tasks."

"Once he's up and getting around, won't he progress much more quickly?"

"We can certainly hope that will be the case . . . . Jasmine, I haven't stated circumstances quite so pessimistically to your aunt. She's been under a tremendous amount of strain, and right now, I think it's only hope that's keeping her together. She's slept very little, and as much as she'd like to help, she can't be in the room with Thomas without crying, even though she knows that what he needs most is encouragement and love. His emotions are dulled. The spark seems to have gone out of him."

"Isn't that natural—for someone who has been so sick?"

"Yes, it sometimes is," Dr. Gannon said with a brief smile, "and we can hope that it will pass."

"How soon will I be able to see him?"

"Any time really. The shot is only a formality, but it will have reassured Cynthia. There's no reason why you shouldn't go up to him now. No doubt you'll find Phillip there."

Thomas's room in most respects appeared completely normal. Clothing lay strewn about, Phillip's bedding lay all in a tangle on the floor, and Phillip himself, in long shorts and a T-shirt, sat sprawled in a chair. Thomas, however, was much changed. He sat up in his bed, his hands folded in front of him, seeming to do nothing at all. His face seemed thinner and much too pale. His eyes were dull, sunken, and ringed with dark circles. He managed a thin smile upon seeing her—in truth, a more kindly smile than she might normally have expected from him—and he offered no objection when she reached out and brushed his hair away from his forehead.

Jasmine exchanged a look with Phillip, during which she was apparently unable to conceal the degree of her shock. Phillip quickly rose up to stand beside her, saying, "The guy looks like some kind of a corpse, doesn't he?"

This caused Thomas to chuckle just a little, and Jasmine too was able to smile in relief.

"I almost was a corpse," Thomas said in a slow, weak voice.

"But your dad says that you're completely safe now," Jasmine said, in a questioning voice.

Thomas managed to nod assent, saying, "It's coming along."

"I'm so glad," Jasmine said, suddenly finding herself overwhelmed with tears, that led to sobs, which a frenzied wiping of her eyes and nose failed to dispel. This feminine weeping seemed for some reason to be a tonic for the two boys. Phillip held her tenderly by the shoulders and looked across at his cousin, while they both stifled giggles. Once Jasmine understood that she was a source of mirth, she tried even harder to muffle her sobs, causing her to emit an unladylike snort that caused even Thomas a small sputtering of laughter.

In the days then weeks that followed, it became clear that Thomas would not soon resume his previous life; and in the same way that a reformed drunkard becomes useless to his former boon companions, Thomas lost favor among his college friends. This was not due altogether to his inability to join in drinking and drug-taking, however. Thomas was changed. When friends visited, he listened to the stories of their exploits and conquests with a cheerful but detached smile, much as he would have listened to an anthropologist recounting the curious behaviors of Cameroonians on the upper Ubangi. His friends went away pleased with themselves for having remembered their friend and liking Thomas for having received them so cordially (for in the past he'd sometimes been considered cold), but shaking their heads at what he had become. Each vowed to return soon, but did not.

This withdrawal from the world manifested itself in other ways as well. Stories which might have bored him in a wink previously, he could now listen to with remarkable patience. For example, while he didn't express any deep curiosity about Jasmine's stay with her uncle, he seemed very much to enjoy her recounting of her days of exile, and even on occasion solicited more detailed information about the state of her Uncle Johnson's house and his habits.

As his eyes tired quickly when he tried to read and the noisiness of the television seemed to irritate him, there was not a great deal else for her and Phillip to do in his presence—other than to make conversation. They talked of nearly everything; but they did not discuss Los Angeles, the Hills, or the events that had led up to Thomas's illness. It was not until early September, two weeks after Jasmine's return, that he received a card from Sherry Hill. He read it and passed it to them, with the same distant smile with which he looked on his former friends: "It's time to get well and get your butt down here. The girls are all weeping for you. Love ya, Sherry."

"Do you think she will ever come back to Arden Park?" Thomas asked.

"I think she'll come back sometime before school starts," Phillip said, with a glance toward Jasmine, "unless something else comes up."

"She probably finds it dull here," Thomas said.

"It's different from LA," Phillip said.

"Arden Park used to seem dull to me," Thomas said. "Now, it just seems peaceful."

This, coming as it did from Thomas, struck Jasmine as wisdom, and she was left to consider the vagaries of the human psyche. A person might be changed by an event in one's life. Whether as the result of a tragedy, an illness, an ordeal, or even a stroke of good luck, lives were reformed and rededicated and changed for the better. That Thomas was changed was no longer deniable. If these changes would be permanent, it was still impossible to know.

The possibility of change led her to think also of Max. He was shy about visiting Thomas, yet this could be explained by a reluctance to interpose himself in what he felt was a family matter. She'd given him little of her time, yet he'd been kind and thoughtful on every occasion when they met. She still could not feel affection for him, yet his patience, his hopeful comments about Thomas's condition, and his eagerness to be of help to the household had earned her respect. Would it not be over-proud to continue to disapprove?

As for Max's own feelings, he certainly believed himself to have changed, especially as evidenced by his newfound ability to wait and persevere. He judged himself to have done all that could be done to earn Jasmine's attention and her to be too honorable a soul to deny him indefinitely; yet, as the days passed and she continued to rebuff him, he concluded that he must assert himself. Patience might be a virtue, but pining was not.

Late one evening, he waited for her in the living room, determined to evoke a more definite demonstration of her feelings. From a chair near the fireplace, he had a view of the window in Thomas's room, next to which Jasmine typically sat. When he saw her rise and the light then go out, he moved to the hallway, where he could view the staircase. He then chanced to meet her at the bottom of the stairs.

He spoke her name softly, and she turned to him with alarm. "I didn't mean to startle you."

"I wasn't expecting anyone."

"I've been waiting a week to have some time with you."

"We've seen each other every day."

"Some time alone. Could we go into the living room for a little while?"

Jasmine did not want to go into the living room with him,

especially not at such an hour in a house that felt very nearly abandoned, but she remembered her admonitions to herself. She thought to say "for a little while," but there was no pressing reason why the while should be little or long, and she did not wish to lie. "Yes," she said, "of course." To her great discomfort, he then seized her hand and led her to sit beside him on the couch.

"I've hardly been able to get a minute with you . . . . Did you talk with your uncle about William?"

"I hope to before he leaves."

"You remember your promise to me?"

"I do," she said.

"All I ask is that you keep your promise." Jasmine nodded and murmured her assent, and he went on. "Thomas is much better."

"Yes. He still tires easily, and he can't concentrate on anything for very long."

"Things like this take time."

"Yes. Dr. Gannon has said so as well."

"That's great then. He's past the worst."

"Yes, I think he is, but there's some concern he won't fully recover."

"A gutty guy like Thomas? He'll be back."

She had never thought of Thomas as especially brave or persevering, yet it seemed kind of Max to suggest that he was. "He lacks energy," she said.

"He's been through a lot. He'll come back."

"He doesn't seem unhappy."

"How could he be, with you there to help him all the time?"

"Phillip is with him even more than I am."

"Nothing against Phillip, but one minute of your time is worth ten of his."

"His reading is very slow and labored. Phillip is very patient with him, and they tell each other jokes. It's so good to see Thomas smile."

"I can tell from what you've said that he's doing great. Because you see him so much you don't see the changes. I know they're huge."

"I hope that's the case."

"But I didn't come here to talk about Thomas. Not tonight. You have your life, too."

"I don't feel . . . ."

"I know . . . but you can't let Thomas's problem become yours too. He's the one that's sick, not you. You can't let this take up your whole life."

"It has only been two weeks."

"But I know you. If we let you, you'll sacrifice everything for him, and that wouldn't be fair to you. Not to anyone."

A poor orphaned girl taken into the very prosperous home of relatives whom she has never met will necessarily have different ideas about obligation and sacrifice than those who have not encountered such misfortune and rescue; yet even Jasmine could acknowledge that Thomas's tragedy should not be compounded. "He's still frightened and insecure," she said, "but I think that will soon pass. He won't need so much of our time."

"And what if it doesn't pass? Phillip won't be here to help. It will be only you then."

"I don't know," Jasmine said.

Jasmine had said this last in a way that implied not indecision but considered awareness of her situation, and Max now ceased his argument. After a moment, he turned and took a small box from the end table, where he had placed it while he had waited. Instead of taking it as he had intended, Jasmine regarded it with something like horror. He reached out with both hands and joined hers, his, and box together.

"I want you to have this."

"How could I accept another kindness from you now?" Jasmine asked. "It is I who should be making gifts to you. You've been so helpful."

"Open it," he said.

When she did not, he drew his hands free and opened it himself. Inside was a thin gold chain, from which hung a clear stone. The stone was to all appearances a diamond, though given that it seemed nearly as large as one of her finger nails, she could only hope that it was not.

"I want you to have it."

"I can't accept this. I can't think that it is in any way right that I should have it."

"It is perfectly right. It's mine to give, and there will never be anyone else I want to have it. After all, I can't wear it myself."

Despite her near horror, he had now managed to clasp the necklace behind her neck. She reached to unfasten it, but he caught her hands. "Don't make more of it than it is. The stone isn't a fashionable cut. It's not worth all that much. Besides, I want you to have it. It wouldn't matter if it was worth millions. There's still no one else I would want to have it. Your neck is the setting it was made for. It would never look right to me anywhere else now."

"It's not glass?" she said.

"No," he admitted, "it isn't glass."

"Then I can't accept it."

"I want you to have it. You have to keep it."

"I cannot."

"Keep it as a favor to me. As a symbol of our friendship."

"But this is much more than a symbol of friendship."

"How is it more?"

Jasmine considered before answering. "It has the appearance of a romantic gift."

At this, Max laughed aloud, then seeing that she remained completely serious, said, "But romance is so much fun."

Jasmine did not deny this. "I don't feel that we are well matched—not romantically."

"I think we are very well matched, and I think when you get to know me better you'll think so too."

She did not respond to this immediately, and this he took as a sign of compliance. Since fastening the necklace, he had never fully released her, having let his hands settle to her shoulders, and he now pulled her toward him, as though to kiss her.

This she could not allow. She turned her head and accepted an awkward kiss on her cheek. A kiss on the lips, with a newly given diamond on her neck between them, was exactly the outcome

Max had sought. A kiss on the cheek was not. Under such provocation, Max could not disguise his ire.

"Jasmine," he said, "isn't it time to grow up a little."

"No matter how grown up I ever am," she replied, "I don't believe that I will ever want you to kiss me in such a way."

"And in just what way is that?" Max inquired, but Jasmine, now in tears, had already risen and run from the room, having forgotten even to remove the diamond from her neck.

Chapter 28

The Lure of Hollywood

Chrissie and Julia had been deeply upset by their brother's illness, so upset that they could not bear to visit him during the earliest periods, while he was still in the Los Angeles hospital. For a time after he'd returned to Arden Park, they went occasionally to his room, but it soon became apparent to both that their conversation held little interest for him. They were themselves bored by quiet reading and conversation, and his therapy, which included belabored repetition and excruciatingly slow oral reading, was painful to them. They had decided to trouble him no longer with their visits. In any case, they were busy with preparations for their departures to college.

After Max turned his attentions to Jasmine, Chrissie had for a time found renewed appreciation of Pudge. Her tender feelings for him had not lasted, however, and she'd ended in quarreling with him over his plans to take a motoring trip to Las Vegas with some rugby chums. The trip was scheduled for the last weekend before she was to leave for Arizona, a lack of consideration which gravely injured her feelings, and she was now refusing to speak to him.

Max, too, was feeling downcast, especially as the diamond necklace had been put back in his hands by his grandmother on the very morning after he had tried so valiantly to give it away. With Jasmine and Phillip always in Thomas's room, it was natural that he and Chrissie would spend time consoling each other.

Max did not intend that Jasmine learn of this. Or do we give him too little credit in thinking so? The human psyche is a complex and unwieldy beast, and certainly one part of Max Hill wished to disguise his renewed adventures—wished even to deny that renewed adventures they were. At the same time, however, another part of him seemed intent on thwarting his wish for secrecy. It made no objection to his pinning Chrissie Gannon up against the fireplace bricks, inserting his hand under her skirt, and lifting it up to her thigh—all in full view from the window of Thomas's room. That Max knew of this unimpeded view we already have learned. That he did not take the precaution of dimming the living room lights may be taken as evidence that he wished no longer to dissemble before Jasmine, that he wished for her to know the whole truth about him—all the contradictions in his character and all the risks that his affection carried with it. Or one might conclude that Max was striking out at Jasmine to assuage a wounded spirit—in the same way a golfer would strike his new three iron against the nearest tree. Or perhaps Max was merely playing what he perceived as favorable odds: How could he have known that Jasmine at that very moment would be gazing out Thomas's window? Or could it perhaps have been some indefinite combination of all of the above. Who really knows? Who truly understands the cunning of another's heart? Who truly understands the cunning of his or her own?

That Jasmine saw what transpired in that living room you may already have guessed, and you may also rest assured that, if Max Hill's psyche operated at several levels, Jasmine Johnson's did as well. First, she was shocked. Second, she was deeply relieved that it was her cousin pressed by Max Hill and not herself. Third, she was alarmed at the danger in which Chrissie placed herself. Fourth, she was wounded on behalf of Pudge. Fifth, she was wounded at Max's perfidy to herself. Sixth, she was ashamed on behalf of the entire family. Finally and persistently, she was angry.

Instead of continuing to witness this scene, she turned and let her face settle into her hands. She also perhaps emitted an involuntary moan, for Thomas's gentle voice now rose up, saying, "You don't need to stay when I'm sleeping."

"I don't mind."

"It's okay now. I always know exactly where I am when I wake up." He now studied her face, on which she already felt the blush of her anger, and it blushed more deeply. "You're upset by something," he said. This was another change in him: he noticed things about others he would never have perceived in the past.

"I'm just too warm," Jasmine said quickly.

Thomas didn't reply to this, though his kindly look suggested that he didn't believe her, and she was tempted to inform him of what she had just observed. In the end, though, she could not. It was true that he was much too divorced from the world, and an increased involvement in the affairs of the household would be a step to the good, but this would be too distressing. Besides, what could he possibly think but that she was jealous of her cousin?

"I was just thinking of my grandmother," she said

"You've talked a lot about her. She's still a big influence on you, isn't she?"

"She is, but just now I was remembering something about her that wasn't very pleasant. Sometimes she would get very angry with William or me."

"Maybe you deserved it," Thomas said, with a smile.

"No doubt we sometimes did, but she got more angry than she should have. Sometimes she blamed us for things we didn't do. We used to hide from her."

"Everybody gets angry sometimes."

"But there's no point in it unless it will do some good."

"I'm sure it made you careful of her feelings," Thomas said. "Like, you know how we're all careful around Tina?"

Thomas had not himself always been as careful as he might

have been, but Jasmine nodded, as she was thinking instead about the good and bad outcomes of anger. The Bible praised righteous anger. Even Jesus had been angry when he drove the moneychangers from the temple. Of course, Jesus had been acting for good, while neither the righteousness of her current anger nor the good result that might come from it were apparent to her. Alas, if nothing good could come from it, her anger must be buttoned up. There was perhaps a time for anger—the Bible said there was a time to every purpose under heaven—but this could not be it.

Later, however, when she observed Max talking with Dr. Gannon out by the pool, standing close, inclining his head toward him confidentially and laughing and smiling with him—in short, acting in every way as though he were a colleague, or at least his social equal—she was obliged to acknowledge that she had not completely let go of her anger. For a moment, she was tempted even to step forward and denounce him. It remained, however, that she could see no particular good coming from speaking out—at least nothing beyond a certain vengeful satisfaction. She held her tongue.

Unknowingly, very nearly innocently, and even while he was not so innocently tugging away at Chrissie's skirt, Max Hill had been fomenting a more complicated crisis than even he and Jasmine imagined. In wooing Chrissie, he had so liberally resorted to flattery that he had convinced her of her eventual Hollywood stardom! Thinking it no more that the necessary seductive babble—and sure that she would not accept—he had invited her to accompany him to Los Angeles, where he had as much as promised that he would soon make her a star. To his consternation, she not only had accepted, but also, in the time it took him to blink his eyes, had begun plotting and planning.

Knowing how much her father would disapprove, Chrissie first took this news to her Aunt Tina. Tina, never inclined to turn a deaf ear to her favorite niece, could not help seeing the advantages of such a move.

"You're a very talented and beautiful girl," she said. "Any director would be thrilled to get you."

"Max says it doesn't matter at all that I didn't do plays and all that stuff in high school. He says I'm already a great actor. With some people it's like the air they breathe. It just comes naturally."

"I felt it was a mistake when your mother allowed you to drop ballet, and I wish you'd had singing lessons."

"It's not like I want to get into the theater anyway," Chrissie said. "What I want to do is movies. I think, really, deep down, it's what I've always wanted to do."

"And I think, deep down, I've always known this day would come."

Tina and Chrissie were not normally very expressive people, but with this, they burst forth into a rapturous hug.

"Max says I'm a whole lot better than all kinds of fabulously successful actresses. You know how I always liked Cybill Shepherd. He says I'm way better than her, and she was a huge success."

"The thing is that you have real depth of character, as well, and I think that always shows in an actress."

"Ac*tor*," Chrissie said. "Max says nobody calls girls actresses anymore."

"Yes," Tina said, somewhat resenting the correction, "but I don't think you should completely give up on dance and voice. You have a real natural gift for both. Your looks are perfect for the camera and that will get you started, but you'll be able to go so much further if you have all the tools. Of course, you're starting late . . . ."

"Which is all the more reason I need to go to Los Angeles right now!"

Tina could appreciate the importance of quick action, given the young age at which most actors began their careers, the ephemeral tastes of the mass audience, and the capricious economics of the movie business. "Max has had a lifetime of making contacts, and you're only getting started. He can be an enormous help to you."

"He says he can find me an agent, and auditions will be absolutely no problem. If nothing else, I can get modeling roles like tomorrow. That means, when I get my break, my face will already be known. That helps. Plus, Max says he can get me in with the best acting coach in LA. The only problem is she's like five hundred dollars an hour. I know in the long-run it'll be worth it and I'll be able to pay it all back a thousand times over, but right now that's a lot of money."

"You'll need your father's help," Tina said.

"He'll never say okay."

"Never is a long time. If you can convince him of your sincerity . . . and your determination . . . ."

"At least I can save money on the boob job. Max says about ninety-nine percent of actresses have theirs done, but I think you can always tell the real thing from plastic."

"You have a wonderful figure," Tina said, "and that's an asset you can use, but I don't think I would mention that to your father."

"Duh. Like I'm that dumb. It doesn't matter what I say though. He won't go for it anyway. If I ask him, he'll just say no."

"I imagine he will say no."

"So why should I ask him? I should just go. I'll send him a letter or something. It's not like he's going to let me starve."

"No, he won't let you starve," Tina admitted, "but he may not be willing to pay for five-hundred-dollar-an-hour acting lessons."

Up until now, they had been talking in the kitchen. While they had not been overheard, their security was dubious, and Tina now ushered her niece back to the guest house. They sat side-by-side on Tina's bed.

"Eventually, it will be essential that you have your father's support," Tina told her. "It may be a while before you can command higher fees. In the meantime, there'll be the acting lessons, a voice coach, and maybe a publicist, though I can help you with that. And you'll need to have a top-of-the-line wardrobe. Not to mention living expenses. All that will take money."

"Mom might help."

"Not without your father's approval."

"Then we can forget it."

"Maybe he won't help *now*, but that doesn't mean he won't help ever. You have to make him understand that acting is a serious undertaking, just like school. You'll be studying hard and practicing your skills, doing everything you possibly can to advance your career. It's no different from college—you'll be working at your vocation—and there's no reason why your father shouldn't be willing to provide for you in the same way he would if he were paying tuition."

"He won't though. He'll just say that I'm being ridiculous."

"He won't *now*, but you can begin showing him it's not ridiculous . . . . You have some money in the bank?"

"Only a couple or so thousand."

"How many thousands?"

"Three, I think."

"That won't last very long?"

"I was hoping you could loan me some money, just until I get started."

"Oh, how I wish I could! The little bit I have—I'd give it to you in a minute—and, of course, if there's anything left when I'm gone it will all be yours, but you've seen how I have to manage and scrape just to get by each month."

Chrissie had not seen this, but she did not contradict her aunt. The economic engine of Chrissie's life had been her skill at extracting money from her father, whom she regarded as a bottomless resource. Other than this, she had never paid much attention to finances in one way or another. She could not be certain her aunt wasn't speaking the truth.

"What we have to do," Tina went on, "is to demonstrate to your father that this is a serious pursuit and make sure he understands how deeply you want this and how you're willing to put your whole soul into it."

"That's exactly how I feel," Chrissie said. "If I could only make him understand that. But he won't. He'll say I'm being childish."

"I agree that it may take some time."

"I can't wait!" Chrissie moaned. "I've been wanting to do this all my life. I can't put it off any longer. I'll never be as pretty again as I am right now."

Tina admitted some truth in this statement, at least in its final part. Chrissie was a big girl. Her active athletic career had allowed her to keep until twenty that youthful bloom that for many big girls begins to fade a year or two earlier. Without a good trainer—another expense!—she was at risk of growing matronly. Moreover, her beauty, while striking, could not be called classic. Her cheekbones were not as prominent as they might be, and they could easily be lost if her face swelled.

"Of course," Tina consoled her, "you can't delay any longer. Even so, you can't just run away."

"He'll never agree."

"You mean that he won't agree right away. But I know that your father loves you very much and he wants the best for you. If we can convince him that this is what you really want to do, he'll come around."

"Really?"

"Yes. But you're going to have to make him understand that you're truly a dedicated actress—ac*tor*—and that this isn't just a passing fancy."

"It isn't. I really want to be an actor. I could be really good at it. Max is sure of it."

"Of course you can, but I don't think you can hope to convince your father of that today. The best you can do is to show him how deeply sincere you are. Then, when he sees how hard you are working and how perfectly committed you are to being successful, he'll come around. It would help if you were taking lessons at UCLA or if you could somehow get a connection at one of the studios . . . ."

"I will be taking lessons, and Max says his friend is the very best acting coach in LA. She won't work with just anybody because she only wants to work with people who have real talent. She's not in it for the money. She just doesn't want to waste her time on a lot of clueless losers. Max says there's tons of them in Hollywood. It's like really pathetic."

As astonishing as the five hundred dollar per hour rate seemed, and as ridiculous as was the assertion that the woman was "not in it for the money," the advisability of Chrissie's disassociating herself from the common run was apparent. A recommendation from a well-placed acting coach would no doubt advance her discovery by many months. It was also possible for Tina to imagine that she would someday become just such a coach herself, or perhaps an agent or producer. It was one of the wonderful things about the entertainment industry. Degrees, credentials, experience—in the end, they weren't necessary. Even a talented hairdresser could end up running a studio.

"You'll want to plan what you say to your father."

"I'll tell him how bad I want to."

"That's important. It's even more important that you convince him of the seriousness of this undertaking. He has to understand that this is every bit as legitimate as college, that it's what you really want, and that you will work diligently to make a success of it."

"He won't agree anyway," Chrissie moaned. "I know he won't."

"No, he won't, not until he understands that it's the *only* thing that can make you happy."

Chrissie managed a slight smile, and Tina was struck with a hopeful thought. "After all, he's been spending a lot on Thomas's tuition. He won't be needing that money now, and there's no reason in the world why you shouldn't have it."

"But Thomas *will* need it . . . .," Chrissie said. "Eventually he will."

Tina patted her knee. "Certainly, we have to hope so. He's working tremendously hard, and he's progressing wonderfully, but it remains to be seen how soon he can get back to his studies." She reached an arm around Chrissie's shoulders. "We have to face the possibility that he may never be able to return."

This information came as a surprise to Chrissie. She had noted changes in her brother, including the new softness in his manner, but had attributed them to a weakness that would soon pass.

"He isn't able to read yet—not for even a full minute," Tina informed her niece. "The doctors feel there may be some damage to the language centers in his brain."

Chrissie's stricken face showed the magnitude of her concern, but she managed to say only, "Weird."

"Life has many twists and turns," her aunt said, patting her again on the knee. "I know how much you would like to help your brother, but no good will come from your punishing yourself. I know that Thomas wouldn't want you to. The best you can do for him is to make the greatest possible success of your life. That's how you can help him most."

This logic seemed sound to Chrissie, who, after all, had very little aptitude for nursing and lacked the patience for therapy, and she now returned to the prior problem: how to gain her father's support.

"But Dad will never give his permission . . . ."

"I agree that he won't give his permission—yet. And that's why you'll have to present it to him as a *fait accompli*." Tina's expectant look was met with blank incomprehension. "You will have to tell him that your decision has already been made," she explained. "Of course, you'll also let him know how sorry you are to disappoint him in his plans, but you have to find your own way in life—your own passion—and now that you are certain of it, you can delay no longer."

Chrissie's look was dubious.

"If you demonstrate how completely committed you are, if you are mature and adult-like," Tina continued, "he'll have to consider the possibility that this a serious undertaking. Make him see how sorry you are to disappoint him, how much it grieves you to hurt him, how much you are suffering for your choice, but that you won't under any circumstances be swayed. Your father is a practical man. You have to make him see that this is a very practical undertaking."

"Max says the Gannon name will help a lot."

"Of course it will. It will get your foot in the door. But you can't let your father think you'll be taking advantage of your name."

"I won't be. It's not like I couldn't make it anyway. Max says it'll just speed up the process."

"Exactly," Tina said, "but I wouldn't say anything about that to your father."

"I can tell him I'll use a screen name."

"Better not to mention it at all.

Chrissie nodded.

They went on in this way for some time, adding details to her plans and considering how they might best be presented to her father. "And no 'likes' or 'you knows.' Don't even describe something as 'cool.' You want him to understand that this is an adult decision, so talk like a grown-up."

"All right, enough, I get it," Chrissie now said. "So, I'll tell him at dinner."

"Oh, no," Tina was obliged to reply, "not at dinner. You have to ask for some time in private. Then, you have to discuss this exactly as though it were the most important thing in the world."

"It *is* the most important thing in the world."

"Talking with him alone will impress on him how serious you are."

"But we always talk about everything important at dinner," Chrissie said. "Everybody's there. I mean, it's just easier that way."

"Don't expect anything about this to be easy."

Thus prepared, Chrissie found herself that night facing her father across his desk. Previously, her daughterly repertoire in relation to him included three roles: Daddy's little girl; crusader for justice; and little, lost puppy. Of the three, as her petitions for justice were always transparently self-serving, the crusader role was the least convincing; yet, as her aunt's advice would require her to appear mature and independent, a role with which she had no experience, she found herself relapsing into protest when she found herself alone with her father in his office.

"Daddy, it's so unfair," she found herself saying. "Everybody else is getting money to do what they want to do."

"Julia's going to college, and we hope Thomas will return soon. I have no objections to paying for college."

"But this is *like* college. For me, it is. I have no interest in college. For me, it's a waste of time. This is what I want to do. It's what I *need* to do. It's who I am."

"Chrissie, I've never heard you say more than two words about acting before this summer."

"That's so untrue. I've always wanted to act. You know how I love television and how I used to pretend I was Cybill Shepherd."

"I remember no such thing."

"I would stand in front of the mirror and do that hair commercial. For hours sometimes. I could do it so much better than her."

Even Dr. Gannon was aware that both his daughters spent considerable time before their bathroom mirror, and he was momentarily silenced. Had his frequent absences rendered him a stranger to his daughter's true nature? Chrissie, seeing him doubtful, pressed her advantage.

"This is what I feel like my whole life has been leading up to. An opportunity like this may never come again. Max knows people. His stepfather is a *producer*," she said, applying both a reverential, whispery voice and wide-open eyes to the term "producer." "This is the kind of opportunity people work years to find. It's way too good to pass up."

While he listened, Dr. Gannon silently reviewed his daughter's school years. He recalled that she had often been eager to participate in sports, but had refused dance and music lessons, and had never expressed any interest in participating in a school play, despite her mother's and aunt's urgings. Certainly, she'd never auditioned for anything.

"No, Chrissie," he now said. "I think this decision is far too sudden. You should finish school. Transfer to a dramatic arts major, if you must. Once you have your degree, if you're still interested, then we can talk again."

This statement was so thoroughly reasonable—and so disdainful of her importunities—that the girl experienced no alternative but to attack. "You've always given Thomas anything he wanted, and you won't do anything for me. Just because I'm not a boy doesn't mean that I can't do something important, too."

"Chrissie . . . ."

"It's true. He got the car he wanted. He went to the expensive school. He always got to stay out late." Her hurt feelings now recalled to her the aching heart of a little deserted girl, standing in her own driveway, as a station wagon carrying a world of wonderful joys disappeared down the street. "And he got to go to Disneyland with the Irwins," she blurted, tears simultaneously beginning to gush from her eyes.

"Chrissie, you were eight years old then," Dr. Gannon said. He'd been startled by her tears, and he spoke in a tender and consoling voice, but her sobs nonetheless grew more intense. He could console her only by patting her arm and head.

Chrissie was the first to emerge from the doctor's office. She gave her Aunt Tina one quick, anguished glance and ran up the stairs to her room. While her teary demeanor had seemed to perplex her father, it had a far different effect on her aunt: it made Tina very angry indeed. The key to the success of their strategy had been that Chrissie display a mature conviction of her purpose. In this, it was all too clear that she had failed. She did not go up to Chrissie immediately, as her sister sat in the family room with her, and such a movement would have betrayed their conspiracy. Instead, she silently cast and recast the harsh words she would apply to her niece at her next opportunity.

A few minutes later, however, when Dr. Gannon himself emerged, she was obliged to reconsider the success of the meeting. Her brother-in-law appeared haggard and lost. He directed a pained, very nearly desolate look at his wife.

"She thinks she wants to be a movie star," he said.

"A movie star?" Cynthia replied.

"Yes, a movie star."

"That's ridiculous," Cynthia now said, in response to the impatience she'd detected in his reply; then, when he did not reply immediately, she added, "Isn't it?"

"Yes, it is," her husband replied, "but it's what she wants."

It did not appear that the battle had been won, but to all appearances Chrissie had made a powerful impression on her father, one that might be used to her advantage in the future. Tina was left to consider the power of a woman's tears, a force which she now regretted not having exploited more effectively in her own affairs.

Chapter 29

Sherry Hill Returns

At this time, Sherry Hill chose to return to Arden Park. She had been informed by her brother both of Chrissie's precipitate decision and Jasmine's rebuff, found the events amusing, and welcomed an opportunity for intrigue. Besides, she was happy to escape LA at the moment, in part because its seemed less exciting with the Arden Park contingent absent, in part because she wished to avoid the attentions of a noisome suitor, in part because she reminisced fondly on Jasmine's friendship, and mostly because she wished not to let her association with Phillip languish.

By the time of her arrival, news of Chrissie's appeal to her father had reached the entire household. It is conventional to attribute the spread of such news to supernatural forces, but this is no more than an excuse used by those who revel in gossip and drama. In this case, the first to let information slip was Chrissie herself. She had informed her sister in no uncertain terms that she was "going to Los Angeles and there's nothing anybody can do about it" and had slammed her door behind her. Julia, having used the time of her abandonment in Arden Park by the other young people to spin visions of revenge that culminated in her own grand Tinsel Town success, had no intention of being left behind again now. Determined, righteous, and fierce with indignation, she had gone to her mother, thence to her aunt, and again to her mother, where she had finally pried loose the essence of Chrissie's appeal to her father. This information had sent her into howls of protest. Under the circumstances, Cynthia had felt obliged to explain events to Jasmine and Thomas.

It was one of Sherry's virtues that she was interested by people who led lives different from her own—even those who led unfashionable ones—and unlike the Gannon sisters, she was capable of conceding that others might not prefer to be exactly like her. Of course, she understood that friendships sometimes could be put to profitable use—even friendships among the boorish and unfashionable—but she set no other requirement than that her friends entertain her.

With most of these acquaintances, such as the Korean woman who owned the dry cleaners where she dropped her clothes and with whom she occasionally had lunch, her involvement never advanced beyond curiosity, though she was quick to admire determination in the face of difficulties. Her talks with Jasmine, however, had cut deeper. She had detected in Jasmine a constancy of character and depth of goodness which she knew herself to lack, but which she had the wisdom to perceive as being not only admirable but also practical. To some, Jasmine's quiet, unassuming manner implied lack of confidence and an acquiescence to others' guidance. Sherry knew better. While Jasmine often deferred to her cousins, this attitude was more the product of a deep confidence than a lack thereof. She was certain of her own feelings and experienced no compulsion to be dogmatic in asserting them; while she was in some respects much less naïve than her cousins, it would be nearly impossible to induce her into any action which she considered merely expeditious or pragmatic.

Moreover, she was intrigued and even gratified by what she perceived to be correspondences between her own personality and Jasmine's. They both were highly attuned to the feelings and reactions of others, and their focus in any conversation often turned to the same person. Their responses to this intelligence were often different, however, and Sherry was eager to assess Jasmine's current state of mind. Soon enough, she heard piano music in the living room. She found Jasmine there, sitting in khaki Bermuda shorts and a snowy white polo shirt—clothes which she would not herself have ever worn, but which Jasmine managed to make look crisp and attractive.

"I know you're not a hugger," Sherry said, smiling, "but I just have to." She leaned over and squeezed Jasmine with heartfelt tenderness, then took a seat beside her on the bench. "My God, you've been through so much! How have you survived?"

Jasmine, who remained inclined to take speech literally, said, "Dr. Gannon said there was really no danger to any of the rest of us once Thomas's fever had passed, though the shots were reassuring."

"Shots or no shots," Sherry said, "it's so horrible to be around sickness all the time, first your grandfather and then this. I know I couldn't have done it."

"It was my uncle," Jasmine replied pleasantly. She was thinking, however, that Sherry, like Scarlet O'Hara, would likely do very well in any crisis, and she went on to say, "I think that if I were ever in real need, there is no one I would want more to assist me than you."

"Not even Phillip?"

"Except for Phillip, of course," Jasmine conceded.

"He's really great, huh?"

"I think that he is."

"All that money, but you'd never know it to talk to him. He acts just like anyone else."

"I think that having money has in some ways affected him very much."

"Really!" Sherry said with honest enthusiasm. "How?"

"It has made him more thoughtful. I think that he is very much aware of how he's been blessed and that has made him more considerate of the needs of others."

"Is that *always* a good thing?"

"I think that it is."

"Doesn't that also cause him to waste his time on fools? I mean he's just too smart to spend his time listening to idiots. Doesn't he have a responsibility to make the most of what he's got?"

Jasmine had no immediate answer for this.

"I mean, he could be on TV," Sherry continued. "He could be in politics. He could start a software company and make billions. Think how much he could give to charity then."

"A very great deal," Jasmine admitted.

"It's not a crime to be wealthy, you know."

"I had not thought that it was."

"Then why would he want to be a *teacher*?" Sherry moaned.

"It is, I think, because he likes the idea of working with children."

"But isn't that in itself being selfish? Why should he limit himself to working with miserable little brats?"

"I suppose that some will misbehave."

"Of course they will, and smell bad too. And they won't care. The fact that he wants to help them won't matter to them a bit. They'll still do everything in their power to avoid learning anything and to get gum onto his chair. It just seems so humiliating."

"It's a job that needs doing," Jasmine suggested quietly.

This Sherry could hardly deny. "But Phillip has so much greater possibilities. He could accomplish so much more by doing something . . . something on a bigger scale. Something more dramatic."

"What a teacher accomplishes may not always be apparent, but it's important nonetheless."

"I don't mean that it's unimportant. Of course, it's important. It's just that it's something that anybody can do. Lots of people who could no doubt be very good teachers couldn't begin to accomplish the things that Phillip could. Why not let them be the teachers?"

While Jasmine understood that Sherry's objections to Phillip's chosen occupation arose more from the unfashionability of the teaching than from concern for the public good, they could not be completely dismissed. "There is the question of how much an individual is called upon to sacrifice for others," she admitted.

"Exactly," Sherry said, "there's no reason why a person like Phillip has to sacrifice himself to something so awful as teaching."

It would have been illiberal to point out that this statement reversed Phillip's and Jasmine's views of which occupations required sacrifice, and Jasmine didn't do so. After all, despite her conciliatory statements, Sherry's view of the teaching profession was clear, and she had made no attempt to hide it.

Instead, Jasmine attempted to reply to the unstated sentiment. "His independent wealth will make the teaching life less constricting."

"But think of the boring people."

"There is that."

"Teachers seem so petty. And they wear such awful clothes."

"That too," Jasmine said.

Sherry laughed so good-naturedly that Jasmine was happy to join with her, then said, "I know you're thinking that what's petty is to make so much of clothes. And I agree with you, I really do. Clothes shouldn't be important. What does it matter what kind of clothes a person wears? It shouldn't matter at all. It's just that it does matter. Symbolically, it matters. Clothes send all kinds of messages. You, for example, you always appear so simply and cleanly dressed. It's perfect for you. It tells people at a glance how absolutely perfect you are. If somebody else wants to signal that they're tasteless and boring, then they only get what they deserve."

"Shouldn't we try to see beneath the surface."

"Of course we should!" Sherry said. "But it's so often disappointing. You hope that someone will be different than they look, and they turn out to be just as awful as their haircut . . . . I'm scared it might turn him into a complete dork."

"I think that he would be free to wear whatever clothing he preferred."

Sherry had momentarily forgotten that Jasmine also intended to become a teacher, and she regretted using the term "dork." Now, as a way of apology, she again gave her good-natured laugh. Even so, she could not deny that hers had been an honest reaction. She had previously dismissed Phillip's stated career interest as a fancy that would pass. His steadfast devotion to Thomas's rehabilitation, however, obliged her to consider that he might prove steadfast in this as well. She had visited with Thomas and considered his condition, sad as it was, to be a lost cause. That Phillip could sit with him for hour after hour, reading children's books and carrying on mundane and even sappy conversations, suggested that he was capable of enduring any amount of boredom.

"Do you think Phillip is sacrificing too much for Thomas's recovery?" she now asked softly. "You know, he's even talked about not going back to school so he can stay with him."

"There are people here to see to Thomas's welfare," Jasmine said. "Phillip should continue with his own life. He should go back to school."

Sherry was cheered by this unexpected response, especially as she knew Jasmine's endorsement would carry heavy weight with Phillip, and she now resolved to make one final effort to extricate him from the whole miserable mess in Arden Park. Yes, Thomas had brain damage, and that was terrible. But how did Phillip's sitting around doing boring, stupid stuff help?

Sherry now rose to leave, but before she did, she turned back to Jasmine. "Let me ask you something," she said. "Do you think that Chrissie really wants to go to Los Angeles?"

"Yes, I think that she wants to."

"But should she?"

"That I can't judge."

"Max doesn't think that she should."

"Cynthia understood that he had given her encouragement."

"I know," Sherry said. "There's some misunderstanding there. This isn't what he wanted. Chrissie needs to know that."

"She would be very disappointed."

"That might be better than the alternative, right?"

"Dropping out of college would be a very big decision."

"A very big mistake is what you mean."

"I can't say that for certain."

"I can," Sherry said, taking her leave.

Sherry had visited Thomas only once since her return and found his room depressing. Now, however, as this was where she knew Phillip to be, she knocked at his door. Thomas's surprisingly robust voice bade her to enter, and she discovered the two young men still in the throes of some joke that had passed between them. Despite her normal poise, Sherry found herself distressed, as anyone is who intrudes on others' laughter. "What are you two laughing at?" she asked, somewhat in the tone of a chastising mother.

Sherry set her gaze on Thomas. He turned to his cousin and burst again into laughter.

"It was nothing," Phillip said, but laughter sparkled in his eyes.

"It was probably something juvenile, sexist, and probably indecent—just the kind of joke I like. So tell me."

They still refused, but as Thomas, who was sitting up in bed with a book on the bedcovers in front of him, was showing more real life than Sherry had expected ever to see in him again, she could not be really angry.

"Little boys playing games," she said, in a mocking though not truly malicious tone.

Sherry now cast her gaze on Phillip, hoping with her eyes to convey many deep messages, in addition to the immediate one, which was that she wanted to be alone with him. To her surprise, it was Thomas who responded. He picked up the book on his lap.

"Okay, guys, I have to see if I can get through one whole page of this without falling asleep." The book, Sherry could now see, was a textbook from a business management class.

"If you did," she said, "you'd be the first."

This resulted in a renewed burst of laughter, which Sherry this time joined.

"I'm already doing better than I was," Thomas said. "I never even picked it up before."

Sherry was shocked. "You were paralyzed for a while?"

Thomas laughed again. "No, I mean I never picked it up the first time I took the class," an admission that struck a new round of laughter from the two young men.

Sherry and Phillip discussed Thomas's condition as they made their way out to the patio.

"He's much better," Sherry suggested.

"Much better."

"Do you think then that he might go back to school?"

Phillip shrugged.

"You'll go back though."

"It's starting to look that way."

"I think you should."

Phillip didn't answer this question until they had seated themselves under the patio umbrella. "I wouldn't have to sit out forever. Not even a whole year. I could take an emergency leave for a semester."

"But that isn't necessary now, right? Since he's so much better . . . ."

"It may not be."

"It's not your job anyway. I mean he has his own family. How much can you do for him that they can't? It's not like you and Thomas were ever that close."

"Am I not my cousin's keeper?" Phillip asked with a teasing grin. "But to answer your question. No, we weren't that close. But we grew up together and family is family. And, no, there probably isn't that much I can do for him."

"He'll have Jasmine anyway. Who would you rather have taking care of you if you were sick?

"No one. But Jasmine has her own life to live."

"No more than you."

"I think we sometimes take unfair advantage of Jasmine's kindness."

"*You* don't."

The implication of her statement—that, yes, others in the family did take advantage of her—did not need to be elaborated upon. Both knew that Chrissie and Julia took advantage of anyone who would allow it and exacted retribution on those who wouldn't.

"Cynthia depends on her for everything," Sherry continued, "now especially."

Phillip agreed.

"They're close," Sherry went on. "Your aunt is like a mother to her."

"In some ways *like* a mother."

Sherry took his meaning. "She's not really the motherly type, is she?"

"Not really with Chrissie and Julia either . . . . She's not a nurse either."

"Still, between the two of them—plus Tina . . .," Sherry began. "And it's not like they don't have enough money to hire therapists."

Phillip acknowledged the correctness of what she said, but he remained thoughtful. "The thing is," he said, "if I'm going to teach, I don't really need to go back anyway. I can get a degree here just as well as anywhere else."

Sherry was not one to argue forcefully for the importance of education, but she could not hide her abhorrence to this proposal. "My God, you'd give up the Ivy League to go to some dorky state college!"

Phillip laughed. "It's not really dorky."

"Maybe not dorky," Sherry admitted, "but if you're going to go to college, and you can go someplace that has a reputation, why not? The Ivy League may be overrated like you say, but it still has that aura about it."

"What will an aura matter if I want to teach?"

Sherry now searched herself for a more telling response. "But think how much more you will *learn*," she intoned. "There's no comparison between what you can learn at a private school and public one."

"All schools pretty much teach the same things. Besides, in the future it's not going to be where you went to school, but what you know."

"But you associate with such a higher level of students now."

"They're not all so high," Phillip averred.

"Still, it's so hard to get in. Everybody there has to be pretty smart. While here . . . ."

" . . . all you have to do is show up?"

"More or less," Sherry admitted.

"That's true," Phillip said, "but I think that's an advantage really. The Ivy League talks a lot about diversity, but for real diversity I'd be much better off here. And if I'm going to teach kids who are from different cultural groups, it might help to have some experience."

Sherry could no longer contain her frustration. "You're not still serious about this teaching thing, are you?"

"It's what I've always wanted to do."

"At one point I wanted to be a nurse, but I got over it."

"You could be a good nurse," Phillip said.

"It wasn't realistic."

"And you think being a teacher isn't realistic either?"

"I think you've made being a teacher into something it isn't, just like I made being a nurse into something it isn't. Nursing is bedpans and bad smells, and teaching is just setting yourself up to be mocked, ridiculed, ignored, and abused. Plus you get the bad smells."

"No bedpans though."

"I wouldn't even bet on that."

"If it's so bad doesn't somebody have to try to make things better?"

"Nobody in the world could be less well-suited to that than you."

"That's not very flattering."

"I don't mean that you're not capable and talented and all that. You are. Maybe more than anyone else I know. It's just that all your intelligence will only get in the way. You'll say something really brilliant and nobody will understand you. In fact, even if you mean something to be really nice, they won't understand it, so they'll hate you for it. Heaven forbid you ever say anything sarcastic or ironic. Nobody would ever understand. Your life's just been too different."

"A little imagination goes a long way in understanding people."

"That's just it. You'll imagine these kids to be nice and misunderstood, and they won't be. You think everybody in the world is basically good. They aren't. They're mean and selfish. And sometimes they're cruel and even vicious."

"I think all people have good traits."

"And when you can't find them, you'll think you've failed somehow and be completely miserable, while in fact it's them who will have failed, just like they've failed in everything else they've done."

"I'm sure it's not as bad as all that. Even if I agreed with you, even if I thought I'd lived too protected an existence to know what's going on, Jasmine hasn't. She's gone to a public school, and she knows what it's like. And she thinks teaching is a very useful profession."

"That's because she's that one-in-a-thousand student who teachers dream about. Teachers are so grateful to have her that they pee all over themselves when she's around. But she's the exception. No, she's more than that: she's unique. Most teachers teach for twenty years without having any students anything like Jasmine."

"She's not a good example," Phillip admitted, shaking his head, "but the fact remains that there are a lot of different kinds of people in the world, and everybody needs a chance to feel successful. Teachers offer people the chance to be successful."

"But what if kids don't want to be successful?" She didn't wait for him to reply. "Because they don't. At least they don't in the way you want them to. They want to drive nice cars and wear nice clothes like everybody else, but they couldn't give one wham-damn about learning anything."

"Every child wants to learn."

"Spare me the sap," Sherry said.

"All right," Phillip admitted. "Maybe some don't. But that's part of the job: to show them how rewarding learning can be."

Sherry shook her head. "You just don't get it, do you? For them, learning wouldn't be rewarding. They have no interest or aptitude for it and they've got just enough brains to realize it. Why not do something for people who will appreciate what you're doing? You act like there's something wrong with successful, motivated, interesting people. Just because they're successful doesn't make them less good. Rich people can be nice, too."

"I didn't say they weren't nice," Phillip said, "or interesting. It's just not where the greatest need is."

"Maybe it's not where the greatest need is, but it is where you can do the most good."

Phillip was far too honest not to perceive a vein of truth in Sherry's argument. Many of his fellow students seemed to champion low culture as a way of disparaging high, despite their having gone to extraordinary lengths to accrue the benefits of an Ivy League diploma. It was as though they believed poverty inevitably to confer wisdom and goodness, while the wealthy were condemned to shallow-mindedness and avarice. In fairness, Phillip was obliged to acknowledge that good and bad traits could be found in all economic groups.

"Your family has a tremendous amount of influence with very powerful people. Think how much good you can do by using that influence wisely. As a teacher you can do what? Help forty, fifty, at most a hundred kids in a year? But by changing laws and supporting good causes you can help thousands, maybe even millions."

Here, Sherry's argument found a tender conscience. Phillip had been advised from the time he was a small boy—even by the tooth fairy it sometimes had seemed—that wealth, for all its blessings, carried with it obligations. He experienced in himself some guilt at his desire to be free of them.

"There is that," he now admitted, but then he went on to defend himself. "Doesn't a person also have an obligation to himself? And don't you always do a better job when you like the job you're doing?"

"I'll bet Chrissie said something just like that when she was talking with your uncle."

They had not talked of Chrissie's plan, Max's role having made the subject a delicate one, and Phillip was given pause. "She probably did," he finally admitted.

This comparison appeared to have had stronger affect on Phillip than she had intended, and Sherry now said, "Not that I think it's the same . . . though I think you're both being selfish, in different ways."

"Chrissie is only doing what she wants to do."

"Oh, sure!" Sherry now said. "But it isn't even what she wants to do, it's just what she thinks right now she wants to do. She hasn't thought about her family or her expenses or any of that. You can decide you want to do something, or you can just do something because it feels good at the moment. They're not the same."

"There's no chance she'll really do anything in LA, is there?"
"None."

"Why is Max encouraging her then."

"I don't think he is . . . I know that he didn't mean to. You know how Max is. He's got that beautiful voice and he just gets going and I think he hypnotizes even himself and just says things. But I know he didn't tell her she should move to LA. That was some kind of misunderstanding. Or Chrissie hearing what she wanted to hear."

"I don't think Chrissie really knows much about acting."

"She has no idea," Sherry said, "but then I could say the same thing about you and teaching."

"You could," Phillip said, speaking with more firmness than he was usually inclined to direct toward her, "but you would be mistaken."

Sherry, who was not accustomed to being so directly contradicted, found herself miffed. She was, however, able to restrain herself from using harsher epithets that came to mind and said only. "That seems so dorky. I'm sure I don't understand you at all."

Phillip shrugged. "What's going to happen with Chrissie?"

"It'll blow over. Max will take care of it. He will, or I'll kill him."

Chapter 30

Dr. Gannon's Conversation With Max Hill

It happened that even while Sherry and Phillip conducted their conversation out by the pool, another was taking place in Dr. Gannon's office, where he had taken Max for the purpose of a heart-to-heart conversation. This was a meeting that Max would have preferred to avoid, and he was now lying very nearly continuously, if not perfectly consistently.

"I've done everything possible to discourage her," he now said, with a voice of fatherly concern, "but you know how Chrissie is."

"I'm not so sure I do know her anymore," Dr. Gannon said.

"All I mean it that she's very determined. Once she's decided to do something, there's no turning her head . . . . And I know that I have to take some of the responsibility for that. I thought that it would be fun for her to get to know a little bit about the business, and she seemed so intent on finding out . . . . I didn't really see how it could do any harm."

"She hasn't any real talent at all, has she?"

"That would depend on what you mean by talent."

"By talent I mean an ability to act."

"The importance of acting ability is a little overstated. I know any number of really fine actors, who could no more get a day's work in Hollywood than a mineworker. And then I know a number of people who can't act, or at least who can't act much, who are doing quite well. Besides, acting is an acquired skill. Anyone, or almost anyone, can acquire enough skill to . . . ."

"What you are saying is that an attractive figure and a famous name are likely to be of more use to her than any actual ability she might have."

"Chrissie's a very intelligent girl. I have no doubt that she can acquire . . . ."

"And in the meantime she makes a complete fool of herself, her family, and her family name."

Max thought it futile to deny this and now said, "Maybe I could have been more forceful with her, but Chrissie has her heart set on giving this a try, and the last thing I would want to do is hurt her."

"She'll be hurt far worse if she goes through with it and fails, as I'm quite sure she will."

Max nodded solemnly, conceding the doctor's point. "Like you," he said, "I would never want to see her hurt."

A look of understanding passed between them, and then Dr. Gannon asked, "Can you talk her out of it?"

"She's very determined," Max replied. Then, he paused as though to think. "If she were introduced to the right people, who offered her the right discouragement, if she met enough other girls who had tried and failed, and if she were made aware of how much drudgery there is in the business, in a few weeks . . . ."

"A few weeks?" Dr. Gannon repeated.

"Maybe not even that long."

"Wouldn't it be far better," Dr. Gannon said, his temples throbbing, "if she changed her mind *before* she missed a semester of school?"

"Much better," Max now said. Then, seeing that Dr. Gannon's hostility had not abated, he continued, "And I may be able to help you with that."

"In what way would you mean to help?" Dr. Gannon said, his tone very nearly contemptuous.

"I mean to say, that I can try to influence her . . . . I understand why you would be upset. Under your circumstances I would be as well, and, for my own part, I agree with you completely. Chrissie has far too much going for her to risk her future. And, certainly, considering your special circumstances, there's no question that she must be especially discreet." Seeing that Dr. Gannon's bulging forehead veins had withdrawn, Max thought it well to continue a little longer with this line of discourse. "I couldn't agree more, and I only regret that I haven't been more forceful in conveying that to Chrissie. She is a sweet girl, and as we both are aware, young in many ways. In what I now see was misguided compassion, I didn't state my position sufficiently directly. Instead of hearing what I said, she heard what she hoped to hear." Dr. Gannon's demeanor remained unsettled, and now, thinking he'd perhaps gone too far in criticizing Chrissie, Max continued quickly. "That was, of course, completely my own fault. I've been in the business long enough that I certainly should have anticipated her reaction. Don't we all have a tendency to believe what we would like to believe?"

This Dr. Gannon could hardly deny, and taking his softened expression for approval, Max continued.

"Sometimes being over-delicate does a service to no one, and looking back, I can see how she might have taken things that were said in kindness—and because I really do admire and respect her tremendously for her wonderful talents and accomplishments— how she could have taken those words for encouragement."

"The girl is under the impression that you did encourage her. She conveyed to me that you would be managing her career."

"Oh, my," Max said, "That's not good."

"It certainly isn't good," Dr. Gannon said, but with a softening of expression that suggested that he no longer felt assured of Max's guilt.

While he did not care tremendously whether or not he had the doctor's good opinion, Max was too shrewd to ignore the risk in creating powerful enemies. At the same time, he'd enjoyed the game of luring Chrissie to Los Angeles, had looked forward to using her name in conversation there, knew that valuable prestige accrued to him by being able to produce her at parties, and found her breasts tempting. In short, he did not wish either to offend Dr. Gannon or to give up any of these possibilities—after all, they were the spices that made life stimulating. Fortunately, he was able, in this moment of reflection, to come upon a plan that would serve both ends.

"I hope I don't need to tell you how sorry I am about all this. I feel responsible, and I'd like to see what I can do to correct the situation. I think if you will allow me to speak with Chrissie, I can clarify for her what my actual feelings are."

"She can be a very determined young lady."

Max met Dr. Gannon's look with a knowing smile. "She can. Very much so. And I'm sure she'll put me over the grill for a while. But I don't think it will be anything I can't survive. She'll probably even forgive me someday." This last he said with an ironical chuckle, which was rewarded with a nod and a thin smile from Dr. Gannon.

"I could, of course, simply refuse to let her go," the doctor now said.

"I'd rather you didn't have to," Max said quickly. "It's much better if we do it this way. I've caused enough disruption in this household without that. In any case, it's much better that Chrissie be brought to see the situation as it actually is and to make the decision on her own."

In truth, Dr. Gannon was very willing to let Max have his try, as he feared his daughter would defy any direct refusal on his part. That would leave only the prospect of cutting her off financially, which seemed the desperate resort of a failed parent. "Yes," he said, "it's always better when all parties buy in to a decision."

"Much better," Max agreed, "and I think you can trust that it will all be resolved quickly—in the next day or so."

"That would be very welcome news."

Max now went on to announce that he would be leaving Arden Park permanently the next week, as it was necessary he resume his career interests. "I know it's not for everyone," he reassured Dr. Gannon, "but this is the career I've chosen, and I feel a responsibility to approach it in a professional manner."

Dr. Gannon always responded well to the word responsibility, something his children had long known. Now, remembering the poise and maturity Max had shown throughout the summer and the example of good manners he had so frequently been for his own children, he expressed real regret at his permanent departure.

"Of course, I'll return from time-to-time," Max said. "My grandparents are here, and I think it's very important for both of us that we maintain that connection across generations."

Feeling optimistic that the dark cloud blown in by Chrissie's acting fantasies would soon be lifted, Dr. Gannon could say with real feeling, "We will enjoy having you return. I know my wife has come to think of you as a member of our family."

Max left quickly, vowing never to return, especially not in the few hours before his departure, and thinking to himself that, while there had been some good times to be had, Arden Park really was an incredibly dull place. Except, of course, that there was Jasmine.

It happened that on his way out of the Gannon home, Max overtook his sister. They walked across the street together.

"What an ass," Max announced.

"Who?"

"Old man Gannon." Not wanting to tell even his sister that he felt he had been treated as a ten-year-old, Max instead said, "He thinks Chrissie has talent."

"Doesn't she?"

"All the talents she has are on her chest."

"He expects her to be successful in LA, then?"

"Oh, no, he understands that she can't act. He thinks her talents would be squandered."

"If she can't act, wouldn't they be?"

"If she had any real talents, they might be. But really there's not much to squander, is there? Chrissie's a good-looking girl, but her high opinion of herself is totally unjustified."

"If she's so untalented, what do you care?"

"She amuses me."

"Her breasts amuse you."

"No, her breasts stupefy me."

Sherry laughed at this. "I take it he isn't going to let her go?"

"She's grown up. She can make her own decisions."

"But she's not going?"

"I've agreed to help convince her to return to school." Then, when Sherry again laughed aloud, he said, "I tell you the man is a complete ass. It was either that or listen to a sermon . . . ."

"You just don't want to admit that you've been beaten at your own game."

"I find I like it best when everyone does exactly what I want them to. In any case, it's only a slight delay. In a week or two, I'm sure she'll succumb to the irresistible pull."

"And how do you think Jasmine will feel about that?"

"One thing I'm sure of is that she won't feel jealous."

"Another case of not getting your way?" Sherry queried.

"It sucks and I'm tired of it," Max said.

"Tired of Jasmine?" Sherry asked, with real surprise.

"No, not of Jasmine. Of course not. But I'm tired of trying to convince her that . . . ." He broke off, searching for the right words.

"That you're someone you're not?" Sherry suggested.

" . . . of my good intentions," he substituted. "Maybe she'll miss me." He ignored Sherry's laugh, and went on. "But, at this point . . . . At this point, she'll have to beg me to come back. You know she refused to kiss me the other night."

"Refused to kiss you?" Sherry mocked.

"Everybody kisses everybody now. It doesn't mean anything. And she refused, even after I had given her the necklace."

"I told you it was a bad idea. The necklace made her take you seriously, and once she took you seriously, she couldn't kiss you."

"What a lot of nonsense."

"You don't understand her at all, do you?"

"I understand that she's a little priss and needs a good . . . ."

"Don't even go there."

"It's true though."

"You have no idea how not true that is."

They had now reached their grandparents home. They settled onto the old leather couch, and, given a moment's reflection, Max's pique abated.

"She's still the most remarkable girl I've ever known."

After a further moment of silence, Sherry said, "Yes, but it was never going to happen. You and Jasmine, that's not a match made in heaven."

"It's not going to happen *right away*," Max said. "I understand that. After all, she's young. I know it's hard to believe, but you realize that she still has another year of high school."

"You think that she's going to change?"

"Of course, she'll change," he said.

"And maybe you'll be able to get her drunk."

"I don't mean that at all," Max said in protest that was to all appearances sincere. "Maybe I'll change. In some ways, I already have."

"You've certainly been acting peculiar," Sherry admitted, but he didn't respond to the smile which she offered.

"You know I'm tired of LA, too. It's better than here, I grant you. If it weren't for Jasmine, I wouldn't ever have come back. But it's gotten to be too much of the same old thing. Everybody out to get somewhere and to screw somebody famous or screw *over* some nobody . . . ."

"Or better yet, screw over some somebody," Sherry interjected.

Max at first refused to acknowledge her smile, but when she rolled her eyes, he relented. "It's got its moments, I admit, but after a while . . . ." He shrugged. "The only time that I really feel good, the only time when there's any real edge to things, is when I'm with Jasmine."

"Maxwell, you just want to get the girl in bed . . . ."

"I don't."

" . . . and can't."

"I don't even know if I would if I could," Max said.

"Of course you would."

"I might, but that doesn't mean I *only* want to get her in bed. I like the feeling I get when I'm near her. I like to do things for her. Haven't you ever felt like that?"

"Maybe when I was six."

"Well, little sis, I think this might be the definition of being in love."

"Oh, give me a break. You're not in love."

Max shrugged again. "I'm in something."

"And that's why you're trying to get Chrissie down to LA, where you can shag her to your heart's content."

"Chrissie's got nothing to do with it."

"I wonder if Jasmine would agree with that statement."

"She wouldn't, but then she's only sixteen. She doesn't understand . . . ."

"I think she understands perfectly, and that's exactly why she won't have anything to do with you. Face it, you're not going to change and neither is she. She has values—actual real values—something you and I have only read about. Plus, you're too far gone to change now. You're stuck in your ways forever."

"I'm not so sure of that," Max said, rising up to go to the bar.

Sherry was now able to meet her brother's eyes, and she could not deny either the longing or the sincerity in his expression.

"Big Brother, for your sake I wish it could be true. I honestly do. I wish you could become the kind of person who could be wonderful for Jasmine, because I know she would be wonderful for you."

"People do mature, you know. They change."

"No doubt."

"Jasmine's very young. People change a lot at her age."

"If she changed, then she wouldn't be Jasmine."

"I don't expect her to change totally. Just a little. And I'll change a little too."

Sherry's matter-of-fact shake of the head seemed to contradict him, but she said only, "I wish you luck. I truly do."

This seemed to end the conversation, and Max went to the kitchen for ice. When he came back he began mixing himself a gin and tonic.

"I'm leaving in the morning," he said.

"Chrissie's not going to be happy."

"That's why you have to talk to her. Tell her that nothing's changed. It couldn't look like we were leaving together, so I left early. I'll be sending her a letter explaining everything."

"I don't know whether to hope you're telling the truth about the letter or to hope that you're lying."

"Just tell her. This thing with Gannon was just too much of a hassle. I'm too old for dealing with fathers of teen-aged girls. If she wants to come to LA, that's up to her. Just tell her that for now she has to let her dad think she's changed her mind. I've got to get him off my back . . . ."

They now turned for a while to discussing Sherry's situation. She admitted that she too might be in Los Angeles soon.

"Not going well with the oil baron?" Max asked.

"He still wants to be a teacher."

"Poor slob."

"Cheap shoes and body odor."

"Look on the bright side," Max said. "You'd have long summer vacations."

"The whole idea of a vacation appalls me. To think of being stuck in some dismal place nine months a year. I mean a person has to be able to go someplace tropical in the winter. And, for God's sake, I don't mean for just two weeks."

"He won't stick with it. Nobody lasts more than five years."

"Five years! One year would be an eternity!"

"Then, you'll just have to speed things along."

Sherry regarded him warily.

"Use your feminine charms."

"I think he's immune," Sherry said. Then, miffed by remembering her previous failures, showed uncharacteristic pique, saying, "Maybe he's gay."

Her brother laughed. "He's not gay. You just need to escalate your tactics. You haven't slept with him, have you?"

"I don't know that that's any business of yours."

"Your problem is that you really don't like sleeping with guys . . ."

"It's all so messy . . ."

"And because you don't like sleeping with guys you give up your most powerful weapon. What do we know about Master Phillip? He's loyal, honest, kind, sincere . . . just the kind of guy who if you sleep with him will become loyal and obedient as a lapdog."

"Good God," Sherry said.

"Awful, isn't it, that life should be simple? But it is. Set your trap."

"You mean to get pregnant? Are you kidding?"

"Not to get pregnant, you dope. Not even to pretend to get pregnant. Just to sleep with the poor boy. After that, he'll be so grateful, he'll follow you around like a lost puppy."

"I don't think he's very interested in sex."

"You little idiot. The only reason he doesn't stare at you is because it wouldn't be good manners, and the only reason he hasn't tried to rip your clothes off is because he respects you."

"Isn't it good that he respects me?"

"Good or bad isn't the issue. What's important is what's useful. What seems to you like an undignified, possibly amusing, but just as likely depressing, little event would be momentous to him. To his way of thinking, it would bind you for life. Loyalty would eternally oblige him to put up with any amount of crap you might want to heap on him. And he'll buy you anything you see."

"You're really horrible. What would people think if they could hear you? What would Jasmine think?"

The smile left his face.

"Now, now, big bro," Sherry went on, "she won't hear a whisper from me. I really hope it will work out between you. I don't think it will, but I hope it will."

"The problem with a girl like Jasmine," he said, "is that she gets into your head. Even when she isn't listening you start not wanting to say certain things. You just imagine her being there."

"Not that she would ever say a word to criticize . . . ."

"Of course not."

"Or, for that matter, show in the tiniest gesture that she disapproved."

"No, but you'd know."

"How is that you always do know?"

"You just know."

"Which is proof that there's good in you yet, brother. It shows that you know what's right even if you don't always do it. Otherwise, how could you know what Jasmine is thinking?"

"It is proof, isn't it?" Max said cheerily.

"She reminds you of your better self."

A look akin to amazement came over Max's face. "If I was with her all the time, I'd get used to it. I could probably be that way all the time."

"Oh, the rapture!" Sherry said mockingly. "Actually, though, I don't want to discourage you. I'm sure she's very good for you. But you should know that your better self is a pretty boring guy."

"If I had Jasmine, that wouldn't matter."

"He'd even bore you sooner or later. Probably sooner."

"That's not true."

"What do we have here? A believer in true love?"

"Why not?"

"True love that lasts for a lifetime?"

"Absolutely."

Sherry laughed. "That's the gin talking."

Max set his glass down. "Maybe a lifetime isn't realistic. But even if it didn't last that long, that doesn't mean it couldn't be a good thing. Nothing lasts forever. Don't those Buddhist monks make those elaborate sand things that they tear up as soon as they're done?"

"Jasmine's not a Buddhist. She'd expect it to be for a lifetime."

"Everybody does, more or less. Nobody gets married, or whatever, admitting that it'll last such-and-such an amount of years and then they'll move on, but it's a question of being realistic. It's okay to pretend it will last forever, but you also have to be aware that it never does."

"Not never."

"Never."

"Some people stay married for a lifetime."

"They don't count, because they believe God will strike them dead if they don't. They stay together out of fear."

"What about the doctor and the former Miss Arden Park?"

"He travels so much, it doesn't matter. She's home base. All he has to do is come back once in a while and check in. Perfect. If he had to spend all his time with her, it wouldn't last six months. He thinks she's stupid."

"I don't believe that he fools around, but I do agree that he thinks she's stupid. What about her? She doesn't fool around."

"If I went to see her at about five o'clock, and caught her after her second drink, I could have her moaning on the couch in about . . . ."

"Shut up. You're disgusting."

"I'm afraid, little sis, you're reluctant to see life as it actually is."

"But it isn't that way for everyone. Wasn't it you who just a short while ago was telling me it was a mistake to assume everybody was just like me? Well, everybody isn't just like you either."

"And it's a good thing, wouldn't you say?"

"Some people do stay married forever, and it's not just because they're scared."

Max shook his head.

"They do," Sherry continued. "It's amazing, I know, but they do, and Jasmine's the kind of person who will."

"I have an open mind. I'm willing to give it a try."

"That's just it. If you start out with that attitude, it can't work. You have to decide in advance that it's going to work no matter what."

"That would be ridiculous. I'm not sure how I'll feel next week, much less in ten years."

Chapter 31

The Gannon Girls Play Their Hands

Julia had never completely surrendered Max Hill to her sister, and she had taken some encouragement from the red eyes, furrowed brow, and hard-set jaw which Chrissie displayed on leaving her conference with their father. Not that she would have behaved differently if she had been in her sister's position: she adhered to no categorical injunction against a girl trading up; indeed, it would be inhumanly cruel—not to mention stupid—to permanently bind a girl to a boyfriend when she had the opportunity to do better. Max was in every respect but money far more desirable than Pudge. Rich was good, but rich and famous was even better, and it seemed probable—almost certain—that Max would soon be both. Placed in the same circumstances as her sister, Julia would have played her cards in the same way. But they in fact had not been placed in the same circumstances—they had been dealt different hands—and different hands called for different strategies.

Certain factors worked in Julia's favor: first and foremost, Chrissie already had Pudge. Dumping one boyfriend for another was one thing; being perceived to have done so was another. Chrissie had made the mistake of keeping Pudge near as a safety. That strategy now worked against her. Julia also believed that her larger bust made her sexier than her sister. Chrissie had been more successful because she'd been more experienced, had flirted more openly, and had exhibited herself to better effect. Having mastered Pudge, she was ready to play the game at a higher level. Julia herself was no prude, and she would certainly someday learn all there was to know, but she knew that she still had tricks to learn. During the critical moments, she had been mortified lest Max detect her nervousness or she make some crucial error. She would not repeat her mistakes.

Julia's distrust of her sister was only exacerbated when Sherry returned to the Gannon house for a private meeting with Chrissie. The whispers of conversation that escaped Chrissie's locked door, the cheerful laughter which preceded the reopening of the door, and especially the self-satisfied glance Chrissie gave her when they passed in the hall fully renewed Julia's sense of injustice over how events had transpired. She had at various times during the summer been angry, disappointed, humiliated, and jealous. Never before, however, had she felt so forlorn. She closed the door of her room, buried her face in her pillow, and cried red-hot tears.

It was not in Julia's nature, however, to dwell long in self-pity, and retributive thoughts soon began to reassert themselves. Her sister's glance, instead of angry and abashed, had been spiteful and haughty. She knew her far too well to believe that this change in attitude was the result of having admitted an error in her ways and having reconciled with their father. Something new was certainly in the works, and any new plan which could so thoroughly restore her sister would necessarily involve Max Hill. If there was to be any justice, this plan must be uncovered and revealed to their father.

Her father was so out-of-touch with the real world that he would never guess what was going on behind his back. It would look bad to rat directly on her sister, and her father hated tattling nearly as much as he did lying; but if it came to that, she could claim that the situation—like fire, poison, or blood—was sufficiently alarming to require her to do something she loathed. Her best move, though, would be to secretly force the plan out into the open. First she needed to find out what the plan was. With this in mind, she arose from her bed, retired to the bathroom to repair her eyes and face, which tended to streak and redden miserably when she cried, and began assembling the cheerful and cooperative countenance that she thought would be most useful for her undertaking. It was a mark of her growing wisdom that she would disdain pouting. More mature tactics would be required.

Dr. Gannon was returning to Washington in the morning, and with Max's departure also imminent, Cynthia had planned to make the evening special. Pudge had relented and agreed not to take his trip to Las Vegas, and he and Chrissie were to all appearances again on good terms. Cynthia had invited Pudge and the Hills to dinner. The evening would be made even more special in that Thomas would be coming down to dinner. He had taken a few previous meals in the kitchen and was expected to be doing so regularly soon, but this would be his first meal taken as a "normal" member of the family.

Cynthia's plans were thwarted when Sherry arrived bearing Max's regrets, but the meal having been prepared, it could hardly be stopped for lack of a guest of honor. Thus, they sat down at the dining room table and proceeded, with palates that would have been just as well pleased with pizza, to eat hors d'oeuvres of grilled dried tomatoes topped with roasted garlic and freshly ground parmigiano reggiano.

"Cool," Pudge said, eating with relish.

"You're really going to stink, you know," Chrissie warned.

This gave Pudge pause. "Not if we all eat it," he said, then having his doubts, added, "Will I?"

Sherry, however, laughed, ate with equal avidity, and said, "This is too good to worry about anyway."

Chrissie could hardly contradict Sherry, but Julia was quick to note that her sister did not eat the garlic-laced tomatoes. "Are you planning to go somewhere later, Chrissie?" she asked.

"I just prefer not to smell like a garlic truck," Chrissie said.

Chrissie had first paused slightly before replying, however, and this hesitation had assured Julia of what she had suspected from her sister's brusque manner with Pudge: that she planned to see Max later. Julia picked up a tomato, wanting to show up her sister's squeamishness, then giving second thought, poised her fork in mid-air.

"It's too bad that Max couldn't come," she said, turning to Sherry, and speaking in her brightest voice. "Is he sick?"

"He got a last minute call, some script or something. He's really in a sweat about getting it prepared for tomorrow."

"Oh, does he have an *acting* job?" Julia asked, glancing toward Chrissie.

"Who knows exactly what. When he gets like this, he just locks himself in his room, and you hear noises coming out of it like he's some kind of madman." Sherry gobbled another tomato. Julia discreetly set her fork down. "God, these are wonderful," Sherry resumed. "This is one of the really great things about Arden Park. The food is so right-off-the-farm."

"After all," Julia said, "we're all just a bunch of farmers up here anyway."

Sherry laughed good-humoredly at this, and seeing that her remark had failed to cut, Julia found herself smiling as well. Indeed, though she still resented the conspiratorial tone between Sherry and her sister, there was no profit in picking a quarrel with Sherry. Much better to leave the door open for a future alliance.

"Then, he really is leaving in the morning?"

"He was even talking about getting a red-eye. But then maybe it *is* an acting job because he mentioned that he was worried about actual red eyes."

"Do you think you'll be back next summer?"

"We've found a live-in for Gram and Gramps. Thank God. Gram has never gotten the hang of a microwave—she nearly blew up the kitchen last week—and neither of them ought to be driving."

"Whatever happens, you'll have to come visit us," Dr. Gannon announced with authority. "You'll always be welcome in this house."

All murmured their agreement, and Sherry said, "And, of course, we would always love to see you in Bel Air." Given the unsettled situation in her parents' household and the makeshift circumstance under which most independent young people live, this offer could only be regarded as ceremonial, at least as it regarded the adults; but Tina, who was inclined to think of herself as something of a companion to the younger set, responded nonetheless.

"We will do that, won't we?" she said, turning first to Chrissie and then to Julia. "I would so like to meet your parents."

Chrissie responded affirmatively but without enthusiasm. Much as she liked and trusted her aunt, she did not wish to have her company in Bel Air, where she would appear to others to be a chaperone and where drinking, drug-taking, and sexual liaisons were conducted more openly than in Arden Park.

Julia, seeing Chrissie's indifferent response, took the opportunity to say, "That'd be great! We should go soon, Tina. We've never spent enough time in Southern California."

"You really should," Sherry said cheerfully.

"We will then," Tina said, as though settling the matter. "When do you think would be convenient?"

Chrissie could let this trend continue no longer and now interrupted, saying to her brother, "You're awfully quiet."

No one else would have mentioned this, as it was recognized by all those who saw him often that this quietness was a result of his illness and might be the sign of some lingering neural impairment.

"I can't seem to keep up with all of you," Thomas said pleasantly, "but it's fun to listen anyway."

"I'm sure you'll be right back in the swing of things soon," Cynthia said to her son, directing on him her splendid smile. Thomas's smiling response nearly brought the whole table to tears of joy.

At this point in the conversation, a remarkable stroke of luck befell Julia. Pudge tapped his glass with his spoon, and when he had everyone's attention, sat back in his chair in baronial complacency.

"I have an announcement," he pronounced. "In honor of Chrissie's and my first date, which took place two years ago yesterday, we are going to Tahoe to see . . . Mr. Tony Bennett."

Chrissie gasped, observed all the smiling faces turned toward her, and quickly removed the initial look of alarm and irritation from her face.

"And when is this that we will be going?" she asked, manufacturing a voice which suggested equanimity if not quite good cheer.

"Tonight," Pudge replied. "Right now, in fact." He looked at his watch. "Eleven o'clock show. We ought to be right on time."

Chrissie looked stunned, then said, "Oh, my goodness, I can't go now. I'm not ready. I have to dress."

"Get dressed," Pudge said. He was probably the only one at the table who had not detected Chrissie's reluctance, and as Chrissie slowly rose, he looked about the table expecting general approbation.

"How wonderful," Julia said, then added, "God, I wish I could go." For a moment, however, she deeply regretted allowing this last to escape, as the silence that ensued implied that an arrangement to include her was being contemplated. Rather than let this go on too long, she now added, "But then, I know you only have two tickets, and, after all, it's kind of an anniversary."

Mrs. Gannon now chimed in, "This is so thoughtful of you, Pudge," and the matter seemed to be resolved.

Had she been forewarned, Chrissie could have prepared a credible excuse. As it was, she gave real consideration to feigning or perhaps even inducing an ankle sprain while climbing the stairwell. Alas, she reached the top of the steps without having summoned the necessary courage. She now consoled herself with the observation that her departure would distract attention from her association with Max. She would, in any case, see him again in two weeks time, and steering clear of him for this one night might protect him from future blame. In this she found something noble to sustain her: she was sacrificing herself for the sake of her career, and for Max.

Not five minutes following Chrissie's forlorn departure from Arden Park, Julia was up in her sister's room, working through her dresser drawers in search of that item (or perhaps *items*, for she did not know what exactly a male of Max's experience might expect), which she hoped would be required for the evening. As she sifted the stray contents of her sister's bottom drawer, a purse, three small boxes of mementos, and a clutch (which she distinctly remembered to have been used for Chrissie's senior farewell dance, and in which she found a string of three of exactly that which she sought), she considered the problem of Sherry's plans for the evening. It was not that she especially feared being found out by her—she had concluded that Sherry would acquiesce to any wish of her brother—but it would be almost impossible to bring her plan to the happiest possible conclusion in the presence of a third person.

Julia had not yet hit upon any plan for securing her privacy before again coming down the stairs. She was, therefore, struck with an impression of divine intervention—with a celestial assurance that what she was about to do was not only right but fated, ordained, and destined for success—when she learned that Phillip and Sherry were preparing to go out to a movie. She wished them a pleasant evening, and immediately retired to her own room to select appropriate attire, make her final preparations, and wait for darkness. Alas, with a brief, unladylike snort, she also took a sharp sniff of white powder from the crease of an envelope.

Later, in the deep twilight, she might have been judged by any member of the household to demonstrate a new dimension to her growing character—a new maturity and depth of feeling—as she strolled contemplatively in the back garden and gave the occasional flower a meditative sniff. A moment later, however, the same observer would have searched the garden for her in vain, as Julia had slipped out the back gate.

She started in the opposite direction of her goal, walked much of a mile to circle her suburban block, crossed a neighbor's lawn and entered the Lees' side yard. She found her way to the back yard, where, much to her frustration, she smelled cigar smoke.

Not wanting to encounter Mr. Lee but seeing some advantage in knowing his exact whereabouts, she advanced in slow gingerly steps, and happily—oh so happily!—she discovered Max laid out on a reclined patio chair, a glass of whiskey in one hand, and the offending cigar in the other.

Julia's figure, which the current fashion allowed her amply to display, had long served admirably to attract masculine attention. Of course, if some undesirable nitwit was so foolish as to misinterpret and think that her attractions were directed *at him*, he was quick to feel the sharp edge of her disdain; or, less commonly, if a desired object failed to respond, he was quickly labeled a dullard. In truth, she was so endowed that she had seldom felt the need of subtlety in her coaxing, nor was subtlety much in her personality.

Now, in this most critical of engagements, therefore, she elected to rely on her strengths. She pulled one spaghetti-strap off her shoulder, wriggled her shorts lower so that her exquisitely tanned belly might better be displayed, and induced her minuscule top to fold so that he might appreciate the full plumpness of 180 degrees of breast. Thus, gunports fully cleared, she went straight at him, taking a seat at the foot of his cot and placing one hand on his bare leg.

If Max was surprised by this display, he was not so startled as either to spill his drink or cough out his Havana. Their eyes met. He allowed a knowing smile to curl his lip. This she returned, before leaning forward to claim his drink, brushing his thighs with her chest as she did. She drank half off in a single taking, still holding his eyes.

Over the previous weeks, there had been ample opportunity to develop a certain tension between them, to turn pegs and tune strings; yet what was achieved was achieved so quickly that the strings made little music before they sagged. Julia herself had not particularly enjoyed this, especially as a certain lack of confidence in her own performance had been exacerbated by what she felt was a tendency to bossiness in how he gave instructions and directed her movements. It was therefore, with some diffidence, that she asked, "How was that?"

"Cool," he said. "Very cool."

"I've never hooked up quite like that before," she admitted.

For the moment, Julia's past sexual experience and the girl herself were matters of indifference to Max Hill, but he was experienced enough to know that this might change in the future, and he was now placed in a quandary as to how he should reply. He was aware, however, that good manners alone called for an expression of the rarity and excellence of her performance and of the intensity of his pleasure. However, he also understood that this expression was called for precisely because it would establish them in a private and unique association, which at least one part of the female psyche instinctively sought and which would imply certain privileges of intimacy.

Another possibility existed: deep-down the girl might really want to be humiliated. If so, she could be turned into a servant of his every whim and wish, which, with a girl of her assets, had strong advantages. If this were the case, she would respond best not to benevolence but to neglect, random verbal abuse, and an occasional "good girl." He could not be certain, however, that she was as yet acquainted with this side of her own character—if, indeed, such a side existed—and she would need to be led carefully to its full understanding. This wearied him, and as he was leaving in the morning in any case, it seemed easiest just to say nothing.

Julia, despite finding herself lying against his legs, began to sense that their intimacy had not advanced quite as she had hoped. It seemed essential to her that they "hook up" in some tighter embrace that would seem both more binding and less perfunctory and one-sided. Julia was too young and inexperienced to have much idea of the cruel indifference of the sated male animal. Instead of waiting for the propitious moment or undertaking those quiet flanking maneuvers that might have speeded his renewal, she pressed ever forward.

To attempt to stimulate where only rest is wanted is to chafe, and Max was not one to suffer any irritation gladly. He did—just—avoid sending her packing, but he could not rouse himself to make a more energetic—or ingenuous—excuse than, "I really need to think about this."

"You *what?*" Julia asked incredulously, rising from her ministrations.

"You know there are lots of things to think about here, lots of considerations."

"You've always thought I was cuter than Chrissie. It was just that you thought I was too young. Isn't *this . . . ,*" she said, spreading her arms to show the tableau before them, "enough to prove that I know what I'm doing?"

This response seemed to Max to be so full of error that he did not know where to begin. He did not think her more attractive than Chrissie; if he had, all would have been much easier. Julia's maturity had never been an issue of great interest to him, and, in any case, he had in his experience encountered fifteen-year-olds who performed with greater expertise than she. And here she was clinging to him—an error that displayed not only deep ignorance but complex character faults as well.

"I just need some time alone," he said, thinking that if he could be rid of her now, he would be gone in the morning.

"I've only been here for two minutes!" Julia persisted.

"Really? Only two?" Max asked, wondering at the great disparity that sometimes arose between psychic and physical chronometers. "I'll bet it was more. However many it was, they were pretty intense minutes."

This being as much compliment as she now expected to receive, Julia received it as such. Her dignity somewhat restored, she now ceased her efforts, sat up, and took from him the cigar, which, while much neglected, had never left his hand. This she puffed experimentally, her face held high in the air as she appraised its taste and effects. She puffed again, inhaling more smoke this time and gagging only a little. This had the fortuitous effect of settling a strange dizziness down upon her. As she gazed out into the darkness, trying to decide whether or not the sensation was in fact pleasant, Max was given a few brief moments to reclaim his composure and to evaluate her form. Impressive it was. So impressive that he began to feel that it would be a shame not to explore it further. The girlish clumsiness with which she had seemed to manage it's very adult proportions—a lack of art that had put him off for a time—now seemed to demand the guidance of a man with his experience. He reclaimed his cigar from her hand and passed her his drink, saying, "It isn't that you aren't hot enough—you're seriously hot. And it sure isn't that I don't want to."

"When two people like each other—I mean when they're really, really attracted to each other—isn't that like enough? I mean that's pretty cool when that happens, right? Like how often in your life does that happen?"

This was a line of argument to which Max typically paid lip service, though he had never given it more thought than to observe that it appealed to many women and might prove a useful avenue for seduction. Now, however, he gave it real consideration, but in a manner far from what Julia had intended. The likes of Julia he had encountered many times before, but he'd never met anyone like Jasmine Johnson. How often *did* such things happen? Might he never feel quite that same way again? Would he never again feel that touching desire to protect or that noble desire to earn someone's esteem? Already the feelings seemed a little distant to him, as though the Max who had made that long drive up the valley and who would have pursued Jasmine's remotest cousins to the farthest corners of the earth had not quite been right in the head.

"Huh?" he said aloud, with a somewhat mystified sigh.

"You know I'm right," Julia said.

Max again nearly threw her off himself; in fact, a thoroughly obscene expression of this wish was right at the tip of his tongue, but again he paused. If Julia were to leave, he would be left alone with this rather empty and somewhat unpleasant sensation that thinking of Jasmine had started in him. He'd rather not.

Instead, he admitted a long-standing wish to snuggle against Julia's bosom, though he expressed himself in more explicit language. Whatever the language, that and every other wish was granted.

Much had been accomplished, and Julia spent the next day in evaluation of the previous evening's successes and contemplation of future rewards. Max had promised that he would delay his departure, and she had hoped that he would appear at the house in the morning, but she was hardly surprised that he did not, given both the delicacy of their situation and the amount of brandy he had drunk. She said nothing smug or suggestive to Chrissie when she returned in the afternoon, nor was her serene demeanor exaggerated much beyond the normal. Imagine then her consternation when Sherry arrived to announce that she had just taken Max to the airport! Imagine her rage at her sister's complacent nod upon receipt of this news!

Her near blind fury was contained only by her recollection of the previous night's events, in which the man in question had been brought to utterly gratifying declarations of her magnificence. Her self-regard was such that she could not even now suspect him of lying to her. No male, she reasoned, would give up such highly prized attractions easily. Instead, his absconding must have resulted from a failure of courage: he was not prepared to face the condemnation and tears which open acknowledgment of their relationship would cause. As he was only delaying the inevitable and necessary, this was weakness in him, but it was weakness she was as yet willing to forgive. After all, he was an artist with an artist's delicacy of feelings. She would need to be the strong one. She would reunite with him and give him the courage to face the condemnation of the world.

Thus, she forgave him, but she could not forgive her sister. She was deeply averse to having her importance to Max underestimated, even if it was to be for only a short time.

"Shut up, Chrissie," she said, in response to one of her sister's knowing nods.

"I didn't say *any*thing."

"Shut up."

"What did *I* do?" Chrissie asked.

"Just shut up."

"What's *with* you?" Chrissie whined.

"What's with *you*?" Julia whined back.

While this type of bickering had once been common in the Gannon household, it had been muted for some years, and all present were both surprised and embarrassed to witness it.

"Julia!" Tina said, "that's enough!"

"*Me?*" Julia protested, with some justification. "Chrissie started it."

"I did not start it."

"Whichever. Both of you. Stop right now," Cynthia said. "Voices like that just make everything so unpleasant."

It was probably just as well that Mrs. Gannon made no appeal to justice in her reprimand, as neither of her daughter's would have been willing to see justice applied. The two young women glared at each other, but nothing more was said.

This elevated tension in the house had prevented Jasmine from experiencing the fullness of relief that ought to have resulted from Max Hill's removal from Arden Park. Moreover, she knew something more of the reasons for this tension than she ought. The night before, having heard a crash outside near the pool, she looked out to find Julie lying beside a toppled chair. She had gone outside to check on her safety and found her struggling to rise.

"What are you looking at?" Julia said, when the moonlight had allowed her to determine that it was her cousin who looked down on her.

Understanding that the question was rhetorical, Jasmine made efforts to right the chair, while Julia struggled to her feet. "Are you all right?" she asked.

"I'm fine," Julia replied, "perfectly fine." The voice, though sloppy, was too firm to suggest injury, and Jasmine now began to retreat. "I'm just a little drunk," her cousin continued. "*Max* and I had a few drinks is all." The pride with which she had said this and the facetious tone told much, if not quite all.

That both Chrissie and Julia should be romantically attached to Max Hill, all while he was himself professing a deep affection for Jasmine, was appalling. It made matters yet worse that her cousins, instead of trusting and confiding in each other, were instead probably separately placing themselves under his guidance. That this guidance would be far from altruistic, that it would be insincere, unreliable, manipulative, exploitative, and self-serving, Jasmine assumed.

This awareness presented a new dilemma. Her cousins certainly did not know the extent of his perfidy. Moreover, they would not want to know of it, would be predisposed to disbelieve any report of it, and would revile the deliverer of any such message and seek any device to vitiate his or her motives. Yet, despite these obstacles, Jasmine felt that something must be done. Her cousins were on a path that might lead to great harm. Beyond general heartbreak and the rupture in family relations that seemed imminent—both horrible enough in themselves—Max Hill seemed disinclined to protect them from the moral hazards that a too fashionable and pleasure-seeking lifestyle presented. Indeed, this was exactly the path down which he would be most likely to encourage them.

Jasmine well knew that it was not her position to advise her cousins on moral issues, nor had she ever been inclined to do so; yet, given what she knew of Max Hill, given Chrissie's arrest in Los Angeles, given that he was paying court to both sisters at once, given that he had at least permitted, if not encouraged, Julia's inebriation, and given that he lied, was not a disastrous outcome almost certain?

It was not in Jasmine's nature to be a snitch, nor did she wish to be a busybody; but when bullets such as these filled the air, were not maneuvers demanded? Julia *ought* to be old enough to know better—certainly Chrissie should—they ought to be trustworthy in evaluating risks, assessing others' characters, and exercising good judgment, and under more normal circumstances they perhaps would have been; but now their judgments were swayed by the competition between them and by the glamour that Max Hill represented. Given time, given the knowledge of him she had, they would no doubt see their folly, but in the meantime, they might bring irreparable degradation and shame both on themselves and the Gannon household. Could not something be done?

Jasmine reasoned thus, but a deep reluctance to meddle posed counter-arguments. Her cousins were not virginal; they had begun drinking alcohol during the summer, now had some experience with its effects, and would not be caught completely off-guard;

her own views had always been old-fashioned and even prudish compared to those of her cousins, and she had no right or reason to expect her cousins to adopt hers. She was not the girls' mother, nor, for that matter, even their sister. Under these circumstances, it was unlikely that her advice would carry much weight. If it was impossible that her advice would be acted upon, wouldn't it be better to remain silent? It was not in Jasmine's nature to covet the moral advantage that being able to say "I told you so" would confer. Such advantage would more likely generate resentment than respect and certainly would never promote affection. Might she not someday prove of more use to her cousins by now retaining their trust and affection—by avoiding the alienation that would surely result from a denouncing of their lover?

These reflections were not amiss, yet she could not escape the conviction that something must be done. Out of her temporizing, however, came one useful conclusion: she must find a way to circumvent her cousins' tendencies to become resentful. This would best be accomplished by presenting what she knew in such a way that they could feel that they were acting as their own agents in rejecting Max Hill—rather than following another person's advice or instruction.

How best to do this? Not, she felt sure, by going to any of the adults. While Dr. Gannon could be trusted to act judiciously, there were aspects of the situation that could not be hinted of in his presence. Her Aunt Cynthia's judgment, especially when she was distressed, ranged from unpredictable to unsound. Her Aunt Tina, in her eagerness to support Chrissie, would likely place a preponderance of the blame on Julia, or perhaps even find an excuse to condemn the messenger who carried the unwelcome news. Even had his past not argued against as a voice of authority and reason, Thomas was not yet well enough to face quarrelling.

There was Phillip. It was not completely fair that he be drawn into this affair, as he was not an immediate member of the family; yet he was close to them all, respected and trusted by all, and was possessed with wisdom and good judgment. As he was not inclined to meddle, any words he did speak would be treated respectfully.

She believed she could bring herself to inform him that their cousins were involving themselves with the same boy—man, really—and even to present to him her supposition that he was plotting mutually exclusive futures with each. How though was she to inform him that the man in question was Sherry Hill's brother?

Though she had never spoken critically of Sherry and had always taken special care to compliment her where compliment was due, Phillip could not have helped being aware that Jasmine did not completely approve of her; and it was natural enough that he would regard this lack of approval as the product of jealousy. It had always been accepted in the family that Jasmine held something of a crush for her cousin. It had been treated as sweet and becoming, like the crush of schoolgirl on her teacher. Would he now doubt Jasmine's motives if she were to present her evidence to him? Would she seem naïve, her concerns overwrought and childish? Would he suspect her of allowing a childhood affection to advance into an unhealthy obsession?

All these thoughts troubled her, but once she'd resolved her course, she was obliged to put her worries aside. If she could save Julia and Chrissie from ninety-mile-per-hour crashes—whether into heartbreak, each other, or both—she must do so. The happiness of the entire household depended upon it—indeed, something beyond simple happiness was involved. Deception, insecurity, and danger, abundant as they might be in the world, could not be allowed to rule the household. They would inevitably create fissures of discontent and distrust, and their home, the rock on which all their happiness was built, would divide. Jasmine was still enough of a child to experience this threat explicitly—in images of the house lying empty and abandoned, the sidewalks broken, and the gardens turned to dry weeds.

At one time, Jasmine could have trusted Phillip to sense her troubled thoughts and make a special trip to her stoop to counsel her; even in the absence of any suggestion of distress, he had used to visit her there once a day or more. Now, however, as their early morning runs had been foregone, and his free hours were typically spent with Sherry Hill, she found it more difficult to arrange a private meeting with him. Two anxious days passed. With Dr. Gannon departed, the two sisters persisted in glaring at each other, openly and ominously, poisoning the house with their ill will; yet she still had not attempted a private discussion with him. Then, late one night, Sherry Hill left town, nearly as abruptly as her brother.

The very next morning she found herself alone with Phillip in the Gannon kitchen. She had recently come in from a morning run and was sitting in her bare feet eating her breakfast cereal when Phillip came down, his socks and running shoes in hand. He sat himself down in the chair opposite her and began pulling on his socks.

"I've run about three times in a month. I'm going to lose it all if I don't get started again," he said, though his manner did not suggest any real concern. "Is it hot out there?"

Jasmine shook her head, saying, "I think it will still be fine for another hour or so."

Phillip applied himself to smoothing the wrinkles in his socks, and Jasmine felt her heart begin to flutter. She did not know precisely why it should be so hard to speak to him of the matter which so troubled her, yet it was. For a moment, it occurred to her that her fear stemmed from an understanding that what she was doing was in some way wrong and that guilt inhibited her; but this idea could not hold its ground against the foreboding she felt at contemplating Julia's and Chrissie's open defiance of their father, the certain breach that would ensue between them, and the degradation to which she suspected Max Hill might yet subject them.

"I would like to speak to you of something," she said, her heart in her throat. He peered up over the table as he fitted his shoe. "It concerns Chrissie and Julia." She paused for a moment, hoping he would guess the source of her concern and spare her the necessity of speaking out first, but he only nodded and continued with the tying of his shoes. "I'm afraid of a serious break between them," she said.

Phillip nearly laughed. "Chrissie and Julia are always fighting."

"I fear it may be serious this time. They're older . . . ."

"Old enough to know better?" he asked; then, without waiting for an answer, he added, "Julia's just upset that Chrissie has Pudge locked up."

"I'm not sure that's fully the case."

"Julia's never been one to let Chrissie have anything she didn't. Not that she's jealous of Pudge in particular. It's just the principle of the thing. I remember her once throwing Chrissie's bicycle in the pool because Chrissie's had more gears."

"I'm concerned that it may involve . . . may involve . . . Max Hill."

Phillip now offered a teasing smile. "If Max Hill was the problem, they'd be fighting with you."

"No . . . ."

"Yes."

"You know that he pays attention to both of them."

"Just like he does every other girl . . . . Max is a flirt. There's no getting around it. But you're the one he's serious about."

"I don't think that's entirely true."

"But it is true . . . ."

"If it is, I wish that it weren't."

Phillip now put his hands up on the table and regarded her intently. "It's okay, Jasmine. He's a little older I know, but you don't have to be afraid of him. He's a good guy. He's got a lot going for him. You ought to give him a chance . . . . Yeah, he may flirt and play around a little, but a lot of guys do that. It's not all that horrible."

Jasmine was considering how best to suggest that Max's flirting went beyond mere play, but she had not yet found the right words to attempt a reply when they were interrupted by their Aunt Cynthia. She entered the kitchen from the patio door, carrying an armful of flowers, and Jasmine jumped to assist her.

"The zinnias just keep coming and coming," she said. "They're really gaudy and cheap looking, but I like them anyway."

"Zinnias are always lovely," Jasmine said.

"And they're so easy to grow. Sometimes I think we need to just take what God gives us in the garden and not fight so hard to grow other things."

This statement showed unusual insight for her aunt, who was generally not inclined to philosophize, and Jasmine now especially loved her for it. Cynthia was not a knowledgeable or proficient gardener—in fact, she grew less temperamental varieties as much out of necessity as preference—but she managed, by taking what God gave her, to keep both the house and garden full of bright flowers throughout the spring and summer and into much of the fall as well. Given time to remove the tears that her current turmoil was helping to push into her eyes, Jasmine would have repeated her Granny's counsel about little things making rich lives. Instead, Julia chose this moment to make her entrance into the kitchen.

Julia, being neither small of stature nor quiet in her manner, was not one to make her presence unfelt, and now, though she did not say a word, she assembled the ingredients for her breakfast with such baleful silence that they paused in their conversation to await some outburst. None arose. Julia buried herself in the newspaper and began spooning cereal to her mouth, and Cynthia began arranging her flowers.

Abrupt and pointed speech is often required to communicate to someone what they do not expect to hear and may not want to know. Jasmine could not continue her conversation with Phillip with others present, but she was steeling herself to follow him out and make a more direct appeal when Julia's voice arose from behind her paper.

"Where's Chrissie?"

"Probably still in her room," Cynthia said, not yet turning away from her flowers.

"She isn't," Julia said, still from behind her paper.

"She must be in the bathroom . . . or out in the pool."

The likelihood of Chrissie having taken a morning swim of her own volition was zero. "Wanna bet?" Julia asked.

Cynthia looked to Jasmine. Jasmine shook her head in honest ignorance, though a foreboding rose quickly in her breast; nor did Phillip have any information to offer.

"Maybe she got up early and . . .," Cynthia began, but she stopped short, and it was apparent she could think of no plausible explanation for Chrissie not being in the house.

"Maybe she followed Max Hill to LA," Julia said, under her breath.

The others regarded her with alarm and consternation.

"Well, she did," Julia said. "She just took off after him, and he doesn't even want her there. What a whore!"

"Julia!" Cynthia remonstrated.

"Well she is! She just dumped on poor Pudge and took off."

"Did she tell you this?" her mother asked.

"Tell me this? Hell no. But that's what happened anyway. Where else would she be?"

"Any number of places," her mother said.

While this could be true of an evening, as Chrissie was considered old enough that her whereabouts need not always be tracked, it was much less true in the morning. When Julia responded by saying "Like where?", Cynthia remained dumb.

"Well, I'll call the Blunts to check, and please, everybody, please just have a good look around the house."

"While you're calling," Julia said, "why don't you just tell Pudge that his slut girlfriend dumped him."

"Julia!" Cynthia again remonstrated. "I won't have that!"

Julia now slammed her spoon onto the table, spilling her bowl of cereal as she did, and burst violently into tears.

"Goodness," Cynthia said, pale with shock.

Jasmine looked toward Phillip who said, "I'm sure there's some perfectly good explanation."

"Some perfectly good explanation?" Cynthia said, for no apparent reason.

"Yes," Phillip said. "I'll call Pudge's house. Jasmine, why don't you check all the downstairs rooms? She may just be sleeping in the living room or something. And if she's not there try the cars. Maybe she fell asleep listening to the radio."

"And what then?" Cynthia asked. "Call the police?" She said these last words in a whisper, they being too horrible to speak out loud.

"We'll drive around the neighborhood," Phillip replied, as he understood better even than his aunt and cousins the undesirability of bringing the police into a family difficulty. "Maybe she went for a walk."

"God, where is she?" Cynthia moaned, very deep worry creasing her face. "We'll have to call the police."

"First let's make some calls and have a look around," Phillip said. "It's most likely just a misunderstanding."

"A misunderstanding?" Cynthia said. Then, when she received only a nod in answer from Phillip, she seemed to brighten. "I'll call Tina," she said.

"Yes, call Tina," Phillip replied. "That's a good idea. She might know something. In fact, Chrissie's probably at her house. But wait until we've checked here and called Pudge. No point in worrying her unnecessarily."

Cynthia did not wait. Even while Phillip was dialing Pudge's house, he saw that the other line was being picked up, and he heard Cynthia's voice in the other room. As for Pudge, he had no knowledge of Chrissie's whereabouts.

"I'm sure we'll sort it out in a few minutes," Phillip said, preferring to end the conversation quickly. "Probably Tina will be able to explain it all"; and for a few moments, it seemed likely that she would. As he was preparing to hang up, Cynthia came into the room looking much relieved.

"Tina says we shouldn't worry," she said. "She's on her way over."

"Did you hear?" Phillip asked Pudge. "She's at Tina's. Sorry to have bothered you." He then hung up, promising to explain everything later. "She's spent the night at Tina's then," Phillip went on, turning to his aunt.

"At Tina's? No . . . . At least, I don't think so."

"But she's there now?"

Cynthia shook her head.

"Where did Tina say that she was?"

"She didn't say precisely."

"But she knows?"

"I'm sure she must . . . . She sounded like she did."

Cynthia's bewildered look now warned Phillip that the effect of Tina's reassurances was quickly dissipating, and he halted his questioning of his aunt. "In any case, I'm sure she'll explain it all when she gets here."

"She was very definite in saying that there was no reason to worry," Cynthia said, breaking into tears.

Chapter 32

Tina Advocates for Her Niece

After hanging up from talking with her sister, Tina Stubbs experienced several moments of very vivid anger with Chrissie. Her reassurances to Cynthia had been motivated by no more than instinct, as she too had no certain knowledge of her niece's whereabouts. She admitted the possibility of her having departed for Los Angeles—it was an idea that they had discussed, and Tina had agreed that it was an opportunity that could not be foregone—but to leave without informing her was spoiled-rotten insolence!

As she made her walk to the Arden Park house, however, and considered what course she would take when she arrived there, her anger softened. The girl's unannounced departure in some ways made her position stronger. She could defend her niece in innocence. No one could accuse her of having counseled her to act against her parents wishes or of conspiring in her departure. Then, once the girl had made her whereabouts known, Tina could speak objectively and in innocence of the opportunities the entertainment industry offered and of the critical importance of both the introductions Max Hill could provide and the guidance he was offering.

Tina had developed these arguments with an increasing sense of her own ability to carry the day, and her step had grown more resolute with her increasing confidence; but she now faltered. What if Cynthia had called David? When she imagined making her arguments to her brother-in-law, they seemed less substantial and unconvincing—he might even think them "womanly"! Without admitting to herself what she was doing—for she professed herself to be in every way the equal of Dr. Gannon in good judgment and moral discernment—she now broke into a scurrying shuffle. It was not, of course, that she was intimidated by the doctor or that he could not be brought to see the wisdom of her reasoning, but it did seem better that she should arrive in the house before he was called. After all, she and Cynthia knew Chrissie's true nature much better than he possibly could, given his frequent absences, and it was important for Chrissie's sake that they present a united opinion when he was called for consultation.

When she arrived, she found them all assembled in the kitchen. Two circumstances were immediately apparent: Chrissie had not yet been found, and Dr. Gannon had not yet been called. Indeed, Cynthia was on the very verge of picking up the phone.

"No," Tina said, "no, no, no. We can't disturb him yet. That would be completely wrong. After all, we know Chrissie best and we know best what to do. Until we learn more, we would only upset him and keep him from his work. We'll call him when we have something more definite."

"What if she's had some accident? Or worse?"

"I'm sure nothing like that has happened."

"Where then *is* she?"

This was a question Tina was not prepared to answer, for she had been struggling for some time to find plausible explanations. "She could be any number of places," she now said, regretting before the words were out the weakness of her plea.

"But where?" her sister asked, real despair in her voice.

"Oh, she might have gotten up early and walked to the store for something."

"Wouldn't she have been back by now?"

"Not if she ran into someone. She may have run into an old school friend. You know how it is with these girls. They've been away for a year, and now it's as though they've discovered a long-lost friend. They go for coffee and end up talking for hours and hours . . . . I'm sure she'll remember us and call in a few minutes."

Cynthia tried to take comfort in this scenario, but since she could not imagine anything short of whipping that would get Chrissie out of bed earlier than ten o'clock, her whitened pallor did not improve. She would have preferred to call her husband, for she always found his counsel reassuring, but she had so often left such decisions to her sister in the past that she could not resolve to pick up the phone.

There passed an hour in which the young people used their father's private business line to make calls to acquaintances, searching unsuccessfully for information while attempting by tone of voice to minimize their appearance of concern. Their inquiries could not have succeeded in locating Chrissie, as she had confided in no one, nor is it likely that they successfully disguised their concern, as their having resorted to calling in itself indicated a high state of alarm. While each unsuccessful call increased the general alarm and anxiety, Tina remained a model of strength and composure, dismissing each failure as not unexpected and her sister's disappointment as "carried away." Thus, the alacrity with which she responded when the kitchen phone rang, leaping past the others and even pushing Phillip aside, surprised all of them.

"Yes," they heard her say. "Of course." Then, after giving everyone a reassuring nod, she added, "You've had your mother very worried, but I can see that you didn't feel you had much choice." This was as close to an admonition as she would come, however. She now listened more than spoke, responding with nods and reassuring phrases. "No, of course not, there's no way you could have known . . . . Yes, you've called now, exactly as I always knew you would . . . . Certainly it's your decision to make . . . . Absolutely, it's your life to live . . . . No one could dispute that . . . ." She continued in this vein for some time before Cynthia, her fear of her older daughter's wrath having been overcome by her sense of motherly indignation, asked if she might speak.

Tina handed her the phone, smiling and saying, "She's upset and overexcited, but remember that she needs our support now more than ever."

While Cynthia usually accepted parenting advice from her sister, trusted her judgment in such matters, and wanted even now to follow her example in conversing with her daughter, her accumulated stress and anxiety were too much for her to contain. After confirming her whereabouts, she burst into recriminations.

"What kind of a person leaves her whole family to think she's been kidnapped?" she wailed. "We'd imagined all sorts of terrible things. Bludgeoned to death, thrown off a bridge. My God, it was horrible. What kind of a person does something like that?" She listened for only a moment before going on. "What do you mean, you thought we wouldn't notice? You live in this goddamn house, don't you? Of course, we'd notice."

"She thought we'd think she was still in bed," Tina said, touching her sister's arm.

"Think she was still in bed?" Cynthia said incredulously.

"She's usually still in bed at this time," Tina said calmly.

Cynthia turned toward the spot on the wall where the wall clock had been a decade earlier, then, without ever finding the clock's current location, went on. "Well, we didn't think you were still in bed," she said, just as though Chrissie had been in the same room listening to Tina. "And you obviously didn't think at all. Or can you think?"

Cynthia now gave a demonstration of why Tina's parenting skills were held to be more efficacious than her own. If Tina's judgment was not always what might be hoped for, she was rarely overcome by her temper, and even then tended at least to be succinct and definite. Cynthia's allegations now ranged far and wide. She accused her daughter of "selfishness" and "immaturity", of "never having given a moment's thought to anyone else in her family", and in response to some comment of Chrissie's, of "trashiness", "sluttishness", and "acting like a tramp." Further, she accused her of never having done anything to contribute to the household, of having wantonly wasted her father's money, and of having dyed her hair so often that it would surely fall out, which would be exactly what she would deserve. She continued on to describe her own failings in giving her everything she wanted in life, even when she knew she shouldn't have, and accused herself of having ruined her daughter's character as a result.

"I tried, but I just couldn't," she wept. "You were just too strong for me. If I gave in on one thing, then you just demanded something else. I just gave and gave and gave until . . . look at you now. Acting like . . . like . . . a bitch in heat. I knew all of this would happen and I didn't have the strength to do anything, with your father gone so much, and now look . . . . Oh, my God, your father," she bemoaned. "How will we ever tell him?"

At this, Cynthia was fully in tears, and Tina was able to take the phone from her trembling hand.

Sincerity, even in the absence of good sense, commands respect, and Cynthia's honest emotion might have had some good effect on her daughter had not Tina now taken countermeasures. She began by assuring Chrissie that her mother was fine—only upset by the realization that her babies were growing up and making their own ways in the world. She then reiterated her earlier statements of support, going even so far as to praise Chrissie for her independence. "It will carry you far in this world," she said.

Though she was already regretting her earlier outburst, this proved too much for Cynthia, and she raised her head from her tear-soaked hands to say, "Far? It will carry her far? Far where? . . . ." She then again hid within her own palms.

Soon thereafter Tina hung up the phone, and Julia, who had been observing all this with intense curiosity, could no longer restrain herself. "Where is she?" she asked. Tina indicated with an upraised finger that she ought to hold her question a bit longer, but Julia would not been silenced. "She's in LA, isn't she?" she said.

"Yes, as a matter of fact, she is," her aunt replied.

"Is she with Max and Sherry?"

"She was only at the airport."

"I knew it," Julia said.

"Of course, I'm sure she'll be seeing them very soon."

"I wouldn't bet on that," Julia said.

The others regarded her with surprise, but she didn't expound further, and it was left to her mother to ask what exactly she had meant.

"He doesn't want her there," Julia finally said. "She's just forcing herself in on them. I wouldn't be surprised if they . . . ."

"Max Hill—and Sherry too—repeatedly mentioned how eager they were to help her and how happy they would be to have any of us visit," Tina now said. "Don't be ridiculous."

Julia rolled her eyes. "Like what people say when they're being polite is what they really mean," she said.

"Don't be silly," Tina said. "They were perfectly sincere. I'm absolutely sure of it."

Julia guffawed.

Julia's comments were a consternation to all of them, except perhaps Jasmine, who could guess at the mixture of truth and vitriol that produced them; yet she did not seem willing to offer more in comment, and it seemed best to let her motives remain mysterious. The others all understood that the immediate and more pressing issue was how to inform Dr. Gannon of his daughter's departure.

Cynthia began by saying that he had to be called immediately. Tina argued that such a call would exaggerate the importance of the events and cause unnecessary alarm. "We'll tell him in the natural course of things."

Cynthia could scarcely bear the idea of possessing such information without her husband's support, and she now moaned aloud and turned to her niece. "Oh, Jasmine! Couldn't you go and bring her home for us?"

As everyone at once understood, this remark was based on a general tendency to turn to Jasmine for help and consolation rather than any particular skills Jasmine had exhibited in influencing Chrissie, and Phillip now intervened before Jasmine was obliged to admit her own impotence.

"If anyone should go," he said, "it would be me. I've been there."

"If your reason for going was so that you could reassure Cynthia about Chrissie's circumstances, that would be fine," Tina said. "If you're planning to bring her home, I think that would be wrong—completely wrong."

"Wrong? Wrong?" Cynthia said. "How could it be wrong to bring her back to her family?"

"It's time for her to make her own way. This is a fabulous opportunity, and I understand perfectly why she feels she needs to pursue it now. She'll never get another chance like this in her entire life. I agree that it's unfortunate that David doesn't see it in this light, but if you were thinking only of Chrissie's best interests, and less of your own, you would agree with me."

This admonishment struck home with Cynthia, for she knew herself to be both capable of selfishness and overly attached to her own comforts, both physical and emotional. She now shook her head and again began to weep. That those circumstances which most made her feel secure and content were often exactly those which best assured the welfare of her children now gave her little consolation. Her immediate motives were typically selfish: she disliked being upset.

"I think it will be best for everybody that we treat this as the most natural event in the world," Tina now said, " . . . as it really is. It's perfectly natural that a girl of Chrissie's age, with the talents she has, will want to strike out and pursue her own path."

Julia again guffawed, and Tina threw her a truly malignant look. "Of course, we could make a great big issue of it, upset her father terribly, and cause the whole world to think that she'd run off and joined the circus. But exactly what good would that do?" Receiving no answer, she now continued. "On the other hand, if we all accept this as being sudden, but otherwise not that big of a deal, I think we'll be able to keep it in perspective."

Although Tina did not say so, all knew that she was referring to Dr. Gannon's perspective; they also knew that Tina would have been considerably less confident and more deferential in his actual presence, as she, like her nieces and nephews, dreaded his anger. Cynthia herself was normally confident of her abilities to soothe and console her husband and even saw this as her one area of unsurpassed expertise. Moreover, she trusted his wisdom and depended on the good effect his authority exerted on the children. Now her confidence was broken. She knew her husband had already had a private conversation with Chrissie on the subject of Los Angeles, in which he had explicitly denied her permission to go there. Never before had he been so blatantly defied, and she agonized over how he would react to this failure of his authority, for she saw in it a very great failure indeed—perhaps even a demoralizing defeat. Moreover, he was now deeply engaged in work which she knew he regarded to be of great importance. There would never be a good time for such a blow, but for it to happen now was horrible. Cynthia silently cursed her daughter, then immediately regretting her thoughts, began to weep, murmuring through her tears, "Oh, what are we going to do?"

No response was forthcoming, and as was often the case when the wisest judgment was sought, they all turned to Phillip. It was not he who spoke next, however, but Thomas. Throughout the exchange he had been watching with his now characteristic look of pleasant curiosity. He said so little that they often ignored him entirely, and Julia for one had begun to regard him as a simpleton.

"I was thinking that I should go. But I'm not sure I'm quite up to it yet." He turned to Phillip. "Would you be willing to go in my place?"

"You're certainly not well enough," Tina said quickly, "and it wouldn't be fair of us . . . ." She was cut off by her sister.

"Oh, would you?" Cynthia said, turning to Phillip. Her face brightened just as though everything had already been resolved. Phillip acknowledged that he would, though he admitted some doubt about his ability to help. Cynthia called him to her, hugged him, then, still holding his arm, sat him on the couch next to her. "Just bring her home," she said, "that's all you need to do. Just bring her home."

"Of course, if that's what she wants . . .," Tina began.

"Oh, what does it matter if it's what she wants?" Cynthia said quickly. "Just bring her home."

"I can't *make* Chrissie do anything, Cynthia," Phillip warned gently.

Cynthia shook her head, saying, "I want you to bring her home right now."

This was a more adamant statement than they were accustomed to hearing from Cynthia, and Tina now answered in soothing tones, "Of course, Phillip will try . . . . I'm sure he'll do everything he can."

It having been resolved that Phillip would go to Los Angeles, his method of transportation became the compelling interest. Planes left the airport every hour, and Cynthia was adamant that he should leave immediately; but because he was too young to rent a car, there was real advantage in his driving. It was decided that they should call Sherry and see if a car could be made available to him. The phone in Bel Air was not answered.

"I can leave now and be there tonight," Phillip finally said. "I'll have a car and that will make everything a lot easier." He turned to Cynthia, stroked her hand, and then lifted it from his arm. "It would be no use being in LA without a car. LA's impossible without a car."

In deference to his aunt's distress, Phillip left without taking time for any orderly packing, only tossing handfuls of items into a gym bag. Nevertheless, the nearly eight hours that passed before his first call were bitterly counted down; even then, he could offer scant relief. He had found the Hills' house locked and empty and had not been able to locate either Max or Sherry. There were acquaintances of theirs with whom Chrissie had developed friendships during her previous stay, but Phillip was unsure of their addresses and phone numbers. He would continue his search through the evening, and then, if necessary, get a motel room and resume in the morning. Of course, he did not report all this directly to Cynthia. Rather, he told Tina, who could be trusted to convey the essential information in the least alarming manner possible. Nonetheless, when Tina first hung up the phone, Cynthia was near hysteria. Only after some hours of coaxing did Tina finally lead her off to bed by offering her one of her own sleeping pills and assuring her that "everything would seem so much brighter after a night's sleep."

The next morning, Julia was gone as well. Cynthia found a note on her bed. She had left for Los Angeles and would call soon. "Don't worry," she wrote. "I know what I'm doing." The note made no mention of where she planned to stay. Her Mustang was no longer in the driveway.

Cynthia presented the note to her sister in grave silence. Tina glanced over it quickly and said, "You'll just have to cancel her credit card." Her sister moaned in response. "As soon as she finds out what it's like to be on her own financially," Tina continued, "she'll come running right home."

This observation, while probably true—and not just for Julia but for Chrissie as well—offered no consolation to Cynthia. Her moans escalated into sobs.

"I cannot believe that Julia would do this," Tina continued. "She's threatening to ruin Chrissie's dream. But I promise you she'll come home when she gets hungry."

Thomas nodded thoughtfully and gave Jasmine an inquiring and hopeful look, but she could not offer him reassurance. She turned to Tina. "Might Julia have received some private invitation from Max as well—or from Sherry?" she asked.

"The Hills aren't fools," Tina said. "They know how old she is. But it would be just like Julia to show up unannounced and crash the party. She's always been so very jealous of Chrissie."

While her preference for Chrissie was quietly accepted in the household, Tina had in the past attempted to disguise it. This degree of partisanship suggested some alteration of her mental state, and they all—even Cynthia—regarded her with a degree of alarm.

Having noted the others' shocked faces, Tina adopted a more judicious tone before going on. "Julia still has some growing up to do. She won't always be able to depend on her sister to make her way for her"; but seeing that Cynthia was not much mollified by her new tone, her face again hardened with impatience. "She's being a little bitch is what she's doing," she said, and in reaction to the horror this seemed to induce, continued, "Oh, for God's sake. This isn't any time to mince words. You know it's true. She's been trying to take Max away from Chrissie since the day he arrived. She's been acting like a little slut."

"Stop, Tina," Cynthia said, raising her hand as though to fend off a blow.

"Well, it's true. Chrissie's found the opportunity to accomplish something extraordinary, and she has a really wonderful young man who's obviously in love with her and . . . and . . . and Julia just can't stand that. She can't bear to see her sister succeed in anything."

"I thought . . .," Thomas began, but his voice broke. His look of serenity was now gone, and he stared at them in confusion and distress. "What about Pudge?"

"What about him?" Tina said in exasperation.

"Yes, what?" Cynthia asked, turning to her sister.

"Nothing, that's what. It was never more than a teenaged infatuation. It only got to seem serious because Chrissie was too soft-hearted to break it off with him."

"I had no idea," Cynthia said. "Pudge is such a sweet boy. He'll be devastated."

"Chrissie should have spoken to him earlier, I admit. She was wrong about that. But don't give me any of that poor little Pudge business. A girl can't hold herself back for a boy who won't admit that she's outgrown him. If he's that dumb, he's only getting what he deserves. Besides, he won't hurt for long. He's too shallow for anything to go very deep."

Jasmine had privately admitted to herself a wearying narrowness to Pudge's conversation, but that he was considerate of Chrissie and always kind and polite could not be denied. Furthermore, had he perceived a need, he would have done anything in his power to assist the Gannon household. This disparagement by Tina seemed much too extreme, even cruel. Worse, it set Thomas to trembling. One aftereffect of his illness was a hypersensitivity to any stress or discord. Doctors had warned that it might be so for some time.

The boy who once would have walked away from this scene with a sardonic smile or a disdainful roll of his eyes was now deeply distressed. He wished desperately to say something to restore tranquility to the household, but he was not yet strong enough: his eyes remained fearful, his lips trembling, and his tongue tied.

Tina was too angry to recognize his symptoms and Cynthia too caught up in her own grief. Neither seemed inclined to take the necessary steps to align their views and reestablish a secure and undivided position. If anything was to be done, Jasmine would have to act. She moved across the room to sit beside her cousin and laid a hand upon his knee.

"Wouldn't we all feel better," she asked, "if Dr. Gannon were called?"

"Oh, yes!" Cynthia said at once, and Thomas nodded, thoughtfully perhaps, though Jasmine felt in it a sad acceptance of his own powerlessness. They all turned to Tina.

Tina huffed her disapproval. "You're being a bunch of ninnies."

"I am not being a ninny," Cynthia said, with renewed vehemence. "Both of my daughters have run away from home."

"They haven't run away," Tina said. "We know exactly where they are."

"Know where they are? . . . Yes, we do know. They're somewhere in a city of twenty million people."

"You're being ridiculous."

"I'm not."

"You certainly are."

A silent impasse ensued, during which Jasmine was again able to speak. "Apart from our own feelings, shouldn't we consider how Uncle David would feel?"

"Your Uncle David has far more important things to worry about than this," Tina said.

"More important than his own family?" Cynthia protested.

"The girls are fine. I agree that Julia has acted very badly . . . ."

"They are *not* fine," Cynthia said. "They're not fine at all."

"You needn't worry so much. They're big girls, and they know how to take care of themselves."

"Julia is only eighteen years old . . . . I would really like to call David."

"And what good do you think that would do?"

"It would make me feel better."

"There are more important considerations than our own personal feelings."

Her heart in her throat, Jasmine now ventured once again to guide her elders. "Might he not want to be called. If he were to come home and discover . . . ."

"Don't give me that Jasmine Johnson," Tina said. "What you mean is that *you* want him to be told, which is hardly surprising for a girl who would steal her cousin's favorite doll."

This final statement referred to an incident that had occurred when Jasmine was still very new to the household. She had understood Chrissie to be giving her the doll in question, as she had been given other of Chrissie's outgrown or discarded items. Whether it was because Jasmine had misunderstood her intent or because Chrissie had later regretted her generosity and changed her mind, the older girl had soon demanded its return. When Chrissie had discovered that a sock was missing, one that Jasmine was quite sure had not been on the doll when it was given to her, she had become inconsolable. The household had been in chaos for much of a day, and Jasmine had felt even Cynthia's reproach.

Jasmine had explained herself then, as well as a child in tears could do, but given Chrissie's certainty that the doll had been taken without permission and the general ambiguity concerning the lost sock, Jasmine had suffered the type of character stain that only months of unimpeachable conduct could erase. Now, inferring from this invocation of past events a form of stress-induced insanity, Jasmine saw no hope that defending herself in the current case would be of any purpose. She spoke no further.

"I'm not at all worried about Chrissie," Tina now said, "not in the least. Julia had no business leaving in the first place and needs to be told to come home at once. You need to make it perfectly clear that she is to come home immediately or face severe consequences."

Though Cynthia knew, in theory, that facing consequences was good for children, she found the prospect of inflicting them on Julia deeply troubling. Indeed, while Tina had often spoken of consequences in the most steadfast tones, she'd never been known much to exact them, and it remained unclear exactly what consequences she was proposing. It had always been left to Dr. Gannon to deny, limit, chastise, and face the wrath of his children.

Tina now paced the room, then stopped and look down on her sister, whose face was again buried in her hands. "Julia has a tendency to poor judgment," she said. "Especially when it comes to her sister, she's absolutely poisoned with her own jealousy. Still, I don't think any serious harm will come to her in a few days. Why don't we give her a week? If she's not home by next Sunday, I'll even go and get her."

"Oh, God," Cynthia intoned. "An entire week! Could they possibly stay away that long?"

"Friday, then. Or Thursday. What if I go on Thursday? I'm sure she'll come home with her tail between her legs long before that anyway."

Cynthia looked up hopefully, saying, "Do you really think so?"

Tina gave a knowing smile. "I wouldn't be a bit surprised if you hear her sneaking in the back door sometime tonight."

"Oh, how I wish they were both back in their beds right now!"

"Yes," Tina said, "it's hard, but I'm sure things will very soon be back to normal. But we have to remember that we can't keep them home forever. Even Julia will be grown up someday"—she turned a brief smile towards Jasmine—"even our Jasmine. Eventually, they all have to leave the nest and make their own paths, and an entertainment career isn't built in a few days, or in a month for that matter."

Jasmine was aware that Tina had been speaking only of Julia's return, while her Aunt Cynthia's comments had applied to both girls. This last comment seemed to confirm that Tina did not expect to see Chrissie at home any time soon and that she was unlikely to work to that end. By Cynthia, however, this message remained unread. "Yes, of course," she said, "but for now we just need to get them home."

It seemed to Jasmine that this breach in understanding promised only grief, yet Tina, who could not have been unaware of it, chose to speak no more. Jasmine's conscience pleaded that she speak out. She knew, however, that remarking the breach would prolong one aunt's anguish and feared it would invoke the wrath of the other. Tina's anger she could bear; Cynthia's suffering she could not. She remained silent.

Much could be envied in Cynthia Gannon's normal life: she'd married a man of means and good character; they lived in a safe and pleasant neighborhood among trustworthy and thoughtful neighbors; until Thomas's recent illness, their family had suffered no serious misfortunes either of health or reputation; she had retained her figure and youthful appearance, and her husband both loved her and lusted after her. People would have said that she had little to complain of, and she would have agreed. Everything was normal, and no one valued normalcy more than she. Yet, while she appreciated what she had, she suffered under minor disruptions: news of a poor grade in school, a contretemps between her husband and one of the girls concerning the length of a skirt or tightness of a blouse, a threatening noise from the washing machine, or any suggestion of obligation to volunteer in some school activity could cast a nasty pall over her day. This disappearance of her daughters, coming as it did on the heels of the near-death of her son, was much worse than anything she had faced before. Over the next hours and days, heartsickness shadowed her every step.

The one certain remedy would be to call her husband. She could not imagine what he would do—it seemed to her that there was absolutely nothing that could be done—yet David always found a remedy. She felt in her heart that once he was called, the entire mess would soon be resolved, or at least the weight of it would fall from her shoulders—And wasn't that almost the same?—yet she always stopped short of picking up the phone. Tina accused her of calling on him too often. Cynthia knew full well how much it pained her husband to see her unhappy, and she had many times been gratified by the lengths to which he would go to relieve her misery. Was she now too dependent on him? Did she bother him unnecessarily with her minor problems and tribulations? Shouldn't she someday grow up and learn to manage some of the family's problems on her own?

Yet, even as she would trouble her way through these considerations, Jasmine's words would keep coming back to her: "Might he not want to be called?" She could not help thinking that her husband would want very much to be called. Hadn't he always said that he wanted to be informed whenever anything of importance occurred at home? Hadn't he told her how being apart from his family and feeling as though he missed important milestones in his children's lives was a great hardship to him? What occurrence could be more important than this? Was this not a milestone even of tragic proportions?

Yet, always, just when Cynthia found herself on the verge of calling him, she would see her sister's bright and confident face and feel herself to be just the worrying ninny Tina thought her to be. Or, when she was most anticipating the comfort of placing everything in her husband's capable hands, Phillip would call and explain some mystery or describe some new development, and plant some new seed of hope. For, while much remained to be explained, some mysteries were now understood.

The reason everything seemed so irregular, Phillip explained, was that the Hills were no longer staying in their parents' house, it having been leased. Max was working exceptionally hard and was seldom to be found—Phillip, in fact, had not yet spoken with him—but Sherry was seeing to the girls' accommodations, moving them about from friend to friend. Yes, there had been an initial battle between Chrissie and Julia, but Sherry was managing it so that they stayed in different places. Julia's anger seemed to have abated, and the girls were talking again. It appeared that they would reconcile soon. No, he had not yet convinced them to come home, nor would he until they'd all had a chance to talk to Max. Both girls were waiting for his direction before plunging into the film world. As for himself, he was now staying with a teammate from his college track team.

Tina seemed to find the substance of these conversations completely satisfying—it was unfortunate that the Hill's house had been leased, but everything else was proceeding exactly as it should. Of course, Max would be busy. Actors worked all hours of the day for weeks, then did nothing at all for months at a time. That was the nature of their business. Julia seemed to be coming to her senses. No doubt she would be coming home soon. They were fortunate that Sherry and Max were so well-known and well-liked—no doubt everyone was eager to host any friends of theirs, especially when they came from such a good family as the Gannons. Plus, Chrissie would be making important contacts. It was just as she had expected. Things were progressing perfectly.

While Cynthia found developments less reassuring, she was accustomed to accepting her sister's constructions of events, and she suppressed her more hysterical thoughts. Still, when Thursday morning arrived with neither of her daughters having returned, she could not resist asking Jasmine to make Tina's plane and auto reservations and to drive her to the airport, nor would she have eschewed tearful begging if it had been needed to get her sister and her bags on their way to Los Angeles.

Chapter 33

All That Can Be Done Is Done

As soon as the car had left the driveway, taking Tina's forceful presence and Jasmine's comforting companionship with it, Cynthia was again in tears. She wandered out to the pool, tried to pick a flower, and found herself kneeling on the grass crying. She then retreated to her bedroom to lie face down on her bed and weep into her pillow. Cynthia liked that her bedroom smelled of her husband, and when he was away for only a week or two, she avoided changing the sheets on their bed. Now, as she soaked his pillow with her tears, the smell of his shampoo found its way through her sobbing, and her heart ached even more fiercely at his absence.

Of a sudden, she sat up. The house was quiet. She was in her own room and her own house, and the telephone, which had once seemed such an evil temptation, beckoned to her. "Might he not want to be called?" she asked herself again. There could only be one answer, yet she still hesitated. Tina would tell her that she was being a ninny, that she should grow up and take care of things like this on her own. David would be disturbed. Worse, he would be angry—very angry. That was only to be expected. He would seethe and suffer, probably remain silent for a time on the far end of the phone. He would demand to know why she hadn't called earlier. He might go so far as to admonish her or even yell at her. He was so awful when he was angry. And wasn't it possible that Tina would have them both home by morning?

She was able to resist for an hour, but the sound of Jasmine pulling the car back into the drive again posed the question: "Might he not want to be called?", and the slamming of the door seemed to provide the answer, "Of course, he would." She picked up the phone and dialed.

Indeed, he was angry, very angry, and her inability to compose her thoughts through her tears only made him more so. Yet through the ordeal of explaining and re-explaining herself, of trying to recount the details of each girl's departure, and what they had said and done before they left, she felt an immense relief. He would know what to do. He always did. All the awfulness would soon be over, because he would know how to put everything right. And his anger would pass too. He never stayed angry at her for long.

He wanted their telephone numbers, and she was ashamed that she could only give him Phillip's and Tina's.

"I'll call them," he concluded, "and if I can't make any more sense out of this, I'll catch a flight tomorrow."

"You can't interrupt what you're doing," she said, while hoping that he would. "It's much more important than this."

"It's not more important," he replied sharply. "You should have called me earlier."

"I expected them to come home . . . ."

"Under these circumstances, it was unacceptable for them to leave even for an hour."

"I know that now. I just was hoping . . . ."

"I'm sure you were."

She hung up with a feeling of reassurance. A great weight was lifted from her shoulders. It would all be solved, or at least he would be coming home. He had not told her he loved her before he hung up or offered a kiss over the phone—perhaps someone was in his office and he could not—but this was not so important. She knew that he would feel badly for not having acted more kindly to her and that he would be ready to make it up as soon as he got home.

She walked out in search of Jasmine and had to go all the way to her room to find her. She sat at her desk reading—so like her, she thought, to sit at the desk instead of lying on the bed as her other children would have done. She could not resist walking over and kissing her on the cheek.

"Thank you," she said. "Thank you for being our Jasmine."

Forty minutes later, when Dr. Gannon hung up the phone from talking with his sister-in-law in Los Angeles, he harbored no intention of going to Arden Park—not that he had been satisfied with what he heard from her, to the contrary. What she had said—and even more the tone in which she had said it—had only intensified his anger, and he intended to go directly to Los Angeles to relieve her of her responsibilities in supervising his daughters. He felt compelled to call his wife first, however, and while she did not directly ask him to come home, he understood her tears, silences, and meaningless questions to indicate that she very much wanted him to stop in Arden Park. This made no logical sense, of course. She was an adult in her own home and in no danger, while his children were as good as lost in the largest city in the country. But logic, at least the logic of the bystander, often plays little part even in the most successful of marriages. He hung up the phone with the knowledge that he must first go home before proceeding to Los Angeles.

Whenever Dr. Gannon was arriving home, Cynthia herself went to the airport to meet him. As he would not arrive until after midnight and she already appeared dangerously tired, Jasmine wondered for a time if this evening might prove an exception. By ten o'clock, however, she had gotten up from bed, showered, and come down in her robe to assure Jasmine that she should herself go to bed. Jasmine gently offered to stay up and go for her uncle, but her aunt's certainty quickly dissuaded her.

"One thing you could do," Cynthia said, "is get the car out of the garage and put it out front. I hardly have time to put my face on, and I don't want to be late."

While the time required to pull the car from the garage was trivial, there was always some small element of stress in assuring that no post was scraped on backing out. This was a small chore that Jasmine was happy to do. When the car was sitting in the drive, with keys left in the ignition, she went upstairs to tell her aunt goodnight.

She found Cynthia before her mirror applying makeup. She looked up briefly, then said, "Damn, I can't find my eyeliner. I wonder if Chrissie took it." She rummaged in her makeup drawer for a moment then huffed in despair. "The problem is that I can't see without my glasses, but I can't put makeup on my eyes when I have them on." Jasmine now stepped forward to help peruse the drawer, and found a pencil. Apparently, it was not the one her aunt had expected to find, but she shrugged and accepted it. "Along with everything else, he shouldn't have to come home and find that his wife has turned into an old hag."

Jasmine made certain to be far away in her own room when the Gannons came home, but she did encounter them early the next morning when she was coming home from her run. Her uncle and aunt were putting his bag in the car in preparation for another drive to the airport. While the doctor's visage was grim, it was apparent in how the couple stood in close relation to each other and leaned yet closer to speak—and no doubt in many other details too tiny to be remarked—that they had been reconciled and were united in their feelings.

When a child dies or is gravely injured, it is nearly beyond the capacity of the parental mind to accept responsibility. Indeed, some lawyers make their livings from exploiting wishes to cast blame on doctors, police, engineers, instructors, friends, supervisors, neighbors, or anyone else with either wealth or insurance. Not even Dr. Gannon, who prided himself on his even-handedness and was respected in government circles for it, was immune. While he could now accept his fair proportion of responsibility in the mishandling of Thomas's illness, he had originally lashed out at his family, Thomas's friends, and even the other doctors. Now, with these events following so closely upon Thomas's tragedy, he once again found himself in a less than charitable—even less than just—frame of mind.

"Maybe if you'd been a little nicer to the boy," he said to Jasmine, "he would have stayed here and none of this would have happened."

Jasmine felt these words so sharply that she could scarcely believe herself to have heard them correctly.

"I've always known that Chrissie and Julia were complete airheads," he continued, "but that didn't mean you had to be, too."

This second statement could not be misunderstood and confirmed the full depth of his bitterness.

"I did not love him," Jasmine said, "I do not love him, nor could I ever love him. I felt it would be wrong to encourage him under the circumstances."

"No one asked you to love him, only to treat him with common kindness."

"Goodness," Cynthia said, again patting her husband's arm.

"You can't deny that all of this might have been avoided if the boy had stayed here in Arden Park."

"No girl is ever obligated . . . .," Cynthia began. "It would be wrong to give false encouragement to any boy if she didn't have any feeling for him."

"No doubt that's true," Dr. Gannon said, "but the devil of it is, why couldn't she have any feelings for him?" He turned to Jasmine.

"For a girl as kind as thoughtful as you can be, you certainly were short with poor Max. You'd think he was some kind of hillbilly."

While Jasmine had known that much of the household thought she'd acted ridiculously prim and shy, she was not willing to accept a charge of snobbery. "On the contrary," she said, "I find him fashionable, witty, intelligent, and very charming—more so in all of these than myself."

"What the devil's wrong with him then?"

"We're different."

"You can't expect everybody to look exactly like you."

"My feelings have nothing to do with his appearance."

"What then?" Dr. Gannon asked, with real exasperation.

"We have different values."

"Do you think you might have been a little more open-minded?"

While it may now have appeared to Dr. Gannon that Jasmine sulked, the reason she did not answer at once was because she was giving real consideration to his question and to a cluster of related questions that surrounded it. Was it time to relinquish some of her Granny's influence? Were Granny's rules not so much superior to the Hills' as merely different from them? Her cousins would not have called her good but "prissy," and her uncle, whose firmness of character she had always admired, now seemed to feel much the same. Had she been a prissy? Was there not something important, even wonderful, in being charming and witty? Max Hill was the type of person who added sparkle and glamour to others' lives. Wasn't this ability a virtue? And was it not possible that she'd misconstrued the scenes she'd overseen between Max and Chrissie? And might not Julia have thrown herself at Max and been rebuffed? And, even if they had not acted so innocently, could it be that all of this was no more than harmless play? Wasn't it possible, even likely, that such play was common among his peers—in the world of actors and celebrities? And even if some of his character faults were real, had she not been wrong in judging him too harshly? "Judgment is mine sayeth the Lord?" Who, exactly, did Jasmine Johnson think she was?

Max had given her very real help when she'd found herself stranded with Mr. Johnson. He'd as much as admitted to poor conduct in the past and had promised to behave better in the future. If he had failed to keep his promise, had she not failed as well—in a hundred ways—at being good? No one was perfect. Failure was only human. Shouldn't she have been less self-righteous and more forgiving?

For none of her questions could she reach a simple or unambiguous answer, yet one fact remained: "I could not have loved him," she now said. "To have suggested otherwise would have been wrong."

Her uncle threw up his hands in defeat, saying to his wife, "It's time."

David Gannon had been the first love of Cynthia Ward's young life; and her love had been reciprocated in full measure. She had never for one hour been obliged to compromise the feelings of her heart and could only imagine how painful such a thing might be. That she *could* imagine, however, was apparent in the consoling look and gentle press on the arm she gave Jasmine before she and her husband settled into the car.

While she believed she supported her husband completely and if backed into a corner and threatened with a knife might even have been able to restate his opinions concerning Jasmine's behavior as her own, she could not in her heart fault Jasmine—not now when she felt so much gratitude toward her, specific gratitude for having encouraged her to call her husband and general gratitude for her having stayed faithfully beside her in Arden Park. The current crisis was of such magnitude that Cynthia had offered no pretense as to her need to keep Jasmine close. Indeed, she was so abject in her worry that she had asked her to sleep in her own bed with her, which Jasmine had willingly done.

In the days that followed, Cynthia craved distraction from her worries. It was not to be found. First of all, she could not leave the house for fear of missing a phone call or (a wish too fond even to be spoken aloud) the unannounced return of one or both of her daughters; yet everything in the house reminded her of her missing daughters and prevented any escape from her brooding. Her conversation could only drift elsewhere for brief moments, before, as though caught at the end of its leash, it returned to its beaten track.

"To leave is one thing," Cynthia would say, "but to leave without telling us first!" . . . "I'm sure they're perfectly all right." . . . "Really, what could go so terribly wrong?" . . . "I'm afraid that I worried David unnecessarily." . . . "Tina's really very good in these sorts of situations." . . . "I'm so glad it's all out in the open now." . . . "David always knows exactly what to do." . . . "Is there some real chance that Chrissie could be an actress?" . . . "I'm sure they'll be home by tomorrow, or the day after, at the very latest."

These and other ruminations were repeated with endless variation and not infrequent self-contradiction. Jasmine could only answer with a non-committal nod, or at most a gentle reassurance, for she knew much better than to join in any criticism of her cousins: it would not have reassured her aunt for her to do so and would have jeopardized future relations with her cousins.

One tomorrow passed and then another, however, without the hoped-for return. They had daily news from Dr. Gannon, but it could not be called encouraging. He had spoken with Chrissie, who was living under ambiguous circumstances with a group of young screenwriters and actors. She had been vague about Max Hill's whereabouts, but she'd been adamant about not coming home. She was, she said, "among very creative people with very pure artistic standards, and with new ideas about almost everything." She had learned that acting lessons were a total rip-off and had started her own screenplay—working day and night—while she was making contacts, getting "headshots" (she was confidant that she'd found the most "dynamic" photographer in all of Southern California to take them), interviewing agents, and working her way into auditions. She'd laughed contemptuously at the mention of her sister, admitted that she had seen her, and opined that Julia was being very foolish and immature. "You need to find her quick because there are scummy types here who will take advantage of her. Some of the people she's been hanging out with are real losers.

Things could get really messed up." She had not been able to tell her father where Julia might be found, and he had not yet seen her.

These conversations had deeply discouraged Cynthia, especially as David admitted to losing his temper, behaving badly with Chrissie, and making enemies among her new acquaintances. Phillip, he said, had been more effective than he. Her husband's speech had been halting, his tone uneven. He had sounded tired and defeated—even aged. She'd felt a great sympathy for him, but also, as she was forced to acknowledge that he could not immediately set everything right, she was frustrated with him and even a little angry.

On the evening of Dr. Gannon's third day in Los Angeles, an event occurred at the Arden Park house that made things much worse. As dark approached, the doorbell rang, and a girl describing herself as a friend of Julia's appeared at the door. Cynthia dimly recognized the pixyish face and guessed that the girl had at some time come to the house with a group of Julia's friends; but she did not know her name, much less anything about her family. She wore a skirt that was at least six inches too short for decency but was nonetheless slit up the side. She asked for Julia, in a voice as squeezed and elfin as her face, then hitched up her pink tube top and waited for Cynthia's reply.

"She's away," Cynthia informed her.

"Oh," the girl simpered. "Is she in *Hollywood* with Chrissie?"

Cynthia found the question troubling and wanted not to answer, but could think of no good excuse not to, and affirmed that this was true.

"Because I just wanted to know," the girl said, while smiling sweetly and pulling a newspaper out from behind her, "if Julia's seen what's in the paper."

Cynthia now identified the girl's attitude as one of impertinence, and she was determined no longer to be agreeable. "I have no idea," she said, stepping back as though to close the door.

The girl flashed a wide, mocking smile, turned and hobbled down the steps in a giggling run, then stopped to remove her platform sandals, exposing her underwear as she did. "You haven't seen it yet either, have you?" she said. Then, when Cynthia did not answer, she squealed and ran for the car. Cynthia now saw that there were at least three other girls in the car, peering intently out at them, plus a boy driver who had slumped down to hide his face. The other girls whooped and screamed as their braver companion dove in among them. The tires squealed, the paper came flying out of a window, and they sped out into the street.

Jasmine, having risen to investigate the noise, found her aunt in the entry, standing with her back against the door. Her eyes were closed, and she wrenched her head slowly from side to side, as though in a spasm of grief. Jasmine called her name. She held her head stiffly to one side for a moment longer, as though she would prefer never to open her eyes again, then, clenching her arms under her breasts and shaking herself, looked toward Jasmine.

"Oh, Jasmine," she said, her face now quivering and pale, "if these are the kind of people Julia's keeping for friends, what terrible things is she getting herself into?"

Jasmine led her aunt into the living room before explaining that she had not seen the car and could not possibly know to what she was referring.

"It was a bunch of wild girls. Horrible wild girls. And a boy was driving them, and he was horrible too." She now broke into tears. "She said something about a newspaper. I think it's what they threw out in the driveway."

Jasmine sat up to look out the window. There in the driveway a rumpled section of newspaper sat. Had it been a meaningless piece of jettison, Jasmine would have gone out immediately to remove it. Now, however, she was obliged to consider both her aunt's condition and the indignity of responding to an impolite act. While Dr. Gannon was not quite a national celebrity, either by his wealth or his fame, he was enough in the news and political fray that he had given his family firm instructions on public relations. He would always politely excuse himself from responding to questions that involved his family, and he would expect them to do the same. Whether the substance of any question was true, false, scurrilous, flattering, or merely friendly, they must always refrain from answering. "No comment" must be their invariable response; otherwise, the day would come when no comment would seem an admission of wrongdoing.

To go and pick up that paper seemed to Jasmine to transgress the bounds of "no comment," and though it sat in the driveway as conspicuous as a dead cat, she would have let it remain had Cynthia not asked her to retrieve it. She did not argue the issue with her, nor did she stuff the paper immediately into a trash can. She handed the paper to her aunt, who took one look at it, gasped, and let it drop. Jasmine picked the paper up. In a photo three columns wide and just as tall, a disheveled Julia was being held back by two young men. A hideous snarl consumed her face as she struggled to break free of the hands that clung to her arms.

Jasmine was able to examine this photo with greater calm than her aunt. The details, however, provided no reassurance. Across from Julia, at the front of a crowd and the apparent target of Julia's wrath, was Chrissie. A uniformed policeman stood beside her. The young men holding Julia seemed to smirk. In the background was a police car.

As the format was that of a tabloid, it had been apparent to Jasmine on picking up the paper that it was not the LA Times, and from its Hollywood imprint, it was apparent that it was little more than a local scandal sheet. Yet she could take only limited comfort in this. Written reports in such a paper as this could easily be dismissed: everyone knew that the writers cheerfully and relentlessly lied, exaggerated, misconstrued, insinuated, and misled for the sake of dramatic effect. But the picture itself could not be denied, and the image of Julia, with the strap of her blouse down and her bosom half-uncovered, her hair wet and plastered to her cheeks, her eyes wild, and her face red and bloated—in short, in exactly the pose in which every photographer hoped to catch a celebrity— was an indisputable fact. Whether her aunt's mind had captured all the details in the photo Jasmine could not be sure; nor did she have any way of knowing if her uncle was aware of it or would have told his wife of it if he'd known.

One need only take a five-minute, remote-controlled, channel-surfing tour of the tube to appreciate that most people are titillated by the betrayals, humiliations, deceits, misfortunes, and even illnesses in others' lives. Some, not content with the exquisite anguish of the soaps, are quick to take any opportunity to spy on the crises and dramas in their neighbor's lives. And wouldn't it be more delicious yet to be right in the thick of such lovely scandal as this! How, they might ask, could Jasmine now not call her uncle—or, better yet, Phillip—or maybe the both of them—and tell them of the shocking photo? After all, they needed to know the extent of the danger Julia had put herself in. Wouldn't this information help them to find her more quickly? If there was to be any chance of keeping the photo from spreading further, wouldn't they need to act quickly? She had a positive responsibility to call them. It was her duty and no one could fault her for performing her duty, no matter how unpleasant.

Alas! Even such strong arguments could not drive Jasmine to the telephone. First, she had to consider her aunt: it would not be good to upset her by inflating the significance of the photo. Second, it was most likely that Dr. Gannon and Phillip both already had knowledge of it, and if they did not, they would soon learn of it from Cynthia. Third, and most importantly, it was essential that no indictments of her cousins be perceived to have come from her lips. She looked forward to the time when everything would be resolved. It would then be time to repair injury, forgive, and reunite the family. When they returned home, her cousins' shame would leave them oversensitive to any insult or perceived criticism. They would be quick to suspect treachery, jealousy, and betrayal. In order that such feelings might soon be overcome, she hoped to provide no grounds for reproach. It would be bad enough that she had stayed home and played the good girl. In the interests of the family, she must not create the appearances of having tried to curry favor with her aunt or uncle or to have elevated herself above her proper role.

Ordinarily, Cynthia might have been expected to call her husband herself, and had there been no news to report, she might well have done so, as she always found his voice comforting. She had, however, already once been a bearer of bad news to her husband. She knew herself to have brought much grief upon him then. She had only with unusual difficulty restored his affections, and she did not wish again to make herself so prominent a figure in his unhappiness. Thus, they passed another fretful night.

By morning, Cynthia so feared a telephone episode analogous to what had happened in the driveway that she refused to answer the telephone. Thus, when the phone rang during breakfast, it was Jasmine who picked up. The caller responded to her hello with an indistinct mumble, followed by a pause.

"Is Chrissie there?" the voice finally asked.

Callers who did not identify themselves placed Jasmine in a dilemma. Dr. and Mrs. Gannon, as well as her Aunt Tina, always asked the party's identity before making any response, and Jasmine always gave her name immediately when calling. The Gannon children, however, neither asked nor gave names and resented such inquiries as intrusions into their private lives. Jasmine had resolved the issue by always asking the caller's name when the call was for her aunt and uncle, but only doing so with her cousins' callers when they sounded like adults. It now seemed to be of particular importance to maintain the family's privacy, and despite the youthful sound of the voice, she asked who was calling.

"Jesus, Jasmine, why do you always do that?" the caller responded. Before the words were fully out, Jasmine had recognized her error: the complaining voice could belong to no one but Julia.

"Julia!" she acknowledged. "No, Chrissie's not home. She hasn't been home at all."

"I knew it!" Julia said. "That was all just a lie."

"I don't understand."

"You wouldn't. It's nothing."

"I'll get your mother."

"No. I don't want to talk with her."

"I know she would want to talk with you."

"I can't right now. Just tell her it was a sales call."

"I can't tell her that. I can give her a message though, whatever you would want me to pass on. Are you well?"

"Yeah, I'm okay. Tell her not to worry."

"Don't you think it would be better if you spoke with her?"

"No."

"I know she will ask where you are."

"As if I'd tell you that."

"She's been worried. I would like to be able to tell her something reassuring."

"I told you I was fine. She doesn't have to worry. I can take care of it myself."

"I'm not certain that she will know what 'it' is."

"I didn't mean for you to tell her that part. Look, I gotta go. Tell her everything's cool. It's Chrissie she needs to worry about."

"Why? Is Chrissie in some kind of trouble?"

"She's going to be."

"If there's anything we can do to help her, I'm sure . . . ."

"Forget it," Julia said. "Forget I even called. Mom's going to find out soon enough anyway." With this, she mumbled a good-bye and hung up the phone.

There was no possibility of hiding from Cynthia that someone had called, and Jasmine met her aunt's inquiring eyes with dread.

"Was it them?" Cynthia asked.

"It was Julia," Jasmine admitted. "She says that she is well."

"You should have let me talk to her," Cynthia said, with near venomous ire.

"I hoped that she would, but she . . . ."

"Are you telling me that she didn't want to talk with her own mother?"

"I'm sure she would have liked to. And if she'd known how much you wanted to . . . ."

"Couldn't you have told her?"

"I did try to explain. No doubt, she had some engagement and only had a minute."

Cynthia could not long stay angry at anyone for long, especially not Jasmine, and with this, she again broke into tears. She stepped forward and settled herself into Jasmine's arms. Nor could Jasmine hold any resentment toward her aunt, who was so obviously suffering. She understood that she had stricken out blindly from her hurt and bewilderment.

"At least we know that she is well," Jasmine offered.

"She knows that she can call home if she needs anything," Cynthia burbled into her niece's shoulder.

"She does," Jasmine affirmed, thinking that yes, if Julia found herself in real trouble, she would always think of Arden Park as a place of safety and security.

"Did she say anything about Chrissie?"

"She thought that she might be here."

"How could she think that?"

"I don't know."

"Could it mean that she's on her way here now?"

"I suppose that it could, though I wouldn't . . . ."

"It must mean that," Cynthia said. She lifted herself from Jasmine's shoulder, and looked into her face, a too-bright gleam of excitement in her teary eyes. "She'll be here by this evening . . . . I'm sure it means that. She's on her way home at this very minute. What else could it mean?"

Is it better, kind reader, to allow someone to remain in despair or to enliven him with false hopes that will inevitably collapse? This was the question which Jasmine now debated. Julia had implied that the report of Chrissie's return to Arden Park had been a ruse. The entire conversation, both its tone and content, had seemed unreliable. Jasmine did not, in fact, believe Chrissie to be en route home. On the other hand, she did not wish to destroy her aunt's hopes, and she was herself so much at sea in the whole affair that she could not positively deny that Chrissie would appear in Arden Park within the hour.

"I'm sure they'll both be home before very long," she said, "even if it isn't today."

Most of us at times choose to believe things which we know to be false. With a part of herself, Cynthia acknowledged the less-than-encouraging message in Jasmine's reply, but she chose to ignore it. Instead, she cheered herself with thoughts of Chrissie's imminent return and began speaking of a plan to build a type of glassed and screened garden house that would serve as an entertainment center for the young people and a venue for entertaining guests, while maintaining the ambience of a summer camp. It was apparent to Jasmine that the structure described was several times too big to fit the designated space beyond the pool and that it would be much too hot for comfort in the summer and too cold in the winter. Nonetheless, she was able to share in this imaginary venture with her aunt, as she too felt the appeal of being indoors and in the garden simultaneously, and, most importantly, of having a cheerful group of young people right here in the backyard.

This happy interlude was interrupted by the telephone. The call was from Dr. Gannon, and it, of course, needed to be passed directly to Cynthia. Jasmine exited the room—and house—to walk in the garden. While she could not hear a word of what was said and would not have wanted to, she looked in through the kitchen window between circuits of the flower beds to know when she might re-enter the house. With each pass, it became more apparent that the straw props of her aunt's cheer had crumbled. She stood unmoving with the phone pressed to her ear, not saying a word, her face drawn and her expression grave.

After Jasmine completed her third lap around the garden, her aunt no longer stood at the phone. She took a deep breath and went inside. Cynthia was not in the kitchen or in the living room. She went down the hall and peeked into her aunt's bedroom. Cynthia lay face-down on the bed. Jasmine hesitated. Isolation of one's self may be a charade designed to evoke pity, an attempt to disguise weakness, or a retreat to gather strength. In some situations, as when madness swarms, it is necessary to intervene in another's sorrow, even when such intervention is not sought. Cynthia was not inclined to self-pity, nor had she been too proud to seek Jasmine's solace in the past. Jasmine stepped quietly away from the door: she would allow her aunt to nurse her wounds in solitude.

When an hour had passed, and no sound had come from the bedroom, she ventured to peek in. Cynthia lay sleeping, her bottle of sleeping pills on the table beside her bed. She hurried to check the bottle, confirmed that no excessive number had been removed, and resolved to call Phillip at once. Her call reached him in his car. She waited while he pulled off from the highway.

"I'm glad you called," he finally said. "We're going to need your help." He then related to her an astonishing sequence of incidents, which made it clear that circumstances were indeed grave.

Yes, they knew of the photo that had appeared in the paper, but that was not the most serious problem they had with photos. The publisher seemed willing enough to relinquish the negative— for a price, of course. Unfortunately, they had learned that far more compromising photos also existed—but these were of Chrissie. Apparently, during her photo session, she had been seduced first into allowing swimsuit photos, then bikini photos, then half-bikini photos. Worse yet, she had unknowingly signed a release for the photos, and the photographer was threatening to sell them to a national magazine.

"These people are pros at this. Apparently, they get a girl and flatter her, and tell her how beautiful she is, and then, in the name of art, they convince her to take some 'very tasteful' photos. The girl thinks she's signing one thing when she signs the agreement, but she's actually selling the rights to the photos."

Dr. Gannon was using all his influence to suppress these pictures, but Chrissie was of legal age, and the release had strong legal standing. Chrissie claimed to have been plied with alcohol and other drugs. If they could prove this, there might be a remedy, but that would create a lot of publicity—which would only make the people involved too happy. If the negatives and the story about them were to be suppressed, a substantial payment would likely take place.

"No one wants to be blackmailed," Phillips continued, "least of all David. If the photos had something to do with his reputation, I think he would just walk away. But since it's Chrissie, he can't. She's put him in an impossible situation. Tina's not being any help. She's gotten it in her head that Chrissie's going to be a movie star, and she even tried to sell David on the idea of the photos being a normal part of the business. He went into a rage with her, and she and Chrissie took off. We don't know where they are now."

The situation with Julia was, if anything, worse. Later the same night that the newspaper photo had been taken, she'd been at a party at a house that had been involved in a drug raid. It appeared that the raid had somehow been orchestrated as there had been a crowd of photographers present at the scene. As far as they knew, Julia had not again been captured on film—at least no photos had yet surfaced—but that was probably only because she had passed out in one of the bedrooms and could not be led out by the policemen. Nonetheless, she'd been taken into the police station early that morning and spent the entire day in jail.

And where had Max and Sherry been during all this?

"Max is nowhere to be found, though I'm pretty sure he's in town. I kind of think Chrissie and Julia have been talking with him, but they won't say a word when his name comes up. It doesn't seem like he's doing much to help. On the other hand, it doesn't seem like he's very involved—not directly anyway. At least, he's smart enough to make sure it doesn't appear that he is."

And as for Sherry?

There was a long silence. "I don't know really."

This was territory that Jasmine could not safely tread. A positive comment, such as "I'm sure she's doing all she can," would invite contradiction; a negative one would be dishonorable.

"She's involved in other things," Phillip continued. "I haven't seen that much of her."

It is an ill wind that blows no good. The shipwreck provides flotsam to the scavenger, the bankruptcy of the grocer on A Street is a boon to the grocer on B, and one man's firing is another man's promotion. Yet how much are we permitted to rejoice in such windfalls? How much joy are we allowed to let show?

Phillip's tone of voice hinted to Jasmine of a more serious breach than his words described—perhaps even a suggestion that "other things" implied other people. We cannot honestly say that Jasmine did not feel a surge of hope at this moment; and we cannot say that she did not a moment later experience a brief instant of satisfaction—what some might even call smugness—when Phillip said, "She has lots of friends here. Lots of them. Arden Park was just a summer fling." Nor can we say that Jasmine now spoke up in defense of her friend Sherry Hill.

We can say that Jasmine made no efforts to induce her cousin to elaborate further or to be more specific. And in reference to the questions above, we will propose the following for your consideration: one is allowed to be more joyful when one feels assured that the other's misfortune is not truly a misfortune at all; and Jasmine let neither dismissive words about Sherry nor the smallest contented murmur or sigh escape into the telephone.

It would have been unseemly to place the importance of his relations with Sherry on the same plane as the more grave circumstances of his cousins, and Phillip allowed a moment of silence to pass. He then resumed in a faster and more businesslike tone of voice. "We'll talk with David's lawyer about the photos today and try to make a deal," he said. "Chrissie was trying to act like they were no big deal, but I know she'd really like to have them back. Even Tina finally admitted that they needed to stay in her control."

And Julia?

"I hope we'll convince her to come home. That may depend on Max though. Julia and Chrissie aren't talking about it, but I think he still has influence. If we can get him out of the picture, I think she'll be okay."

The police charges?

"If Julia will just cooperate, I think that can be managed. As much as you hate lawyers, you appreciate them when you need them. I'm not sure she will cooperate, though. At first, she was pretty scared, but now she's talking like it was all just a prank. I think somebody gave her the idea it was a great publicity stunt, and she's using that to save face . . . . Even Sherry said it would probably do her good if she were in the movie business. People down here have got some pretty screwed up ideas. Some people treat this whole thing like it's a joke. I know you've always said that it's important to expect the best from people, but I'm not sure in this case. Some people just take advantage. They go along doing what they want to do for their own selfish reasons and are perfectly happy to let you figure out excuses for them. We've come up against some people who are just plain creeps. They're just out to take what they can get. They're total jerks."

Jasmine chose not to respond to this, and Phillip, perhaps sensing that he'd been too sweeping in his criticisms, began making preparations to end the call. "In any case, tell Cynthia that we've been talking with both Chrissie and Julia, that they're safe, and that we hope to be home soon."

"She will ask me questions."

"I know, but I think it's best to leave the details for Uncle David. Besides, we're not clear on all the facts and circumstances yet, and to tell her more would just worry her."

"If she thinks that there are secrets being withheld from her . . . ."

"I know, I know. And you can tell her as much as you need to, but everything I've said was intended for you only, and you're not obliged to tell her any of it."

"How much do you think that I should tell her?"

"I have no idea. None of us knows what we're doing exactly. All I can say is use your own judgment. It's probably better than any of the rest of us anyway. Just do your best."

This she did understand. It was how her grandmother would have advised her: she would do the best she could and leave the rest in the hands of God.

Phillip now interrupted his farewells to ask if she had been running. She admitted that she hadn't, because they were waiting for phone calls at every minute, and she did not like to leave Cynthia alone.

"I haven't either," he said. "When this is all over, let's go for a long run out to the river and find a nice shady place under some poplar trees to sit down and watch the water go by."

"I'd like that," Jasmine said.

"Why is it that people who should have so few problems in their lives have to go out and make them?"

"Sometimes it's difficult to recognize our blessings until we're threatened with losing them."

"I guess," Phillip replied, "but some people do a better job of it than others."

Chapter 34

Our Story Concludes

That meeting of our two young people out along the river was to occur, but not nearly so soon as they would have hoped. Many phone calls, disappointments, and vanquished hopes would intervene.

As concerns Julia, when she finally met with her father for a second time, she appeared red-eyed, intermittently demanding and morose, volatile with false pride, and inclined to fidget and perspire. She could not account for the disappearance of her Mustang, and was unable even to indicate whether it had been loaned, stolen, misplaced, or sold; nor did this failure of memory seem unnatural to her. In short, it became apparent that her behavior was very much being influenced by the use of drugs. It was possible to reason with her only through a herculean effort by Phillip to assemble not only her father and mother, but Max and Sherry Hill and even her Aunt Tina, all of whom urged her to go home immediately and seek counseling. She did not do so willingly, of course, but with her credit card having been cancelled, Max having betrayed her, and her newfound friends having deserted her when she became a net consumer rather than net supplier of their preferred stimulants, the alternative was street living. Even her extreme pride in her own judgment would not admit to the ignominy of filth and begging.

Exactly how Julia had planned to live in Los Angeles and what she had hoped to accomplish (other than "be a success") had always remained obscure. Chrissie, however, was able to state a specific objective: she intended to be an actor. This goal, given her family name and good appearance, could not be totally discounted, and with her Aunt Tina giving support and encouragement, Chrissie would not be discouraged. Despite a threat of total removal of family financial support, despite her father's repeated promises that if she studied theater in college and graduated, he would support her move to Los Angeles, despite her mother's impassioned pleas, she could not be induced to return home. She was supported in this decision by her aunt, who dedicated what resources she possessed to establishing herself and her favorite niece in a Hollywood bungalow.

But we get ahead of ourselves, you may say. What of Jasmine and Phillip and that meeting on the river? In fact, we do not get ahead of ourselves, for that meeting would not occur until Thanksgiving!

Having been delayed in his departure for school by his adventures in Los Angeles, Phillip was obliged to travel directly from Los Angeles to San Francisco, where he picked up his clothing and flew on to Providence without a stop in Arden Park. While this would allow him a short visit with his own parents, who were temporarily in San Francisco, and while he knew that the Arden Park house would be very quiet with the Hills, Chrissie, Tina, and Dr. Gannon in Los Angeles, he felt himself curiously homesick at this omission, a condition which he attempted to remedy by calling Jasmine so often that he began to wonder if he were not becoming something of a pest.

Their first phone conversation concerning Chrissie and Julia, when the girls' situations were just beginning to be understood, had initiated Jasmine and Phillip into a level of conversation that was now more adult, more equal, and more intimate. Because they understood each other well and implicitly trusted that each wanted only the best for their cousins, aunt, and uncle, they were able to discuss the advisability of extreme measures without fear of rebuke or disclosure. Their joint counsel was of considerable use to their aunt and uncle. Where David's and Cynthia's propinquity might bias their judgment, they could suggest reason and restraint; where their aunt and uncle's love of their children made them blind, they were able to provide insight. It was Phillip who had proposed the family meeting that had drawn Julia back into the fold, Jasmine who had argued for the inclusion of Max and Sherry Hill in that meeting (on the grounds that representatives of her new friends were essential to its success), and Phillip who had applied the necessary pressure to secure Max Hill's attendance. They had also advised against placing ultimatums and setting harsh conditions for Chrissie. She remained resolute in her goal, and given her more advanced years, her determined personality, and the support of their Aunt Tina, they saw no potential reconciliation. The best that could be done would be to remain in communication, keep the family's arms open, and hope.

Though it is rarely admitted to and is even more frequently sanctimoniously denied, there exists a very nearly universal human tendency to feel some excitement and even exhilaration in the presence of other people's tragedies. Jasmine and Phillip had recognized that they were not immune to this human weakness and were wise enough to distrust themselves. They had resisted every impulse to draw self-importance from their involvement in their cousin's problems or to revel in their intrigue. In the end, all the family, even Julia, would be grateful for this.

Yes, yes, the meeting! Phillip had found himself that November longing for a return to Arden Park. It was to him as though something had been left unfinished—something that had for the past months proved a distraction from his school affairs, which rightfully at his age and time should have become the primary interest of his life. Fortunately for Phillip, his family was wealthy, he had earned the trust of his parents, and they were happy to pay for anything which he presented to them as being of real importance. His guilt at extravagance having been allayed by booking a discounted overnight flight, Phillip was able to find himself in Arden Park on a crisp, autumn day, under unusually unpolluted skies, and jogging out along the river with Jasmine at his side. They were in high spirits: Julia had been uncharacteristically cheerful that morning, Thomas continued to improve, and the family had begun to accept Chrissie as the Hollywood, daring-do of the family. It seemed that Arden Park might almost return to the happy household of their childhoods. They did not run at a pace to test themselves, the air was delightful, and their feet seemed to float above the ground.

They talked for a while of Jasmine's college applications. Her academic performance was extraordinary by any measure, and as her senior year got under way, it had become apparent that she would have a wide selection of colleges from which to choose. Indeed, her record, when combined with a check mark in the box designating African-American ethnicity, would gain her admission to any university in the country, and in most cases, a full scholarship as well. This check mark she had declined to make, for she was as much European- as African-American and was hardly disadvantaged. Moreover, Dr. Gannon had come to see both the real perfidy of Max Hill and to appreciate the exquisite good character of his niece. He had, for the present, been relieved from responsibility for paying for his own children's educations and wanted to make amends to Jasmine by paying for hers. Even more remarkably, Mr. Harold Blunt had offered her a private scholarship, against a promise of taking employment in his company upon her graduation. Indeed, he had spoken of opening an entrepreneurial foundation for non-college-bound students of which he hoped she might someday serve as director. Both these offers she had for the moment deferred, for new developments had caused her to reexamine certain of her previous plans.

Jasmine and Phillip chatted for a time about the facts of her position and what progress she had made with applications, but these things were well-known to both of them and were not for the moment at the forefront of their thoughts. It happened that they soon found themselves next to a small grove of poplar trees, with a picnic table ensconced therein, and Phillip suggested they sit for a moment. Thus, they perched themselves on the table top, their feet on the bench, and looked out across the water.

Alas, the river where it passes through Arden Park is not among the more beautiful in the world. It is channeled, and thus runs flat and with little variation in its current. The vegetation tends to the brushy, thorny, and perpetually heat-weary, and at this time of year, when the new winter's green shoots have not yet overgrown the past winter's dry remains, brown. Yet, the river does have its scenic qualities. For one, autumn leaves linger until Christmas, and a gentle breeze now kept a bright yellow confetti of poplar leaves twisting overhead. As they ran, they had stirred flocks of valley quail, which have a remarkably perfect and colorful patterning, and followed them as they ran down the trail and off into the berry thickets, their topknots flicking forward preposterously with each step. Cottontails had dashed along the edge of the trail ahead of them, and they'd been made to imagine bright salmon running through the green waters by fisherman who had crossed the running trail and wandered down paths to the river's edge. Then, finally, a pair of geese, always harbingers of the changing seasons, had flown by so low and quietly that they could hear the beating of their wings.

As they sat side-by-side on the concrete table top, they both felt a poignant sensation of change. It was understood between them that the Arden Park household was forever altered; both knew that Jasmine's circumstances would change greatly in the coming year; even the geese seemed to signal that it was a time of moving on—and of leaving behind.

Remembrances of Jasmine's first days in Arden Park were in the air, as were a particular sensation of humility, pride, and self-acceptance at their summer's successes and failures, and a certain deep gratitude that they had themselves escaped the most horrible of the summer's consequences. While you, dear reader, might enjoy hearing all of these sensations and more discussed between them in some detail, unfortunately our protagonists are not so loquacious on topics of sentiment. Besides, it would have been ignoble and thoughtless to discuss some of them and a temptation to fate to discuss others. All this was understood between them, and at a far deeper and more secure level than words might ever convey. Indeed, words at this moment might well have circumscribed these feelings in ways that would have defined and limited them unacceptably. It was better to watch the sparkling water pass and listen to the leaves rustle overhead.

But, yes, there existed one area of understanding that must not and could not remain implicit between them. After they had remained silent for a time, sitting at this table, their shoulders not even brushing, it fell upon Phillip to cross this divide; yet even after he had accepted this awesome responsibility, he allowed himself to sit for a moment longer with his heart in his throat. Finally, he turned his face toward her, until she felt him looking and turned to face him.

"Jasmine," he said, "you are the most beautiful person I know."

Jasmine might well have said that *he* was the most beautiful person she knew. Instead, she blushed exceedingly.

"You are also," he continued, "the most beautiful girl I know . . . . And, the most beautiful woman."

Jasmine's response was to let a tear fall down her cheek. This he caught with his finger and kissed away. Fortunately, yet another tear was to avail itself, and this he kissed directly from her cheek. Then, finally, he kissed her very so ever so gently on her lips.

Epilogue

If you are of a certain age and disposition, dear reader, you may perhaps be as happy to depart from our story here. Some, however, having followed us this far, will like to know a little more of what the future holds for our protagonists.

Let us then begin with Julia. When Julia first reappeared in Arden Park, the arrival of even this very sullen and unhappy prodigal cheered her mother, but the hoped-for return to normal was not to be. It was determined that Julia had been sampling various drugs since her early teenage years, had escalated this to regular use during the summer, and in Los Angeles had been using drugs steadily, indiscriminately, and, alas, habitually. It would require weeks for her to admit that this constituted a problem, and even then, as she was very reluctant to admit that the problem was one she could not control through her own will alone, her prognosis would remain doubtful. Indeed, it is understandable that it should have been difficult for her. The drugs she consumed made her feel capable of great feats and, combined with the support of her fellow consumers, superior in all ways to the uninitiated. What more had she come to ask from life?

As for her sister, it is correctly understood that acting talent is not a prerequisite for success in Hollywood. Chrissie, however, was too proud to perform the pandering or groveling that would have been necessary for success in its absence. She would, however, in her first spring in Los Angeles experience a brief bloom of success. She was given the lead role in an independent production, which was described to her as a futuristic, post-modern horror film that would deconstruct the clichés of the genre to show that horror of all kinds was a device to subjugate women. Unfortunately, these points would never quite be made, and in order to recoup their

461

investments, the producers were obliged to trumpet the only marketable qualities the film possessed: the Gannon name and Chrissie's completely exposed bosom. Reviewers reacted with glee to the opportunity to savage a famous-named ingenue with delusions of talent, and even Chrissie and Tina were forced to admit that the film was a horror.

For a time, Chrissie's future looked bleak, but it is an ill wind that blows no good: a preposterously well-to-do, Southern California car-dealer saw this execrable film, fell in love with the young Ms. Gannon—or perhaps with her bosom—and arranged to meet her at a party. Given her experience with Pudge, Chrissie knew exactly how to handle tedious men of extraordinary wealth who adored her. While it was he who arranged their introduction, she would arrange that he divorce his wife and marry her. Given differences in age and education, the shortness of their courtship, Chrissie's resolute determination to be free of her parents' tyranny, and the circumstances under which her lover had abandoned his previous family, Dr. and Mrs. Gannon saw the prospects for this union as dismal. They could take solace, however, in knowing that she would be so well financially provided for that she would not soon be induced to take further movie roles. And, dear reader, you can feel assured that if this husband does not last, another will be found.

As for Tina, her niece would remain faithful to her, employing her as a personal assistant, domestic consultant, and event coordinator and keeping her comfortably ensconced in her Hollywood bungalow. Indeed, largely as a result of Mrs. Stubbs's astute planning, invitations to Chrissie Gannon's parties would become among the most sought-after in Beverly Hills. Not even Max and Sherry Hill, no matter how diligently they might seek, would ever receive one.

Thomas, both in his appearance and by the measure of all tests medical and psychiatric, was soon recovered; yet, to those who had known him before, it was undeniable that he was changed. He became a less aggressive person, a less assertive one, and a less ambitious one. His attachment to the Arden Park household, which he had once seemed to disdain, grew so profound that he scarcely could be induced to leave the house to buy milk or bread. Only months of urging and reassurances could bring him to expand his horizons and enroll at the local university. There were those who saw a great tragedy in what had befallen him; others felt that his experience had improved his character, making him more understanding and kind. His father was more grieved than his mother; Cynthia was secretly pleased to have him close to her in their home.

And William . . . . Jasmine went so far in taking Max Hill's advice as to speak with her uncle before informing her brother about the circumstances of his nomination to the academy. Dr. Gannon implored her to understand that no doubt as to William's merit had ever arisen, that he would himself have long-since advocated his nomination had it not been for the family connection, that William had in any case been well on his way to obtaining admittance independent of any outside influence, and that Max's congressman's nomination of William had perhaps been the single most distinguished act of his career. When Jasmine had protested that no such intervention should ever have occurred, her uncle had informed her that she would be doing her brother a deep injustice if she spoke to him on the subject and positively ordered her not to do so. Jasmine submitted. Over time, as William distinguished himself at the academy in every way, her misgivings retreated, and she could take complete and unalloyed joy in his achievements.

Now, patient reader, as for our heroine . . . . In another era, we might have let her story conclude with that kiss by the river, but in this age of indiscriminate noodling, some of you will want to know a little more. On that fine November day, eros had joined forces with agape and logos, and together they proved more powerful than any concerns propinquity or propriety might present. The couple's first episode of hand-holding within the family compound caused quite a sensation— and think how Cynthia must have felt when she first observed her niece and nephew kissing one another!—but awe soon gave way to an expanding effervescence of joy.

Much advice was given. Dr. Gannon, whose admiration for his wife's niece had become fierce and uncompromising, had been among the first to call Phillip to a private meeting. With unheard-of sternness he reminded his nephew of his niece's tender age, warned him against injuring her in any way, and forbade precipitate decisions that would blight or limit their futures. Yet, he was the first, and certainly not the last, to come away from such a meeting with a renewed belief in the power of true love.

Phillip's own parents, on learning that the couple contemplated marriage, were at first quite shocked, in some measure because of the racial difference between them. When they came to understand that no marriage was imminent, and that certainly nothing would happen before Phillip's graduation, their fears were relieved; and after meeting with the young people and seeing the maturity and even wisdom of their plans for the future, and, of course, how happy they were in each other's company, they began fervently to hope that such a marriage would come to pass. Phillip's father (who was after all a plant geneticist) was even reported to jest that the Gannon clan had grown "too pale" and would "benefit from a little hybrid vigor."

Thus, two years later, Phillip having secured the promise of a teaching position in Arden Park, a date was set—the Saturday after his graduation. Many felt that he was too young for such a step, and all agreed that Jasmine was; yet there are always extending circumstances. Never were there two young people of better judgment; nor ever were there two people more in love. If love could anywhere, here it would last forever.